Praise for

The Accidental Marriage

"A thoughtful, heartbreaking, and often laugh-out-loud romp that captures the complexities of a new marriage that's falling apart. Annette Haws also explores the more interesting question: What keeps a marriage together?"

—TERRELL DOUGAN, columnist for the *Huffington Post* and author of *That Went Well: Adventures in Caring for My Sister*

"In *The Accidental Marriage*, Annette Haws has created rich characters, so real and flawed you want to shake them, yet so lovable you want to invite them to dinner. Haws delivers a story that makes you want to rush to the end to find out what happens and prose that makes you want to slow down and savor it."

—KAREY WHITE, author of *For What It's Worth*, *Gifted*, and the recently released *My Own Mr. Darcy*

"Annette Haws, the acclaimed author of *Waiting for the Light to Change*, has just done everyone a favor and written a new book, *The Accidental Marriage*. Annette writes the story of two mismatched people in love, and wraps their lives around your heart in a way that won't let go. If you want a story with plot, character, and real, deep meaning that will leave you thinking long after you're done, this is the book for you.

—SHANNON GUYMON, author of *Makeover*, *Taking Chances*, *The Broken Road*, and *Do Over*

the accidental MARRIAGE

the accidental MARRIAGE

ANNETTE HAWS

Bonneville Books
An Imprint of Cedar Fort, Inc.
Springville, Utah

This is a work of fiction. The characters, names, incidents, places, and dialogue are products of the author's imagination and are not to be construed as real. The opinions and views expressed herein belong solely to the author and do not necessarily represent the opinions or views of Cedar Fort, Inc. Permission for the use of sources, graphics, and photos is also solely the responsibility of the author.

ISBN 13: 978-1-4621-1374-3

Published by Bonneville Books, an imprint of Cedar Fort, Inc.
2373 W. 700 S., Springville, UT 84663
Distributed by Cedar Fort, Inc., www.cedarfort.com

LIBRARY OF CONGRESS CATALOGING-IN-PUBLICATION DATA

Haws, Annette.
  The Accidental Marriage / Annette Haws.
     pages cm
  ISBN 978-1-4621-1374-3 (perfect bound)
  1. Marriage--Fiction. I. Title.
  PS3608.A897A66 2013
  813'.6--dc23
                                    2013034885

Cover design by Shawnda T. Craig
Cover design © 2013 by Lyle Mortimer
Edited and typeset by Melissa J. Caldwell

Printed in the United States of America

10 9 8 7 6 5 4 3 2 1

*To Betsy, Charlotte,
Nollie, Lucy Jane, and Lauryn
with love*

Also by
Annette Haws

Waiting for the Light to Change

Contents

CONTENTS

Part One
The Romance

∾ 1 ∾

Explorers and Revolutionaries

Nina Rushforth was not raised to be a failure. The lofty expectations in her parents' stately brick home are almost palpable, and she can't believe the disappointment her life has become. With thirty-six pairs of young eyes watching her, Nina grasps a stick of chalk in her fist and, using a yardstick, draws an intricate web of white lines on the blackboard. Swallowing hard and forcing a tight smile, she bisects the baseline with a quick horizontal stroke and hands the chalk to a freckled boy sitting in the front row.

"Okay, George, do your stuff. Fill in the subject and the verb."

In the back of the extraordinarily long room, a spit wad flies through the air and sticks with a silent splat to a construction paper daisy decorating the edge of the bulletin board. Giggling, Robbie Eder peels another strip of paper off his assignment and crams it in his mouth like a couple of dry sticks of gum. Nina notices, but she doesn't care. Rowdy boys throwing spit wads are at the bottom of her list. Newlywed or not, her husband didn't come home last night—that makes eleven days in a row—and she wonders if he's ever coming home at all. How will she keep breathing if he doesn't?

Slapping her palms together as though she's announcing a party with streamers and hats and a box of silly favors, she asks the class, "And the direct object?" The guest at this party. "Where does it go?"

As if she's responding to a dapper game show host, Amanda Church sings out, "After the verb." Nina can only give the girl a significant nod, because at that particular moment nothing can bypass the lump lodged in her throat. But crying is not an option, not in front of a classroom of farm kids—not in front of anyone. Jill Ferney tiptoes to the front of the room and hands her a wrinkled pink tissue.

Sighing, Nina drops the chalk in the railing next to the black felt erasers. Blaming her well-intentioned father or her domineering mother-in-law, blaming the vile type teacher out in the portables or the curmudgeon in the front office, is simple during the day but not so simple at 3:00 a.m., when she dreams the sound of her young husband's key in the lock. Night after night she stumbles out of bed, blinking through her thick glasses balanced on her nose—and opens the door to nothing. Standing in the cool breeze, feeling the goose bumps rise on her skin, she know she has only herself to blame.

When did her interesting, well-organized life begin to unravel? Nina knew the exact moment. Eighteen months ago, before Nixon was reelected. The fall of 1972. It was a hazy afternoon, and she was sitting in an auditorium at St. Andrews University listening to a lecture: History 204, Explorers and Revolutionaries 1680–1830, except the lecture had devolved into a rant.

Her cheek resting on her left palm, Nina glanced toward the lectern and squeezed one eye shut. A torrent of words spewed from Professor Galsworthy's mouth as he criticized the Vietnam War. She wasn't inclined to listen. *Excuse me,* she thought, *at this very moment, how many young British soldiers are occupying Northern Ireland?*

His reedy voice felt like fingernails scraping a blackboard. "Heaven knows we Brits were guilty of imperialism during Vicky's sixty-year reign, but isn't it time civilization pushed past The White Man's Burden and all that rot?" Tufts of gray hair haloed his flushed face, and bits of spittle fired from his lips into the front row. He waved a tight fist and exposed a frayed cuff under the sleeve of his tweed jacket. A first act, that's what he was, warming up the class for the peace demonstration. The campus was papered with flyers whipped by the wind, caught in bushes, stuck against windows, and littering doorways.

"Four o'clock!" Galsworthy shouted with his last possible breath. "Market Street." The class collected their belongings and washed out of the building into the pale afternoon sun. It was like a street carnival.

4

"Amazing," Nina whispered to herself. Were any students still in class? The musty odor of weed drifted through the air in the courtyard, and Nina sniffed a couple of times like a vegetarian at a barbecue. Throngs of shaggy-haired students milled about, talking and flirting, enjoying the endless possibilities of a Friday afternoon, as the rally on Market Street exerted some strange gravitational pull.

She whipped her knitted scarf around her neck and buttoned her navy peacoat before she passed under the six-hundred-year-old stone archway from the courtyard of St. Mary's College onto South Street. A stiff breeze from St. Andrews Bay stole her breath, and the light tang of salt air tickled her nose. The surge of the students pushed her along, her feet barely touching the cobblestones. A voice, amplified and strident, pulsed over the chatter of several hundred students: "Withdraw troops from Vietnam! Now!"

Six foot one in her stocking feet and with butter-blonde hair that stood out like a beacon, Nina was a girl people noticed. She knew exactly who she was, an eager, absentee American spending a semester abroad, a bit of an escape in a medieval town in Scotland, on a spit of land that jutted out into the cold deep blue of the North Sea. She certainly knew who she'd been, the youngest child and only daughter sharing the familial stage with two domineering brothers and a third who wasn't.

One hand raised to shield her eyes, she scanned the gathering. Where was Colum? Stretching on tiptoe, she glanced over the crowd looking for hair so black and curly it blanched his skin, made him look like he'd never seen the sun, made him look like he'd spent his first twenty-six years hiding out in caves along a craggy Irish shore. Maybe he had. *Humble* was the only word he used to describe home. There he was. Rail thin and clean-shaven, Colum was only one of six or seven males in the entire throng without a beard or a straggly mustache. He elbowed his way through the mob and gave her a quick nod. His bony shoulder pressed against her. At such close quarters, amateur repairs were hard to miss in the worn black overcoat that hung to his knees. Standing under a streetlight, a young stranger raised both hands and made the peace sign before he flicked his cigarette lighter at the toes of a stuffed effigy of Richard Nixon. The dummy burst into a fierce blaze, momentarily quieting the crowd. Smoke stung Nina's eyes under her contact lenses. Black ash and burning shreds of fabric caught in the wind. Suddenly, the day had an ominous feel.

"The dummy's innards were doused with petrol. Come this way." Colum ducked toward a narrow side street and ran past the doors of a dozen shops. He grabbed her hand and pulled her out onto Market Street. Laughing as though they'd been clever, they strolled hand in hand toward the edge of the gathering as if it were a Sunday afternoon. She caught her breath and whispered into his ear, "Will it get nasty?" A half smile on his face, Colum turned to face her. "Ah, this is nothing. The crowd's mellow. Don't open that lovely mouth of yours. Just smile. Does every kid in the States go in for straightening?"

She felt like she'd been held up for public scrutiny and found lacking because her teeth weren't bunched together. She couldn't wait to tell her mother that five years of orthodontia were a social liability.

A feisty redhead climbed onto the makeshift stage, a couple of orange crates slapped together with a length of plywood hammered on top. The girl gripped the neck of a mic, pulling it to her mouth like a kebab she was ready to bite. Earsplitting reverb screeched through the air, and the girl scowled before she started to chant.

"What do we want?"

The students yelled, "Peace!"

"When do we want it?"

"Now!"

Wearing raggedy bell-bottom jeans, T-shirts stenciled with catch-phrases or silhouettes of rock groups, and corduroy jackets to stave off the chill, students rocked back and forth, rose on their toes, and yelled rhythmic slogans for five or ten minutes, until a slender professor from the history department took a turn at the mic. Colum gripped her hand more tightly.

Broad shouldered and red-faced, a rough crew of Scots, townies by the looks of them, had enjoyed one too many pints and turned away from the third or fourth speaker railing about the war a half world away. Their blood was up, and the local hooligans shoved their way through the students and swaggered down the street ready to inflict peace on anyone whose looks they didn't like. Nina stepped out of the way but not before she heard one sneer, "CIA," which was ridiculous. If the CIA were here, these buffoons would never know it, but she glanced in the direction they were taking. A couple of young men looking like freshly minted FBI recruits stood on the corner of Market and City Road, a poster between them and a stack of navy books at their feet. Nina pressed her fingers against her mouth. Mormon missionaries, hoping to chat up a stray student or two when the demonstration wound down, seemed to be the target. She'd noticed them once or twice, clean-cut boys walking down the narrow streets with two-story stone buildings on either side of them, and she'd turned away. She'd resisted the encounter, not wanting to know if they were boys from her high school, or Salt Lake, or some small town of hardworking farmers in Utah or Idaho.

Colum's eyes followed her gaze before he muttered. "Here's trouble. That same bunch of toughs tossed a couple of Jehovah's Witnesses into the bay last spring. Pamphlets and all. Not a pretty mess."

Her books wedged in the crook of her arm, she leaned forward and blinked twice. "We've got to warn them." That's all there was to it. Tugging on his hand, she eased her way through the stragglers on the edge of the crowd.

"They won't get hurt," Colum smiled. "Just the old heave-ho and into the drink."

"Not a chance. What would you do if a handful of thugs wanted to toss one of your Irish buddies into Lake Michigan?"

"I'd ask my buddy what he did to their sister," he said cheerfully with a grin and a wave of one hand. She could smell ale on his breath.

Skirting the toughs, Nina sprinted down an alley, the breeze whipping her hair. Standing by as a clutch of drunken Scots roughed up a couple of missionaries and tossed them, scriptures and all, into the bay didn't feel like a patriotic option. One boy was tall. He wouldn't go down without a fight. Blood. Broken noses. Calls home in the middle of the night from the mission president. Not the story to tell at a homecoming in a packed chapel.

"Go!" she cried out, her scarf coming unwound. Pushing at the air with one hand, she reached the missionaries. "Be off. Right now." She handed the shorter guy the poster and started collapsing the easel. "Head to the bus station."

More than a little surprised, the young men gawked at her. "Excuse me, Miss," the shorter boy said, his glasses skewed on his nose.

Colum strode up. "Lads, time to relocate." He nodded over his shoulder at trouble sauntering down the street. "Not the best day to be American."

The shorter missionary, Elder Twitchell according to the black-and-white name tag, grabbed the easel and hurried down the road as though he were dancing the rumba in double time with a stick figure he'd only just met. The other reached down to collect their copies of the Book of Mormon.

"Faster." Nina gave the tall missionary a gentle shove. "No kidding, you've got to move." A stone whizzed by, barely missing his ear. With strides that matched her own, he started running and didn't stop until the four of them were panting hard, hands on knees, collapsed on an iron bench outside the bus station. Catching his breath, Colum started to wheeze, "Could those blokes even find Vietnam on a map?"

"CIA." Nina started a giggle that grew into a laugh. "Not-very-secret secret agents." The taller of the two red-faced missionaries gave Colum a sideways look. "Is she always like this?"

"You tell me, Yank." He gave him a wink, his lips twitching. "I just met her last week." He shrugged. "Do American girls come any other way? Women's lib. Isn't it a national craze on your side of the pond?" His speech was so quick and clipped, and the look on Elder Twitchell's face was so blank—he hadn't understood much—that Nina had to smile. Dry yellow leaves floated down in a wan blue sky, and Nina savored the moment, one perfect, ridiculous moment she didn't want to forget. Sitting beside her on the bench, the three young males joined in a hearty laugh.

The taller missionary studied her face, careful to keep his eyes above her neck. "Why the bus stop?"

She nodded toward campus security across the street.

He stretched one long arm across the back of the bench. "I know you from somewhere."

Not wanting to begin the whole where-did-you-go-to-high-school rigmarole, as though three years in a brick box were somehow defining, she said, "I played tennis for Highland High."

"You play tennis?" His dark eyes glittered.

"Doubles. The only girl in the state." She tipped her head to the side and started to laugh. "What can I say? I'm remarkable."

"This is exactly what I've been telling you." Colum thumped the

8

bench with his fist. "Women's lib. The next thing you know, they'll be stealing our bats and staging a sit-down on the cricket pitch."

"You must be good. At tennis." Elder Spencer, according to his name tag, looked past Colum and met her blue eyes. A blush spread across his face and red-splotched his neck.

"I have a wicked two-handed backhand," she said, raising both shoulders.

"I'll bet you do," Elder Spencer said. "So how did that work? Getting on the team?"

"I beat two-thirds of the guys at tryouts, and my coach likes to win."

And suddenly, she left the small shops that opened directly onto cobblestone streets and the arched walkways that led into grassy courtyards shaded by ancient oak trees, and she remembered hot spring afternoons and tennis matches held adjacent to the track where this guy probably ran the 440. Elder Twitchell started to whistle "Thy Servants Are Prepared," missing more notes than he hit.

She moved her head to the rhythm of the spotty whistling and started to sing, "Thy servants are prepared to teach Thy word abroad."

Elder Spencer's jaw relaxed. He'd figured her out. She was on his team, a fellow Mormon. She'd attended all the same church youth groups, listened to general conference twice a year, and, with a stubby red pencil, underlined the same scriptures in seminary. If his family had been members long enough, he was probably a third or fourth cousin—removed once or twice.

"I accompany the ward choir," Nina said. "You know, in Salt Lake." She ran her long fingers up and down an imaginary keyboard.

"You're a member?" he said, confirming a fact already in evidence.

"Sure. Do you think your girlfriend's the only one left at home?" She gave him a quick wink.

"How do you know I have a girlfriend?"

Everything about this boy—from his missionary haircut and his knitted vest to the tips of his polished shoes—looked comfortably familiar, but this spasm of homesickness wasn't going to topple her newly achieved independence.

She glanced at him and shook her head. "Guys like you always have girlfriends." Probably a pale little thing who loved to pluck at his sleeve and gaze into those soft brown eyes.

"We haven't seen you at church."

"It's in Dundee." She raised both hands and laughed. "How am I supposed to get there?" She wound her scarf around her neck and settled her books against her chest.

"There's a bus," Twitchell offered.

"And a two-mile hike uphill." She'd checked it out but that was all. She turned away, looking past his shoulder to where Colum, one foot crossed casually over the other, was leaning against a parked bus.

Elder Spencer's voice was low. "You should come on Sunday. Both of you."

"Thanks for the invite," Colum said, "but when I require a dose of guilt, I visit St. James."

With a quick wave, Nina turned and started up the hill. Colum walked alongside, his hand on her shoulder. "Any more surprises?" he asked.

"For you or me?"

2

The Lanky American

He didn't see it coming, and why would he? Elliot Spencer had always kept the rules. He was his mother's golden child. "My firstborn son" she called him, and though the whispery way she spoke the phrase rankled him, the feeling of something biblical stuck. One of those rules, certainly in the top ten, was all young men of upstanding moral character should spend two years in some far-flung corner of the world spreading the good word. And so Elliot boarded a plane for the first time in his short life and landed in Edinburgh, initially a shock to his provincial sensibilities, but he'd adjusted quickly—not being much more than a boy.

In two months, he would cross some imaginary finish line and become part of a crowd of students at another university and the black-and-white name tag on the worn suit coat would be put aside; occasionally, the thought gave him a moment's disquiet, a cramp in the pit of his stomach that passed quickly. He enjoyed the regimented lifestyle of a missionary. The choices were simple and easily made, and he'd thrived. His height, his pleasant tone of voice, and his friendly American handshake were God-given tools, and he combed his hair carefully each morning and grinned at the guy in the mirror who was brushing his teeth. He'd stopped by the Royal Mail that morning and two letters in his breast pocket, one in his mother's firm script and the other in his girlfriend's stylized scrawl, both began with "Dear Elliot, When you come home . . ." His eyebrows pinched into a V. Returning home, nothing would be simple; choices would be complicated and consequences could kink and knot if he weren't extremely careful; and so, for the past year, he had pushed thoughts of home out of his mind—until today.

The breeze off the North Sea was blowing up a storm, and a pale sun hung low in the sky. Elliot breathed in the sea air and watched the girl as she meandered up Market Street with the skinny guy's hand on her shoulder. Several students exiting a pub grinned when they heard the soft trill of their laughter. Her smile was easy, relaxed, and so American. After the Brits, her voice had sounded slow and smooth, almost like a drawl. A wave of homesickness tightened across his chest.

Twitchell punched him in the arm. "Breathe."

"Come on," he said to Twitchell. "We've done enough for today. Grab the easel and the poster. I'll carry the books."

"Where are we going?"

"I told Sister Buchanan we'd stop by and stow her flowerpots in the shed. Check on her after I leave. A couple of times a week."

Elder Twitchell shoved his glasses up the thick bridge of his nose, tossed the easel over his shoulder, and jogged along, trying to keep up with Elliot's long strides.

"You need your gym shoes tonight," he told Twitchell. "You ever played soccer? After we teach the McMurphys, you're in for a rough game with their kids. They're brutal." But they weren't really; they were just kids, not so different from his own little brothers, and they loved the rough and tumble in the back pasture with the lanky American.

Three days later, the cold weather arrived, and the trek to the Laundromat on their preparation day was wet, but after folding his laundry and ironing his shirts—at least the collars and the cuffs—Elliot was determined to visit the ruins high on the bluff. With a dry cheese sandwich in his pocket and an apple in one hand, he strode up the crooked streets of this medieval village that had clung for protection to the castle and the cathedral built on the heights.

With Twitchell nearby, he wandered through the wet grass past gravestones so old the names were long since obliterated by the persistent wind and driving rain. For several long minutes, he stared up at massive stone walls, all that was left of the nave and the west gable. The sun was trying to break through the thick layer of clouds. Why did those Scots build here on this point of land exposed to the North Sea and Viking raiders? He shook his head.

"Let's head over to St. Rule's Tower," he called to Twitchell, who was rubbing the surface of a gravestone with his thumb.

And then he saw her in a sudden shaft of sunshine, leaning through the stone openings on the top of St. Rule's, the blue sea behind her and the wind whipping her hair. He'd never seen anything so beautiful— grass, sea, stones, and the girl. He didn't know her name, but he knew whenever he thought of Scotland for the rest of his life, he'd treasure this one perfect moment.

She looked down and noticed him standing in the tall grass. "Hallo!" She waved her hand. "Grab Elder Twitchell and come on up. You can't believe the view." The wind caught her last word and strung it out like an echo.

He inhaled the cold air and signaled to Twitchell, who was shaking his head and mouthing no at the same time.

"Eleventh century," she called down. "It's older than the cathedral, but the stairs are safe. At least that's what I've been told." A couple of other girls stood beside her, bundled against the wind with cameras in hand, leaning against the stone walls.

He squared his shoulders, put a token in the turnstile, and started up the metal circular stairs, his hands touching the dank, rough stones on either side. Narrow and dark, the stairs circled under slits in the rock walls the height to fire off an arrow. He climbed until his head was level with the landing. "That's like climbing up an elevator shaft."

She shouted into the stiff breeze. "St. Regulus shipwrecked at Muckross—isn't that a funny name? He was escaping with what was left of St. Andrew, because Emperor Constantine wanted the bones for Constantinople. How's that for nervy?"

Elliot laughed and rested his palms against the rough wooden railing. Standing in the wind, he felt like a kite soaring high above the village, the beach, the ruins, and his companion, who was panting his way up the last of the 156 stairs.

"So St. Andrews knee cap"—she wiggled her fingers—"several digits, a thigh bone, and perhaps a forearm ended up here. A cathedral was built to house the relics. It's kind of funny to think of bones as religious capital."

He knew he should say something interesting or profound, some spiritual insight, some lofty bit of wisdom about the fleeting nature of life, but his tongue stuck to the roof of his mouth, and he glanced down the stairwell watching for Twitchell.

It was after two, and the sun wouldn't last. The girl shoved her hands into the pockets of her navy jacket. The thick collar of the fisherman's knit framed her face. "The newer cathedral was dedicated in 1318, and Robert I came to the dedication and *rode his horse up the aisle*. That was Robert the Bruce. A big Scottish deal, if ever there was one."

Grinning, a pert English girl with brunette curls elbowed the blonde. "She's such a pro on all things Scottish."

A disgruntled Twitchell stepped onto the landing. "We're up at least six stories." Clutching the railing with his left hand, he moved around to peer down cautiously at the miniature version of St. Andrews village.

"That's everything I know in a nutshell." She smiled at Elliot. His heart was about to erupt out of his chest.

"It's nice to see someone from home," she said. The smile she gave him felt like a warm squeeze or a soft hand pushing a drowning man under water.

He turned his face toward the tide. Rushing in, rushing out—he couldn't remember which. All the muscles in his neck constricted on cue, and he could feel the blood coursing up his carotids. "So what brings you to St. Andrews?"

She studied Elliot intently with a gaze that felt intrusive. "Robert Burns," she announced as though the landing were a podium. "The Romantic Period. He was the pioneer of that entire movement." His face must have looked as blank as his brain felt. "You know, Robert Burns, Scotland's poet. 'Auld Lang Syne'?" She gave him a sideways glance. "No one's mentioned him to you? You look just like him. All you need is a kilt, and if you've got decent knees, you'll be in business. A professional Robert Burns impersonator."

That explained the quizzical looks she'd been giving him. "So is that good?" he asked.

Her flicker of a smile felt like a laser scoring a direct hit. "Burns was so incredibly handsome he could melt hearts at fifty paces."

He willed himself not to blush. She laughed, and he was pretty sure she was laughing at him. "I'm not in the heart-melting business," he said, his own heart thrashing around his rib cage. He brushed a moist palm against his forehead.

"You think?" She grinned. "I bet there's a large collective sigh from the female congregants every time you walk into church." She leaned forward over the wooden railing. "Anyway, the Romantic Period is my emphasis, and I want to have some fun before I student teach, but I love it here. I'm thinking of coming back after Christmas, maybe transferring."

"I love it too. It's going to be hard to leave." He glanced across at her, but she was surveying the waves and the stretch of beach beyond. "So here you are, and you're going to be a schoolteacher?"

"So here I am and uncertain about the schoolteacher thing. This week I've been giving some serious consideration to joining a circus." Nodding toward the north, she touched his hand with her fingertip. "That's what's left of the castle."

He felt like he'd been jabbed with a cattle prod. An electric current passed through his body, standing his short hair on end. She stared at him like he had smoke coming out of his ears.

Eyes wide, she jerked her finger away. "Sorry. I didn't mean to invade your personal space."

He held up both hands, laughing. "I'm a little gun shy."

"Listen, you're totally safe with me. I'm dating someone."

"The guy you were with last week?"

"Who is teaching a poetry seminar as we speak." She glanced down at her watch.

"Do you think he'd be interested in hearing the discussions?"

"No. He's Irish. Irish Catholic."

He raised an eyebrow. "If you were my little sister, I'd tell you to be careful." The expression on her face said, "Blunder. Major blunder."

"But I'm not your little sister, and the last thing I need is one more brother. I have more than enough, thank you very much." Frowning, she looked away. "Someday we'll all read Colum's novels, watch him being incredibly glib on talk shows, and say we knew him when. He's lived through 'the troubles,' as he calls it. Can you imagine growing up in Belfast? It's another world. A war zone." She gazed down at the water breaking against the fingers of rock extending into the bay.

Her hair smelled clean, like cut grass. Elliot wanted to hear her say *he* was clever, notice *him* for being taller than she was, or for being a missionary, or for making the climb up the tower in record time, anything. Her wide blue eyes were set in a face as symmetrical as her teeth with only one dimple to distinguish left from right.

"He's very chatty," she went on, "unless I ask him anything about home or Ireland, and then I get these one-adjective conversation stoppers: abysmal, wretched, grinding poverty. But of course, he's kidding because he's a product of his upbringing, and he's brilliant."

"There's no shame in being broke."

"No. Of course not." She appraised Elliot in earnest as though, until that minute, she hadn't been able to see past the name tag he'd left home on his suit coat. "I've known a lot of guys before they leave for missions and plenty after they've come home, but I've never actually met a person in the act of being a missionary." More mischief in those blue eyes. "Talking to strangers, knocking on forbidden doors, and making appointments."

"Fending off attacks." He glanced at her out of the corner of his eye. It was her turn to blush. He put his head back and laughed.

"Did you think I was launching an attack?"

"I was terrified. I'd never been accosted by a . . ." He paused, kicking himself for being beyond stupid.

"Amazonian warrior. Don't worry. I've heard it all before." She raised an imaginary bow and shot an arrow though the slit in the wall beneath her. Then she raised that bow and fired at him, point blank.

His skin tingling, he slapped a hand over his chest. She shook her head and laughed. He was certain he wouldn't just remember this moment—this moment would divide his life into two halves, everything that came before, and all the delightful complications that would come after. Consciously, he took a deep breath and stepped into the curious lightness that seemed to envelop them both.

Her hip anchored against the railing, she stretched her arms toward the sea. "Such an amazing world out there."

"We should go back down." He flinched. "I mean, I should go back down. You can do whatever you like." But calling to her friends, she led the way, and he followed her with his hand outstretched to grab her if she stumbled on the rough steps.

Standing in the wet grass, his socks felt damp as he waited for Elder Twitchell to follow the three girls out the doorway. The sea grass rippled along the expanse of beach. His mother chided him for mentioning the coasts and the rough water when inspirational stories were what she wanted to embellish to her friends at church, but on this island, eighty-five miles was as far as a person could be from the Atlantic or the North Sea, and that was where these people got their strength, their seagoing courage.

Smiling, the blonde girl waved them over to the edge of the cliff. "Be part of my photo op. I'll get doubles made and send you a copy." Twitchell dropped his bag and leaned against one of the stone walls. "Smile," she demanded. "Not a grin, a smile. Like you have a fun secret." She clicked the shutter as Twitchell stuck out his chest and tried to look older than his nineteen years.

"I'm from Mesa, Arizona," Twitchell was saying. "I go to ASU." As though a girl this pretty needed to hear impressive credentials, that he was a college man when he wasn't into being a cosmopolitan religious adventurer.

"Now you, Elder Spencer. You stand right over here. Let's get the North Sea in the background." The sun behind her, she clicked again. She moved in for a closer shot, just his head and shoulders. He was suddenly aware of the frayed cuffs on his high school sweatshirt, so faded the red had turned pink.

"What do you want me to think about?" he asked.

"You don't want to know," she said, looking into the viewfinder, but her cheeks flushed, no mistaking it.

He waited until Twitchell turned his back, then he leaned over and whispered. "I don't even know your name."

"Nina," she said, suddenly very businesslike. "Nina Rushforth. And I have to go." Two figures, with their backs against the wind, stood on the bluff. The tall young man with dark hair waved to her, his black coat billowing around him. Brilliant or not, he resembled a scarecrow more than anything else. "Colum," she announced. "His seminar must be over." Avoiding Elliot's eyes, she turned away.

He watched her saunter through the grass with her friends, heading toward the brick seawall below the castle. She waved a mittened hand over her shoulder before vanishing down the steps. Not moving, he stared at where she'd vanished. If anyone had asked, he couldn't explain what he felt. A romantic epiphany or perhaps a spiritual manifestation. He wasn't sure. All he knew was that he was blissfully euphoric about a strange girl he'd only talked to twice.

He climbed onto a three-foot block of chiseled stone. "I'm going to marry that girl," he whispered to the ruins and the wind with his arms outstretched.

"That's one tall girl. Her feet have to be a size ten," Twitchell grumbled. "She could ski without skis, and she probably does."

"No one's looking at her feet." By the time his eyes arrived at that lowest extremity, his brain was filled with so many amazing possibilities that shoe size became about as important as lunch on Tuesday.

"Her hair's crazy," Twitchell said. He shook both hands by the side of his head. "And her hands are huge."

"Her hair's beautiful."

"You've lost your mind," Twitchell said. "Your girlfriend's sending you pictures of wedding dresses, and your mother's reserved the ward cultural hall for the reception. You've got a bad case of cold feet." He waved his hand in the direction Nina had taken. "Five bucks says we never see her again."

"Oh, I'll see her again. Next Sunday at the Dundee Ward. Count on it."

"But she's with another guy."

"She's just infatuated—nothing serious. Besides, she's going to fall for me."

"Why not? You've already fallen for yourself."

"You dumb jock" was all over on Twitchell's face—Elliot had seen it there before—but it wasn't coming out of Twitchell's mouth, so he didn't care. Today nothing Twitchell said, or didn't say, mattered. He was just a bump in the road, an ant at a picnic, a short kid from Arizona who wore thick, dark-rimmed glasses.

"Nina," he whispered to himself. "Nina Rushforth." Her name sounded like a lyric to a song. A shaft of sunlight pierced the gray clouds and enveloped St. Rule's in light. Theirs was no chance meeting, no cosmic accident. Nope, fate had brought them together. The fortress of rules that had protected him his entire life was in danger of toppling, but at that particular moment, Elliot didn't care.

* * *

The pale-blue aerogram sat on the makeshift desk. Prodding himself for some glimmer of feeling, Elliot thumbed through the stack of pictures: candid shots he'd taken of Pam plus her senior yearbook picture with a fur drape covering her shoulders. For the last six months he'd needed pictures, because when he closed his eyes, he couldn't conjure her face, but tonight he felt surprisingly free from the immense strain of holding back the tide of smothering expectations. The girl next door, pretty and eager, that's what Pam had always been. A wave of guilt irritated his stomach as though an ulcer had been gnawing at his insides for two years. She'd eased her way into his family, and he'd been her oblivious accomplice so sure of the predictable life they'd share: four or five kids, Sunday dinner at his mom's, mowing the lawn on Saturday morning, shoveling snow the same day it fell, mortgage and car payments, and coaching Little League. Not now. Nostalgia and convenience weren't a reason to marry, not after the way his heart flip-flopped on the top of St. Rule's Tower. Clutching his pen, he began to write.

> *Dear Pam,*
>
> *Late October is cold and wet, and the days get dark in a hurry, but the North Sea is beautiful. I wandered around the ruins today with Elder Twitchell, and I'm amazed at what those faithful people built with their hands and a few rudimentary tools. What an inspiration.*
>
> *Two years is such a long time. I'm not the same person who left you at the airport. I've changed in so many ways, and I'm sure you've changed too. There's no easy way to say this. I'm just not sure how I feel about us. I tried to explain that a year ago, but you brushed it off as a misunderstanding. I've had a lot of time to think about how we just slid into a relationship. We didn't really choose each other. Circumstances chose us. I asked you to wait, and I know this is a rotten thing to say, but you should know what I'm thinking before I get home. I don't want to make any firm plans until I get my bearings and see how I negotiate this new time in my life. I'm going to want to date other girls.*
>
> *I feel terrible about all this. I hope you can forgive me.*
> *Elliot*

He stood at the post office the next morning and held the pathetic excuse for a letter in his hands. The blue aerogram wasn't a letter; it was a bomb.

∾ 3 ∾

Needles Knitting

chill wind blew, and Sunday or not, it was a nasty day, and Nina was sorry she'd ventured out. She'd wrapped her woolen scarf around her neck and over her mouth, but the tip of her nose was freezing. Wally Prescott, a plump junior studying medieval languages, was hovering next to her, bumping her side and invading her space. She pushed open the chapel door. A worn couch behind him, Elder Spencer was standing in the foyer with a firm grip on a squirming four-year-old, but when he saw her, his face broke into a smile as though a ray of sunshine had pierced the dreary winter's layer of gloom. He gave the boy a gentle shove. "The washroom," he said, "second door on the right." He watched her expectantly as she unwound her scarf, and then he extended his right hand.

Her fingers were so cold they burned. Her mittens had vanished under the clutter in her dorm room and her hand looked like a misplaced lobster she'd discovered in her pocket. His hand, strong and hard, held hers an uncomfortable moment too long.

He whispered, "I'm glad you came."

"Yes, well, there you are."

He raised one eyebrow, and she gave a quick nod at Wally, who was perspiring profusely under a hooded woolen coat and seemed reluctant to abandon her side.

"We didn't discover we had the same destination," Wally said, pleased with this sudden turn of good fortune, "until the bus dropped

21

us at the station. I gave her a bit of a start until we sorted it out." He'd pursued her up the hill. Not much of a contest there—a chubby hedgehog chasing a hare—but he was huffing so loudly and obviously gaining on her, so she finally turned and confronted him. "Why are you following me?" The poor guy fell all over himself apologizing for nothing he'd done wrong and rattled on, nonstop, for the last 'eg of their journey. She gave his arm a gentle pat to disengage before she unbuttoned her coat and glanced at her surroundings, which were like no church she'd ever attended before.

The building wasn't more than ten years old, but it was humble and boxy, not much in the way of carpet or draperies or couches. Still shivering, she pulled her coat about her, thinking she'd bolt for the door if Wally inched any closer. The opening notes of "A Mighty Fortress" pealed through the building.

"Violet McKenzie. She donated the organ," Elder Spencer intimated as though they were sharing a private joke. "She's the only one who knows how to play it. Rumor has it she was a Presbyterian in a past life."

"Bring it on, Violet," Nina said. The three of them filed into the chapel, and Elder Twitchell made a dramatic point of standing to let her scoot across the hard wooden bench, then followed her immediately, which left Wally near the aisle looking displeased.

Wrapping her hands in her scarf, she sat very still. Elder Spencer was a picture of pious reverence, nothing moving except his eyes, his strong jaw set and determined. Twitchell was fussing with the hymnbook. The walls were whitewashed cinder block, and the working-class Scots in heavy sweaters heartily sang hymns with familiar music and words that were strangely unrecognizable to Nina. The first speaker was the branch president, a ruddy-faced man with a shock of hair as white as his shirt. She understood one word in ten of his clipped Scottish brogue, and she finally quit trying at all and remembered instead Colum's angular cheekbones under his deep-set gray-green eyes. They'd been sitting in a pub the night before, a drenching rain rattling the window. His rough hand covered hers on the cheap Formica tabletop, and his voice was low, almost musical. "Institutions are all about self-justification, Nina. Political, religious—they're all the same. Why one is right and the other isn't. Ordinary folk get caught in the middle, or in the crosshairs, if we're not lucky." He shook his head sadly. "Everyone's shouting 'heretic' and pointing fingers at their neighbors, and God's in heaven wringing his hands and weeping at the cruelty."

"So I guess that means you don't want to go with me in the morning?" She pushed a stray lock of hair behind her ear.

"Darling girl, you can't understand me any more than I can understand you." His smile was gentle, and he raised her hand to his lips and kissed her palm. "My worry is you don't understand yourself."

She tried to empathize, but how could she begin to understand generations of hatred so fierce that a man could hide a bomb under a truck, not knowing who would be pulled bloody and dead from the carnage. The only real problems she'd faced were what selections to make in the smorgasbord of opportunities her parents laid before her.

After the last hymns were sung and the announcements were made, everyone headed for the small cluster of Sunday school classes, but Elder Spencer gestured toward the foyer. He stood with his hands clasped behind his back, biting his lip. His hand-knit sweater vest was a complicated maroon pattern of twisting cables, an extra layer of protection from drafts and inclement weather. His worn coat pulled tightly across shoulders that had filled out since the suit had been purchased two years ago.

"This is the real deal, isn't it?" she said. "Pure religion."

"What do you mean?" He tilted his head toward her. "Pure religion?"

"No frills. No ambition. Simple folk. Big hearts." She felt relieved.

He nodded. "Good people. Working class." As though that said it all.

She fumbled in her purse and extracted a white envelope she pressed into his hand. "I had those pictures developed." He opened the flap and glanced at the contents. The close-up of him? Not there. She'd hoped he wouldn't notice.

"I seem to be missing," he said.

"Really?" She shrugged. "I wonder how that happened." She laughed a quiet sort of laugh, reverent and low, church appropriate, before she spoke. "I need to head out. Beat the crowd, if you know what I mean. I can't do an hour on foot and then another hour on the bus with soon-to-be Brother Prescott." She smiled up at him. "But my roommate's curious. She wants to hear the first discussion. You met her last Monday." She wiggled her fingers by the sides of her head. "Curls. Her name's Liz Wycombe."

"Can I have your number?" He cleared his throat. "To call."

"We're never there." She jotted their phone number on the back of the envelope. "But you can leave a message at the desk in the residence hall."

"Another person needs to be there for the discussions."

"I can do that." He'd nicked his cheek shaving, and why that made her smile was a mystery. She raised one hand and turned to leave.

"When are your exams over?"

"The eighteenth of December. I leave the next day out of Edinburgh."

"I'll be back in the States the end of December or the second or third of January." His eyes traveled over her face, then stopped and met her frank gaze.

She lifted her chin. "I'm coming back. Maybe we'll cross paths at the airport."

His face crumpled. "Winters here are awful. Dark and dreary. No Utah blue skies."

"That's what people keep telling me."

"Colum?"

"No. He paints a different picture. Cozy firesides and the telling of tall tales in flickering lamp light. Needles knitting. Mulled cider. The whole bit." She'd started making a list of things she'd need winter quarter: ski underwear, more sweaters, a pair of Wellingtons, and a couple of jars of peanut butter.

He rested his weight against the window. "Why, Nina? Why put yourself at risk?" Did having her name in his mouth give him some small part of her, give him permission to question her choices? Who did he think he was? She felt heat rising in her cheeks.

"Risk? What risk? You think I'll get lost in the fog and freeze to death on the eighteenth fairway?" She wet her bottom lip with the tip of her tongue. "Elder Spencer, it sounds ridiculous to keep saying that. What's your real name?"

"Elliot." He studied her until she wiggled uncomfortably. "You're giving up student teaching?"

Colum's words flowed out of her mouth, "I can do anything, be anything. The what and where aren't as important as the passion I feel"—she touched her chest—"about whatever course I choose."

She was trying to sound mature, businesslike, and put a "Let's get a few things straight, Buster" tone in her voice. "Elliot, in addition to braving a Scottish winter, I'm considering law school in three or four years."

"Law school?" He looked like the words scorched his tongue.

"It's in the genes. Rushforth, Rushforth, Rushforth, Brewster, and McGregor. Like it or not, my dad wants me to be," and she wiggled three fingers, "Rushforth number three." "Like it or not" had slipped unannounced out of her mouth. How odd. "Or maybe I'll be a public defender. Not sure about the details." She laughed at the incredulous expression on his face. He was trying to be impressed, wanted to be impressed, but he couldn't get his head past that log on the train tracks.

His arms folded tightly across his chest, he said, "I'm trying to picture you in a courtroom buttoned up in a black suit arguing with a judge." But he seemed to be having trouble with the image. "Being a schoolteacher is more compatible with a family," he said. "Summers off, holidays." He sounded lame, and he probably knew it.

He was taller than she was, but not by much, and her blocky heels gave her the inch or two needed to engage him eye-to-eye. "I am woman. Hear me roar. Welcome to the seventies." Then she pushed the metal handle of the door. "Tell Wally I'm sorry, but I'm off to the races without him."

The rush of cold air slapped her across the face. She whipped her scarf around her neck a time or two until it covered her ears and mouth, and then she strolled down the hill.

* * *

His shoulders fell, and every bit of air in his lungs escaped through his nose until he was completely deflated and staring down through his hands at the worn, industrial strength carpeting. He thought about sending up a quick prayer, and then his mother's voice murmured in his ears, like a long distance call: "Son, be careful what you pray for. You might get it."

He wiped the fog off the window with his forearm and watched the girl until she vanished over the crest of the hill. A young Scottish member came up and hung his arm over Elliot's shoulder. "Quite a pair of shanks on that girl, if you know what I mean?"

Twitchell, a half smile playing across his face, was observing him from across the foyer. "You don't know anything about her. You could get burned and badly. That girl's a total stranger."

"I know this sounds completely crazy, but standing on top of St. Rule's Tower last Monday, I felt like I've known her forever."

"Well, I'm just worried that you'll *know* her while you're my companion, and then we'll both get sent home. Merry Christmas, Mom and Dad."

"Give it up." He punched Twitchell in the arm, harder than the crack warranted. "I'll be home in a little more than a month. Mission accomplished."

～ 4 ～

Two Hearts That Beat as One

Steel gray. The whole world looked steel gray. Twinkling Christmas lights and wreaths on the doors didn't dispel the gloom. Winter solstice was coming up fast, and the days were one continuous blur of fog, drizzle, low-hanging clouds, and darkness crowding twilight and dawn. Elliot rested his head against the glass door of the small Dundee church. The interior of his brain was as bleary as the sky outside. It had been three long weeks since he'd seen Nina. There was no reason to look for her now, but he couldn't rid himself of the shred of hope that glued his face to the frigid glass.

For the past two weeks, he'd worked hard, crowding thoughts of her out of his head. Knocking on doors with a Book of Mormon in his hand, he'd hauled Twitchell up and down the Scores, the street bordering the village and the sea, and Market Street, and every side street in between. They'd met Liz for the third discussion, but she politely sidestepped questions regarding Nina, and he was too proud to press her. They haunted tree-lined lanes by the student residence halls and set up their street display by the bus stop, but as hard as he tried to forget her, she was always in the back of his mind like a blurry presence in his peripheral vision.

Was it something he'd said? He racked his memory of their last encounter in a tea shop where he and Twitchell had stopped to read their mail and discovered Nina, her hair damp from the wet drizzle, with hot chocolate steaming on the table in front of her. She sat across

27

from him, a wry smile playing across her face, flipping through a three-page letter from home. Slipping it back in the envelope, she said, "Looks like I'm bereft of funds."

"I'm sorry," Elliot said. "What happened?"

Her cheeks were dry, but disappointment etched across her face. "No winter quarter. I'm being reeled in." She mimed the motion, her right hand turning in circles as though she'd hooked a sleek trout on the end of her line. "After due consideration, my illustrious father decided funding Colum's Pulitzer is not something he's inclined to do. No Irish grafts on the family tree."

Score one for the home team. "Your dad. He said that?"

"Not exactly." She shook her head. "I need to find Colum. Of course, I already know what he'll say: 'You're a grand girl, and you'll weather worse.'" She tapped Elliot's letter with her fingertip. "You're not opening your mail?"

"I know what it says. I'll read it later."

"'Two minds with but a single thought. Two hearts that beat as one'?" She raised one eyebrow. "Yeats?" she said softly.

He laughed. "No. Recriminations."

She gave him a quizzical look and eyed the pink envelope on the table. Trying to be clever, Twitchell made some inane remark about a firing squad at the airport and shot Elliot a couple of times with his finger and his thumb. Nina shoved her chair back abruptly. She placed a threepence next to her untouched hot chocolate.

"Elder Spencer, you're a heartbreaker." And then she was gone, back into the drizzle under gray skies. *Heartbreaker*—female code for one of the bad guys.

And here he was Sunday morning with his head pressed against the glass door and an epistle from his mother in his jacket pocket, fulfilling some need he must have to punish himself for breaking mission rules—in spirit if not in deed. He read it when he wanted to feel more miserable.

Dear Son,

We haven't heard from you in several weeks, which distresses me, but your father's patience is always a lesson in dealing with you children. He says letters or not, you will arrive home on January

2nd. *I hope you're keeping the rules. Don't be afraid to call the mission president if something is bothering you.*

Your letter to Pam has certainly taken the shine out of Christmas at the Baugh home as well as ours. I don't know what prompted your change of heart, but I'm sure everything will work out for the best. We've known Pam since she was little, and I know for a certainty that a better girl doesn't exist. She will make some man a fine wife, and I can only hope that man is you. You could certainly do worse.

Do your best. This isn't an experience you get to repeat. Know that you are always in our thoughts and prayers,
Mother

"Sister McKenzie just called." Elder Twitchell leaned around the office door. "She's got a bad cold, and her daughter says bringing her out in this weather will kill her for sure. The fog settles in her lungs." Twitchell coughed twice. "No organist for the Christmas program. What now?"

Elliot looked down at hands that could palm a basketball, but he'd quit piano lessons after two miserable years. Listening to the choir's final rehearsal, he followed Twitchell down the hall but paused when a rush of cold air lifted the hair on the back of his neck. He didn't turn around. For the last two Sundays, he'd turned around every single time the door opened, his heart in his throat, and his heart couldn't make the trip one more time.

Elder Twitchell sighed and smiled broadly. "Nina, how are you on the organ?"

Elliot glanced at her out of the corner of his eye. She and Liz were standing in the foyer wiping their shoes on the mat with Wally Prescott attached to Nina's arm like a large fleshy barnacle. Maybe the sense of betrayal Elliot felt wasn't justified, but he didn't care. Listening to Twitchell snore, he'd lain awake at night and driven himself crazy wondering where she was. He was easy to find. He was right here at church every Sunday.

Nina's hair was wound up in a soft-looking knob, but loose tendrils curled down around her face. She had on a powder-blue dress, the color of her eyes, and the lace ruffle around that slender neck stole his breath away. Her coloring and clothing were so pale in the sea of tweeds and heavy woolens, Nina looked like a tall angel balancing on a narrow beam of light. Elliot didn't trust himself to speak to her. He wasn't sure what would escape out of his mouth, so he turned away and spoke to Liz. Nina nodded to Elder Twitchell; she would give the organ a try.

She slid onto the bench. A lock of hair kept escaping down her neck, and her left hand nervously looped it back into place. She nodded at the choir director, a stern woman with iron-gray hair pulled away from her face in a tight knot. The director raised her strong arms for the choir's opening hymn as though she were Moses parting the Red Sea and the Pharaoh and his legions were just a stray bit of nonsense. Elliot and Elder Twitchell stood with the rest of the choir. "Angels We Have Heard on High" started on the beat they'd rehearsed the previous week, but Nina's hands danced across the keyboard, and during the second verse, she picked up the pace to the director's surprise.

Elliot leaned forward, the backs of his calves touching his chair. When Nina finally glanced up, the director was holding an unmoving baton in her fist and staring at Nina with such fierce exasperation that Elliot expected a spontaneous Scotch blessing in front of the entire congregation.

He burst out, "Hail the heav'n born Prince of Peace!" in his strong baritone, and the rest of the choir followed him into the third verse. It was tense. Finally, as the last notes of "Glory to the Newborn King" settled over the crowd, Brother Fraser stood to read the Christmas story. Nina mouthed "thanks" at Elliot, and he flashed her a quick thumbs-up, her lengthy absence forgotten.

After the closing prayer, forty people jammed into the foyer, looking for boots, coats, and scarves and wishing one another a happy Christmas. Small children squawked underfoot. Shivering, Nina stood with her coat over her arm, staring out the window at thick flakes falling against the dark winter sky.

"We're giving you and Liz a ride to St. Andrews," he said. So many bodies were packed into such a small space that she had to twist her neck to see his face. "It's a nasty out there." He wanted to tug affectionately on an errant curl by the side of her face as though she were one of his little sisters.

Her lips turned up in a half smile. "What about Wally?"

"I'll find him."

In a few minutes, buttoned against the cold, they started out in five inches of new snow. Flakes settled in their hair and eyelashes. Laughing, Nina and Liz clutched each other to keep from falling, and Wally, not willing to be excluded, grabbed Nina's other arm. If they slipped on the ice, she'd be split down the middle. Elliot handed Elder Twitchell the keys, a first, and climbed into the passenger side. Beaming, Wally scooted in beside Nina.

"So," Elliot asked, "you've been studying for exams?"

"That's what I should have been doing. I visited Edinburgh. My last chance to walk the Royal Mile and poke around those two castles." Her voice dropped as though she were confiding a secret millions of people didn't know. "I stood on the very spot where David Rizzio was murdered."

Wally, who'd been raised on royal gossip, modern and ancient, volunteered, "They stabbed him fifty-six times right in front of her."

"Who?" Elliot asked.

"Mary, Queen of Scots," Nina replied. "The bloodstains are still on the floor. They won't come out."

Wally gave a loud harrumph, and Liz laughed. "Americans are obsessed with the royals."

Nina stretched her arms past Wally and closed her eyes. "I tried to reach out and feel the ghosts."

"Her husband was one of the murderers," Wally said. "She never forgave him."

"And then Bothwell murdered her husband and kidnapped her and took her away to Dunbar Castle." Nina spoke in an indignant rush. "Can you imagine that journey on horseback in weather like this?"

The interior of the car was silent as they imagined the kidnapping of a queen; only the wipers made noise, indifferent to the drama.

"The man who controlled the queen ruled Scotland," Nina whispered.

The car slid, and Twitchell said, "Sorry. A bit of ice." The interior of the car smelled like wet wool, and their breath fogged the windows. Elliot reached across Twitchell and turned the wipers on high. They skirted a stalled car.

"And this all happened when?" Elliot grinned. "Last week?"

Wally cleared his throat. "Elizabeth beheaded her, you know. She didn't know what else to do. She'd locked her up in the Tower of London for almost twenty years. Mary had long red hair, and after the deed was done, the executioner held up her head for the crowd to see. But she'd been in prison for so long her own hair had turned gray, and the red hair in the man's hands was a wig. Her head fell out of the wig and rolled across the platform."

Elder Twitchell grasped the steering wheel at ten and two. "I would have thrown up. All that blood."

"And my parents named me Elizabeth. What were they thinking?" Liz giggled.

Nina whispered, "In the sixteenth century, half the girls were named either Elizabeth or Anne, interchangeable girls."

Elliot could see the lights on the bridge over the River Firth. In thirty minutes they'd be back at her residence hall. On Friday Nina would vanish.

The headlights shot faint beams through the blizzard. Elder Twitchell navigated the narrow streets and pulled up to the curb. Bare headed, Elliot jumped out to open the car door, and as Liz walked toward the entrance, he hurried alongside Nina. "We have an appointment with Wally at two on the seventeenth in the lounge of the psychology building. I need to see you before you leave."

Thick snowflakes landed on her face and shoulders. She glanced away from him toward the door Liz was holding open. "Thanks for the ride. I'm glad I'm not trudging through snowdrifts in Dundee." And then she gave him a sideways look. "There's a walkway. Off South Street. It opens into a courtyard between the divinity school and the psych labs. There's a tree there. Legend says Mary planted it herself."

* * *

It was almost five on the seventeenth. An eerie cloud shrouded the village, softening the edges of rock and brick and muffling every noise. The light from shop windows, decorated for Christmas, shone like elongated squares on the cobblestone street. Elliot and Twitchell huddled under the walkway, shivering in their soaking socks and shoes.

"Five more minutes," Elliot pleaded. "She'll come. I need to talk to her. Nothing will happen."

"Nothing will happen?" Twitchell rolled his eyes. "That's probably what Bothwell told his troops when he shoved Queen Mary inside Dunbar Castle and pulled up the drawbridge."

"Maybe she's already in the courtyard." Elliot glanced at his watch anxiously. Striding through the walkway, Elliot abandoned Twitchell, his insurance policy against temptation, looking in the pharmacy window at a Christmas display of shortbread in red plaid tins.

Glancing through the high windows, he could see students, copying machines, and secretaries sprinting to finish a semester's work, but the exteriors of the original buildings were hundreds of years old, built with lichen-covered stone. He turned slowly but he didn't see her until she stepped out of the mist, out of the shadow of the ancient tree with her coat pulled tightly around her and a scarf covering her hair. He thought for a minute that maybe this wasn't Nina at all, maybe this was one of the original inhabitants.

And then she smiled at him and all preconceived conversations and agendas vanished. "Nina," he whispered, touching her gloved fingertips. "Do you feel what I'm feeling?"

Her fogged glasses were propped on top of her head like a tiara. She took a deep breath, as though she were a kidnapped queen resigned to her fate. "I have to admit you were something of a shock. I walked out of Professor Monroe's class that morning—he's the only real Scot in the whole department—and he'd been reading *Tam o' Shanter* as it was meant to be read. An hour later I'm looking down from St. Rule's Tower, and there you were standing in the sunshine, and my head was full of Burns's amazing language." She sighed. "And, Elliot, it was like I'd stepped back two hundred years."

He was drunk on the sound of her saying his name.

"You climbed up the stairs, and Robby Burns was standing next to me on the top of St. Rule's, so incredibly handsome, and the terra firma just moved beneath my feet."

He wasn't sure he liked this. He felt like a stand-in for a dead poet.

"And all the amazing parallels," she continued, "oldest of seven children. Ploughman Poet. Incredibly humble beginnings. Do you think you might have been Robert Burns in a past life?" The sly hint of a smile was in her eyes, and he wondered if he were a blur.

Was she toying with him, flirting with him, or had she just given him the excuse to gently explain that Mormons didn't believe in reincarnation? He'd always been himself, no extra souls crowded in with his spirit, but he was caught in the ephemeral web she was casting as he drowned in those risky blue eyes. If she wanted him to be Robert Burns, okay. If she wanted to be Mary, Queen of Scots, okay. In thirteen days, he'd gladly cart her off to any of the castles they had around here. There wasn't a shortage. They could adopt a clan, wrap themselves in plaid wool, sit in the icy wind, and gag down haggis if that was what made her happy. He leaned toward her.

She stepped away, and her lips parted slowly. "No, Elliot. No way am I going to be a guilty memory. And that's all that I'll be if I'm a mistake you have to confess at your last interview with the mission president." She rested a hand on his arm. "I want to be one of your memories of Scotland, not some guilt trip."

The thick mist enveloped them. "Why, Nina? Why do you have to be a beautiful memory? Why can't we see each other when we get home and date like normal people?"

"Because I'm sorting out feelings about a baffling Irish poet, and because you're going to slip back into your previous life. No doubt about it. None of this will seem real."

Well, she had him there. But he didn't need to wait. None of this seemed real now. This was the most romantic setting anyone could imagine, it was Christmas, and he was standing in the mist inches away from this beautiful, surprisingly strong girl, who was keeping him at arm's length.

"And, Elliot, I've known a million guys like you, and you and I are on a completely different trajectory."

He cleared his throat. "Nina, I have to see you again."

"You're such a romantic." She broke a bit of greenery off the ancient oak and pressed it into his palm. "Keep this. It's a promise. When you get home, if you feel the same way, find me." She touched his cheek with her fingertip. And then she was gone, vanished back into the fog.

He stared at the bit of green in his palm. Mistletoe.

∽ 5 ∾

Lock Her
in the Basement

*B*ill Rushforth set his briefcase down next to the kitchen table. "There's a beat-up VW van parked in front of my house."

"That's very perceptive of you, Dear," his wife said, brushing his forehead with her lips "Someone is here, but he and Nina have taken off for a tromp through the snow. He borrowed your boots."

"Who's wearing my boots?"

"The boy she met in Scotland."

"I thought she wasn't taking his calls."

"He sent her a rather terse note. He has an IOU she promised to honor, and he said he would be here today to collect. No ifs, ands, or buts."

"She told you that?"

"Not exactly." Barbara, Nina's mother, set a rather elaborate ham sandwich in front of her husband and poured Sprite into a cup filled with ice.

"What's he like? Other than persistent."

"Tall and very handsome. Five bucks says he was the star of his high school basketball team. He's very comfortable in his own skin. A guy's kind of guy."

"How's Nina?"

"Fluttering. All morning."

He leaned back in his chair and pressed his steepled fingers against his chin. "She needs to focus on the LSAT. I don't know why she's student teaching this quarter."

"Let's see." She wagged her finger at him. "Who insisted on a teaching certificate if she wanted to be an English major?"

"I thought she'd change her mind."

"Well, we know how that worked out, don't we?"

He took a large bite of his sandwich and chewed for several minutes. "She's only twenty."

"I know, but she's your daughter, so I'm sure there's a plan here somewhere."

"I can't have her getting married. She's too young."

"Whoa. You're jumping the gun. No one was smiling around here when they left."

"I send her to Scotland to save her from Lars the Lutheran, she takes up with a tragic Irish novelist, and now she comes home with a returned missionary?" He bit down on a pickle.

"Maybe you should lock her in the basement."

* * *

Six new inches of snow sparkled under a bright blue sky, and the tree that afforded such convenient shade for golfers teeing off in August was dripping water from snow crystals clinging to its bare branches, and that made the bench where they were sitting something of a water hazard, but neither Elliot nor Nina seemed to notice.

He tossed a handful of snow at her, but she refused to smile. He looked over the bluff at the twisted path they'd left in the snowy fairway, their side-by-side tracks the only sign of humans. He could see where their conversation had faltered, where their feet had stopped shuffling, where her lips had been pursed. If he hadn't spotted the bench, they'd be on their way back to her house—and his family's van.

"Let me explain what was going on at the airport," he said.

"I don't need you to explain." She cocked her head to the side. "I was there." He tried to see the disaster through Nina's eyes, but she didn't know the players, which complicated everything.

His last weeks in Scotland, he'd waged a letter writing campaign. On preparation day, he filled four or five aerograms with Scottish jokes the locals were happy to share and an exaggerated reports of the nasty Scottish weather Nina was missing. He and Twitchell thought the descriptions were hilarious:

Birdwatchers announced a glimpse of sunshine near Aberdeen and set off a stampede of sun-starved Scots who nearly capsized the British Isle.

After 142 consecutive days of gray skies and drizzle, flocks of sheep contemplate suicide.

Each morning he dropped a letter into the Royal Mail. His parting shot was a thin volume of poetry with a note inside the front cover announcing Robert Burns's 200th Anniversary Tour beginning at the Salt Lake Airport on January 4, United Flight 2466, where Mr. Burns would make himself available to personalize the book. He'd scrawled a quick note to his mother and dad: *Please don't invite Pam and her family to the airport*, but he didn't tell them why.

What had he expected as he walked out of the Jetway, his heart thumping under his name tag, his hands trembling, and his knees weak? Gone for two long years, he had looked around hoping to see his brothers and sisters, his parents, and Nina, all laughing at his corny Scottish jokes and smiling, because—of course—they would have introduced themselves.

How could he have forgotten his mother's penchant for producing huge familial extravaganzas? As the oldest son and the oldest grandson he always played the starring role but never a rehearsal, never a collaboration on the script. Now here were dozens of relatives stacked layer upon layer, and at the pinnacle, just like a wedding cake, he'd arrived on the scene to hold Pam's hand and listen to everyone sigh. The adorable couple reunited at last.

"Welcome Home, Elder Spencer" signs, balloons, and at least fifty people—aunts, uncles, a handful of cousins (some he hadn't seen in years), his mother's mother in a wheelchair, and the entire Baugh clan—filled the waiting area under the harsh glare of fluorescent lights. Loud speakers, unaware of the brewing disaster, kept calling flights. Travelers elbowed their way through the jovial crowd. There was Pam, the nail-biting presence, the petite girl with teary eyes, standing so close to Elliot's mom that everyone within a mile radius knew exactly who she was: the girlfriend. "Spurned" was not information she'd shared, but anyone who saw her face could make a case for "desperate."

He hugged his mother. He grasped his father with his right hand in a clumsy embrace. It was mayhem. He felt like a carved chicken with everyone clamoring for a favorite body part. All these people wanted to shake his hand, or hug him, or call him "Elder," or ask obvious questions, "Elder, I bet you're glad to be home." His mother had not spread the news that *something* had happened quite recently in Scotland, and his Uncle Mark pumped his hand and said, "Well, I guess the next family get-together will be when you two kids tie the knot." And someone shoved Pam at him, and then she was hugging him, and he squeezed her shoulder and said hello. She grabbed his hand and hung onto him as though she were drowning. People were pressing against him with their eyes, everyone anxious for a bit of a story, some detail they could share later. It was so awkward and horrible that he wanted to sprint back down the Jetway and hide in the cockpit. And then he saw the marble replica of Nina staring from the magazine stand across the concourse, unsmiling, conspicuous without a carry-on or a purse.

He only had eyes for her, and so everyone else followed his gaze to the tall girl in the plum pantsuit with her blonde hair piled on the top of her head. She looked like a fashion model compared to this small-town crew. He caught Nina's eye, but she shook her head and drifted into the stream of tired travelers moving down the concourse to baggage claim. She was gone, and he had a sick feeling in the pit of his stomach. Despair etched across his face as the whispers began. "Who was that?" "Who was she?" "Did Elliot meet her in Scotland?" The tears sliding down Pam's face added to the whispered asides. The wrong girl was standing on top of the cake. His mother's solution was to invite Pam to make the two-hour drive home to Logan with their family of nine packed into the VW van with everyone talking at once, and Pam and Elliot wedged into a corner.

Now sitting on the snowy bench, Elliot tried to look sincere, but what he really felt was panic because this was his final roll of the dice. "I didn't want Pam to come to the airport. I'm avoiding her." Which was difficult because the stake president had called Pam and him to lead the young adults, a position of some responsibility. He was the victim of a conspiracy that had his mother's thumbprint all over it.

"You were holding her hand," Nina said.

"She was holding mine. If I'd had a referee's whistle, I would have blown it and called a time-out. It was one big mix-up, and then you disappeared. You have a way of doing that. Disappearing." He was released from his mission, Nina was sitting two inches away from him, and he couldn't touch her. He waited for her to speak, to say anything, to look at him instead of the pine trees loaded with fresh snow.

He rested his hand on her shoulder. She flinched. "Nina, give us a chance." He lifted a sandwich baggie out of his pocket with a dried shred of green inside. "Here's your IOU. Remember what you promised?"

With a skeptical half smile, she lifted her face to be kissed, and he did kiss her, long and hard. He felt her eyelashes fluttering against his cheek and her heart pounding through layers of coats and a sweater. Fireworks, no question, and the Tabernacle Choir singing the "Hallelujah" chorus. He kissed her again before whispering in her ear, "I'm so sorry about the mess at the airport. Can you forgive me?"

Breathless, she murmured into his chest, "It was just so awkward. I felt like the 'other woman.'"

"All I thought about was finding you."

The snow sparkled in the bright sunshine, and the sky was unbearably blue. She slid a handful of snow down his back, and then, laughing, she raced down the hill, inviting him to chase her. He closed his eyes and let the snow and cold air remind him of what it felt like to be a little kid. Sitting on the snowy bench with the sprig of mistletoe clutched in his fist, he felt something unwind inside him; he was finally home. He stood up and sprinted down the hill.

Hours later, red-cheeked with damp hair and soggy gloves, they burst through the kitchen door, laughing.

"Leave those wet boots in the garage." Nina's mother was stirring something in a copper saucepan, and the kitchen smelled like chocolate. Black-and-white houndstooth-patterned pants and a white sweater were not what Elliot expected a normal mother to be wearing in the kitchen, but nothing about Nina's family was remotely normal, not even close.

Eyebrows raised, she looked innocently at Nina and then gave her a quick wink. "Your father and I are leaving to run errands. Don't you think Elliot should meet him?"

"I don't know. Is this the only fresh Christian you could find? Or has the lion already been fed?"

Standing across the kitchen from Mrs. Rushforth, an attractive woman in her own right, Elliot had no choice but to say, "Nina, I'd like to meet your dad."

"Okay." She didn't say, *You asked for it*, but the thought was implicit in her firm grip on his hand.

The living room they crossed felt like the lobby of a swanky hotel. "Your dad's been successful," he said.

"And my mother's father started Interstate Trucking. He sold everything during the Depression and bought an old truck." She grinned at him. "My parents' marriage is a classic case of new money marrying newer money, but Dad's brilliant. Wily when cornered, but brilliant nevertheless." She rapped on the glass door of his study.

"Elliot." Not waiting for an introduction, Nina's father stood and extended his hand. "Bill Rushforth. I'd like to say Nina's told us all about you, but she's kept us rather in the dark. I assume you're adjusting to being home and back in school?"

"Yes, sir. It's great to be home."

"Well, don't let me keep you. I can see from your faces that you're enjoying the snow." He smiled a warm, gracious smile that he probably used right before he skewered someone on the cross exam. "Nina, you and I have an appointment tomorrow afternoon at four o'clock."

"Dad—"

"No arguing, young lady. Four o'clock."

Following Nina, Elliot nearly tripped on the Persian rug in the entry. She laughed and closed the front door behind him. But climbing into the van, she slammed the car door as Elliot fiddled with the ignition.

"What was that about? Four o'clock?" He pulled out of the driveway and headed north.

She huffed, "A discussion entitled 'What Are You Going to Do with Your Life?' which translates into not fooling around and spending more time studying for the LSAT. There will be several salient points on the dangers of early marriage and children having children."

He whistled under his breath. "How old are you?"

"Twenty, and too old for *appointments* with Dad."

"You're just a kid."

"I'm graduating from college in June, magna cum laude. I am nobody's kid."

Stopped at the light on Sunnyside, he squeezed her hand. "I don't get this whole law school thing."

"Why would you? No one was drubbing constitutional amendments into your brain before you could talk."

Elliot raised his shoulders. "I'd like to understand."

Nina put her stocking feet up against the glove compartment. "My mother is a lady who lunches. She's very social and philanthropic. She's also," Nina held her thumb and finger an eighth of an inch apart, "as smart as my dad."

"Doesn't she tend your nieces and nephews?"

"She's crazy about them, but Granny Nanny? Not a chance. And she's not the Primary president either. So that's the way it is. And law school is a matter of pride for my dad. He loved it when I was clobbering guys on the tennis court."

"What does Nina want?" He tapped his fingers nervously on the steering wheel.

"I want to see *Casablanca* at the student union." She pointed with the flat of her hand. "Turn right at the next light."

*　*　*

Five hours later they were parked in the dark in front of the large red-brick residence with only the streetlights creating shadows. The air outside the van was brittle cold.

"I thought you were student teaching spring quarter."

"A spot opened up. Someone, a very smart someone, quit."

"Tell me about it."

"I have four classes of Honors English." She rolled her eyes. "They're only three years younger than I am."

"Do they know that?"

"They're figuring it out."

He let out a long sigh. "I can't come next weekend. We only have one car, and when I take it, everyone walks." He waited, trying not to hold his breath. How badly did she want to see him?

She twisted a lock of hair around her finger and quoted a line from *Casablanca*. "Well, we'll always have Paris."

He laughed. "I have to see you. I'll hitchhike down here if that's the

41

only way, but if you could come up, that would be great." But where could she stay? Nine people shared the only bathroom at his house. If she were Pam, he'd just toss her in the mix. But Nina as number ten in the lineup on Sunday morning? Not a chance.

"I'm not ready to be a houseguest." She shifted uncomfortably. "Seems a little quick. I'm still getting used to the idea of you."

"How am I doing?"

"Well, there are some talented guys auditioning for the part of boyfriend. Nothing's certain. You did pass the *Casablanca* test. Have you ever read *Rebecca*?"

"It's at the top of my list."

"Then I'll call my friend, Cindy. Maybe I can come up in a week or two and camp on her couch."

He exhaled audibly. "That might be easier."

"That bad?"

"My mom's holding out for a Pam revival." And she'd do everything she could to scare Nina away, a risk he wasn't going to take. He felt both of his pockets. "I've misplaced the mistletoe."

"No, you haven't. I've got it." Neither spoke until he lifted her chin with his finger so he could see her eyes. "Elliot," she said, "I'm not in the market for a serious relationship."

"We'll take it slow," he murmured, lifting the hair away from the side of her neck, but his heart felt like he'd stepped onto a roller coaster that was seconds away from cresting the first hill.

She lobbed him a quick glance. "I've lived in Utah all my life. I know about returned missionaries. You're a desperate breed."

* * *

Nina's parents heard the kitchen door close.

"That's a two-hour drive home for that boy at this time of night." Barbara folded the pillow behind her back before she rested her magazine on the bedspread. "I should have invited him to stay."

"We're not encouraging a long-distance relationship," her father replied.

She chuckled and patted the back of his hand. "The stars in that little girl's eyes were huge."

6

Long Distance

Sleet was falling on a dreary Friday afternoon in the middle of March. Standing in front of a classroom of thirty-five restless sophomores, Nina pressed her fingers against her forehead as though she could take her emotional temperature and diagnose this disease, a fluttery heart and a scattered attention span. She'd been counting the minutes since lunch—one hundred and seventy-five—until she could toss her satchel stuffed with lesson plans and student essays on the backseat of her high school graduation present, a 1970 Mustang, and zoom north.

She wasn't sure when it had happened or how it had happened, but Elliot Spencer was all she could think about, which was silly. *No longer "I am woman, hear me roar,"* she thought. *I am kitten, hear me mew.* She'd lost her mind and whatever good sense she'd been blessed with. Every other weekend she drove to Logan and slept—with her feet hanging over the armrest—on the DI special in her friend's miniscule apartment and waited impatiently for the handful of hours Elliot could snatch between the two weekend shifts he worked in the hospital lab and his endless studying. They haunted the third floor in the library and plopped down on lumpy couches in the student union. Cramped in her car's bucket seats, they picnicked on barbecued chicken and Fritos. It was an odd arrangement, nothing she would ever have predicted in her rational past life.

She checked her watch for the hundredth time, and Mr. Stewart, her forty-something supervising teacher, rolled his eyes. "'Cupid is a

43

knavish lad, thus to make females mad.' Name the play, and you're out of here."

Nina focused on the checked scarf knotted around his neck and made a lucky guess. "*A Midsummer Night's Dream.*"

"Come back Monday morning quenched. Please, for both our sakes." He nodded toward the door.

On Saturday night, music from a spring formal in the adjacent ballroom filled the student lounge, a barnlike room with a glass southern wall creating the feeling of a cathedral filled with beat-up couches and chairs. With her leg tucked beneath her and a paisley scarf tied in a bow under her ear, Nina drank every word coming out of Elliot's mouth. No barber since his mission, his dark hair curled over his shirt collar, and she smelled the faint tang of hospital chemicals when he shifted on the couch. His revelations about the NCAA playoffs, embroidered or not, were the most fascinating explanations she'd ever heard a human utter. His hand grazed her neck. Her skin tingled.

"I was thinking," she said, curling a lock of his hair around her finger, "that we might go to church together tomorrow morning. At Cindy's ward."

He shook his head slowly, not pulling away. "I need to go with my family. It's the glue that holds my mother together. It makes her feel like I'm still . . ." He pressed his hands together as though he were gripping a ball.

"Part of the team," she filled in.

Elliot sighed. "Exactly." And his mother owned the franchise.

Nina straightened the bow on her throat. "They don't know about me, do they?"

He rubbed his jaw. "Oh, I'd be willing to bet they've figured something out. They're not dumb."

She grabbed his hand and started to nibble on his little finger. "Elliot," she spoke without turning her head toward him. "We hang around here. We almost live in my car. But we never go to your house. Seems kind of funny."

Her inflection on funny sounded more like *peculiar*, like he was hiding something sinister from her, a younger brother with webbed toes or a tattooed uncle with a dozen felonies on a twenty-inch rap sheet.

Elliot rested his head against the back of the couch and stared at the ceiling three stories high. When he spoke, it was to the skylights and any ancestors who happened to be listening. "There's not a lot of privacy at my house. Emotional privacy."

"I get that. I grew up with brothers."

"Nine people in a small space," he continued. "We share everything. Clothes, pencils, shampoo, toothpaste, diseases, you name it. I have two drawers that are mine and eight inches in the closet. I don't own anything that my little brothers haven't plundered. No one would hesitate to go through my drawers if they were looking for something." Or if they were curious. "Am I making any sense?"

"I'm following you." But not really, because nine people sharing one bathroom was difficult to imagine. His mother must stand outside the door with a stopwatch and a buzzer. And nine towels? Where did a family hang nine towels? The logistics intrigued her, but she bit her tongue.

"When I take you home," he touched his chest, "my Nina will become common property for everyone to discuss, criticize, and toss around the front room. I like having you all to myself."

"That sounds a little crazy."

"I know."

"The library isn't all that private."

"Compared to my house, it is." He laced his fingers together and stretched his hands above his head. "My life's black and white and blurry, and then you arrive in a burst of living color like the NBC peacock."

"You poor thing." She grabbed him by the shoulders and examined his face. "You've been missing me something terrible."

"You're right." His soft brown eyes latched onto her face before he kissed her. A couple of guys two couches nearer to the windows started to applaud. She felt light-headed, dizzy, and suddenly the corny lyrics from dozens of love songs made perfect sense.

The opening beats of "I Heard It Through the Grapevine" pounded through the lounge. The jangle of a tambourine launched her off the couch. Her shoulders swaying, she tossed her blonde hair back and forth and snapped her fingers in time to the music. "How do you feel about crashing that party?"

He grabbed her hand. "I'm for it." A grin on his face, they sauntered down the wide hall into the darkened ballroom. Fractured light
from a disco ball shot beams into the mob of college students. The
dance floor vibrated. Elliot turned toward her and bumped her hip
with his own. She twirled and shimmied as the bass pulsed. She turned
toward Elliot. He matched every move she made. He reeled her in next
to his chest and then spun her away. She laughed. He was behind her,
both hands on her waist, and then he was at her side. This guy loved
to dance. So many delightful revelations. Who was this Elliot Spencer? A circle of students formed around them, swaying back and forth,
watching her and Elliot move in perfect sync with each other. At the
end of the room under the light of a couple of long-armed lamps, the
disc jockey set a slow song on the turntable. Nina wrapped both arms
around Elliot's neck.

"Nope." He put his left hand firmly on the small of her back. "Can
you follow?"

"Try me." She'd always thought of a waltz as fairly benign, but not
dancing with Elliot. Initially, their circles were small, but gradually, he
maneuvered her out of the herd of students hanging on to each other,
slowly rocking side to side. He twirled her without missing a beat or
losing direction. Holding her tightly against his chest, they moved as
one, flying across the floor—all she was missing was a hoopskirt, a
twenty-inch waist, and dainty shoes, size five. An hour later, sweat drib-
bling down her hairline, the music stopped, and she untied her scarf
and lifted her damp hair off her forehead.

"Don't lose that," Elliot whispered into her ear. She tied her scarf
around his bicep. A couple of junior high girls stood behind a serving table ladling fruit frappé into paper cups. As the lights rose, Nina
blinked and loosened the first two buttons on her top, fanning herself
with the flat of her hand.

Sweating and red-faced, Elliot said, "Let's go."

"What? You're turning into a pumpkin? It's only ten-thirty."

"Time to bite the bullet." He pointed her toward the lobby. "Everyone else in my family will be asleep, but you can meet Diane and Gordy."

"Right now?"

"This very minute."

He pulled her car to a slow stop in front of his house. With the exception of the single porch light, the moss-green pebble-dash home was blanketed in darkness and quiet. When Elliot opened the door, only shadows greeted him. No Gordy stretched out on the floor watching Johnny Carson with the volume on low. No Diane perched on the couch. Elliot stood quietly next to the front door as though he were a stealthy intruder.

"Is there a TV room downstairs?" She could almost feel seven unconscious people breathing in unison.

"No. The ceiling's too low. It's a real basement." What did that mean? An earthen floor? Black widow spiders?

"Where's your room?" She squeezed his hand in the dark.

He nudged open a door just off the living room. Two bodies were asleep and snoring lightly on the bottom bunks. He nodded toward the top bunk near the window. "That's mine."

"Claustrophobia?"

"Not for me. For me it's normal." And silent and peaceful for the moment. He shed his coat and flipped on the dim, twenty-watt bulb over the stove. Bright orange Formica covered the countertop, and not a dish was out of place. No empty water glasses by the sink. No signs of human habitation. Standing in the shadows, he opened the freezer and reflexively grabbed for a carton of Daisy Mae chocolate chip ice cream, a brand Nina'd never heard of. Shrugging off her coat and kicking her shoes under the kitchen stool, she rested a sweaty foot on the rung and leaned her chin on her palm. "Elliot, I have something I need to tell you," she whispered, "about the LSAT."

Headlights filled the room with garish light as a car pulled into the driveway. "It's Diane." A spoon of ice cream in his hand, Elliot leaned across the counter for a last lingering kiss.

And then, with a rush of cold air, Elliot's mother whooshed into the room in her practical navy coat. His father, two steps behind, switched on the overhead light.

Awash in harsh fluorescent light and prepared to smile, Nina twisted away from Elliot, her right hand extended. Elliot's father's face bloomed a berry red, and his mother slumped into a kitchen chair as though her knees could no longer be held responsible.

With a spoon dripping ice cream still clutched in his right hand, Elliot, with his free hand, patted Nina's wild hair, which resembled, more than anything else, a dandelion gone to seed. The four of them faced each other, like victims of a crash, silent and overwhelmed by shock and loose body parts. She and Elliot looked disheveled and oddly red-handed. A funky odor was rising from Nina's stocking feet, but she hadn't done anything wrong and didn't understand why everyone was staring at her.

Elliot nudged her. "Your top's unbuttoned." His voice was low, not a whisper, more emphatic. Taking her coat off, putting her coat on, some sinister motion had tugged those slippery little buttons loose and exposed a glimpse of white lace. Too surprised to avert their eyes out of politeness, everyone watched Nina's fingers, which seemed to be stuck together, refasten five buttons. Heat rose up her neck and settled in the hollows of her cheeks. And there was her scarf tied to Elliot's arm, like some kind of male trophy, his lady's favors carried into battle.

After a long and horrible pause, half of Elliot's mouth curved up. "I thought you were home. Asleep."

His mother didn't answer him. A fringe of bangs was glued on her forehead, the rest of her dark hair was swept up in a simple French twist, and her cheap pearl and rhinestone earrings sparkled in the light. She cocked her head to one side like an angry robin whose nest had been invaded by a cat, and her glittering, dark eyes peered at Nina.

Nina's toes frantically searched the linoleum for her shoes. She pushed Elliot's hand aside and combed through her hair with her fingers. She extended her hand a second time. "I'm Nina," she blurted as though she had misplaced her last name as well as her shoes.

His mother stared at them both. "Well," she huffed. "Well," she said again.

Nina slowly lowered her hand. The edge of Elliot's dad's mouth was starting to twitch, and his leathery face seemed pleasant under a receding hairline, but his wife, two or three inches taller than her husband, just nodded her head and said, "Nina," as though the word were a bitter taste on her tongue. "I'm assuming you don't live around here." It wasn't a question; it was an accusation, a piece of incriminating evidence.

"I live in Salt Lake." The far side of the moon.

"Nina," his father said, "we're very glad to make your acquaintance."

His mother turned to Elliot. "I can make up the couch, or I suppose she could sleep with Diane." But what she really wanted was Nina out of her house.

"I'm staying with a friend, a friend from high school."

Her lips pursed, Elliot's mother nodded knowingly as though a critical bit of information had been tricked out of an informant. "Well," she said. "It's getting late."

Keeping his eyes focused on her face, Elliot's father eased his arm around Nina's shoulder and gave her a surreptitious hug while his wife removed her coat and hung it in the closet.

Clutching her jacket and one shoe against her chest, she whispered to Elliot, "I guess I won't be seeing you tomorrow."

"I'll walk you out to your car." But he paused halfway down the front walk, reaching for her hand. "This is my fault. I'm such an idiot. I should have set the stage. Prepared them." He stared over her shoulder at an immense pine tree and couldn't meet her eyes.

"Beginnings are important. This one was past awful." Her heart was pounding, and she desperately wanted to be home, back to being Bill Rushforth's much-loved daughter. "You get your looks and your height from your mother. What did your dad contribute?"

"Long suffering. Plus, I'm smart and kind, and I'm an Eagle Scout." He tried to smile. "The list goes on and on. You had something you were going to tell me?"

"Not tonight. I'm too rattled." Blocking the light, Elliot's mother's dark figure filled the front window.

With his hand on Nina's car door, Elliot spoke. "Listen, about tomorrow. I've got a meeting right after church. And I have to be to work at three." This felt like a brush-off. "Can you meet me in that waiting room in the hospital at two? We could be together for an hour?" Damage control.

"I don't know, Elliot." She shook her head and turned away.

"I better go in and unwind this mess." He thumped the hood of her car a couple of times before he strolled back to the house. She heard the storm door bang. No way was she going to be an inconvenience. The interior of her car felt safe, smelled familiar. She found a box of Junior Mints in the glove box and popped one in her mouth. Her fingers played a nervous melody on the steering wheel before she groped in her purse for keys that weren't there. They were in Elliot's pocket. Her stomach clenched. It was all she could do to make her legs move up the sidewalk. Climbing the front stoop felt like she was scaling Everest. The front door hadn't closed firmly, and the one-sided argument was easy to hear.

A voice low and smooth flicked at Elliot like a leather whip in the hand of a master. "What's happened to you? You walked off that plane two months ago, let your hair grow, and turned your back on your family. I don't even know who you are." There was a pause, and Nina imagined a couple of significant sniffs and a Kleenex daubing at tears. Nina raised her hand ready to knock. "And this half-dressed girl in my kitchen? What if one of the little kids had come in for a glass of water?" Her voice rose. "This isn't the girl for you. Nothing feminine about her." She thumped her fist twice on the top of the piano. "And who are her people? How was she raised? You need to cut this off, right now, before it goes any further. You're going to write her a nice letter in the morning—I'm sure you'll think of something kind to say—and end this."

"That's not going to happen." Elliot's voice was tense and low.

Nina held her breath waiting for a heartfelt, romantic defense. Silence. Hands shaking, she knocked softly on the door.

Tired creases across his brow, Elliot's father exhaled when he saw her, as though every ounce of oxygen had been siphoned out of his lungs. "Oh, Honey, have you been standing here long?"

"I need my keys." So she could leave. So she could get in her car, head south, and never lay eyes on any of these Spencers again, because she was not like them, not one iota. Thank heaven.

His jaw clenched, Elliot fumbled in his pocket and retrieved her loaded key chain. She raised her palm to catch the toss, but he was across the room in two strides and slammed the door behind him. The glass in the front window rattled.

"Keys, please," she mumbled. He pressed them in her hand. She turned on her heel, stalked down the sidewalk, and climbed in her car. The drizzle had stopped, but the temperature inside the car and out was chilly. He leaned his forearms against the open window.

She bumped her head repeatedly against the steering wheel.

He reached through the window and touched her shoulder. "I'm sorry you heard that." He stroked her hair. "Nina," he said, "let's run away. Back to Scotland. We could open a little bed-and-breakfast some-where in the Highlands. Call it the Mistletoe Inn."

She tried to laugh, but it sounded more like she was choking.

He took a deep breath. "I love you, Nina." Something he'd never said before, but there were no bells and whistles, no flowers and soft kisses, no lilting music in the air.

"You didn't contradict your mother."

"No one ever does. She goes off on her tirades like she's in charge, and then we all just do what we want." Pathological, that's what this was. Nina felt like she was a Declaration of Independence signed in invisible ink.

"Maybe we can talk tomorrow," she said, "but I'm not coming back up here anytime soon. No way."

He kept his eyes on her face. "Mom's having a hard time letting go. Her kids are her whole life." Nina gripped the steering wheel tightly. She could see his chest rise and fall under his faded plaid shirt.

"I don't know, Elliot." She hadn't been the hulking girl slouching in the kitchen since she was nine—it wasn't a space she wanted to revisit. "Maybe this isn't such a good idea."

"What if I come down for spring break? I'll try and get off work." A muscle twitched in the side of his face.

"My parents are starting to call you the phantom Scot." She mim-icked her father perfectly, "Who's doing the courting here? You or him?"

"I feel like I'm on the bottom of some cosmic game of pile-on with school, this church assignment, my mother, my siblings, my job." He didn't say, "And you," but there it was all over his face. "The last two months you've been the only reprieve I've had. I count the days in three-minute increments until I can be with you." But what was he really saying? That she was making demands too? Nina felt a sense of disquiet, out of balance, and unwanted.

She turned her key in the ignition. No one was shouting, but this felt like a fight.

* * *

The only bottle of nail polish in Cindy's apartment was bubblegum pink, but garish was better than mannish, so sitting on the couch the next day after church, Nina painted her fingernails with tiny brush-strokes before she wound toilet paper between her toes and painted them too. She could do feminine. She could do adorable. She'd watched her mother out-gracious hordes of high-powered philanthropic types since Nina was old enough to pass tiny cream puffs and stinky squares of cheese stabbed with cocktail toothpicks. Nina sprayed perfume on both wrists and clasped on a thin gold bracelet, shaking her hand to gauge the effect. She glanced in the full-length mirror on the bath-room door. Her powder-pink minidress was perfect—no question. She checked the clock, squared her Rushforth shoulders, and headed back to Elliot's house, a.k.a the Lion's Den.

A small person in a starched, white cloud of dotted Swiss answered the door, stared at Nina, stared past her at the Mustang convertible—the day was sunny and the top was down—and finally pronounced, "You have a swimming pool," but the words coming out of her young mouth sounded more like "You have a communicable disease that my mother doesn't want me to catch."

Nina smiled expansively, "Yes, I do. And it has a very deep end. Twelve feet." *Where we routinely drown snippy children.*

An older female nudged her sister out of the doorway. She looked like she'd borrowed Elliot's face and shrunk his features in the wash.

A smile stretched across her face, Nina extended Elliot's biochem book toward the storm door. "You must be Diane. Elliot left his book in my car."

Diane craned her neck and looked past Nina. "Nice ride."

If Nina had been thinking clearly two or three days ago, she would have borrowed her sister-in-law's celery green, rusted out Dodge Dart, but this morning that inclination left her. "Yes, it is. May I speak with Elliot for a minute?"

Diane shot a hand out of the partially opened storm door and snatched the book before she nodded at the old brick church across the street. "He's in a meeting."

"It was nice to meet you." And waving over her shoulder, Nina crossed the street, opened the heavy oak door, and followed the sound of subdued voices down an empty hall. Holding her breath, she waited outside a classroom door. Funny how in the last twelve hours she'd turned into an inadvertent eavesdropper.

A young adult service project was under discussion, cleaning the litter on the highway between Logan and the next little town down the road or maybe a stretch of highway up the canyon. A petite girl with luminous brown eyes and sticklike fingers was writing on the blackboard with a broken piece of yellow chalk, although it was more like she was performing on a brightly lit stage. Eyelashes fluttering, she was smiling shyly at Elliot as though the other six people in the room didn't exist. Pam. No question.

Nina nudged the door open with her foot.

The color drained out of Pam's face and puddled on the floor. "We're having a meeting."

Nina shrugged. She didn't care if they were having a meeting or not. One eyebrow raised, she nodded at Pam. "I need to borrow Elliot for a quick minute, and then you can have him back."

Elliot jumped from his chair.

Her heels clicked against the linoleum until they were out of earshot, then she turned on him. "I left your biochem book with one of your sibs. She didn't introduce herself, but it might have been Diane." Nina had marched up to his house thinking she could charm her way past last night's false start, and she'd been treated like a king-size soiled dove he'd picked up on Twenty-Fifth Street in Ogden.

He grasped the back of her arm and nodded his head toward the couch in the foyer. She jerked free, dropped onto the couch, and crossed her long legs at the knee.

"This whole long-distance romance thing isn't working for me," she choked out, but she didn't stand up to leave because her knees had turned to jelly.

He swallowed hard and didn't speak.

"I sleep on Cindy's floor. Except no one really sleeps. Marjorie tripped over me at three this morning. That was a lot of fun. They're sick of having me here. I'm up and in the shower at seven-thirty so I don't get in anyone's way. I tag along to church. I hang around so I can see you for an extra ten minutes, but of course, today that wasn't convenient because you have a meeting with Pam. And never in my life has any group of people treated me this badly. Never." She bit down on her thumbnail and scored the polish with her tooth.

He stood in front of her with his hands outstretched. "You're tired and upset. Let's not say anything we'll regret."

She stared at him. What did her mother always say? *When a person's behavior is inconsistent with what is coming out of his mouth, believe the behavior.* She was off the couch and heading for the double glass doors. He caught her waist. Her heart was pounding. "You're missing your meeting."

He shrugged.

This was her big exit scene, but he still had her in a firm grip.

"I love you so much," he said. "It feels like I'm going to implode, right here in the middle of the building where I've attended church my entire life. A fitting end." He held her more tightly, but this was not going well. "You're my best friend, but the people in that crummy house across the street are my family. I'm not gc'ng to apologize for them, and I'm not going to apologize for you. Not to anyone."

She broke free, shoved open the exterior door, and slumped down on the concrete steps. A stiff breeze ruffled her hair. She bent over and rested her face against her knees. He watched her for several moments before he walked out into the chill sunshine. He sat down beside her, his back pressed against the railing.

"I'm sorry," he murmured. "Please don't cry." That must be what girls did in his experience, but Nina raised her head, dry-eyed and feeling perplexed. "I'm not sure what crying would accomplish. It never really worked for me, and I gave it up years ago."

His back straightened. "What did you want to tell me last night? What's the question I'm too dense to ask?"

"I scored in the ninety-seventh percentile on the LSAT. I nailed it." She wasn't sure what she expected to see in his face, jubilation, pride, tiny fireworks mirrored in his eyes, but what she got was a blank stare.

A skinny, acne-scarred committee member in a tight suit chose that moment to push open the glass door. "Elliot, we need to make a decision."

Elliot's fingers slowly clenched into a fist. "Pick a date to clean the canyon," he said, barely turning toward the interruption. "Deal with it, Larry." Then he nudged Nina. "Let's get out of here."

Standing, she snagged her panty hose on the concrete. "Sorry, Elliot. I'm going home."

7

Serious Thinking

Elliot wasn't invited for spring break. Serious thinking time was Nina's excuse. He wondered if she had to make an appointment with her brain. Maybe that was the way it worked in her family—appointments even with themselves. He was clearly the topic of this inner dialogue, and he felt more than a little irked that he wasn't included in the discussion. This Nina roller coaster that he was riding made him dizzy and left his stomach in odd places, but he wasn't ready to get off, and he wasn't about to let her off either.

Robert Burns in a past life? Okay. He could work that angle, so every other day he sent her a short love letter, cajoling, flattering, and usually containing a joke or a couple of lines of poetry. He hadn't heard a single word from her in ten days; but nevertheless, he was particularly pleased with

> But to see her was to love her,
> Love but her, and love forever.

Success! By return mail, she let him know that those lines were from a poem about a breakup. Was that his message? Lost love? Infidelity?

The message was he had to read Burns more carefully and out loud. He didn't give up; he was sending a letter every day now, and it paid off big. On Monday night his mother gave him the message that *she* had called. "Nina," he said. "Her name is Nina." His mother just gave him her pinched face look and told him stamps were cheaper than long-distance phone calls.

It was late, but Nina answered on the first ring. "Elliot." No mention of her prolonged silence. "Why don't you come for conference weekend? The whole family's coming for dinner on Sunday."

Maybe that sounded like Disneyland to her, but not to him. He'd be tripping over her brothers and their kids and not getting any of the inside jokes, and Nina had told him her family was big on inside jokes. But she wasn't going to make the drive to Logan anytime soon, that was clear. This was his shot at reconciliation, and he was more than a little anxious.

"I work on Saturday and Sunday." But he knew this was a test he had to pass. If he could wow the brothers, it might tip the scales. "Let me see if I can trade for Friday night, and maybe I'll just give that Sunday shift away." Hey, it was only money—for tuition, his future—but not a problem.

"I'll come and get you," she offered.

"No. I'll figure it out." He suddenly felt cross, imposed upon with little encouragement. "So, Nina, how's the serious thinking going?" When she didn't answer him right away, he tapped his pencil against the kitchen counter and wondered which part of her brain would respond, the pros or the cons.

"I have a few things we need to discuss," she said.

Great. An agenda. "Do you want to give me a heads up so I can do my own serious thinking in advance?" *Or would you like to blindside me?*

"No. We can talk on Saturday."

And the girl chooses Door Number Two.

He set the phone in the cradle and decided not to broach the subject of conference weekend with his mother, because he knew what that conversation would be. A truckload of guilt. Conference weekend was something of a holiday in his family. The family slept in Saturday morning, and his mother made waffles with strawberries and whipped cream. They lounged in front of the television on the living room floor strewn with pillows and blankets. It was like going to church in pajamas. The kids took notes or drew pictures with colored pencils, and his father rewarded high scores on the conference pop quiz with movie tickets or an IOU for ice cream cones at Baskin Robbins, an unheard-of luxury. Sunday dinner was amazing because his mother would duck in and out of the kitchen all day when the choir was singing.

Conference weekend was the stuff of family traditions, and family tradition equaled sacrosanct. He'd have a private conversation with his dad about borrowing the van and then squeeze out the door Saturday morning and head down to Rushforth Central, where a couple of dozen chaperones, in all sizes, were ready to pounce. It ought to be a great weekend.

Saturday morning, right after the choir's last song—he'd been listening to the van's radio—he stood on the welcome mat, looking two stories up at the large-paned window over the massive oak door. Had the house grown an extra floor since January? This brick monster looming over him was bigger than any of the churches he'd attended in Scotland if he didn't count the cathedrals. He pushed the doorbell, and it didn't just ring, it played the University of Utah fight song. What was that about? They needed five measures and a cause to find their way to the entry? He ran his fingers through his hair and grasped the broken handle on his high school gym bag.

He'd get inside and discover that this probably wasn't a house at all. It was a maze full of booby traps and daunting obstacles, a test for intrepid suitors to determine their worthiness. A brother was probably waiting inside the door with a blindfold in hand to escort Elliot to the maze's entrance. If he could make his way back, intact, to the front door in less than two days, he'd win the hand of the beautiful but reluctant princess, who probably would need more time for serious thinking, so what was the point anyway? Maybe he'd fall down a trapdoor after a few wrong turns and vanish.

He heard someone turn the dead bolt, and the door swung open.

"I thought you'd never get here," Nina said. She gave his cheek a soft, wet kiss, then she tugged on his hand and pulled him into her father's unoccupied study. Her arms around his neck, she lifted her face to be kissed, but he held her at arm's length. His eyes searched her face.

"What's wrong?" she whispered.

"You tell me." But immense relief flooded his chest, and he dropped his gym bag at his feet. There was no time for Nina to answer, because her mother's shoes clicked across the parquet floor.

"Elliot." She extended her hand. "Call me Barbara." She gave Nina an amused look. "I phoned Aunt Lenore. You can park at the Eagle Gate. She'll have a token waiting for you."

"Do you want me to drive?" Nina asked.

"No," he said, trying to be pleasantly assertive. "But I would like to know where we're going."

"Temple Square."

Tickets and parking were impossible. Lines of young people formed before dawn outside the Tabernacle for the handful of unassigned seats. Hundreds of others, less determined, sat on blankets and listened to General Authorities' addresses piped outdoors under a cloudless blue sky along with thousands of tulips and daffodils blooming in concert to celebrate April conference, Nina's destination.

Throngs of smiling people coming for the two o'clock session filled the sidewalks. It was like the twenty-fourth of July, a holiday, a festive occasion, and no one worried about being jostled by the crowds dressed in Sunday best.

Because Nina was Nina, she found an unoccupied section of grass under a crab apple tree in glorious bloom. It was like she had a reservation. Her stage was set. Elliot lay down on a denim quilt, rested his arm behind his head, listened to the opening strains of the choir, looked up at the prettiest girl in the world, and determined to hold his ground.

She traced the side of his face with a blade of grass. "I've missed you."

He squinted at her with one eye closed. "Everything feels empty when I'm not with you. Even if I know you aren't coming on Friday, I still look for you. Listen for your step on the linoleum in the library. Imagine you've changed your mind to surprise me."

She took a deep breath. "It's really hard for me to drive to Logan every weekend. There's nowhere to land, nowhere to be."

He raised himself on one elbow and kissed her palm. "I know," he said slowly. "I think about that too. I'm not sure what the answer is."

"One of us needs to move. You could transfer to the U."

He laughed and glanced up through the tree branches. He'd handed her the first item on her agenda. "I have a job that's going to look good on my applications. The pre-dent adviser thinks I'm great. Oregon always takes the top student from Utah State. That's my best shot."

Her mouth twisted to one side. "I didn't really like student teaching." Item number two.

"No one does. It's no-man's-land."

"It feels like educational sound bites. Forty-five minutes isn't long enough to explore ideas, and then *riiiiing.*" She shook her hands as though the ringing of bells triggered a seizure. He shrugged. "No one's pressuring you to be a schoolteacher. Certainly not me."

"You didn't mention my test scores in any of your adorable notes."

Here we go, he thought. Nina's fingers were playing with the daisy button in the middle of her lavender sweater. It was impossible to look anywhere else. His heart started to pound. He took a deep breath. "My hand couldn't make the pen write those words."

She opened her mouth to speak, but he cut her off.

"Don't get me wrong. You're amazing, but I don't see why you'd subject yourself to three expensive, grueling years unless you really want to be an attorney." He swallowed hard, but he might as well be hung for a sheep as a lamb, so he plowed ahead. "I'm totally in favor of a lot of what the women's movement is pushing. If women have to work, they should get equal pay and have equal opportunity. No question. And a woman needs to have an education she can fall back on if her husband gets sick or disabled or *dies.*" He smiled as though that last bit about dying were a joke. "But a law degree feels like a demanding career away from home, and being a parent is demanding enough. Call me old-fashioned, but that's how I feel."

She stared at the tulips as though they were somehow complicit in this small skirmish of the sexes. A comforting, familiar voice boomed through the loud speakers, but Elliot couldn't make himself focus on what was being said, not with Nina's face in front of him. She looked pensive and not happy, not happy at all. He sat up and put his arm around her. He smelled the fresh scent of her hair and wanted to brush his lips across her cheek, but sitting here in the middle of all these people listening to conference, he felt like he was in church. Not the place to be kissing Nina.

She inched away from him on the blanket and held her face up to the sun. She leaned back on her elbows and closed her eyes. He tried to look away, but his eyes kept returning to her, gauging her expression.

"This is a pretty amazing time to be alive, 1973," she said. "Women have so many choices that didn't exist a generation ago. I'm smart, Elliot, but I'm not what anyone would think of as domestic. Not at all." Leaning next to his ear, she whispered, "The last casserole I made was in seventh-grade home economics—tuna and peas in cream of chicken soup. I've never cleaned a bathroom."

"You're kidding."

"No. Mrs. Thatcher comes twice a week."

"And she—what?"

"Does the laundry, irons, scrubs the tub, vacuums, you know, all that household stuff."

"You never did chores on Saturday?"

"Oh no. I practiced the piano like I was glued to the bench. Cleaning a bathroom would have been a reprieve. Time off for good behavior." She shrugged. "Sometimes we went skiing. In the summer we hiked in the Albion Basin or up Millcreek Canyon.

"You didn't work in the yard?"

"Ernest worked in the yard."

"A yard guy?"

"Exactly."

"No one worked?"

"Your idea of work is sweating with a hoe." She held up one finger. "The expectations in my home were almost palpable. If I'd come home with a B on my report card, it would have a three-alarm fire. We all worked hard—just not at domestic sorts of things. Two hours a day on the piano, rain or shine, and endless tennis lessons in stifling heat." She had circumnavigated the globe and was ready to plant her flag in the turf. "I'm not lazy," she insisted, "but cooking and cleaning, all that," she waved it away with the back of her hand, "doesn't really interest me. Being a fifties sort of domestic diva doesn't play to my strengths."

He had a hard time imagining a cleaning lady showing up in student housing. "And who raises your kids? A nanny?"

"Being an attorney and being a good parent aren't mutually exclusive," she said, shielding her eyes from the sun with her upturned palm. "Children grow up. Babies go to kindergarten." She shrugged.

"Teenagers need a full-time mom more than little kids." He was channeling his mother's voice and he knew it, but his mother was right. He needed to get Nina away from her father's influence, but that was going to be tough. She worshipped her dad when they weren't going toe-to-toe. "Have you been listening to any of these guys this morning?" He nodded toward the cone-shaped loud speaker. "Nothing's more important than family." He picked up a handful of crab apple blossoms and started to decorate her hair. "It's not about holding on to a different generation; it's about faith. Do you have enough faith to stay at home and raise children?"

She turned her face toward him and muttered, "Are you for real? You sound like you're reciting a text. I mean, come on, Elliot. What if I told you you had to stay home and take care of kids 24-7?"

The familiar cadence of a soothing voice filled the air around them. Elliot held tightly to her hands, nervous that what he was about to say would pop their pretty balloon, and she'd sail away from him. "I don't want my wife to work. There. I've said it."

Her breathing was shallow. He could barely see her chest move. He wanted to touch her throat to feel for a pulse.

She wouldn't look at him. "I don't want my mother's life," she said, "so I guess that's it."

"Make your own life." He swallowed hard. "But, Nina, make it with me."

She turned toward him. "You haven't heard anything I've said."

"We can figure it out. Compromise." He clutched her hands more tightly. "Marry me," he whispered. "Marry me tomorrow or a week from Wednesday or the first Saturday in May."

She shook the pink petals out of her hair before she leaned forward and kissed him softly. "And do what? Iron your shirts and wash your socks? Bottle peaches and pears? Find a job? Teach while you go to school?"

She freed one hand from his grip. He was losing her. She was floating away from him on a cloud of notes from "Lead Kindly Light."

"Our lives don't have to change much." He reached for her. "Think of us as best friends sharing an apartment. Roommates." He thought his head was going to burst. He'd never loved anything in his life as much as he loved Nina. He was going to get lost in those blue eyes of hers, because she was staring at him, looking right through him.

"Do you really mean that? Equal partners?" she asked. "Do you love me that much?"

"Absolutely, completely, and forever," he whispered.

61

❧ 8 ❧

Run, Nina, Run

Sunday morning, before the last speaker could return to the red, upholstered chair, Barbara clicked off the television. "Highland High Tennis" spelled in black block letters across her T-shirt, Nina was tying the laces on her running shoes. The pleasant slackening of religious muscles Elliot experienced at home during the closing hymn was absent here.

Oliver handed the baby to his wife and asked, "Teams?"

"Dad and I will stand you and Elliot and Nina," Benjamin said.

All weekend Elliot had observed Nina's father speak with understated authority, the professorial asking of questions, some rhetorical, some not, from the back of the auditorium.

"That's not particularly fair," Bill said. "Don't you want to play, Dorothy?"

Barbara nodded toward the three-month-old baby asleep on a blanket. "I'll come and watch," Dorothy said.

Elliot was waiting for the after-conference discussion about inspirational insights. Evidently that wasn't going to happen. Maybe at lunch.

Nina gave him an exaggerated wink. "Are you ready for this?" But he wasn't sure what *this* was. "Football," she whispered. She nodded at her brother Oliver. "Region champs." Then she thumbed at Benjamin. "All-state running back." Tall and muscular, the brothers—because Elliot was starting to think of them collectively—loved to mix it up. Everything was a contest, the more physical the better.

The day was clear. April—the perfect time of year. The sap was running. The Rushforths were jogging to the playground at the local elementary school. Everyone understood the drill, everyone except Elliot, who felt slightly ill at ease. Nina's family was a country unto itself.

Oliver slapped a hand on Elliot's shoulder before the kickoff. "Okay, you keep Ben off balance and then block for Nina." Nina was the receiver?

Oliver chuckled at the expression on Elliot's face. "You've never seen her run?"

Elliot snapped the ball, Nina headed down the field, and Oliver faded back and yelled, "Go long, Nina!" And then the ball sailed through the air. Nina was running backward, her arms outstretched. Her father charged down the field toward her. She shouted, "Block, Elliot!"

She caught the ball, hugged it against her chest, and twisted to the right. Her dad was coming at her. Elliot held up his hands in protest. "I'm not going to knock down your father." But Nina was gone, racing down the field, laughing, holding the ball over her head as she danced across some imaginary line between the swings and the slippery slide.

"Okay, next play," Oliver said. "Quarterback keep." But everything got confused; Benjamin rushed the center and clobbered his brother. Nina leaped on the pile while her father, his hands on his hips, laughed. Elliot just shook his head. There were definite rules but none that made sense to him. Rushforths played their games their way and they played to win.

An hour later, Elliot flopped on the damp ground, panting. Going down hard and coming up laughing seemed to be the cardinal rule. The first new sports shirt he'd owned in two years was covered with grass stains. No one seemed worried about breaking the Sabbath, because they were smashing it. His mother's lips would be in a line so tight her mouth would vanish.

Nina's father looked at his watch. "Lunch." His hair damp with sweat, Oliver loped down the sidewalk as Benjamin tossed the ball to him, back and forth, down the street. New green leaves shaded the trees with the suggestion of chartreuse, and everywhere, daffodils decorated immaculate lawns.

Nina held back and sat down in a swing. A streak of dirt down the side of her sweaty cheeks and her hair pulled back in an elastic, she pushed off with her toes and swung forward until Elliot caught the chain and twirled her around.

"So, young man, you want to get married?" She looked down her nose at him as though she were a bishop commencing an interview. "And how are you planning on keeping this young woman happy and supplied with food stuffs?"

He stepped behind her and gave the swing a push. "I'd be more motivated if she'd take a shower."

She leaned back, hanging on the chains, until her ponytail touched the gravel. "How often?"

He laughed and stretched out his arms. He wanted to embrace the entire playground. Last night, sweaty, frustrated, and buried in the cushions and pillows in front of the television, he'd tried to fill in some of the blanks for her, but she'd just shaken her head and gazed off into space. Now there was a lively interest in those blue eyes. He grabbed the chains, and she lurched forward into his arms. "What changed your mind?" he asked.

"Sucker punched by love."

"Are you serious? Is this a yes?"

"If you'll meet me halfway."

"What about August?" he said.

"What about December? That would make it a year."

"A year?"

"That we've known each other."

"You want to keep doing this every other weekend craziness, sleeping on Cindy's couch for an extra five months? Wouldn't you rather live with me?"

She opened her eyes wide. "This must be what it feels like to be one of those South American cliff divers."

Blissfully euphoric, he felt like climbing to the top of the slippery slide to make the announcement. "Let's go home and tell your folks."

"No." She held up a stiff palm. "We do this by the book. You need to talk to my dad first. And the lion will roar—loudly."

He squeezed one eye shut.

"We'll wait until we have a firm plan before we tell anyone. You've got to trust me on this." She looked up at him. "You are so incredibly cute," she said and started to stroll down the street. He watched her for a couple of minutes until she waved at him over her shoulder. He jogged to catch up.

"Where's the other Rushforth brother?"

"The draft dodger marooned in the Canadian wilderness? John's waiting for some kind of amnesty so he can come home."

Elliot whistled.

"No kidding. In World War II, my dad fought with the 101st Airborne Division, the Screaming Eagles, and he made sure Oliver and Benjamin got in the National Guard so they wouldn't go to Vietnam, but John was smoking a ton of dope and flunked out of college. Draft bait. So he burned his card at a peace rally and thumbed his way to Canada."

"Was your dad there at D-Day?"

"No. He went over two weeks later, but he fought in the Battle of the Bulge, which was really awful, and he never mentions it. Ever."

"Where does John fit in?"

"We're two years apart. I'm closer to him than anyone else. At least when I was growing up." Her bright smile dimmed. "I cried and cried when he left, but it didn't do any good. It didn't bring him back."

"I've never heard his name before."

She shrugged. "John's not tall. He's not an overachiever. Which is fine, but he made being an underachiever something of a personal mission, and he could be pretty nasty. Savage about my parents' lifestyle. He was into the whole counter-cultural thing. Sex, drugs, and rock 'n' roll. The last time I saw him, he had greasy hair down to his shoulders."

"I bet that didn't sit well."

"He always confused concern with disapprobation." She knelt down to tighten the laces on her shoe. "I wish he were here. We could tell him. Of course his advice would be that you don't need to be married to sleep together."

Elliot pulled her down on the neighbor's damp grass. "Don't think that. This isn't just physical. I love you, but I also really like you. I like talking to you. I like your take on things. My parents aren't always friends. I don't want us to end up like that."

She tipped her head to the side. "You can live in the same house with two people your whole life and not understand how their marriage works. Not know all the secrets and the ins and outs." She took a deep breath. "I want John in our life."

"Let's call him."

"He doesn't have a phone."

"Does anyone know where he is?"

"I'm sure my dad keeps loose track of him, but he's not someone we discuss." She glanced up at him. "So don't bring him up."

* * *

Smells of garlic, spaghetti sauce, and a loaded diaper filled the kitchen. Oliver was hustling the toddler into the bathroom. "Poop alert." One daughter-in-law was cutting bread. Barbara poured water into glasses. Nina's father was shaking spaghetti in a red enamel colander. Everyone was talking and no one was listening, but when a little blond-haired boy jerked his thumb at Elliot and asked, "Who's this guy?" Nina laughed. And when Nina laughed, everyone smiled.

"Dad, do you think Haldeman and Ehrlichman are long for this world?" Benjamin rolled a handful of peas onto the high chair tray. "Watergate: The gift that keeps on giving."

"Nixon thinks he can save himself by sacrificing them, but I don't think Sam Ervin is going to let go of this bone."

"Didn't anyone wonder about Nixon when he picked such a crooked attorney general?" Nina patted herself on the chest. "Who is the only person in this kitchen who was for McGovern?" She cupped her hand by her mouth and whispered loudly enough for the entire family to hear, "Although I'm sure in a year or two, it will be unanimous."

"Hey, Nina," Benjamin teased, "How's Lars?"

One eye closed, she laughed at him. "Happy on the hill working for Senator Bennett. I'll tell him you asked."

The banter stopped long enough for Nina's father to bless the food, and then platters were passed counterclockwise.

Benjamin took a sideways look at Elliot. "Is there any way to turn off the grin on this guy long enough to eat? The light reflecting off his teeth is going to trigger my seizure disorder."

Barbara made a slicing motion across her throat. "I was a stranger and ye took me in."

"What's the count, Nina? Stranger number two hundred and thirty-three?" Benjamin poked Elliot in the side.

Nina rolled her eyes. "We want this one to come back. How about passing him the bread?"

Oliver leaned forward over the table. "This sounds serious. Has little Nina discovered there are more interesting things to do with men than beat them over the head with a tennis racket?"

"You're still pouting from the drubbing you took from me last week."

Barbara tapped her chin with her finger. "Two friends gave me copies of Ira Levin's new book for my birthday. *The Stepford Wives*. Has anyone read it?"

Nina whispered to Elliot. "She just took one for the team."

Benjamin started to laugh. "It's frightening, but probably not a reflection on Dad."

"In my book, your mother is just about perfect." Nina's father nodded at Barbara.

"Thank you, Dear."

Benjamin poured a glass of water for the little boy seated on his left before he turned to Elliot. "Mom says you're applying to dental school. When?"

"A year from this fall."

"Have you taken the admissions test?"

"I'll take it a year from now."

Nina interrupted, "Are you now or have you ever been a member of the Communist Party? What's with the inquisition?"

"Relax, Nina. This is guy talk." Benjamin turned toward Elliot. "Elliot doesn't mind. Look at him. He's euphoric. What's your science GPA?"

"Three-point-four."

"You need to bump it up a point."

"I'm working on it."

Benjamin leaned back in his chair. "Don't worry about it. Most guys' grades go up after their missions or when they get married."

Elliot wiped his mouth with his napkin. "Well, I'm planning on both."

Nina dipped her head and groaned. The toddler kept smacking the tray with his cup, the little boy kept driving his car along the edge of the table, and the baby in the bassinet in the next room started crying, but the adults were all eerily quiet, as though a sudden spring storm had dropped a layer of snow over the kitchen table. For the longest ten seconds of his life, no one met Elliot's eyes except Nina's father, whose face had turned that shade of crimson only fair-skinned men can achieve so perfectly.

"Hey," Benjamin finally said. "That's great. When?"

There was no real reason to feel humiliated and clumsy, but that's how he felt, and he wanted to bolt. If there were a window close, he would have jumped through it. Elliot cleared his throat. "August."

Dorothy came around the table and kissed Nina on the cheek. "Congratulations. I'm so happy for you both."

"We'll be shopping for a wedding dress." Her mother smiled.

He'd been so close to the finish line, and then he'd tripped the trap door with his own big mouth. Why hadn't he listened to Nina? In his own small world, he'd always been made much of, but no one sitting around this table was pleased. It was as though he'd sneezed spaghetti sauce in all their faces.

Nina glanced at her wristwatch. "Conference started ten minutes ago." She slid back her chair and touched Elliot on the shoulder. He wasn't sure his legs would move, and if they did, he wasn't sure they would stop before he reached his family's van parked at the curb.

He followed her into the television room. His cheeks burned. He sat on the couch as Nina turned up the volume. "I shouldn't have said anything."

"Too late."

"Should we go in and help with the dishes?"

"No, no, no." Her voice sounded like she was wagging her finger. "Stay put."

Elliot cleared his throat. "Should I go and talk to your dad?"

"When the time comes. Until then, I'll deal with my father in my own way."

No one seemed particularly interested in the afternoon session of conference. The sun faded behind thick clouds, and Barbara turned on a couple of lamps before settling into the couch with her little grandson and a couple of picture books. Nina's father never came in, and Elliot heard a hushed conversation between Oliver and his father over the noises of dishes being washed. Before President Lee could give his final address, Benjamin lifted his little boy, sound asleep, from his mother's arms and headed for the door, stopping just long enough to smile sadly at Elliot. "Alas, poor Elliot. I knew him well."

Nina narrowed her eyes at him.

"Yorick, Elliot. Same difference." Benjamin grinned.

His palms sweating, Elliot was starting to think about home and the swarm of siblings who stole his socks and never saved him the last piece of pie but who loved him nevertheless and prized every word that came out of his mouth. He envisioned his father's quiet face. He wanted to hear his mother's interesting rehash of conference, including garbled quotes she'd direct at her children's moral failings. He was ready to lean over and tell Nina he'd better shove off, when a strong hand settled firmly on his shoulder.

"Elliot, could you spare me a few minutes before you leave?"

The deep, calm voice penetrated the depths of Elliot's queasy stomach. What could he say? No? He shook his head at Nina's frown. "Yes, sir. How about right now?"

Bill didn't sit behind his desk. Elliot wasn't a client. No, he gestured at his easy chair, and Elliot sank into the cushion and heard a soft whoosh and the crackle of expensive leather. Bill leaned gracefully against his desk, his hands at his sides. He didn't look angry.

"Well, Elliot. I guess you've discovered what we've all known for years—what a wonderful girl Nina is." He paused and smiled. "Of course, she's more than just a delightful, warm girl. She's blessed with a solid intellect, something you might not appreciate just yet, but I think you will in time. She's also very young, only twenty years old." He picked up a fountain pen and rolled it between his fingers like a cigar. "How many years do you have left to complete your undergraduate degree?"

"Two."

"Yes, that's what I assumed." He glanced away from Elliot at a piece of mail on his desk. "You're a bright, talented young man. I'm sure of that, or Nina wouldn't be in interested in you. I think chances are excellent that you'll be accepted to dental school and become an orthodontist or an oral surgeon, but have you considered what you'll do if you're not? Do you have an alternate plan?"

Elliot shrank slowly into the chair. He didn't matter to this man. He was just a mild irritant, an obstacle to be dealt with, a mosquito to be swatted. Call in a specialist, Utah Disaster Kleenup, or a pest exterminator.

"No, sir, I don't. I suppose I could work in my family's business." The minute those words came out of his mouth, he wished he could suck them back in.

"What business is that?"

"My dad and his brother have a feed and seed store. It's been in the family for a couple of generations."

Bill raised his eyebrows. "Well, Elliot, taking on a wife is a big responsibility. What if Nina were to become pregnant? You have to consider all the possibilities. You've got years of school ahead of you. You and Nina are young. Why don't you give this romance a year or two to mature? Really get to know each other. Maybe spend a little time apart. Nina's always dreamed of working in Europe before she starts law school." He laced his fingers together slowly as though the placement of each finger required a great deal of thought. "If you'd be willing to take that more prudent course, in a year or two, if you and Nina still want to marry, I'd be pleased to help you with your tuition and setting up your practice. Ease some of that financial burden off your shoulders."

Elliot sighed heavily. Why hadn't he kept his mouth shut? "I know your advice is kindly meant, and that's an incredible offer, but Nina and I have it figured out. We'd like to get married in August before fall quarter begins."

The calm, steady cadence of Bill's voice didn't change. "If you're determined to act precipitously, you must understand," he pressed his palms together, "you won't receive help from me. I can't be a party to something I disapprove of this strongly. You've only known each other five months."

"Yes, sir, but I couldn't love Nina more if I'd known her for a hundred years." He didn't bring up their past lives, but the thought crossed his mind. Elliot stood up. "I'd like to say good-bye to her before I leave."

Barbara was waiting outside the door. She smiled. "Nina's in her room. Go on up. Second door on your right."

Nina was pacing, her hands clasped behind her back, and he would have laughed if the bayonet weren't stuck so firmly in his chest. She turned when she saw him. "You look awful," she said. "You're white as a sheet." She kissed both his cheeks. Her fingers were like ice.

"He was very nice," he said.

"I'm sure. What are his terms?"

"We wait a year or two."

"And what's the plum?"

"Tuition."

"Oooo. He's playing hardball."

Elliot looked around her room. An enlargement of the picture of him she'd taken on the cliff in Scotland was tucked in her mirror. A shabby pink bear nestled between the two pillows on her four-poster bed. She picked it up and clutched it next to her chest. "So, Elliot," she said, patting the bedspread next to her and studying his face closely. "Do you want to wait? What did you tell him?"

"I told him we were pretty definite about getting married in August."

Her nostrils flared slightly, and she tugged on her left earlobe before she spoke. "Thank you for that," she exhaled softly. "He thought he was making an offer you couldn't refuse. And you let him know you can't be bought." She grabbed his hand. "If you'd said yes or even considered the money seriously, it would be over between us. I won't be a pawn in my own life."

He didn't have the energy to kiss her. He was exhausted. Pitfalls everywhere disguised as generous offers or proffered friendship, and Nina was as adept at playing this chess game as any of them.

"What else?" she demanded. "You're not telling me everything."

"What if I don't get into dental school? What if you get pregnant right off the bat?"

"Ah, yes. The hothouse flower scenario. Who will take care of little Nina? Keep her and her unborn child from starving?"

Elliot's shoulders drooped. He'd never seen Nina in attack mode. "You've got the wrong idea. He's just concerned."

"Here's a news flash. I can take care of myself. Second, he's not in favor of this union. He's holding out for a newly minted thirty-year-old junior associate or a Wall Street whiz kid. He'll just keep sending me away—Europe right?"

Elliot nodded.

"Until I come home with someone he likes or someone he arranges for me to like. I'm telling you, Rapunzel has nothing on me. I've got the braided hair and the tower without a door all down pat."

How many boyfriends had been frightened away? Two hundred and thirty-three? He felt sick. He was just a small-town bumpkin with a dad who ran the local seed and feed and a mother who shopped at Sears. He'd never be sophisticated enough to fit in this family. What would happen if they ever tried to get their two families together? What would his mother say about this house and these people? What would they say about her?

Nina took one look at his face and put her arms around him. "I hope you know this has nothing to do with you. You're completely, absolutely perfect, but no one will ever be good enough for the Rushforth princess, and I have no intention of being this family's Vestal Virgin, thank you very much." She nibbled the edge of his ear until color returned to his cheeks. "We're going to be happy even if we live in a dump and exist on stale bread and contaminated water."

He'd never experienced an anxiety attack before, but he had an overwhelming desire to hide under her bed. He stared at the plump pillows and the rumpled bedspread until his eyes found their way to Nina's face. She was an angel, an angel with a serious attitude, but an angel nevertheless. "I love you," he whispered. A crummy apartment, if she were in it, would be heaven.

"Okay," she said. "Your mission, should you chose to accept it, is to charm my mother. Don't be a sycophant; just be your adorable self." She straightened her back. "My job is to find a job. Pronto." She sat on his lap and kissed him long and hard before she put her arm through his and walked him to the entry. She paused at her father's study door, leaned her head in, and announced, "You have an appointment with Nina," she glanced at her watch, "at seven o'clock."

The front door closed, and Elliot walked across the driveway to the van. In two hours he'd be home, but looking up as he fumbled putting the key in the ignition, he saw Nina standing in the paned window on the second-story landing. An anxious smile on her lips, her hand was raised, pressed against the glass. She wasn't going to let her father and brothers tell her what to do. They'd shoved her into Elliot's arms. He should write her dad a thank-you note.

Cranking down the window, he stuck out his arm to wave back. He'd rescue this Rushforth princess from her parents, her affluence, and perhaps from herself. August couldn't come soon enough.

Part Two
The Reality

9

Sharks and Cowboys

Thatcher Valley, Utah, August 1973

For the last three months, Nina starred in an action/adventure blockbuster that was her own life. She survived familial shootouts, car chases, romantic interludes, shrieks, laughter, ribbons and lace, and a fairy-tale, climactic wedding. But now, eager and nervous, she walked out of the darkened theater and found herself standing alone in a hot August sun, a dry wind rifling her hair. It was as though the theater were a portal into an alien world, and she stood in the gravel parking lot, knees a bit wobbly, staring at an old brick warehouse sort of building. She could not go back; entering was the only way forward, and so she strode down an empty hall toward an office, every small sound echoing in the silence.

Smiling, she extended her hand, her fingernails painted a glossy pink, but the man just nodded at the chair across from his desk. She knew his name—it was painted on the pebbled glass office door: Principal Warren Killpack. She lowered herself into the oak chair and placed her hands on the armrests. She tucked her feet under a rung until she remembered to cross her ankles neatly.

"Nina Rushforth," he stated as he opened the district's manila folder.

"Spencer," she replied. "Nina Spencer. I was married over the summer."

The expression in the cold, dark eyes behind the black-rimmed glasses was lifeless. His short forehead extended into his broad nose, and his wide, humorless grin settled into his thick chest—he seemed to be missing a neck. The glasses, the white shirt, and the side-parted hair slicked back with Brylcreem were a ruse. This guy wasn't human; he was a shark. Nina breathed rapidly as he flipped noiselessly through the contents of her file. A window fan directly behind him blew papers on his desk, and he looked up as he dropped a painted rock, purple and gold, on the pile.

"What were you doing in Scotland? Were you on a mission?"

The slightest flicker of a smile on his face, and she would have gushed, "That's where I met my husband," but instead she cleared her throat before she spoke. "I did a semester at St. Andrews University. My emphasis was the Romantic Period."

He stared at her.

"You know, Robert Burns." All she got was a blank stare.

"How old are you?"

"Almost twenty-two." In eleven months. "I graduated ahead of my class." The end of her sentence slipped out of her mouth, unnoticed.

He kept flipping through the file, scrutinizing each page like a meticulous KGB agent. Had he found some incriminating document she hadn't submitted? Some devastating surprise? Pictures taken with a telephoto lens through their open bedroom window, black-and-white 8x10 glossies or maybe something garish in color. Her cheeks burned. The contract was signed and dated: Nina Rushforth, May 28, 1973. She had a copy in her purse sitting right there on the floor. She needed this job.

Irritated, he pushed the file to the side of the desk. "You'll be teaching seventh-grade English in the morning. Third hour prep, first lunch. Sixth and seventh hour you'll be in the ninth-grade rotation. Everyone teaches a mini course fifth hour."

"Mini course?" She knew about miniskirts and mini-marts but nothing about mini courses.

For the first moment during their interview, he looked slightly pleased; obviously mini courses were his brainchild. "Everyone teaches a four and a half week course outside their regular subject area." He slid a paper toward her, a shopping list of last year's offerings: photography, candy making, Christmas crafts, soccer, wood working, auto repair, volcanoes, Pacific Battles in World War II. It was an impressive list. She turned several pages. Short stories. Her heart skipped a beat. There was hope.

She sat up straight. "Would you like me to choose one of these? No one mentioned mini courses at the district." And no one mentioned sharks.

"You'll be teaching girl's charm."

Dumbstruck for only a moment, she smiled slowly, wondering if he were joking, testing her sense of humor, or seeing if she'd slip up. "Girl's charm?"

He nodded.

"I used to teach tennis lessons to kids this age." She almost said, "At my parents' country club," but she was starting to get the drift. Nix on anything about travel, country clubs, and Robert Burns.

"Thirty-four seventh- and eighth-grade girls are registered for girl's charm. That's the job."

"What will a course in girl's charm involve?" She tightened her grasp on the armrests.

He snorted and bumped her file with his fist. "A sorority girl like you won't have any trouble figuring it out."

Sorority girl? She nodded at him. Of course. How to snare a man. Tricks of the trade. Never too young to learn. "So you don't have a set curriculum you'd like me to follow?" As soon as the question came out of her mouth, she realized how ridiculous it was. What did this man know about being charming? Zilch.

He handed her a book with a worn brown cover: *Be the Girl You Want to Be.* She flipped it open. The publication date was April 1956. Where had he found this relic? There were chapters on tidy nails and complexion and posture and appropriate conversation and how to smell fresh all month long. But there was no mention of painting toenails fire engine red or interpreting risky body language. No mention of rising expectations for women, educational opportunities, equal pay for equal work, or tales of exceptional women who veered off the beaten path. Nina smiled politely, but she felt like she had on haircut days when she was a little girl with the sandbox all to herself and all her brothers' forbidden tractors at her fingertips. In six days, thirty-four little girls were going to learn about Nina's version of charming.

She looked up at him and batted her eyelashes. "Mr. Killpack, mini courses are inspired." She stood and brushed imaginary dust off her navy, polka-dot skirt. "Would it be possible to get the keys to the classroom?"

He leaned his head back and shouted, "Ruth. Can you get Janice's keys for Nina? And," he said, pretending to have an afterthought, "your faculty assignment is the school play."

"A play?"

"Before Christmas."

She knew nothing about producing a play, but she knew what his response would be: "That's the job." Christmas w: ~ four months away. There was plenty of time to figure it out; she'd write it on her list of things to worry about another day, maybe next week.

A heavyset woman appeared in the doorway. Salt-and-pepper hair styled like a scrubbing brush, she looked just like the Rushforths' housekeeper, Mrs. Thatcher, sans mustache on her lip. Nina, realizing she'd been holding her breath, exhaled. She liked Ruth immediately; they could do business.

In the outer office by Ruth's desk, Nina stretched out her legs and filled out tax forms, health insurance forms, and an agreement to donate ten dollars to anyone working in the district who up and died. Ruth handed her the faculty list with addresses and phone numbers, each preceded by a name in parentheses.

"It's a phone tree," she explained. "For emergencies."

"Great idea," Nina said. "There are only five women?"

Ruth ticked off numbers on her fingers. "Two in home economics, Bobbie and Jean. Bobbie's new like you. She's Marlo Fletcher's wife's cousin. Marlo's dad is on the school board. Then there is Cora Lee, who teaches PE full time. Marsha Lundgren teaches English in the room next to you in the morning and PE the rest of the day." She leaned forward as though she were about to divulge some weighty bit of news. "She was in charge of the drill team at Ridgecrest until she had that last 'oops' baby."

"The drill team." Nina opened her eyes a little wider. "An oops baby." And she wondered what those kids got named. Missy Conception? But she repeated, "Only five women on the entire faculty?"

"And forty-three men." Ruth nodded. "I need to be getting home for lunch. Duke's coming in."

"Your husband?" Nina smiled hopefully.

"He drives truck long-haul. We've been married twenty-seven years. And you got married . . . ?"

"Friday."

She clicked her tongue. "That's what I thought. I put the wedding announcement on the bulletin board in the faculty lounge." Ruth pursed her lips. "So you're starting a new job and a new marriage all the same week? That's a lot to take on. Oops!" She winked at Nina.

Oops, indeed, Nina thought. The keys in Ruth's competent hand, Nina followed her down the hall.

This whole business of having a serious job—seven thirty to four with a half hour for lunch—had been on her back burner all summer. She'd tried to look over Elliot's shoulder or under his arm to the reality of building a life, but then he'd kiss her and thoughts of the honeymoon blocked out a job, and a classroom, and hordes of prepubescent farm kids. *Besides*, she'd told herself in stray moments of misgiving, *thousands of people taught in junior high schools. How tough could it be?* She'd do this a couple of years while Elliot finished his undergraduate degree and then on to her real life.

She was not prepared for Principal Shark or the classroom she'd just entered. It was the length of a tennis court, long and narrow, with a blackboard against the west end. Children in the back would need binoculars. Maybe the janitor could set up bleachers. Miles of blank bulletin board met her gaze when she glanced to her left. The ceiling was fifteen feet high with suspicious, rust-colored spots of peeling paint, and a bank of dirty windows covered the southern wall. It was already hot at ten-thirty in the morning and there were no young bodies. She'd be able to cook children by two in the afternoon.

Ruth laughed at her expression. "The school was built in 1911, and this was the girl's gymnasium. That's why there's doors on both ends of the room. The building's been condemned twice." She handed Nina the keys and escaped the ancient building for her rendezvous with Duke.

Nina shoved open a grimy window and settled her gaze on the wheat fields beyond the parking lot. Next Monday would bring tough little farm kids with scrubbed faces who needed to learn to speak like Walter Cronkite.

That was her mother's parting bit of advice Sunday night as Elliot was loading wedding gifts in the backseat of Nina's car. "Elliot has a bit of a twang, dear." She held her thumb and index finger close together to indicate his twang wasn't terminal. "Make sure he watches Walter Cronkite every night. You know, while you're fixing dinner."

"We don't have a television. Maybe I'll have him read a couple of pages of Jane Austen out loud before we jump into bed."

Her mother had hugged her and given her a coy smile. "Well, here you go. Hang on for the ride." An odd thing to say, and Nina gave her the fierce smile she reserved for occasions when her mother was cryptic.

Nina rested her elbows on the peeling window ledge, thinking about the wedding—such high drama. At the end of July, a letter arrived requiring her presence at a district orientation for new teachers, Monday morning at eight o'clock, three days post nuptials. Nothing in her contract had mentioned an orientation meeting. Five boxes of embossed invitations stacked on her mother's desk announced a date that could not be changed. Their hurried, four-day honeymoon was sliced in half by a single sheet of mimeographed paper. Two days in the bridal suite at the Hotel Utah. That was it.

Monday morning in their tiny apartment, she'd grumbled around searching for her purse and the car keys lost in the clutter. With tousled hair and sleepy eyes, Elliot had grabbed her shoulders. "Nina, the honeymoon isn't over. This is just the beginning of the beginning. We have each other for eternity. I'll be waiting for you right here at four o'clock." He was so completely adorable. "I'll plan a family home evening," he said. "Our first one."

She laughed. "With a lesson and everything?"

"Short on the lesson and long on the everything." Before she hurried out the door, he kissed her good-bye.

* * *

That morning, songbirds warbling outside the screen window woke Nina, and sunshine coming through the nubby, beige curtains cast the room in a pinkish glow. Her four-poster bed was familiar, but the large person sharing it wasn't. It took her a moment or two to remember what she was—a bride. She stretched her arms over her head and wiggled her toes. "Elliot," she'd whispered, "sleeping with you feels like a secret."

"It's called intimacy." He rolled over on his back. "When we close the front door, we're in our own little world. Just us. Best friends and lovers." He kissed her nose. "I've got five hours this morning. How can I help? Do you need anything typed? Stapled? Scrubbed?"

Now, standing by the dirty windows in her classroom watching a couple of high school kids toss bales of hay onto a rack with the ease of jugglers tossing oranges, Nina hummed a little snatch of a song. Elliot had to go back to work this afternoon, but he'd promised to have the miniscule kitchen organized before she got home. There were only two burners on the stove, and the oven was so narrow that a chicken would have to climb in and roll over on its side if it wanted to be cooked. How could they stuff all the wedding presents into four cupboards? Squashed into a small space or not, it would be wonderful to settle into a comfortable routine, because the summer had been straight-up nuts.

The wedding seemed like one last errand to pick up a husband on the way to the main event. Grim faced, Elliot's mother, Rachel, had sat in the temple looking like her firstborn son was climbing a gallows. Nina's father didn't bother to hide his own obvious displeasure. Her mother kept glancing at her watch, and Nina was sure any minute she'd excuse herself to check with the caterer one last time, and Elliot's father had forgotten to shine his shoes, but none of that mattered. Nina gazed across the altar at Elliot, her hand firmly in his calloused palm, and a wonderful sense of peace floated around her, calming her fluttering heart. The crystal chandelier, the elegant mirrors, and the crowd of faces receded until Elliot was all she could see.

"Do you feel what I'm feeling?" he whispered. She nodded. When that first kiss went on moments too long and everyone twittered, she had to remind herself that there were other people in the room.

"We need to remember this moment." His lips brushed the back of her hand. "Always."

Elliot was the perfect groom. Her mother could have ordered him from *Bride's Magazine* for the photo shoot. Six foot four with soft brown hair and dark eyes, he was deliciously handsome, enough to cause the most cynical hearts to quiver. Rachel was a different story. The only adjective to describe her was *annoyed*.

Waiting at the country club for the photographer to set up, Nina's mother fussed with the neckline of the wedding dress and gave Nina a large wink before she whispered, "Well, I'm glad we decided against a formal receiving line. The less Sister Spencer says to people, the better." Nina was sure that if her mother had found a soundproof linen closet, she would have pulled a key out of the pocket of her lavender silk suit and locked Rachel away without a backward glance.

* * *

Nina walked to the back of the ancient classroom and shook the door handle. The glass in the transom rattled. She knelt down to investigate the large opening in the back wall the size of a fireplace, but there was no grate, no ashes. Slipping off her sandals, she crawled into the opening and shouted, "Hello!" No response and not much of an echo. A three-foot square shaft went up ten feet and then made a ninety-degree turn. Must be some sort of cold air return. As she backed out, barefooted and her skirt filthy, she heard a wolf whistle, long and low. Brushing cobwebs off her face and out of her hair, she turned to face a good-looking man, probably thirtyish, slouching by her door.

With the inches his cowboy boots loaned him, he and Nina were eye level, and she liked what she saw: an impressively muscular guy with a two-tone face, tanned to a crisp on the bottom and white from the eyebrows up. Every inch of the lower half of that face was covered in a huge grin. "I heard we had a looker coming."

This guy's trying to be complimentary, maybe flirting, she told herself. She threw back her head and laughed before she walked over and extended her right hand. "You must be Tex." She could play this game.

"No. Did someone tell you my name's Tex?" He gripped her hand. "My name's Nathan Hillyard. Why do you think I'm called Tex?" This guy was all about twang. He'd probably never heard of Walter Cronkite.

She wanted to sing, "I see by your outfit that you are a cowboy." She could mention the pearl snaps on his shirt and white, side-wall haircut, but she didn't. She just withdrew her hand from his firm grasp. "I'm Nina. It's nice to meet you. What do you teach?"

"Ninth-grade science."

"Science. That's great. I'm getting ready to measure these bulletin boards. I guess everyone comes back tomorrow? I'll probably see you at the faculty meeting?" She nodded to end the conversation, analyzed the beige expanse of bulletin boards, and picked up the yardstick lying across her desk.

Splashes of color, that's what she needed. Colored leaves covered with thought-provoking quotations or snatches of poetry. Redirect those wandering eyes and daydreamers. An interactive display on the left. Questions they'd see over and over with an answer under a paper flap. And that back wall? She put a finger to her lips. Maybe college recruitment posters? A dozen. She could get them for free. She'd send off requests tonight.

She glanced up. Nathan was still leaning against the doorjamb with that same lazy grin stretched across his face, watching the yardstick in Nina's hands go end over end down the length of the bulletin board. She wondered if he knew how to use a lasso. And bales of hay? This guy could toss them in the back of a truck with one hand.

10

SOS

Awash in yards of pale blue paper early Thursday morning, Nina looked up to see a put-together redhead in tight denim jeans.

"Don't use thumbtacks. That's asking for more trouble than you can possibly imagine." The woman pushed the lever on a stapler and it magically extended. "You just press it against the paper." She popped the stapler against the bulletin board with her fist, and the blue background was firmly affixed.

"How do you get the staples out?" Nina asked.

The redhead pulled a small claw out of her pocket. "Watch." The metal teeth grabbed the staple, and with a quick jerk, out it came. "I'm Marsha. Next door. Eighth-grade English."

Nina grinned. "You just saved me a couple of hours."

"I saved you more than that. Thumbtacks are lethal."

"There's so much I don't know."

Marsha raised one eyebrow, and the look on her face whispered, "Honey, if you only knew. How did you get along with Killpack?"

"Okay."

Marsha glanced over her shoulder at the open door. "He promised your job to his niece's husband. There was quite a brouhaha when he found out the district signed you. He's supposed to have the last word. Of course, the last word would have been no, which is why Mr. Patterson didn't ask him."

Nina whistled. Tread softly.

"Ken Patterson is a great guy. He's the assistant in charge of second-ary ed."

"I met him."

"He wants to punch up academics."

"Politics. It's everywhere."

"He's trying to break Killpack's stranglehold on this school. You're the only woman teaching an academic subject all day."

She'd been dropped into the middle of a turf war between two entrenched men. She'd parachuted with the 101st into enemy territory when the pilot missed the drop zone, and school started on Monday. One hundred and eighty days. It sounded like forever. Marsha was clearly recruiting for the resistance, but her news was grim.

Marsha rested her hand on Nina's shoulder. "You'll be okay. You're smart. You're the only magna cum laude in the whole building." She winked. "And only married since Friday."

"How do you know that?"

"Everyone knows." Marsha glanced over her shoulder. "The two other guys in the ninth-grade rotation are great, real pros. They've got the curriculum buttoned up. Just keep your head down and your door shut. You'll probably be okay." She waved good-bye and stepped out the door.

Probably? Nina looked down at the small claw in her palm. Not much of a weapon. The hot air was stifling. Both doors and all the windows were open. She was ready to hire a breeze. Her pink blouse stuck to her skin. She caught bits and pieces of conversations float-ing down the hall. An occasional face glanced in the doorway; some actually smiled. As Nina rolled the elastic off her wrist and pulled her flyaway blonde hair into a ponytail, Ruth hustled in, all businesslike.

"I've got your class lists. They're not permanent. Monday we'll find out who's moved out and who's moved in. We've had open registra-tion all August, but people put off getting it done." Ruth pointed at a few names. She knew the genealogy of every student back at least five generations.

Nina glanced through the lists. Two hundred and fifteen students? She'd see two hundred and fifteen students each day for one hundred and eighty days—if she lived. Chances were good that she wouldn't, and every employee in the district would have to give Elliot ten bucks.

"I don't have enough desks."

"You've got plenty of room in the back for another row. I'll have Mr. Mumford bring in a few more." She turned to leave. "One more thing: the boss is real particular about having the roll taken at the beginning of each class."

"I was thinking of taking roll from a seating chart." Her education methods teacher suggested starting class with a bang, a hook, a puzzle, a question, or a contest. Take roll after the class is in motion. Use a seating chart. Be inventive. Don't get bogged down. She looked down at her desk she'd cleaned yesterday. There was a new layer of dust. She looked up. Hovering beneath the high ceilings, low-lying clouds rained down ancient chalk dust. Mount Vesuvius was up there somewhere. In a couple of thousand years, someone would excavate this ex-girls' gym and find her body encased in hot, dirty chalk dust. She wanted to grab Ruth and scream, "Run to the sea! Run!"

Ruth was giving her a worried sideways appraisal as though she'd seen smart girls before. They were fragile, needed a lot of bolstering, took a lot of hand holding, and Ruth was too busy for all that foolishness. "You need to call roll at the beginning of each class. That's how we get our funding." She spoke slowly as though Nina were hearing impaired.

"Okay. I'll call roll."

Ruth patted Nina's arm and started back out the door.

"Hey, Ruth, what are the chances I could get a portable chalkboard?"

"Don't know. I'll ask the boss."

Armed with a stapler and listening to KCPX turned up another click or two, Nina didn't notice the rattle of someone carrying a rack of pop bottles down the hall. Her arms raised above her head, she smacked the stapler against the wall in rhythm to a triple of Three Dog Night. She stepped back, pleased with the look of the trim and ready to put up red lettering, when she noticed three men standing in the front of her room ogling her intently.

Nathan she already knew. That grin must be carved on his face.

"This here's Marlo." With his thumb, Nathan indicated the middle man with black curly hair cut short and amazingly thick lips. "And Zach."

"Lead her out, Nathan," Marlo crowed, "and let's have a look at her. She's eighteen hands if she's an inch."

88

Larry, Moe, and Curly had come to check out the new girl in town. If the guy with the curly hair tried to pry open her mouth to look at her teeth, he was going to be peeling himself off the floor. Shoulders back and her head raised, Nina lifted her hands shoulder level. "Now, don't tell me. Let me guess. Which one of you guys teaches boys' charm?"

Elton John's "Honkey Chateau" leaped out of the transistor radio, and Zach, the short man with bad teeth, did a couple of dance steps. Marlo took a long swig of Coke from a bottle, then he wiped those thick lips with the back of his meaty hand.

Zach chuckled. "When you finish your bulletin boards, you could come out and do mine."

Hands settled on her hips, Nina nodded at them. "Sorry. Every man for himself." *Marlo? What had Ruth said about him? His father's on the school board. That made him Killpack's first lieutenant. And his father's truck stop supplied the faculty room with pop.*

"Hey, Boss." Marlo grinned broadly as Killpack entered the room, then he sauntered out the door.

Zach puffed out his chest and tossed off a parting remark. "If you don't get too close, she looks almost normal."

Stepping across the threshold, his arms crossed against his thick chest, Mr. Killpack ignored Zach and surveyed the room. "You have a chalkboard," he said.

"That's true, but it's at the end of the room, and it would be useful to have one more centered. The way it is now, the kids on the last row can't read the board."

"Janice used the chalkboard where it is," he said. "She didn't have any problems. The only portable chalkboard is down in the gym." He looked at the bulletin boards, then he looked at her. "Learn to adapt."

"Okay." She smiled.

He ambled off down the hall. Why was the problem so apparent to her and so oblivious to everyone else? The chalkboard could have been moved over the summer, over dozens of summers. She sighed and took a hard look at the rows of desks. Not okay. An education course slide presentation of uninviting classrooms had desks arranged just like this, in sterile rows. "Mix it up," the professor had said. "Don't let anyone start class feeling too complacent."

It took her a half hour to arrange all thirty-six desks into two elongated horseshoes. Smiling, she leaned against her desk surveying what she'd accomplished.

Oops. The kids would all be sitting across from each other, and the girls would be wearing skirts. She angled the desks toward the front of the room.

She'd checked off all the items on her list. The noise level in the hall had diminished when she picked up five ditto masters and her purse, and, locking her doors, she walked down the hall toward the parking lot. A dusty breeze moved the leaves in tall maple trees. Her car was one of the last parked on the gravel, and she sat in it for a moment staring at the maroon brick building, feeling a shiver of excitement. With the car windows rolled down, she felt the hot air dry her skin as she drove past miles of golden fields. In Scotland this would be an inspirational pastoral landscape, but in northern Utah she felt like she was sitting on the edge of an unfamiliar world, swinging her legs.

She pulled into her spot in front of the apartment and tapped her horn twice. She glanced at her watch. The drive took seventeen minutes—maybe a little longer. The front door opened and there was Elliot, a wicked grin across his face. His hair curled over his ears and down the nape of his neck. She grabbed books out of the backseat and hauled them into the apartment.

"I don't have to be at work for another hour," he whispered, running his knuckle down the side of her cheek.

"Elliot, I don't get paid until October."

"You're kidding." His arms fell to his sides, and he stared at her. "I bought my texts today."

"Everyone was groaning at lunch. Three paychecks the first of July, and by September, everyone's broke."

His shoulders drooped, and his eyes rolled up toward the ceiling. "I was counting on your check for rent and groceries and my check for tuition." He set her books on the wobbly card table before he started unfastening the buttons on her blouse.

"I'm hot and sweaty and disgusting," she said.

Perplexed, he leaned back against the steal of a couch they'd found at the DI for ten bucks. "How much money do you have?"

"Fourteen dollars and some change."

"We can't pay the rent. What about your parents? A short-term loan?"

She pictured her mother's checkbook. Access denied. "Not a chance." She shook her head and kissed him on the cheek. "What about your parents?"

"My dad gave me the money for tuition the first quarter after I got home. I can't ask him for anything else. They just don't have it."

Her parents did but wouldn't be forthcoming.

"What about your brother?" he asked.

He meant Oliver, soon to be the second Rushforth in Rushforth, Brewster, and McGregor. Her own precarious position as Rushforth number three was fading into a nebulous future, particularly if she starved to death, and it might come to that, because she'd never seen her father's face as angry as when she'd announced the slight reprieve, a year or two off to put Elliot through undergrad.

Her father had enunciated each syllable. "You're going to bury yourself in some junior high in Clarkston?" He'd been counting on unemployment to bring her to her senses.

Witness for the defense, she'd stood on the oriental rug in her father's study that last Friday in May, her contract gripped firmly in her sweaty fist. "Clear Creek," she'd corrected him, which also didn't sit well. "It's by the Idaho border. The kids are probably charming. It's only for a year or two. Law school is definitely still on the table." But law school had taken a distant second. What she really wanted was Elliot.

Her father had loosened his red-striped tie and tossed his jacket over the back of his chair. She walked around the edge of his desk and kissed him on the cheek. "I love you, Dad, but I'm getting married August twentieth. We'd love to have both our families there. We don't want a big wedding, maybe just lunch in the backyard."

Her dad had been too clear. "If you marry that boy," he'd waved a finger in her direction, "don't expect any help from me. You're on your own. I won't bail you out."

"If I have to grub for roots and live in a cave to be with Elliot, that's what I'll do."

Her response surprised him, and he breathed loudly through his nose, "You've never indulged in theatrics, Nina."

"Well, you know what they say about desperate times." But she hated disappointing her father. They'd sent her off to broaden her horizons, and she came home in love with a missionary, a boy from northern Utah. No Ivy League connection. No name in lights. Not a story worth repeating. And the subtext had been clear from the beginning: Elliot was in the market for a free lunch. But he wasn't. He turned down the bribe. Elliot was wonderful and completely responsible.

Later that evening, she'd eavesdropped on her parents sitting on the terrace. Her mother patted his shoulder as her father grumbled, "Twenty years ago George Fowler told me, 'If your eighteen-year-old daughter comes home leading a bear and announces she's going to marry it, don't be surprised.'" He shook his head. "But Nina's always been so reasonable. What's the rush? They've only known each other six months."

"Goodness, Bill, are we that old?" Her mother's soft laugh floated through the kitchen window. "I'm proud of them for wanting to wait. Think of all the kids who don't care, wandering across the country in those psychedelic vans. Making love and not war like a bunch of bunnies." Her mother tapped her polished fingernail on the glass-topped table. "And Elliot isn't a bear. He's just madly in love. In fact, he reminds me of you." She paused. "And we are going to have a wedding—no backyard picnic for my little girl."

Nina frowned at Elliot. "Nope. I can't ask Oliver." Because thirty seconds after the phone hit the cradle, he'd be around the corner in his dad's office telling the tale, "You were right, Dad. Six days post wedding, the guy's looking for a handout."

Elliot scrunched up his nose. "You know, a tenth of what that reception cost would have kept us alive for a year."

"I know." Her stomach growled at the prospect of short rations.

"My mom thought the whole deal detracted from the wedding. If she'd been in charge, we would have had cheesecake on paper plates in the ward cultural hall."

"You didn't tell me that."

He shrugged and examined the checkbook he'd pulled out of his pocket as though it were written in Sanskrit. "I guess the only solution is SOS."

"What's that?"

"It's temp work with a pick and shovel. Outdoor work no one wants. I'll call job service." He held up one finger. "The good news is they pay you twenty bucks at the end of each day. I'll have to let them know I have to be at my other job at four."

She touched his cheeks with her palms and kissed his mouth softly. "Come on. I'll walk you down the hill."

"My mom invited us to dinner on Sunday," he said.

"Free food." She laughed.

He studied her face. "Nothing free about it."

~ 11 ~

Food Fight

*I*t was a good day for a fight, sunny and warm with thunderstorms forecast in the late afternoon. Elliot strode into the apartment, his stomach growling. He'd filched a desiccated slice of pizza in the break room hours ago, but that was it, the only thing he'd eaten all day. His eyes traveled over Nina's short-sleeved sweater and stopped on her pink bell-bottom pants. "What's going on? Why aren't you ready?"

"I am ready."

"You didn't wear that to church."

"I didn't go. I slept in. I don't want to be just half of the lovely young couple. We'll go together next week when you have the afternoon shift." She winked at him. "I finished typing those ditto masters, so I won't have to do it tonight."

He looked past her at the typewriter on the card table. "This is no good, Nina. You can't stay home if I can't go."

"It's just one morning. We'll be there next week."

They needed to leave. They'd sworn off gas and taken up walking. She made broad hand motions toward the door. He stood planted on the peeling linoleum.

"You need to put on a dress. My family wears their church clothes all day."

"My family doesn't. No way am I going to put on panty hose and high heels to walk a mile in this heat. Nothing doing, Buster. Let's go."

Nina sauntered ahead of him out the front door, and the temptation to slap her fanny was more than he could resist.

Startled, she turned around. "Hey, I'm not one of your little sisters."

Heat shimmered off the asphalt, and dry patches of grass looked like yellow sores on the lawns they passed. It had to be over ninety degrees. They didn't hold hands. Nina strode along in sandals, her toenails painted a cherry red. The closer they got to his house, the faster they walked. Someone—it had to be his dad—was grilling something in a garlicky marinade in the backyard. Gordy and his mother were sitting on the front stoop in the shade of two ancient ponderosa pines. An old rope swing hung, not moving, from a bottom branch, and a strip of dirt, pounded hard from endless feet pushing off, circled half of a tree.

Elliot sighed, relieved to be home and out of the heat. His house looked smaller than it actually was because the single-car garage wasn't attached. The steep gabled roof hid a spacious attic that his father had always intended to finish—add a couple of bedrooms and a small bath—but in spite of the unfinished attic, they had managed, all nine of them, with one bathroom and a dose of humor. Nothing in the house was extraneous, no duplications. His mother could have been the captain of a sub, she was that organized and that fastidious, and her crew was well trained. Her devotion to cleanliness was second only to her devotion to righteousness, which she had streamlined into a series of quantifiable rules. As her eyes settled on Nina's trim figure in bell-bottom pants, he thought he heard a siren signaling man overboard—that would be him.

Nina stood patiently while Elliot received his mother's embrace. With an unflinching gaze, Rachel searched his face. "How are you, Son?" That's all she ever called him. Son. His three younger brothers had names.

She touched Nina tentatively on the arm. "Some of the neighbors brought over gifts. Nothing fancy, just practical." Fancy. In his mother's eyes, the Rushforth wedding was all about fancy and a complete lack of substance, but Elliot thought it had been wonderful.

Candles had flickered on tables amid fresh flowers, and three sets of French doors opened onto a terrace set with flagstones above the first tee. A soft canyon breeze had lifted Nina's hair as she grasped the crook of his arm. They stood alone in the middle of the parquet floor as the musicians started to play the "Sleeping Beauty" waltz. Nina lifted the train of her dress as he held her waist and they started to dance.

"Walt Disney?" He winked.

"Tchaikovsky," she whispered. "This is a metaphor for the rest of our lives. Hold hands, smile, and don't step on each other's toes."

Okay, so the reception at the country club was fancy, but it was also magical. Nina's father cut in as the nine-piece orchestra played "Sunrise, Sunset," and Elliot found his mother. She daubed at her eyes as they waltzed awkwardly around the floor. "This isn't what I had planned for you," she'd mumbled. But he'd squeezed her hand. "Mom, this is the happiest day of my life. Be happy with me." He had to give her credit; she'd tried to smile.

Now a week later, his siblings spilled into the kitchen giving Elliot knowing looks, appraising looks, trying to determine if some shift in the familial tectonic plates had occurred post wedding. No one could mention it, but a neon sign was flashing above the kitchen sink: *Elliot is married.* He wanted to laugh. He could kiss Nina till his lips were numb or wrestle her onto the couch, and it was all legal. He wasn't breaking any rules. Right there in front of all of his siblings, he rested both hands on Nina's waist and nuzzled behind her ear. "Let's not stay long." The starch in Rachel's back stiffened.

"Well, those steaks must be done," she said. She gestured toward the concrete slab in the backyard that they called the patio, where Elliot's dad poked at charcoal briquettes with a stick.

Ten people crowded both sides of an ancient picnic table. Along with the tomatoes, the corn had been picked Saturday afternoon from their quarter-acre backyard garden. Nina was ravenous. Long after everyone else rested knives and forks on the paper plates, she was reaching for a fourth roll and her third cob of corn. Other than china, crystal goblets, a mix master, two silver pitchers, and a stack of crisp dish towels, the cupboards in the tiny apartment were bare. Nina hadn't listed food in the bridal registry.

"Well, at least she has an appetite," Rachel announced to no one in particular. The picnic table grew quiet. His siblings were watching Nina eat as though they'd never seen a girl spread jam on a hot roll, as though, at any moment, she might turn into a rubbery green alien and start chomping on Elliot's arm. Nina looked up, glanced around the table, and then laid her roll on the edge of the paper plate. She reached for his hand under the table. Her palm was sweaty.

Rachel cleared her throat. "How does your family know Elder Maughan?"

Nina laced her fingers through his and took a deep breath before words tumbled out of her mouth. "We don't know him at all. One of my dad's partners is connected to the powers that be. He called in some favors."

"I suppose one of the regular temple officiators wouldn't do?"

"Nope. No reverb when one of those names is dropped. I went to high school with Elder Maughan's grandson." She dropped her voice a notch. "A total pothead." She raised her eyebrows at the six siblings scrutinizing her every move. "You know, if you never start, you never have to quit."

Please, Elliot thought, *don't mention your draft-dodging brother.* Eyes wide, his youngest sister covered her mouth with her hand. No one spoke. No one moved. Forks sat on the oilcloth, untouched. He ran his fingers through his hair. He couldn't believe what Nina had just said. Here. At Sunday dinner. In his house. If she inched any closer to him, she'd be sitting on his lap. His mother folded her napkin deliberately and dropped it next to her plate.

Elliot's father gave Nina a sly smile and said, "And tomorrow is your first day teaching children to speak English."

"Two hundred and fifteen children at last count." A half smile flitted across her face. "But that could change. There are twenty extra feet in the back of the classroom. Plenty of space for Mr. Mumford to haul in a couple dozen more desks." She pressed her palm against her chest. "I was thinking of keeping my own name, but I'm so glad I didn't. That school's lost in some kind of weird time warp—back in the fifties. Those men would have freaked."

His mother put her on notice. "You're married. Your name is Spencer now."

"Yes. That's what I just said." Nina gave her an even gaze. "But it's not a moral choice. It's just a personal preference. Lots of my friends are keeping their own names. It's hard to give up your own identity. I wouldn't ask Elliot to become a Rushforth."

Elliot rolled his eyes. No mention of names before this second. He nudged the side of her foot.

"What about children's names?" Rachel asked.

"I don't know. I guess you could toss in a hyphen."

Rachel stood. Regal. Determined. Elliot's two sisters jumped up and started stacking plates and glasses and loading utensils onto a tray. It was a signal, and Nina missed it. Elliot circled her waist with his warm hand and let his fingers drift to the small of her back. He gave her a soft shove. "Help," he whispered.

"What do you need?" she whispered back.

He nodded toward his sisters.

"Got it," she mumbled. She crossed her eyes at him before she hooked a pitcher with her arm and balanced five or six dirty plates in an awkward pile as she started up the back steps toward the kitchen.

A deafening crash shattered the Sunday stillness, followed by Nina shrieking a colorful expletive. That half-inch rise between the back porch and the kitchen linoleum had never been a problem before. Gordy ducked reflexively, Elliot's dad put both arms over his head, and Elliot hesitated, marshaling his strength, reluctant to pick a side, as he fought the urge to flee, maybe back to Scotland. Tears leaked from Winifred's eyes. Marijuana and naughty words all on the same day.

Over Nina's profuse apologies, his mother's voice sailed out through the screen door. "No harm done. The pitcher has no real value. It's just a thing and things don't matter. Diane, get the broom." Then Rachel spoke slowly in a soft, even tone. "I've found that if I put dishes with anything sugary or greasy stuck to them in hot water with a couple of drops of soap and leave them for a few minutes"—he envisioned his mother waving her hand toward the sink—"they come clean with just a couple of swipes." He listened for Nina's response. None came, and his mother continued, "I've found the same thing works with difficult stains in the laundry. I soak them. Sometimes with a little bleach."

"Great," Nina said. "Thanks for the tip."

Elliot could almost hear the drumbeat over the back fence, with his mother chatting to her quilting group or muttering on the phone to her sisters. *Bless her heart, she's irreverent, disrespectful, and swears like a sailor, and I've never seen a girl so clumsy. Grandma's blue vase, shattered. It's the only thing I had of hers. Poor Elliot.*

For a minute or two, the males on the patio just sat, his brothers blank faced, looking anywhere but at him. Before he eased himself away from the picnic table, his father tapped the side of his head as though he could jostle loose what he'd just heard. "Maybe we should join the party." The screen door banged and his father stood surveying the shards of glass and scattered debris on the kitchen floor. Dustpan in hand, Diane glowered as she swept up the mess.

"Girls, these dishes can wait," Rachel said. "Let's open the gifts." The family shuffled and bumped past the disaster and into the living room, where the pile of neatly arranged packages waited on the carpet. The seating wasn't assigned, but over the years each sibling had laid claim to his own particular spot on the couch or one of the chairs or the piano bench or a pillow near his mother's feet. He watched Nina take a quick inventory. There was no room for her on the couch, so Elliot relinquished his position, slipped onto the floor, and patted the carpet beside him. She plopped down cross-legged and rested her back against his knee. Touching him seemed to calm her.

The gifts were a predictable assortment of dish towels, ceramic candy dishes, mixing bowls, an electric can opener, and an interesting collection of kitchen utensils and gadgets, which unfortunately, Nina didn't recognize. The meat thermometer was uncharted territory. The pastry blender and cloth were a mystery. She held up the stocking for the rolling pin and asked, "I'm sorry, but what's this? Has someone broken an arm?" In Elliot's family, that was tantamount to being oblivious to the function of a heart-shaped cookie cutter on Valentine's Day. By the time she unwrapped the lemon zester, she was savvy enough not to tip her hand. "Oh wonderful," she exclaimed, "I don't think we have one of these yet. Now we won't have to buy one." But Diane was onto her and innocently asked, "What is it?"

"Well, all those tiny holes across the top. I'm sure you could use it for a million things." Which made everyone laugh—at her. But happily, Nina laughed harder than anyone else. "I have a lot to learn."

Elliot wanted to poke Diane, but in the next few minutes, he wanted to strangle her. Diane nudged the last box in Nina's direction with her toe.

"Open this one." She smiled. "Pam brought it over last Monday."

The collective hush was the first he'd ever experienced in his noisy family. Pam Baugh was the unseen presence in the room, the family favorite who'd never dropped anything in recent memory and knew instinctively when to be silent. His old girlfriend was hanging on to her position as third party in a love triangle that didn't exist.

Nina gave the box a quick shake. "Nothing ticking." She laughed. He exchanged a look with Diane. She knew what was inside that box, and she was waiting to phone in her report. Nina tugged on the ribbon and slid her finger under the paper. She lifted the lid off the sturdy, white box and saw a small doll perfectly dressed in Scottish regalia nestled against a tartan scarf. She lifted the little Scot out of the box. "I sent a doll like this to my nephew." Elliot had sent this one to Pam.

It was the card resting on the scarf that drew everyone's attention. Elliot's name was firmly printed on the envelope; there was no mention of Nina. She handed the card to him and watched as his cheeks started to burn.

A wicked grin flashed across Diane's pretty mouth, and she hissed at Nina, "She waited for two years. She didn't even date anyone else, and she could have if she'd wanted to."

"I think I already knew that." Nina picked up the doll and turned toward Winifred, the already traumatized eight-year-old Spencer. "Would you keep this for me? I have a stuffed bear who is extremely jealous." Then she spoke softly, "My stake president is totally opposed to girls burying themselves for two years. It's archaic. He says a girl waiting at home is like a widow throwing herself onto a funeral pyre. I mean, what sort of a person would want a girl he loves to twiddle her thumbs for two years?" Diane and Sharlene pointed fingers at Elliot.

Nina blinked at him. "You're kidding." She glanced around the room at this family of faces, then she leaned back against his leg as though she were trying to hide—as if she were an intruder, an outsider, a thief who'd snatched him from a girl they all loved and he was a brainless Ken doll incapable of being an active participant in his own life.

"Pam was crying hard when she brought the present over," Sharlene announced. "Mom had to take her for a walk."

This wasn't a wedding present. Pam was returning everything he'd ever sent her. A melodrama in a box.

Nina's icy fingers clutched the back of Elliot's calf. "Okay," she whispered. "Jump in here. Now would be a good time." But he was occupied reading the card.

Dear Elliot,

How many times have I written those two words? I'm return-
ing your gifts. I wish I could return your promises as easily. We
both remember what they were and why you made them. We both
remember the plans we made for this August, but I hope you're
happy—if anyone can build happiness on deception. I just want
you to remember one thing: People who marry for money pay for
every cent.

Sincerely,

Pam

"I was waiting to talk to you, Son, until she was at work next week," Rachel said. "I haven't been holding anything back."

Why did they all refer to Nina in the third person? She was sitting right here in the middle of the living room. He wondered what the family called them when they weren't here. She 'n' Son? They'd sound like a Korean electronics firm.

"Now, Rachel," Elliot's father, Melvin, started in slowly. "Let's not spoil the afternoon for the newlyweds."

Nina stood, straightening her legs. "Thanks for dinner. It was delicious. I'll stop by Monday on my way home from school and pick up the gifts." Perhaps it was because they were all sitting on the floor, but when she stood, she looked as if her blonde hair were brushing the ceiling and his family had all become midgets. "Big day tomorrow. I have a few things I need to finish." For a second or two, her strong hands plucked at her pant leg, and then without a backward glance, she was out the door and took Maple Avenue at a brisk trot, sandals or no.

No one spoke. It was the longest stretch of continuous quiet the old house had experienced during the Spencer occupancy. Elliot had missed all the signals, or maybe he'd ignored the signals. No one in the neighborhood had hosted a bridal shower, and only a dozen of his relatives showed for the wedding. His mother had established a perimeter to keep Nina out.

Elliot eased himself up to his position on the couch, rested his elbows on his knees, and clasped his hands. "Okay," he said. He took a deep breath and said it again. "Okay." Not looking at anyone in particular, Elliot extended one finger. "You're not giving her a chance. You don't know her. She's wonderful, quick to smile. You've never heard her play the piano." He'd spent happy hours stretched on his back under the baby grand listening to the girl in cutoffs make beautiful, complicated music. Mesmerized, he'd studied her slim ankles and feet as they pressed the pedals. "And she's always got her nose in a book, and then she'll say, 'Hey, Elliot, listen to this,' and she'll read something to me. Something funny or interesting." She said "Hey, Elliot" all the time because he and Nina were friends. He trusted her. If they'd been seven, he would have let her play with his marbles; he would have let her join his club.

He looked around, weighing the heavy silence. He wasn't getting through. He was trying too hard. They didn't want to understand, didn't want to risk crossing their mother. Elliot cleared his throat and started again. "You know how this feels? It feels like you're cheering against me. Cheering for the other team." Nodding slowly, he pointed his finger around the room. "All summer you've acted like who I marry should be a decision made by a committee and you all should get a vote—but you don't." He shoved the white box with his foot, but he was staring at Diane. "This was mean."

Winifred spoke up, "Mom says Nina thinks she's too good for us."

Elliot picked up the pile of wrapping paper and crushed it and the note into a tight ball. "Oh, Mom," he said, "don't do this. Not to Nina."

"This stops now," his father said. "Nina is a member of this family. Elliot, see if you can get her to come back, and we'll all start over."

* * *

His hand shading his eyes, Mel stood on the front porch and watched his son jog up the street. The boys wandered out onto the grass and tossed a football back and forth, careful not to get grass stains on their clothes. Rachel slipped out the screen door and stood at her husband's elbow.

"Those kids were hungry," he said. "Something's going on."

She shrugged.

"Her family's money isn't a sin," he spoke quietly, not turning toward her.

"It's easier for a camel to go through the eye of a needle than it is for a rich man to enter the kingdom of God. I don't want my boy caught up in that lifestyle."

He touched her hand. "Thou shalt love thy neighbor as thyself."

She shook her head slowly. "Love has to be earned."

He watched his youngest boy chase the ball into the street. "No. Love is a gift. You dig in your heels about people you don't like. You've argued like a Dutch uncle all summer, but Elliot wouldn't budge. He's pursued her. It wasn't the other way around."

"That just made him want her more. She's clever. Not like poor Pam wandering around with her heart on her sleeve."

Mel sat down heavily on the step. "Loving Nina is a gift you and I are going to give Elliot, because if you chase her away, we'll lose him."

"I've spent twenty-three years of my life raising that boy."

"You don't own him."

She tied the frayed apron strings tightly around her waist and marched back inside the house.

* * *

Elliot caught up with Nina three blocks away. Panting, he lifted his hair off his sweaty forehead. "We're all new at this. We're going to make mistakes." He sucked in air trying to catch his breath. "Come back and have dessert. Mom made raspberry pie because I told her you like raspberries."

"Not a chance. I'll never be that hungry."

He leaned against a crumbling concrete retaining wall and pulled her toward him. "Please. I don't want to get off on the wrong foot." He was still breathing hard. "If we don't go back, everything's going to be awkward."

"Going to be awkward? What do you think just happened? That was an ambush." She pushed against his chest with both palms. "When did you break up with her?"

"Four days after I saw you." He sighed. "Nina, it was a done deal. Love at first sight. I thought I might feel something for Pam when I got home, but I just didn't." He lifted her arms up around his neck and pulled her tight against his chest.

Her soft breath tickled his ear. "Let's go home."

"Come on. Be a good sport. Come back and have a piece of Mom's pie."

She shook her head. "We teach people how to treat us. I've heard my mom say that a million times. If someone lobs a fireball into your lap, you're not obligated to hold it until it burns your legs. It's their fireball, not yours."

"No more fireballs, just pie." He didn't need a lecture about his family. "Let's go back. Give them a chance to make it up." Standing on the sidewalk, feet spread in a firm stance, he frowned at her. "Do you think that family of yours has been easy for me?"

That made her laugh, and she mimicked his stance. Her arms hanging loose, her trigger finger twitching. "You've run your fingers through your hair so many times, you look like a porcupine."

"You say provocative things to your brothers to get a rise out of them. On purpose. Then you all take the idea for a test drive around the dining room table, and your parents are completely entertained. My family's not like that. You can't talk about church leaders' kids smoking pot. It's disrespectful, and you know it." There was a time, maybe a week previous, when he would never have been this blunt, but now he felt caught in the middle, trapped, and she had played a part.

"The free flow of ideas is important in any group—or family."

"But your family can't talk about the Battle of the Bulge or a brother who seems to be missing." He squeezed her arm.

"Cheap shot."

"I'm just saying that every family has unspoken rules. Yours is no exception."

"Are there any secrets in your family?" She tipped her head to the side.

"I don't know." He tried not to smile, but it was all starting to feel a little ridiculous.

There were no tears on her cheeks, but the afternoon had taken a toll. She shrugged. "When I wake up tomorrow morning, I have to start being a grown-up, a schoolteacher. That's pretty scary. I was hoping you could stand in for thirty-six thirteen-year-olds, and I could practice my opening spiel."

"I need to negotiate a truce," he said. "I'll be back soon." A bolt of lightning crackled in the distance.

"I'm going home." Her hands jammed in her pockets, she started up the hill.

He watched her. Home? Their apartment didn't feel like home to him. It was a cramped motel where he slept with Nina, a couple of rooms filled with boxes and clutter, a place to drop off belongings or stray gifts. Stale cooking odors hadn't moved on with previous tenants, and the refrigerator was empty.

He strolled into his family's yard, negotiations forgotten. He played catch with his brothers, ate two slices of raspberry pie, and stood next to his mother on the front porch as arcs of lightning split the night sky. It was nearly eleven when Diane's boyfriend finally dropped Elliot off. He was ready to deliver his rehearsed apology until he saw his pillow and a sheet folded neatly on the couch. The bedroom door was closed, a faint line of light beneath it.

"Nina," he spoke through the door. "Don't you remember? Elder Maughan said never go to bed angry."

"Then be happy on the couch," came her muffled reply.

∾ 12 ∾

The First Day

She dropped a repentant Elliot at job service on her way to school. Sitting in the passenger seat, he fiddled with work gloves he'd borrowed from his father, not speaking until she stopped in front of the redbrick building.

"I'm sorry about yesterday." He leaned over and kissed her cheek.

"Can we talk about that later? Maybe tonight?" Maybe a week from Tuesday when she had an extra minute to look around her life and remember who she was.

He nodded. "Have a good first day."

Wide-eyed, she raised her shoulders and forced a grin. "What if they eat me?"

A suggestion of a smile on his face, he gripped the worn leather gloves and got out of the car. "I'll see you—or what's left of you—tonight."

* * *

With trembling fingers, Nina unlocked her classroom door and sang to herself, "Head down, door shut," but she was ready. Handouts were copied, the bulletin boards were a work of art, and her name in large script was splashed across the chalkboard. Clutching her books against her chest, she turned on one heel. Her carefully arranged, elongated horseshoes had been shoved into rows. Six rows, six desks per row. A grid. *This won't do*, she thought. And six more chairs since Friday? Well, the horseshoes would have to extend a little longer, and she moved fast, pushing desks and listening for noise from the hall.

Yellow buses started arriving, disgorging hundreds of excited, noisy students. They hit the school doors with a wave of noise, a tsunami of pint-sized seventh-graders and man-sized ninth-grade boys, a surge of hormonal crosscurrents. They filled her room with the smell of fresh morning air and excitement and the faint scent of brand-new, unwashed clothes. Recent haircuts left a band of white skin on boys' necks and around their ears. Her roll book in her hand, Nina stood at the front and looked over the sea of expectant faces.

With a small, self-conscious laugh, she said, "I'm Nina Spencer, and this is seventh-grade English." She felt like a game show host. "I'm your homeroom teacher, and if you have any problems, I'm the person who can help." She smiled broadly. It was a bluff, but no one called her on it.

She pronounced each name carefully, asked politely for nicknames, and tried to remember what name went with which scrubbed face as she seated students alphabetically. Not totally smooth, but smooth enough, and the morning proceeded.

She was wearing her favorite summer dress, a silky polyester knit, pale blue—her mother's suggestion. "It brings out the color of your eyes." No coins for the Laundromat, she washed her things with hand soap in the bathroom sink and hung them over the towel rack to dry. Unfortunately, static cling and fabric softener were words in commercials she ignored, and the dress stuck to her. As she slipped in and out of her classroom and traipsed down to the washroom third hour, she was unaware that every pair of male eyes past puberty was on her lithe shape.

Nina read the third name on the list fourth hour. "Amanda Church."

"Yes, mum." A British accent came from a demure little face with that perfect English complexion and mousey brown hair.

"Oh, Amanda. You're British."

"English, mum."

"I spent last fall in Scotland. That's where I met my husband."

"I hope he's not a Scot. Scots are rotters."

Trying not to laugh, Nina raised her fist to her mouth. "No, not a rotter. He's an American. How long have you been here?"

"Since June, mum."

"That's lovely. We're very glad to have you," Nina said as though

Amanda had been invited to this garden party she was hosting. Nina could have done with a cucumber sandwich and a couple of small iced cakes about now, because the effects of the graham cracker she'd grabbed running out the door this morning had worn off. Her stomach growled, and a boy in a front seat giggled, but that was the only mishap fourth hour, and then the bell rang loudly. First lunch.

At least it was lunch for hundreds of children and half of the faculty. She'd forgotten to stick anything in her purse, and she didn't have money to spend. She couldn't see walking into the cafeteria, plunking down a dollar fifty for straight starch and setting her tray next to complete strangers. Perhaps the PTA brought opening day treats to the faculty lounge? Or there might be a vending machine. Fifty cents. Surely their meager budget could stretch to allow fifty cents to stave off starvation. She thought of her mother at this very moment having a lovely lunch with well-dressed friends at the Tiffin Room in ZCMI. A Reuben sandwich and a slice of banana cream pie. Nina started to salivate.

Looking nonchalantly around the faculty lounge for a nonexistent vending machine, she dropped down on a worn brown plaid couch. No vending machine. No treats. Just dozens of glass bottles of pop stacked in crates.

The talk died down at her arrival. Marlo, with the large lips, sat on the end of the couch. His lips smacking, he munched a bologna sandwich, and nothing had ever smelled that good in Nina's life. He mashed his brown sack into a tight ball and lobbed it into the wastebasket across the room.

"Two points," he bellowed. Marsha had whispered his history during a shared moment between bells. He'd been a seventeen-year-old football hero dazzled by rumors of scholarships that never materialized; now he was stuck in the past, a land of "if onlys" and "might have beens." A fifties guy in the world of the Beatles. A common enough story.

She watched him as he sauntered over to grab a bottle of Coke and popped off the lid with a practiced flip of his thumb.

He held the bottle at arm's length as though he were about to propose a toast to the first day of school. Instead he spouted, "You have to wonder how many people have drunk out of this bottle." Then he tossed out an ugly racial slur as easily as he'd tossed his sack in the trash. Nina gasped at the word he used, clutching her palm to her abdomen as though she'd been punched. He gauged her response out of the corner of his eye before he wiped his ample mouth on his shirtsleeve. She'd heard about people like him, but she'd never actually met one. She thought the species was extinct.

She glanced around the room, ready to make a quick exit, when she noticed her cream-colored wedding announcement pinned with a thumbtack to the message board. Several other invitations had arrived that summer. Photographs of fresh-faced kids smiling broadly, with extended hands displaying rings, were covered with print inviting the recipient to a reception at the local church cultural hall. Her large engraved square—sans picture—stood out snobbishly, not as a notification of the happy event, but as a testament to her youth and inexperience and an implication that her world was not like theirs. Mr. and Mrs. William Rushforth, in an elaborate engraved script, wish to announce the marriage of their beautiful, only daughter, Nina, a bright girl with a silver spoon caught in her throat. She'd come in tonight when everyone was gone and take it down.

As though sensing her discomfort, Mr. Hansen, another teacher in the ninth-grade rotation, smiled at her and set his newspaper on his lap. "Your husband's still in school?"

"Yes," she answered.

"How much longer does he have?"

"He's just starting his junior year."

He whistled. "He just get home from a mission?"

"Last January," she said, feeling the blush rise in her cheeks.

Marlo turned toward her. "How old are you?"

"Almost twenty-two."

"Heck, you're just a kid." Surprise covered his face, and a stray bit of mustard lingered on his chin.

She should have lied. She should have tacked on a few years. They would never have guessed, and twenty-one probably sounded like fifteen to them. A baby, a little girl, only six years older than her students. She started to rise as the door opened. The school counselor entered the room followed by Nathan Hillyard, who was slapping him on the back.

"Hey, everybody," Nathan called out. "The bishop here's going to be a daddy again." Raucous male laughter filled the room.

Marlo stood to shake his hand. "Good for you. We've had our caboose. Shucks, we don't even practice anymore."

Trying to be inconspicuous, Nina edged toward the door, but Nathan turned and gave her dress an appraising stare. She returned his look with what she hoped was the mature smirk of an adult who could enjoy a joke and strode purposefully out into the hall, but she heard another roar of laughter when he said, "That little filly's not writing lesson plans at night."

Gasping for breath, she felt naked and humiliated, as though her four-poster bed were suspended in an improbable surgical amphitheater under fluorescent lights before an audience of male faculty members. Hurrying down the hall, she tried to keep her weight on the balls of her feet so the sound of her heels clicking on the linoleum wouldn't draw more attention.

Thirty-six twelve-year-old girls clustered around the door as she jiggled the key in the lock. One little redhead touched her arm and looked at Nina through thick glasses with aqua frames. "Mrs. Spencer, you have big red splotches all over your neck."

"It must be the heat." She felt light-headed. She should have stopped at the fountain. "I'll be okay in a minute." But the room was stifling. Ninety-two degrees, if she believed the thermostat. Waves of heat rose from the wooden floor. It felt like a sauna.

Sitting in the middle of the two carefully arranged horseshoes, she introduced herself before she held up a picture she'd cut from the cover of a *Time* magazine.

"How would you describe this person?" she asked.

"Old," a little girl answered. "She has a big nose." And iron-gray hair, a bit on the kinky side. Nothing about her clothes recommended her.

Nina nodded. "She's a grandma. She grew up in Milwaukee, Wisconsin. Her dad was a grocer. When she got married, she and her husband moved to Palestine." A piece of chalk in her hand, Nina drew a rough outline of the Mediterranean Basin, and above it, she wrote, "Ordinary People Can Do Extraordinary Things." She underlined it twice. "The United Nations created a tiny little country. Right here. Israel." She pointed to the board. "It's about an eighth the size of

California. And, of course, the surrounding countries were furious and declared war, and the Israelis had no money to buy any guns or planes. So this woman, a grandma, packed one small suitcase and headed to America to ask other people who shared her religion to help. She was hoping to raise a few million dollars. She went home with fifty million dollars. She saved her country." Nina raised her eyebrows. "Golda Meir. Eventually she became the prime minister." Their faces looked a little blank. "That's like being the president."

She held up another picture—Marilyn Monroe. "Dead," she said. "A suicide or an overdose. Not a pretty story."

Nina rested the pictures side by side on the chalk rail before she walked around the room, placing a piece of blue-and-pink-wrapped bubble gum on each desk. "I mean, looks are important—no doubt about it. It's hard to erase a bad first impression, but they're no substitute for substance."

Exchanged looks flew across the room. The baffled students had signed up looking for secrets to obtain the unobtainable: a simple, pretty life with better appliances than their mothers used and two or three kids. Nina wasn't sure they understood what she was saying, but they listened with eyes wide and sweat glistening on their faces.

She popped a piece of gum into her mouth and started to chew. "Let's do it." She nodded at the class and blew a pink bubble half the size of her face, relieved that talents acquired in childhood had not abandoned her. Enamored with a teacher this young and lively, the girls were ready to do whatever she asked. Some chewed gum and blew bubbles while their classmates wrote comic descriptions of their facial contortions. "Would anyone chew gum if they knew how they looked chomping away?" She'd given them a sound bite to share at home.

At three fifteen, Nina stood at the open window and watched the last bus pull onto the highway. She fanned herself with a pamphlet. Her throat was parched, but she wouldn't leave her room until the halls were empty.

When quiet settled over the old building, she slipped off her high heels and tiptoed out to the fountain. She splashed water on her face and neck, then heard a long, low wolf whistle. She turned quickly, fist raised, ready for battle, but the hall was empty. Fuming, she grabbed her purse and drove home. A brown paper sack waited by the front door.

Peeking inside, she saw a dozen ears of corn, tomatoes, a zucchini, three eggplants, six or seven summer squash, and apples—lots of apples—and a note from Elliot's dad.

> *We're so glad that you're going to part of our family. Elliot made a wise choice when he chose you.*
> *Love,*
> *Dad*

She sat down on the concrete step and touched the note to her cheek. She never cried, but a couple of unbidden tears trickled down her sweaty face. She held an eggplant up in the late-afternoon sun. The color was beyond purple. Completely beautiful. She gouged a tiny circle with her fingernail and stuck it in her mouth. She had a couple of cookbooks somewhere in the bottom of a box. She couldn't just plunk raw vegetables down on a plate—she'd need to do something to them, stir them in a pot, or slice them with a serrated blade. She smiled and tucked the note in her pocket as she walked in the door. Wolfing down her second apple, she noticed the pile of Elliot's work clothes, gritty and stinky, on the bathroom floor, a reminder that he'd spent a long day with a pick and shovel. Should she dump the clothes in the tub with a couple of drops of bleach? She didn't have any bleach.

A year ago she'd been heading to Scotland, her head full of Robby Burns, and now she was contemplating her new husband's dirty laundry. How had any of this happened? She wandered into the bedroom but paused and touched a finger to her lip when she saw a crumpled twenty-dollar bill sitting on her dresser and wondered how many times he'd swung a pick ax to earn it.

13

Beam Me Up, Scotty

Nina picked up the neat stack of papers on her desk. She called them essays, but after she read the first two or three, she realized they were—in some cases smudged and wrinkled, but in all cases adorable—letters to her. In an attempt to learn something about the names attached to the faces, she assigned her seventh-graders a task: discover the story behind your name. Today, the twelve-year-olds had written busily. Thursday, or Friday at the latest, they needed a response.

She realized on the drive home that she'd only read ten of one hundred and eight essays. At five minutes per essay—the bare minimum—she had eight hours of correcting ahead of her. She had several acetate overlays to draw for ninth-grade English and a mimeograph to type. She was demonstrating egg white facials in girl's charm and needed to practice separating whites from yolks, a tricky maneuver. She pressed on the accelerator.

When she walked in the door, Elliot, sunburned and sore but fresh from the shower, kissed her wildly, leaving her out of breath and giddy. "I'm crazy about you," he said, "but I'm late for work. Can you give me a ride?" Tucking his shirt in his pants, he nodded over his shoulder toward the bathroom. "I don't have any clean clothes to wear to work in the morning. I called Mom, and she said we can run a load through at her house."

"We?" She dropped the load of essays on the card table.

"And, Nina, there's nothing to eat in this apartment. I'm starving."

It was a subtle accusation, as though she had shirked her duties. Squinting, she measured him with one eye. He was a large person, and the size of his stomach was probably impressive. She'd not realized filling it on a daily basis was detailed in her job description; in fact, it had never occurred to them to discuss the division of domestic duties: who paid the bills, changed the oil, shopped for groceries, or washed Elliot's dirty laundry.

He talked while she followed him out to the car. "There's a day-old Wonder Bread store down by the high school. Dead bread. Very cheap. Can you swing by there and then bring me a sandwich?"

Errands? Dinner? She'd planned on eating a spoonful of peanut butter while she read essays.

She dropped Elliot at work and drove home to collect his work clothes. Picking up a grimy pair of jeans with two fingers, she realized she didn't own a laundry basket, a paper sack, or a plastic bag. Finally, feeling rather proud of her ingenuity, she peeled the pillowcase off her pillow and stuffed in the filthy clothes. Her mother-in-law was expecting her and showed her out to the back porch.

"You know how to sort laundry?" Rachel asked with worried creases on her forehead.

"Of course." Nina waved dismissively and laughed as though she and Rachel were good friends. "I'm an old hand with laundry." A Pakistani laundry. A pleasant recent immigrant to St. Andrews had returned her soiled clothes smelling fresh in a brown paper bundle tied with string—the perfect laundry solution, but not today.

Rachel turned to finish a phone conversation with her sister. Wrinkling her nose at the smells, Nina shoved the grimy clothes into the washing machine, dumped in some soap, and remembered Rachel's admonition about bleach. She unscrewed the lid from the white plastic bottle—one strong odor could combat the other—poured it in, and shut the door firmly. She spun the knob until it pointed at heavy soil, but nothing happened. No sound of running water. She spun the knob again. Nothing happened. She read every setting on the control panel. Nothing said "start." If she could decipher a complicated rhyme scheme, she could make this machine wash clothes. She stood for five precious minutes, the equivalent of one essay, before she smacked the side of the washer with her palm. The tinny noise ricocheted around the back porch like a garbage can dropped from a second-story window. Rachel stalked out and gave the knob a quick tug. "Really, Nina, if you don't know, ask."

Nina ducked past her and headed for the front door. "I'll be back. I have to run a couple of errands."

The machine was spinning away when she returned. She pushed the wet clothes into the dryer and was very pleased to see a start button prominently displayed but had no idea how long drying Elliot's clothes would take. Fifteen minutes? Twenty-five? She set the dial and hit the button. Sitting on the step by the back door, she ran her hand over the pale green bead board and planned the egg-white facials. Mixer, eggs, towels, two bowls, headbands, toner. Seven things. She ticked off the items on her fingers. Egg-white facials tightening young skin was great cover for her stealth lectures about higher education, career choices, and macroeconomics.

Rachel stepped out on the back porch. "Don't hide out here. Come in the kitchen. I have something to show you."

She followed Rachel into the brightly lit kitchen. Two stacks of 6 x 4 cards sat on the kitchen counter. One stack was blank.

"These are Elliot's favorite recipes."

Nina swallowed hard. Elliot was always hungry and he loved food, so of course, the number of recipes counted into the thousands. "I have a hundred essays waiting at home that I need to correct. Another day . . ." she drifted off. *I might have time to spin straw into gold.*

The woman's sheer strength of will was as daunting as an avalanche that swept huge granite boulders and pine trees down the side of a mountain. Nina had never experienced a force of nature like Rachel. "Yes" was the only possible response. She dropped into a kitchen chair and copied Peachy Delight onto a lined card. Melba's Saturday Night Stew was next. Her compliance softened Rachel a bit, and Elliot's mother decided to chat.

"It's important to keep a balance. It's hard to learn everything at once. If you can, you need to leave work at work."

Her pen in hand, Nina said, "I have one hour of prep time at school. There's no way I can get everything done."

Rachel patted the back of Nina's hand, but the expression on her face was cheerless. The buzzer rang, but the Levis were still soaked. This was not good. Nina made her way through casseroles and cookies to the tune of clothes tumbling.

Finally, the buzzer rang again. Standing out on the back porch, Nina shook warm T-shirts that were now a light grayish blue. White splotches covered the jeans. It was mean-spirited of the laundry to behave so badly when her back was turned. Eyes closed, she lifted her head to the ceiling and mumbled, "Mrs. Thatcher. Where are you?" If only she could follow her around for a day, notebook and pencil in hand, for a senior seminar in detergent, laundry, and difficult stains.

Rachel touched her shoulder. "That T-shirt," she said, pointing to the one with a scattering of new holes over the grizzly logo, "was from the year Elliot was All-State basketball."

Nina clutched the shirt in her hands. Her ignorant use of undiluted bleach had destroyed a treasured memento. Under Rachel's stern gaze, her fingers turned into thumbs as she stuffed the clean clothes into the pillowcase, also a dingy gray, and hurried out to her car. Rachel followed her with the recipes in her hand. "You forgot these," she said. "You'll want them for your collection." But they both knew she didn't have a collection or even a metal flip-top box.

Rachel hitched up her left shoulder. "You've never done a load of wash in your life, have you?"

Pretending a rapid onset of deafness in her right ear, Nina leaned forward to put the key in the ignition.

A rueful smile on her face, Rachel leaned into the open car window. "Learning new things is nothing to be ashamed of. No one is born knowing how to do laundry."

Nina eased the car out of park and waved at the handsome, uncompromising woman standing on the curb. She'd been so critical of the way the entire family kowtowed to Rachel, but now she understood. She knew how David must have felt when Goliath lumbered up the valley, but she didn't have a sling, and she was short on rocks. And Custer, she'd never criticize him again for underestimating all those Indians. One thing was sure, she wasn't going to repeat any of this to Elliot. She wasn't going to risk losing him in a barrage of friendly fire.

Sitting in bed that night with a pillow tucked behind her back, her green pen flew across the lined page as an exhausted Elliot came through the door.

116

"I didn't know you were All-State your senior year. Was Pam Baugh the head cheerleader?"

He winked and managed a tired grin before he wandered into the bathroom.

"It's too bad her parents didn't name her Sis-boom," she muttered.

"I didn't catch that snide remark. One more time?"

Nina sat up straighter in bed. "I said it's too bad her parents didn't name her *Sis-boom*. It would have been perfect for a cheerleader. Sis-boom Baugh." *Think of the essay old SB could have written*, Nina thought, writing "Delightful!" on the top of an essay.

Elliot climbed into bed beside her. "What kind of a grade is *delightful?*"

"Listen to this, Elliot. This boy's father was watching an old movie while his mother was in labor, so they named him Cary. He's named after Cary Grant. I wonder which movie it was. *Bringing Up Baby?*" She looked over. Elliot was sound asleep with his mouth hanging open.

The next morning, pulling on his jeans, he said, "What's this?" She'd scribbled blue magic marker on all the white splotches.

"A laundry mishap."

"I'd say."

Friday morning she pulled one leg of her panty hose over her calf and felt Elliot's famished gaze on her back. It had been a long week, and the hands that reached for her were rough from blisters not healed. They left together in the morning, but when she arrived home at five, he was gone. He cleaned up from his first job and then walked down to his second in the hospital lab. His shift finished at eleven, and she was usually out cold by the time he walked home, exhausted. But tonight there would be five twenty-dollar bills hidden in her jewelry box. The rent.

She pushed him away, but her heart was pounding at a dizzying rate. "We're late. We've got to hurry."

"I can't stand this."

"Yes, you can. It's the weekend. Come on."

Minutes later, he jumped out of the car. "I'll see you after school. I don't have to work. Don't forget we promised Mom we'd come to their ward's fall social. Everyone wants to meet you."

"You're kidding. Can't we call in sick? It's our anniversary."

"Two weeks?" His mouth was smiling, but the look in his eyes was desperate. "I'm not going to kiss you good-bye. It just makes me crazy."

She nodded. She had to hurry. Every morning the desks were in rows. Every morning she put them back into two concentric horseshoes. It was a war of attrition she was determined to win. Yesterday, a note scrawled on a piece of scratch paper had been clipped to the front of her roll book. "Leave the desks in rows. It's easier to sweep." Mr. Mumford, the ancient janitor, was in charge of classroom management? He moved so slowly he could die standing next to his push broom, and it would take hours for anyone to notice.

She'd picked up his note and started for the office to register a complaint, but she stopped, crushed the paper into a ball, and tossed it into the wastebasket. She pictured the principal, filling the chair behind his large oak desk and looking right through her. She shuddered. No, she would deal with Mr. Mumford herself. She would be assertive but pleasant.

"Door shut. Head down." She chanted the mantra running in from the parking lot, but leaving the door shut all day created a crematorium, so the last two days she'd devised a system. The sound of bottles rattling meant that Marlo, who brought the pop from his father's truck stop, was carrying crates down the hall. Half the time, he shouted something ridiculous to disrupt her class, so door closed. When the noise passed, door open. The twenty-five minutes of lunch, door closed. When enough kids filled the halls to create a buffer, door open.

Each day she waited until school was over to run off mimeographs in the workroom while the male crew was swilling pop and swapping lies in the faculty lounge. With a little luck, in a couple of weeks everyone would forget she even existed. The faculty lounge was dangerous territory, but she'd navigated the last three days with a degree of success, and this morning she felt confident enough to grab her mail during her third-hour prep.

She hugged her mail against her chest as Marlo stuck his head in the faculty lounge and gave a low whistle. Did the man ever stay in his classroom? *Be pleasant. Make small talk*, she told herself. She held up an unsharpened pencil she'd discovered at the back of her box. "Is someone passing out free pencils?"

He leered at her. "What does it say?"

She read the logo, "Climax II."

He roared with laughter, but she didn't get the joke and gave him a blank stare.

Jerry Stewart, her next-door neighbor, who was reading the newspaper, rolled his eyes.

The pencil, it was Marlo's little joke. She'd been avoiding him and his buddies; they'd been waiting in the weeds for her. Grown men behaving like silly juveniles. *Smile*, she told herself. *Giggle a little*, but she couldn't.

"Don't you have anything useful to do? Pop to transport?" she asked. "Students who need your expertise?" Marlo taught Introduction to the Keyboard. She'd always been good at hitting nerves. His eyes narrowed and he wagged his finger at her, and then he was gone, out to the portables.

Jerry set the paper down on the floor. "I thought you were smarter than that," he said as he passed her walking out the door.

By seventh hour, the movement of the second hand on the clock was agonizingly slow, but finally, the last bell rang just like a starter's pistol, followed by a burst of noise in the hall and the sound of lockers slamming. Nina heard the tires of the school buses crunching on gravel. The buses left six minutes after the last bell rang, and drivers didn't wait for errant children. At 3:40, Nina stood with her ear at the door and a mimeograph master in her hand. The coast was clear, and she tiptoed into the workroom adjacent to the faculty lounge. Friday afternoon, Mr. Killpack joined the crew.

"Well, she's better than that other woman, the one who taught math," he was saying. "At least she's married. That other girl was a hippie."

Nina closed the door slowly so the hinges wouldn't squeak and wondered what branded that other woman as a hippie? Round pink glasses? Waist-length hair? A camouflage jacket?

"I told that other girl if she smoked on campus, she'd have to find another job. And if she'd burned all her bras, she'd have to buy some new ones. They're mandatory at my school." Mr. Killpack wheezed an asthmatic sort of a laugh, and the rest of the crew barked on cue.

When it quieted down, Marlo snarled, "This new gal is just another of Ken Patterson's intellectuals. She won't last till Christmas. Tall or not, those ninth-grade boys will eat her alive." Why did he want her to fail?

She couldn't hear the next remark, but judging from the snickers, she could imagine what was being said. Her ears stung. In a mimicking tone, Marlo spoke, "Her reception was at The Country Club. I didn't realize there was only one golf course in Salt Lake City."

Another voice sneered, "Only one that counts."

Following the faded list of instructions taped to the drum, Nina turned the handle quietly, expecting a perfect duplicate to separate from the cylinder, but the master peeled off on one edge. She bit her bottom lip. It had taken her two hours last night to type the stupid thing. She was trying unsuccessfully to reattach it, when Ruth side-stepped in from the front office.

"Ruth, could you help me for just a second? I followed the instructions perfectly, but I can't make the darn thing work."

"Go home, Nina. It's Friday afternoon." Her tone implied it was risky to be out after curfew. Then expertly flipping the metal catch, Ruth set the counter and whipped the handle around in an efficient rhythm, spitting out peach-colored duplicates. "They shouldn't let you kids out of those colleges until you know how to use the machines. How many years has it been since those professors were in a real school?"

"Thanks." Nina tried to smile and wondered if Mr. Killpack could make a hundred copies without losing a finger or two. "What would we do without you?"

The telephone was ringing in the office, and Ruth, too wise to be taken in by flattery, hurried away.

Nina tapped the papers on the table until they made a neat stack and then attached the next mimeograph. She was cranking the handle quietly when she sensed someone standing behind her. Moist, heavy breathing made the hair on her neck stand, and her knees melted like Jell-O in the sun. Stepping away from the machine, she turned slowly to face Nathan. His feet in a firm stance and a feral gleam in his eye, he'd boxed her into the corner—and he knew it. She pressed her back against the wall and smelled his Bay Rum aftershave. The fine white lines by the corners of his eyes vanished as he grinned at her. His western shirt was crisp and new with those ever-present mother-of-pearl snaps, and if the small check was a bit juvenile, she didn't care. She inhaled through her nose. If she screamed, the faculty room would empty into the workroom at once, but Nathan would be long gone, and she'd be there with ink on her cheek and a ridiculous complaint: "He was standing too close?"

His hand grazed her wrist. "I apologize if you heard any of that rough talk."

She pressed her fist, an imaginary transporter, against her lower lip as if she were Captain Kirk surveying a desolate planet. "Beam me up, Scotty. There's no intelligent life down here." To her surprise, Nathan laughed and stepped aside, leaving her to collect her peach duplicates.

Back in her room, she was watching out the window when she heard Jerry locking his door. She grabbed her purse and the stack of papers on her desk and ran out the rear door. She caught up to him as he opened the heavy exterior door. Curious, he smiled at her.

"Safety in numbers," she said, panting slightly.

"Safe from what?"

She shrugged. "Space aliens."

~ 14 ~

A Very Bad Day

Elliot hit the alarm early Monday morning—6:15 to be exact. In the quiet predawn light, a bleary-eyed Nina swung her legs over the side of the bed, but he grabbed her and pulled her back into the blue-and-white flowered sheets.

"I can't be late."

He ran his mouth down the curve of her neck.

"I don't have time," she murmured. She glanced over his shoulder at the clock.

"You don't have to drop me at SOS," he whispered.

Thirty minutes later, she was hopping on one foot, trying to put on a shoe and find its lost mate in the back of the closet. Her toothbrush stuck out of the side of her mouth.

"Hey, Elliot, toss an apple in my purse." Then she raced out the door. She revved the engine at the stop sign and glanced at the clock on the dash. Late, she was so late. Driving down the tree-lined, main street in Greenville, she passed a school bus collecting children. Thirty seconds later, lights flashing rhythmically filled her rearview mirror.

"I can't believe this," she whispered, reaching for her wallet and rolling down her window.

"All lanes of traffic have to stop for a stopped school bus." The patrolman's hair was slicked back, and his leather boots shone. She got a whiff of fruity hair tonic as he leaned in her window.

"I'm so sorry, officer, but I'm late for school. I teach at Clear Creek."

He just shook his head and started filling out the ticket, taking five minutes per letter. Two yellow buses passed with sixty little faces smashed against the windows gawking at her. Her palms started to sweat. She had to be in front of her class when the second bell rang. He finally handed her the ticket and shook his finger in her face. "Be more careful. A child was hit near here a year ago." She didn't have time for a lecture. Another yellow bus lumbered past. She flashed the officer a broad smile. "I'll be careful. And I do apologize."

He tipped his hat and strutted back to his patrol car. She flipped on her signal and eased back into traffic as the fifth bus rolled by.

Her heart pounded. She couldn't be late. She'd have to have a serious talk with Elliot, but for that she'd need to schedule a time, make an appointment, pencil herself in on the calendar he'd hung on the closet door. Two minutes after her meager dinners, he left for the library and, she suspected, a quick detour home to forage for food. Familial tentacles snaked out from the house on Maple Drive and bound Elliot to his past life. On Saturday if he worked the morning shift, a family project in the afternoon required his presence, painting the boys' bedroom or helping a cousin move. If he worked the afternoon shift, a family project in the morning required his presence, helping his father put the garden to bed for the winter or putting on the storm windows. His remaining hours were spent studying or preparing his Sunday School lesson or falling asleep on the couch. The fifty-cent movie at the student union was a thing of the past.

On Sunday the time slot wedged between church meetings and work was spent eating Rachel's scrumptious dinners. Nina felt like their small apartment was an extension, a spare bedroom, a lean-to against the main Spencer domicile, and she was just a roommate in a dress.

Sunday afternoon, their presence on the wooden pew, second row, was an unspoken requirement, and she had whispered her objection to Elliot yesterday afternoon during the Bach organ prelude.

"My family doesn't sit on the second row. We're side section, third-row-from-the-rear people," she confided behind a raised hand. "We didn't really care for the second row family in our ward. My brothers called them Brother and Sister Seen and Be Seen with their flock of scrubbed kids."

Elliot started to laugh.

"Your family anchors the ward," she said. "Every Sunday someone's doing something, giving a talk, teaching a lesson, leading the music, running the show. If you all weren't sitting right here, the whole business would go belly up." Nina put her arm through Elliot's. "Where are we going to sit?"

"What do you mean? We're right here on the second row."

"No. I mean when we grow up. Where will we sit?"

He gave her a sideways look.

After church the Spencer clan meandered across the street and assembled on the front lawn, where the boys tossed a football back and forth hundreds of times and the womenfolk served up dessert. Later, Nina and Rachel cleaned the sticky plates to have a little quality time together; at least, that was how it was billed. Elliot, the quarterback, was an integral player in this whole scenario, but his mom called in all the plays.

Nina itched to kick off her high heels and play wide receiver in this game of football lite. No tackling, no grass stains, and not much in the way of sweat, but any game was infinitely preferable to Remedial Domesticity 101. Rachel had taken her in hand. Nina was ready to get down on her knees and plead for a pardon or at least a reduced sentence.

Last night at eight thirty, she'd beckoned to Elliot with one finger. "I'm walking home."

"What's the rush?"

"No rush. I'm going home." She had kissed him on the cheek and didn't see him until eleven thirty.

That was yesterday, and now she was late. She couldn't flip on her blinker and pass all these school buses, so she just crawled along eating their fumes. She joined the throng of children shoving each other outside her classroom door. The first bell had rung. Hurrying, she unlocked the door and stepped inside to thirty-six desks arranged neatly in six rows.

"Mrs. Spencer, where do I sit?"

"I don't want to sit by Del Mar. I want to sit by Karalee. We share a book."

"I don't have my homework finished. My mom was sick over the weekend."

Nina stuffed her purse in her bottom drawer and grabbed the roll book. "Just sit down. It doesn't matter which seat." She lowered her palms forcibly. "Just sit down. Now."

Timothy, a small freckle of a kid, asked, "Did the cop give you a ticket?"

"Do I look happy? Do I look like a person who talked her way out of a ticket?" She winked at him. "This would be an excellent day to behave perfectly."

He grinned. "My dad says they catch people the first weeks of school on purpose."

"If only you'd told me that Friday." She ruffled his hair.

* * *

Second hour, her back to the class, she was diagramming a compound subject on the board and speaking above the squeak of the chalk. Marlo tiptoed into the back of the class, collared two little seventh-grade boys, and shouted, "Listen up when your teacher's talking!"

Nina leaped around. Everyone jumped. Round-eyed and terrified, one boy looked like he was ready to cry. Unsmiling, Nina jerked her thumb toward the door. "Marlo. Out," she said, furious at herself for leaving the back door unlocked.

The braver of the two boys said, "We weren't doing nothing."

"Anything," Nina said.

"That right," his friend said. "We weren't."

At the end of fifth hour, little Amanda Church walked up to Nina's desk, her hands behind her back as though she were hiding a secret.

"Mrs. Spencer," she whispered. "Someone has written filthy things on your bulletin board."

"Where?"

"There." The girl pointed in the general direction of the north wall before she skittered away. Nina stepped to the side of the room. One of her interactive flaps had been torn. She lifted "How does a verb become a verbal?" and blushed. Checking "What makes a clause subordinate?" she discovered more obscenities splashed over the answer, but the young vandal, unclear about the act, didn't make much sense.

Her cheeks burned. She worked so hard on her bulletin boards; she couldn't stand copycat criminals using them for salacious graffiti, so she grabbed one of last week's questions from her file. Pulling the disgraced flap off the wall, she heard a quiet knock, and Marsha stepped in.

"Your dress is unzipped." She reached behind Nina and zipped it up. "It was only down twelve inches. No harm done."

"How did you know?" And why hadn't she felt a breeze?

"I heard it in the faculty lounge. How much was your ticket?"

"Too much."

Marsha searched her face. "Do not cry. I mean it. Whatever you do, don't let anyone see you cry. Ever." She patted Nina's shoulder before she left.

Why hadn't anyone told her? Why didn't some little seventh grader whisper in her ear? They were happy to get within an inch of her face if they were going to throw up. If some little criminal was cheating on a test, an informant waited until the proverbial coast was clear to tattle in a hushed tone, but not one of her seventh-grade students had the spark of human kindness to mention her unzipped dress? She was undone and outflanked, and she still had to finish the afternoon.

With a few exceptions, the entire ninth-grade boys' basketball team was in her seventh hour. Nina was stapling on the new flap as the herd of sweaty boys spilled into the room. A fight! A fight by the lockers in the lower hall had everyone's adrenaline pumping. Jeff Wilkinson had thrown the first right hook, but he was provoked. Friends punched his arm and slapped his back, and Jeff made no attempt to hide the tender redness on the side of his face or comb his disheveled hair as he reveled in the glory.

Nina tried to direct the boys to the seats she'd rearranged at noon, but most of them ignored her high-pitched attempts and dropped into a convenient spot next to a friend or leaned over a desk, describing his particular take on the fight.

Nina managed to get two or three boys into their correct seats. The four girls in the class complied beautifully, but Caleb Godfrey, a pale, scrawny boy, a year behind in the onset of puberty, stooped unseen behind her, a large brown grasshopper twitching in his fingers. When she took a step, he tossed it up between her legs. Startled at the scratching flutter between her thighs, her shrieks filled the room. She danced frantically back and forth, slapping the back of her navy sheath inside the concentric half circles of boys roaring with laughter.

Growing up with three brothers had taught her something. She caught Caleb Godfrey by the ear with a firm twist. He yowled as she shoved him in a seat—not the one assigned on her chart. The class quieted. With the heel of her shoe, she squashed the fallen grasshopper, straightened her shoulders, and adjusted her paisley scarf. But the boys weren't looking at her; they were looking past her to the door—at the principal—who stood with his beefy arms crossed against his broad chest.

"Wilkinson." He jerked his thumb toward the hall. Every ounce of bravado drained away as Wilkinson slunk toward the principal, who cuffed the boy roughly about the neck and shoved him down the hall toward the office where a wooden paddle hung on the wall.

As the door closed behind the hapless Wilkinson, Nina clutched the stack of lemon-colored handouts to keep her hands from trembling. "Try the first five questions on the front page," she snapped. "The quiz is tomorrow."

Taking a tissue from the box on her desk, she wiped the gooey remains off her shoe and dropped the small corpse in the wastebasket. She collapsed heavily in her desk chair and watched the clock above the door. Caleb elbowed his neighbor, giggling and gesturing toward her, but Nina was out of her chair and leaning over him, her fingernails biting into the flesh of his neck. "One noise, one anything, and Jeff Wilkinson will have company. Do I make myself clear?" And because Caleb, like every boy in the school, knew the principal was a firm believer in corporal punishment, he nodded sullenly.

Forty long minutes later, a bell rang, and in sixty seconds the room emptied. Crumbling into her chair, she stretched her arms across her desk and rested her head on a lemon handout. She felt like the silver ball in a pinball machine. All day, every day, some unseen hand pulled back on the spring and flung her spinning against walls and obstacles, lights flashing, people laughing. For eight hours every day, she lived in this alien world, and for the other sixteen she was haunted by it. Her life, her rational, interesting life filled with friends and professors and ideas and books, was lost in this alternate universe. When had she crossed over? When she got married? But Elliot had gotten married too, and he was opening the pristine pages of new texts, probably this very moment.

No crying. She grabbed a tissue and held it tightly over her mouth and nose like an oxygen mask. She heard the doorknob at the back of her class turn. Her stomach clenched, and she gulped back a sob.

Jerry stuck his head in the door. "It's four o'clock. I thought you might like a little company walking to your car."

✑ 15 ✑

A Little English Snake

Rain in the air. She could smell it. Nina shoved the classroom window open and stuck her head out. Dampness touched her skin. The leaves in the trees outside her window, washed clean, were turning a magnificent red. No need for a cross draft. The rear door could stay locked all day. No Marlo or Zach disrupting her classes.

The room was deliciously cool. A miracle. She retied the flowered scarf in a bow around her neck and pushed the sleeves of her brown-cabled sweater dress up past her elbows. When she'd worn it last winter, Elliot had raised one significant eyebrow. She'd laughed then; she smiled now.

Sounding anxious, a commentator on her little transistor radio predicted a constitutional showdown if Archibald Cox subpoenaed the White House tapes. She dropped her lesson plan on her desk and turned up the volume. Wow. This train was roaring down the tracks. President Nixon impeached. Nothing had seemed as important as the paycheck she'd be taking home tomorrow afternoon—three hundred and eighty-five dollars, thank you very much—but a president going down. Earth shattering.

The drizzle became a torrent midway through first hour. Ten minutes later the first ominous drips saturated the ceiling and splashed on the floor.

Timothy grabbed the wastebasket and twirled around under the drips as though he had to catch each one individually.

"Right here." Nina tapped the floor with her toe, but another dark spot was appearing in the back of the room. What would happen if the entire ceiling caved in and her bulletin boards were washed away in a flood of lathe and muddy plaster?

"Nobody move," she demanded. "I'll get Mr. Killpack."

He didn't jump up from his desk to run and inspect. He didn't even seem particularly impressed. "I'll send a work order to the district."

"What about today?"

"Adapt."

At least he didn't say, "That's the job," or "It didn't bother Janice." Who was this unflappable Janice who rolled with every punch? The rust stains on the ceiling hadn't magically appeared this morning.

Nina hurried back to her room because the slow dribble and thirty-six twelve-year-olds required constant supervision. The bell rang. One class rushed out and another rushed in to gawk at the leak starting in the back of the room.

"Okay, everybody sit down. No one's going to drown."

"Mrs. Spencer, something's dripping in my hair."

"That would be Robbie flipping you with water from the wastebasket." As though that little girl didn't know. "Knock it off, Robbie." Nina twisted her mouth to the side in a smile. She grabbed the roll book.

A rattlesnake lay coiled on her desk.

A scream exploded inside her throat. Twenty little girls echoed the shriek. Her heart racing, she motioned with her forearms. "Move! To the back of the room." Children bounded over desks and knocked each other onto the floor amid screeches and shouting. Looking over her shoulder as she ran, Nina caught her foot on the handle of a pink floral book bag. Grabbing at the air, she fell, her head striking the edge of a desk. Everything went black.

* * *

A hand, warm and strong, patted her back. Elliot. But musky pomade didn't smell like Elliot. Her mind tried to swim to the surface. Cool air touched her thighs. Her knit dress had ridden up. Someone tossed a cotton blanket over her legs. A rough hand lifted her head and placed a towel on the pillow, then gently untied her scarf. Pain throbbed in the back of her skull. Something sticky dribbled down her neck. Nauseated, she struggled to open her eyes.

"Stay still. You've got a nasty bump."

Not Elliot's voice. This twang was deep seated, a verbal rodeo.

She heard Ruth. "Grab that wastebasket in case she throws up."

Blinking her eyes, she winced. Ruth and Nathan were staring inches away from her face. "You tripped, Honey," Ruth said, "and hit your head a good one on your way down. Nathan heard the commotion and carried you in here."

Here seemed to be the sickroom, a pale green, cell-like room with one small window and a narrow bed across from a filthy porcelain sink. She pictured herself splayed against the wooden floor in her classroom, loose as a floppy doll, and Nathan, always lurking close by, carrying her limp form snug against his chest.

Marsha stuck her head in the door. "Jerry's got her class. The kids said she went down hard." She frowned at the blood on the towel. "Let's have a look." Nathan nestled one arm under her shoulders and lifted her. Marsha moved her hair away from the cut.

"Stitches," Ruth declared. "Five or six. I'll call the clinic."

"There was a rattlesnake," Nina mumbled.

"It's dead," Nathan said.

Glad the slimy reptile wasn't loose in her room lunching on seventh-graders, Nina wondered what brave child had rushed to the desk and done battle with the snake. Maybe farm kids killed snakes all the time out in the fields or up in the haylofts. Maybe there was a trick to killing snakes. Maybe they really did grab them by the tail and, with a quick whiplike crack, pop off their heads.

"Amanda Church found it at the bus stop and thought it would be real funny to bring it to school." Marsha huffed though her nose. "She washed it off in the girl's bathroom and nearly scared the stuffing out of a couple of ninth-graders. Then she stuck it under your roll book. Mr. Killpack has her in the office now."

Little Amanda Church? What did she know about snakes? "How did she keep from being bitten?"

Nathan choked into his free hand, and Marsha laughed out loud. "It was dead when she found it."

Ruth's mouth puckered, exposing the dimples in her cheeks. "That little girl will be suspended the rest of the week." She checked the bright red blood on the towel. "Is there someone you can call?"

"Elliot's in school."

"I'll take her to the doc," Nathan said.

Marsha and Ruth exchanged a quick glance.

"No," Ruth said, "I'll run her down. You don't want to miss third hour. We'll get her fixed up and back in time for lunch."

Nina watched clumps of her blonde hair falling onto the floor as she sat in the exam room. Chewing a pink wad of gum, the medical assistant didn't seem particularly concerned about shaving off a third of the hair on the back of Nina's scalp.

The young doctor with a clipped mustache put a blood pressure cuff around her upper arm and whistled. "Low blood pressure."

"Every time I have it taken, they ask me if I'm dead."

He laughed and started to pull the needle through her skin with tiny pliers. "You're not pregnant, are you? I should have asked you that first."

Ruth's ears grew several sizes.

"No," Nina said, "that would be about the last straw."

The doctor shrugged. "Not for everyone." He clipped the suture. "Keep this clean. Have someone check it every day for any redness, and let's take the stitches out in a week or ten days."

* * *

Elliot was sitting at the wobbly card table in the kitchen when she stepped gingerly in the door. Her head felt the size of a melon, cracked, and she was holding one bruised elbow close to her side.

"Hi." Seeing her but not seeing her, he twirled a pencil in his hand. "My anatomy lab was amazing. We dissected a pig's heart. It was so fresh the chambers were still full of clots."

Nina slapped her good hand over her mouth and lurched into the bathroom. She wasn't sure she was going to come out.

He knocked on the locked door. "Sweetheart, are you okay?"

"No, I came close to dying."

"What's wrong?"

Wiping her mouth on a towel, she unlocked the door and revealed her stitches. "They cut off my hair."

131

He touched her scalp gently. "There's a lot left." He led her to the couch and wrapped his arms around her. He kissed her cheek. "So where's all that pretty hair, and what was the near-death experience?"

"A rattlesnake under my roll book."

"Did anyone get hurt?"

"Excuse me." She pointed at her head. "Stitches."

"Did the snake bite anyone?"

"The snake was dead, but I didn't know that before I tripped and crashed into a desk."

He nodded his head slowly, and then he burst out laughing. "You were running away from a dead snake? Nina, you'll be famous forever. A legend."

She rolled her eyes. "Just what I need. More notoriety."

His strong hands massaged her drooping shoulders. "What do you mean, notoriety?"

"Things aren't going well." She tipped her head forward so he could rub her neck. "Actually, that's not totally true. The seventh graders are great, and the little girls in girl's charm love me, but something's going on in the ninth grade. I can't control those last two classes."

"How out of control?"

"Oh, last week a couple of guys were fooling around. I told them to knock it off, and one looked right at me and shoved a twenty-pound dictionary onto the floor. His two friends did the same thing. It sounded like cannon balls hitting the deck. I don't get it. How those darling little kids morph into drooling, acne-covered delinquents."

He kissed her forehead and took another look at her stitches. "Why didn't you tell me?"

"I am telling you." She opened her mouth to describe Nathan's rough hands, but the words wouldn't come out. She felt cheap and a little dirty, as though she invited his attentions. "I'm having trouble sleeping at night. I spend the entire day dreading sixth hour."

"You're having trouble sleeping at night because I wake you up."

"I want *you* to wake me up. I don't want Nathan keeping me awake."

"Nathan?"

"Ninth-grade science. A little intrusive."

He erased the creases across her forehead with his thumb. "I played on the varsity squad when I was a sophomore, and I took a lot of guff. It's just part of being new and a little different. Be pleasant and work hard. That's all you can do."

"I had all that stuff playing tennis, but there's something more insidious going on. Weird vibes in the faculty. Good teachers stay in their rooms with the doors shut, marginal teachers wander the halls. It's like a bad Western. If Ruth quit tomorrow, the whole place would grind to a halt."

"They're just bored and restless." He walked into the kitchen and returned with ice cubes wrapped in a dish towel and held them next to the cut. "You sit here. I'll fix dinner."

"What is there?"

"I'll make a BLT without the bacon or lettuce." He laughed, "And maybe without bread."

She stood, but he held up his palm. "With a brain injury like that, you better stay on the couch."

"I get my paycheck tomorrow. That means a trip to the grocery store and a movie and quarters for the Laundromat. A whole new world."

Mel's vegetables had kept starvation at bay, but now so close to the finish line, she was reaching saturation. She handed Elliot the second half of her sandwich, and while he chewed, he studied her. "I love your hair, but I think it's got to go."

She could feel the missing locks, sort of like phantom limb pain, as her fingers touched the stubble. "I was thinking a low ponytail—at the base of my neck."

"A third of your hair's gone. We better just cut it off." He left, then walked back into the kitchen with a towel and shampoo. She leaned over the kitchen sink while hands large enough to palm a basketball tenderly washed away dried blood. Sitting silently on the kitchen counter, she felt him snip off her hair with the kitchen scissors. He held her chin in his hand to be sure the sides were even.

"Hey, I thought Nina was the girl who never cried?" The tears turned to heaving sobs, and he held her tightly against his chest. "It will grow back," he murmured. "You'll conquer the ninth graders."

"But Elliot," she wept into his shirt, "it was Amanda Church, one of my adorable seventh graders. I thought she liked me, but it's like I'm not a real person. It's a game without rules, no holds barred."

He whispered into her wet hair. "I understand. Our collective confidence is going through the meat grinder. The only time in my life I ever felt second rate was when I met your parents."

She sniffed and wiped her face on the towel. "You don't feel that way now, do you?"

"Not around your mother, but every time I think about studying at home, every time I think of slacking off, I hear your dad's voice in my head. It keeps me taking those steps up College Hill at a run. I'm not going to fail." He leaned back so he could see her face. "I know why you couldn't call your dad for a loan, Nina. He thinks I'm a freeloader. I'll sell my blood before I'll ask him for anything."

She couldn't meet his frank stare.

He glanced at the locks of her hair lying on the counter. "We need a ribbon."

He left, and she heard him rummaging through a box in the top of their closet. He came back with the large envelope that held their marriage license and a bit of pink ribbon he'd stolen from a sachet. He tied the ribbon around the soft curls and dropped them into the envelope. "Someday we'll show little granddaughters how beautiful your hair was at our wedding and tell them the saga of the snake. It might not feel funny now, but it will be hilarious then."

She reached up to touch her head. "I look awful."

"Not to me. Come here. I'll paint your toenails."

"You have a foot fetish?"

"You know, I just might."

She sat on the couch, knees bent, with her feet propped on his thigh and watched him stroke the tiny brush.

"Let's stay home this weekend, Elliot. Let's pretend it's last April, but you won't have to leave me at Cindy's. We'll go to the movie at the student union and have a picnic on Old Main Hill. We'll fix dinner on Sunday. Just us."

"Sunday is a day for families."

"So what am I, Elliot? The second-string girlfriend who sleeps with Rachel's firstborn?" She bit down on her thumb. "This isn't a new problem. I mean, what's that great two-thousand-year-old scripture. 'Cleave unto your wife'? I don't think your mother's read it lately."

"Nina . . . ?"

"No kidding. Your family tolerates me, but just barely. They think of me as yucky Nina, who sadly isn't Pam Blah."

"Pam isn't a blah." He screwed the lid on the bottle. "Mom will be upset if we don't come for Sunday dinner."

Nina arched her foot. "See this? I'm putting it down." But he caught her ankle and tugged on her little toe.

"Lie down for a while." He stood up. "I'll be back at ten."

"You're leaving me?" After her terrible ordeal? After she'd been stitched and pawed and lugged and shorn all in the same day?

He gave her a knowing smile. "You interrupt me every fifteen minutes, and I can't concentrate when you're right there on the couch. Your friend Cindy called earlier." He paused with his hand on the door. "Cute toes."

"I love you."

"I know. Tomorrow will be better." And he was gone.

She glanced around the shabby apartment. No pictures on the walls, no rugs or furniture other than this hammered old couch in desperate need of a makeover. Last night's dishes were still in the sink, her head ached, and the stitches were oozing blood. She dialed Cindy's number.

Bridesmaids owed a requisite amount of hand-holding, and Cindy produced the necessary empathic noises as Nina told her story, then the petite redhead jumped in with opinions of her own.

"Sorry, Nina, but I never thought teaching was a good fit for you. Plus, you've always been a city girl. Those kids grow up with snakes—not a big deal for them. Your credibility just took a serious nosedive. So what are the kids like really?"

"The seventh-graders are adorable. They're still little kids, and then some strange hormonal malevolence invades their bodies. The boys grow noses too big for their faces, or they grow gigantic hands and feet stuck on the ends of skinny arms and legs. It's so weird. It's like there's no central organization." Nina twisted the phone cord around her elbow. "I don't want to teach school forever. It's not my thing. I'm wondering if I should go ahead and apply to law school."

"How will that sit with Elliot?"

"I won't tell him just yet. I probably won't get in. Schools are only accepting one woman for every ten men."

"But if you do get in, it could get murky real fast. What if you and Elliot get accepted in different parts of the country?"

"Well, the first semester might be tricky, but he could finish where I am and transfer his last credits to graduate here. We could make it work." It was a convoluted plan, and she wasn't surprised when Cindy didn't respond.

Next to the duplicate gifts she was waiting to exchange, Nina kept her transcripts and LSAT scores under the bed tucked next to the record of her immunizations and her Treasures of Truth scrapbook—dreams stuffed in a white dress box. She touched the oozing back of her head while she listened to Cindy.

"Lars is back," Cindy said. "He's going to call you for a tennis game. I wish he'd call me."

"How is the debonair Mr. Liljenquist?"

"Pumped about his summer in DC. Watergate is all he talks about." There was a long pause before Cindy said, "My roommates are back, and we're headed to that free concert on the quad. Come with us. Take a night off."

"I can't. I'm leaking blood, and I have a million essays to correct."

"Well, expect a call from Lars."

16

Painful Penance

Saturday afternoon Elliot stood at the kitchen sink, elbow deep in greasy suds, tepid water, and dirty plates and glasses. After working the early shift, he'd arrived home to a mess days in the making. Gristly remains of a meat loaf—or a meat loaf attempt—stuck to the pan like they'd been baked in a kiln. Outside, a car pulled into the narrow parking lot, and he heard Nina laughing. His jaw clenched, he wiped his hands on his shirt and pulled the curtain aside. Elliot's eyes traveled up her bare legs to her short tennis skirt, the racket tucked under her arm, and a red-and-white bandana tied in a bow around her head. She was chatting through a car window. Her nose and cheeks were sunburned, but she looked happy, happier than he'd seen her in days.

"So I fuss with the dials on the washing machine," she said, "and absolutely nothing happens. I can't believe I'm so dumb. Finally, I smack the machine, because that always makes machines work, right? And it sounds like a garbage truck's been tossed off the roof. Elliot's mom marches out on the back porch, and with a flick of her wrist, the whole thing comes to life. And I get the evil eye. 'Nina, if you don't know, *ask*.' It was hilarious."

She double slapped the top of the car with her free hand. "Thanks for the game."

As she walked in the door, Elliot turned, leaning against the sink. "Where have you been?" His chest rose and fell as though dirty dinner plates required heavy lifting.

"Playing tennis. Such a beautiful day." She wiped the sweat off her forehead with the dish towel sitting on the counter. "Do I need a signed permission slip?"

"What happened to spending the weekend together? We were going to the warehouse sale." He was adding weight to his anger, building a case. He'd mentioned the sale on his way to work, an afterthought tossed over his shoulder at her sleepy body buried in the covers.

"Sorry. I lost track of the time."

"I assumed you'd meet me after work. That's where the warehouse is. You're the one who wants to find a table. I tried to call you twice."

"I'm only a half hour late. Let's hop in the car and go now."

He stared at her. "Like that?"

She jerked a pair of sweatpants out of her tennis bag, shoved in each leg, and knotted the tie. "There," she said. "Let's go."

"Have a shower and change, if you can find anything to wear in that mountain of clothes on the bedroom floor."

The smile drained off her face. "I had a great afternoon. I got in most of my serves. Lars told funny stories about being an intern on the Hill." She eased herself down on a folding chair. "What's really bothering you?" she said. "Don't hold back. Give it to me straight."

He squashed an ant crawling in breadcrumbs. "I shouldn't have to come home to a disaster when I've been working and going to school all week."

"Listen, Buster, I spent the morning at the Laundromat folding clothes and correcting essays. You're not the only one working." She extended a finger in his direction. "But anything else? If you're going to be horrible, you might as well be really horrible."

He took several deep breaths. "You don't have tennis dates with old boyfriends when you're married." He slung a dish towel over his shoulder. "I'm not being horrible. I'm just telling you what I will and won't tolerate. And no tennis dates with Lars." He remembered the glum-looking guy from the wedding reception who stood next to a potted palm for more than an hour with an uneaten slice of cake on a napkin.

"I've been playing tennis with Lars Liljenquist since I was in the seventh grade. He's my friend, and if I want to play tennis with him every single Saturday, that's what I'm going to do. Playing tennis with Lars is nothing compared to what I put up with at work."

His voice rose, "When a man and a woman say they're just friends, one of them is lying."

Breathing hard through her nose, she stared at him. "I have to backstroke past leering men to get to my mailbox in the faculty lounge. I get whistled at if I step out of my room." She sputtered, "You have no idea how trustworthy I really am." Her chest started to heave. "You should be proud of me." The words barely made it out of her mouth, because she was sobbing and running to flop on the tangle of sheets on their bed.

He ran his fingers through his hair and squeezed his eyes shut. When had Nina turned into a weepy female? He loved her, but she made no sense. Why couldn't she understand what seemed obvious to him? After the wedding, he'd jumped back into his life with the blissful addition of Nina, her clothes touching his in the closet, her makeup cluttering the bathroom counter, her panty hose flung over the towels, and her shoes kicked off by the front door. Even when he was gone at night, he loved the thought of her correcting essays or typing away on the wobbly card table. A dozen times a day her voice echoed in his head, "Hey, Elliot . . ." He'd never been happier in his life, and he didn't understand why she wasn't. The thought stung. Scrubbing filthy pots, he stood at the sink and listened to the unfamiliar sound of Nina crying.

He paused at the side of their bed. He studied her almost as if he were seeing her for the first time before he stroked the back of her thigh gently.

"I guess we just had our first fight." He sat down beside her. He pulled the bandana off her hair and touched the sad line of stitches. "Do you want to talk?"

She shook her head.

"Why didn't you tell me about the washing machine?"

She mumbled into her pillow, "I've gone from being a competent person to being a total schmuck. I've never had people actively dislike me before—your mom, other teachers. What did I do to them? Why go to the trouble?" She rose on one elbow. "And you want me to give up Lars? It's the seventies, Elliot. You don't get to pick my friends."

"Great. No problem." He shrugged. "I'll take Pam out to lunch while you're playing tennis with Lars." The second those words jumped out of his mouth, he regretted them.

That evening, he pressed the phone against his chest. "Are you sure about this? I think it's a mistake." Penance came at a price.

Nina shook her head. "Please, just one day."

He tucked the receiver between his chin and his ear while he played with the tie on Nina's blouse. "Mom, we're going to stay home tomorrow."

He listened for two or three minutes, nodding his head, while Nina whispered, "If you capitulate, I'm not going with you."

"No, Mom, we're going to have dinner here. Nina has it all planned, and I think we'll stay here in the evening too. Her head's still sore."

"You're waffling," she mouthed.

"Okay. We'll talk to you soon." He hung up the phone and gave her a large wink. "Okay. Pull out the cookbooks. Let's do this."

* * *

It was a mellow afternoon. After sacrament meeting in their very own ward, a slow meandering walk home through the fall leaves felt like heaven. They'd listened to Professor Wheelwright discuss ancient Mesopotamian cultures while Elliot played with Nina's fingers. No one said hush. No one looked disapprovingly when she played with the hair on the back of his neck.

Now, sheets, still new enough to rustle, were tangled around their feet, and the late afternoon sun cast the room in pearl-gray shadows. He kissed the tip of her nose. She wiggled her toes. "I feel so decadent."

"Don't. This is exactly what we're supposed to be doing. It's healthy and normal."

"Who does the dishes?"

"Forget the dishes."

She closed her eyes sleepily, one arm stretched above her head. "Wouldn't it be lovely if we didn't have to go to school tomorrow?"

"Is it so miserable? Aren't you making any friends?" He brushed his lips across her forehead.

"Jerry. He's my next-door neighbor. He's a little younger than my dad. He's like this small island of calm in a sea of craziness."

"What about Marsha?"

"Jury's still out. She's a spy."

Pushing her pillow up under her head, she traced her fingertip along Elliot's clavicle and outlined his sternum with her fingernail before she reached up to kiss him under his chin. He pulled her against his chest. He couldn't imagine anyone not loving Nina. "You'll make new friends soon."

They heard a firm knock on the front door.

"Ignore it," she whispered. "They'll go away."

A determined knuckle rapped again. Elliot bolted up straight. "That's my mother," he rasped. "Is the door locked?"

Eyes wide, Nina gulped, "I thought you locked it."

"Grab some clothes. Quick." He shoved his legs into his jeans and pulled a sweater over his head. She plowed through the mess on the floor as though the clothes were unfamiliar, belonged to another girl with questionable taste and sloppy habits. He threw a sweatshirt at her. She shot her hands through the arms and grabbed a pair of cords. Horrified, he heard his mother sing, "Anybody home?"

He wanted to throttle his mother. The entire clan had not arrived, just his parents and a few stray siblings, but nevertheless, the living room was packed. Uncorrected essays were scattered across the carpet. Nina plucked her trail of clothes off the floor like Gretel following bread crumbs. A chocolate layer cake in her outstretched hand, his mother glanced at the dried remains of dinner on Nina's wedding china. Pots and pans and every bowl Nina owned were heaped precariously in the sink. Stacked like building blocks, a half dozen cardboard boxes filled one corner.

"Newlyweds." Mel shrugged and winked at no one in particular. Rachel looked down at Elliot's bare feet and then up to his tousled hair. His cheeks burned. Alan giggled.

No one spoke for several long minutes, but his mother knew she'd stepped over some imaginary line of good taste. "I wish you'd called first," he said.

"Well," his mother replied, "we can't stay long."

Diane gestured toward Nina. "Your hair," she sighed. "Your poor hair."

"They shaved off so much at the doctor's office that Elliot whacked off the rest."

He watched Nina retreat inside the expression that tightened across her face. She became a cardboard cutout of the girl he loved. She spoke softly, choosing her words carefully. *She knows any gaffes will hit the air-waves*, he thought. His sisters examined the stitches, but Alan sat cross-legged on the worn beige carpet waiting for his fair share of the cake.

Rachel looked worried. "You fainted?"

"The snake was on my desk," she said. "I tripped in the melee."

"It was a joke." Elliot smiled. "A little English girl who loves Nina. She was just horsing around." Nina stared at him.

"We missed you today," Rachel said.

"Cake?" Elliot said. Nina leaned against the wall, immobile.

"Let me cut that for you, Son." They didn't have enough clean plates, so Rachel put the stopper in the sink and plunged into soapy water. It was amazing to see how quickly his mother could plow through dirty dishes. Elliot stood at her side, dish towel in hand, wiping and stacking each plate neatly on the counter. Her hands resting for a moment on the sink's porcelain edge, she leaned into Elliot and whispered softly, "Would it be helpful if I jotted down a housekeeping schedule for Nina?"

"Nope, not helpful," Elliot said. "Nina's smart. She'll figure all this out."

Rachel grabbed a knife from the drawer. "Let's cut this cake."

Her lips in a fixed line, Nina refused the slice Elliot pressed on her. "Thanks, but no thanks."

"You love chocolate."

Significant glances flashed between the siblings, but Nina wouldn't look at him.

Mel grinned at her. "I've never liked snakes, myself. Dead or alive."

No one responded. The only noise was forks against fine china.

Rachel picked up her sizeable purse. "Well, next week we'll get things back to normal. You'll have dinner with us at home." She touched the top of Nina's hair. If she noticed Nina flinch, she didn't show it. "The nice thing about hair is that it grows. You'll be fine before you know it."

"Actually, I'm fine now."

"I have a few free hours next Saturday morning. I could come and help you get unpacked and organized. If we twist Diane's arm, I bet she'd help too."

"I won't be here next weekend," Nina announced. "I'm going home for a couple of days." This was the first he'd heard of it. "I haven't seen my mom and dad since school started."

"Is Elliot going with you, Dear?"

"No. He has to study."

"Well then, Son, we'll enjoy you for the entire day." Uneasy, the siblings filed out the way they'd come. Rachel paused, her hand on the doorknob. "Enjoy your afternoon."

Nina sucked in the sides of her cheeks.

Elliot closed the door tightly and pushed in the lock.

"A housekeeping schedule?" She bit off each word.

"Shush. The window's open. They'll hear you."

"I don't care. This is a turf war. It's so ridiculous, I can't believe it."

A muscle worked in the side of his jaw. "It wouldn't have killed you to eat a piece of her stupid cake."

She grabbed a handful off the plate on the floor and threw it at him. Missing him by inches, a glob of frosting stuck to the refrigerator door.

"Grow up." he shouted. But she'd already turned away, licking the hateful stuff off her fingers.

~ 17 ~

Repairs

Nina lifted the lid on the baby grand and flexed her wrists. She flipped open a Chopin exercise book and played her favorite preludes as the sunlight through the French doors gradually faded. Her mother turned on the lamp behind the keyboard. Nina closed that book and opened another. Gershwin. She sighed. Every ounce of frustration and sadness flowed through her fingers. She paused, studied the fingering, and began again. "Rhapsody in Blue" filled the house.

Her father set his briefcase on the floor next to a wingback chair. "Our Nina's home," he whispered to his wife.

* * *

A single candle flickered on the table. Her father laid his spoon down and looked at Nina. "The stitches came out yesterday?"

"But today, two little girls in second hour were wearing scarves in their hair." She laughed. The pretty silk scarves she usually tied around her neck, she now arranged around her head. One day, she'd worn a kerchief tied in the back with just a fringe of blonde hair around her face. Another day she'd folded a blue silk scarf like a headband and knotted it on the side. She'd spent a week covering up the stitches, not realizing she was making a fashion statement. She'd walked into the office that morning and Ruth had a scarf, not tied around her bristly hair, but looped around her shoulders—and it looked nice, very becoming.

"What about a movie?" her dad asked. "Anything good playing?"

"You know, I'm tired," Nina said "Worn out, really. I'd just like to go to bed."

Her father turned his head to the side, just slightly, and glanced at her mother. Nina picked up her dishes and set them in the sink so the dish fairy could load them in the dishwasher later when the family was asleep.

She stood at her old bedroom door waiting for her mother to walk down the hall. "Can the dentist see me in the morning?" Because that was Nina's excuse for the visit: bilateral toothaches. She'd called her mother Monday to plead poverty and ask for a trip to the dentist.

"He'll work you in."

Saturday morning at nine, Nina sat in the waiting room with a *Time* magazine unopened in her lap. The bell on the door rang, and Mr. Felt, one of her favorite high school teachers, walked in. Surprised to see her, he pulled up the opposite chair, and sticking his reading glasses in his coat pocket, plied her with questions. "A junior high? I can't see that. You're better suited to high school." He pursed his lips. "I thought you were going to be an attorney?"

Nina held up her left hand. "I got married."

"So how do you like teaching school?"

How much of the truth did Mr. Felt want to hear? "Not much. There's too much I can't control. I can't protect myself from other people's unpleasantness."

"Welcome to life, Nina."

She found herself telling him about the snake and the grasshopper and the principal who wanted to hire a relation. He nodded sympathetically before he said, "You need to make your mistakes in a location that won't be permanent. Then move to where you want to live. You don't need to be the teacher who ran from a dead snake for the rest of your professional career."

She nodded. A practice round. She understood that, but suddenly she wondered if that explained her new marriage. Was it a practice round too? Nothing was going well. They both kept tripping. Double faults.

The assistant showed her into the exam room, clipped a napkin over her shirt, and wedged a sharp bit of cardboard between her cheek and her gums. "Now don't move."

After prodding and poking, the kindly dentist examined the X-rays on the small light box and shook his head. "No cavities. I don't see anything. I'm willing to bet a dollar to a donut, you're grinding your teeth in your sleep."

She exhaled. Even her teeth were in on the conspiracy to complicate her life.

"Is there anything new going on? Anything that worries you?"

Everything worried her, but she shook her head.

"I'm going to make you a mouth guard to wear to bed at night."

That would be lovely. A thick hard plastic guard between her teeth. Wouldn't Elliot be thrilled? But maybe he wouldn't even notice. Last week the climate had cooled both inside and out of their apartment. She'd gotten into bed Wednesday night and decided to put her feet on the pillow and her head under the covers at the bottom of the bed. Admittedly, it was dark, but she waited and waited for him to lean over and kiss her cheek and be surprised by her feet on the pillow—and have a bit of a laugh—only he didn't. She nearly suffocated until she leaned over and pinched his little toe, hard. He'd yelled and thrashed in the covers, sure rats had invaded their bed. He didn't even notice her missing face. He'd scolded. She rolled away from him and covered her head with a pillow. She didn't realize he had an important test in the morning. Too many mistakes.

Her mother picked her up post-dentist and took her shopping for a slipcover for the battered couch. She suggested something in denim, maybe light blue, something that could be laundered. And attractive posters from art museums. Impressionists mounted on foam board. Cheap. A nice look, but no expensive framing. They stopped in front of an exclusive shop, the Chalk Garden at Trolley Square, but Nina refused.

"Mom, I just can't go into a store that has anything to do with chalk," Nina said, so they strolled over to the shoe store and finally selected a pair of boots and then stopped for lunch at a little restaurant by The King's English Bookshop. Nina was starting to relax.

At one o'clock, Nina sat draped in black, watching the hairdresser's distressed face in the mirror. His own hair was shoulder length, and a tight, white T-shirt covered his bony chest. Her mother stood at his side.

"Whoever did this should be shot." Geoff shook his head. "There was no reason to cut away this much hair."

"What can you do?" her mother asked.

He held up the hair on her crown and made scissor motions with his fingers two inches away from her head. "Light and fluffy on top. Layer it all the way down. But nothing short of a wig will cover these stitches for months." He tapped his foot against the floor. "Such a shame after all the work we went to for your wedding."

"I've been covering it with scarves," Nina offered.

"That's a bit Jamaican for a blonde. I say cute dangling earrings and keep the attention on the front of your head." He lathered her hair with something that smelled like rosemary. "Now, let me know if this stings the wound." He toweled her hair before he started snipping. Strutting and fretting, he stood to the side, stared at her hair, and snipped some more. Finally, he measured the bottom layers against her ear lobes.

"It's cute, Nina. Your eyes look huge." He brushed the hair off her neck. "You tell that little Brit the next time she pulls any tricks, we're going to feed her to a python."

* * *

Driving into the garage, her mother tapped a manicured fingernail on the steering wheel. "Now, you just take these things we bought and put them in the trunk of your car. What your dad doesn't know won't hurt him."

Nina waltzed into her father's study to show him the repair. He was pulling volumes off the dark oak shelves, and the outline of a Sunday School lesson on a yellow legal pad sat on his desk. He'd rolled the sleeves of a faded Pendleton shirt just below his elbows, ready to dig into his task. She made a slow circle.

"Elliot called," he said.

She glanced down at her watch. Four twenty-five. He'd just gotten home from work. "I can't believe he sprung for a long-distance call."

He reached over and closed the door. "Okay, Kitten. What's going on?" He motioned her to the green leather chair.

How many times had she sat in this chair? Plenty. Hot seat or favorite spot, depending on the day. She and her dad would strategize solutions to her problems with boys or teachers or her mother. Sometimes he'd talk to her about interesting cases. But today, she felt a lecture coming—not the first.

"Things aren't going well at work. I mean, at all. I wake up in the morning dreading everything about it."

"What exactly?"

Grasping for the right words, she looked around the room at the hundreds of books alphabetized on the oak shelves. Pictures of her mother and her brothers stared down at her. And there she was in a silver frame, a new addition, in her wedding dress surrounded with summer flowers. "I'm the only woman who teaches an academic subject. I'm the youngest woman on the faculty. A day doesn't go by that I don't get at least two or three wolf whistles in the halls. I'm being marginalized by crude remarks."

Nothing betrayed his composure except the rise of color in his cheeks. "Go on."

"The day I got hurt, when I came to, the ninth-grade science teacher had carried me into the sickroom. He's a real cowboy and kind of lurks around, but the ringleader is a guy named Marlo Fletcher. His father's on the school board, so he thinks he's bulletproof."

"What does he teach?"

"Type. Can you imagine? All day long. I'd go nuts." She tucked her legs beneath her.

"Marginalized how?"

"Lots of sexual innuendo. And it's hurting my ability to control my classes. The seventh graders are great, but the ninth-grade boys give me a run for my money every single day."

"Where's the principal in all this?"

"Ha. He's a large part of the problem. The district forced me on him. He'd promised the job to a relative, some guy who'd fit in with the faculty lounge crowd and be loyal to him."

Her father made a steeple with his fingers. "You disdain these people."

"I guess I do."

"And that's probably transparent." He smiled at her gently. "Nina, there's more to being clever than performing well on a test."

"Dad, I'm so unhappy." She sighed wearily.

"I know you are. I can see it in your face, and your mother can too. You've probably got a carful of things I'm not supposed to know about."

"In the trunk."

He laughed. "What motivates the type teacher?"

She shrugged. "Who knows?"

"Think about it."

"Well, if I were to hazard a guess, I'd say being a star high school athlete was probably the high point of his life, so he wears his hair the same way he did in his glory days. He married his high school sweetheart." She picked up a book, glanced at the cover, and set it back down. "He's bored to tears. So he amuses himself by making my life miserable."

"Nina, he was probably flirting with you in the beginning. He wanted his pride stroked. And you turned up your pretty nose at him. Now when he sees himself through your eyes, what does he see?"

"A loser."

"He's not going to thank you for that. You have to be marginalized so your opinion isn't worth anything to him or anyone else."

"His wife would have a fit if she knew what he was doing."

"Men have convinced themselves that this sort of thing is harmless. It goes on everywhere if the boss tolerates it."

"But, Dad, they're trashing my ability to be a good teacher, and I can't do anything about it. I don't have any power cards."

"You never did. I just loaned you mine. And to be really useful, those things have to be earned." He drummed his fingers on the desk blotter. "What does Elliot say about all this?"

"He doesn't know much." And now her father looked worried. "I'm afraid he might care too much and do something stupid, or . . ." Her voice trailed off.

He finished her sentence. "Or he might think less of you?" He frowned. "My advice would be to have Elliot show up at school. That might change the way you're perceived. Makes you appear less vulnerable."

"But we only have one car, and I drive it to school."

"That's not insurmountable. You'll figure that out."

"Is there anything you can do?"

"There isn't any legal remedy. You haven't been assaulted, unless more happened with the cowboy than you're telling me."

She shook her head, but who knew for sure. She'd been unconscious.

"An interesting case is making its way through the courts. It's based on the '64 Civil Rights Act. You can't discriminate on the basis of gender, and sexual intimidation is a form of discrimination, at least that what this case purports. It'll go all the way to the Supreme Court. It will be interesting to see what comes of it. There's another bit of legislation that was signed this summer, Title IX of the Educational Amendments. It's illegal to discriminate against girls in schools. Interestingly, we're going to be representing a group of girls who want to play high school tennis. Pro bono, of course."

"The right to play tennis doesn't seem that earth shattering."

He studied her over his reading glasses. "No, but it's all part of positive forward motion. Working women only earn 53 percent of what a man earns for doing the same job. The Equal Pay Act is going to change that, but each case will have to be challenged in the courts until the law becomes clear."

"And I have to hide a slipcover in my trunk . . ."

"Touché!" He laughed. "That's my little girl."

Before he could wander off on one of his legal ramblings, Nina said, "Dad, I've been thinking hard about the whole law school thing. I want to apply. If I can manage to get in, it would be a better fit."

He nodded without speaking.

"Will you finance the applications?"

"Yes, and I'd help with tuition too, but what does Elliot say about law school?"

"Well, I wanted to talk with you first."

"Oh, Nina, you're swimming in dangerous waters. Don't keep secrets from your husband." He hugged her, and she smelled the starch in his shirt, his favorite cologne, and something that was just uniquely her dad.

She wandered into her mother's sewing room and picked up the phone.

Elliot answered the second ring. "It feels like you've been gone for months. When are you coming home?"

"Sunday night. Do you miss me?"

"Do I miss you? Does Wilt Chamberlain play basketball?" She could hear quiet tension in his voice. "I have a surprise for you."

"I have one for you too. My mom's friend is going to let us have her condo in Park City for a few days before Christmas. I get out of school on the twentieth and we can stay until the twenty-fourth and then spend Christmas Day with my family." It would be so wonderful. She and Elliot could ice skate at Treasure Mountain or walk up and down Main Street looking at Christmas displays in the shop windows. They could sit by the fire and read. "We didn't have much of a honeymoon."

Silence on the line. Why wasn't he thrilled? When he started to talk, she could sense the tension in his voice.

"I'm sorry. My mom wants us to spend Christmas Eve and Christmas Day with them. She's been talking about it all day. Could we come home a day early?"

"Are you kidding? The bed in that condo looks like an aircraft carrier. We could actually sleep together without getting clobbered. Not coming home early. No way."

* * *

When she pulled into the parking lot late Sunday night, Elliot filled the open doorway, an anxious smile on his face and the light behind him. "I've missed you. I dreamed last night I couldn't find you anywhere. It was awful." He whispered into her ear. "Don't ever leave me, Nina."

"If I vanish, I'll take you with me."

She could smell something unusual—not the usual lurking odors she couldn't identify. Something fresh. Paint? She looked over his shoulder into the kitchen. A forty-inch square table painted fire engine red with a tan Formica top sat where the card table used to be.

"I found it at the hospital warehouse sale."

It was the most amazing table, strong enough to hold a baby elephant at a well-baby checkup. If there were ever an earthquake, she and Elliot could dive under the table and be perfectly safe. She was thrilled. Two Windsor chairs, one a bit wobbly—but who cared?—were painted the same brilliant shade of red. She threw her arms around his neck as they stood admiring their first major domestic acquisition. They'd weathered their first separation.

~ 18 ~

Happenings

*L*ast month's colorful autumn leaves had turned into dried refuse clogging the storm drains or hiding under shrubs. The weather outside had a decided chill, but the climate inside the newlyweds' apartment improved. Using an old brush, Nina splashed cinder blocks with Elliot's leftover red paint and then erected a spectacular bookcase against the living room wall. The denim slipcover fit perfectly, almost. Striped throw pillows were a colorful punch against the blue denim. She hung posters with string, some glue, and a few thumbtacks. Standing back with her hands on her hips, she decided the apartment could be an art major's loft, maybe near the Sorbonne in Paris. Everything had been clean when they moved in, and she hadn't seen any reason to disturb the status quo, but this afternoon she opened the tiny linen closet and pulled out the vacuum cleaner, a wedding present from an aunt who didn't understand the utility of silver trays, and sat down to remove the tags and read the instruction manual. She pushed it across the floor several times and was delighted with the result.

When a tired Elliot came home at eleven, he found a bookshelf in his living room filled with Nina's texts and dog-eared novels, pictures of Scotland, a silver framed wedding portrait, and a small blue lamp giving off soft light. He looked around the immaculate room and heaved a large sigh before he raised his head and offered a silent prayer. "Thank you," he mouthed.

Inspired by the new furnishings, Nina started adding a chopped hot dog to the mac and cheese, lettuce to the tuna sandwiches, and a tea-spoon of brown sugar to the cans of baked beans. Her confidence was bolstered by being on top of things, and so one evening as Elliot tucked into a thick bowl of Campbell's cream of chicken soup, she announced, "I'm no longer willing to be your mother's bungling, unwanted fourth daughter, the one who spills the milk and is locked in the closet when she's not being trained to do menial tasks." She cleared her throat. "I'm through with all that. If I get hauled in for dish duty, you're my wing-man. If you're playing football with the kids, I'm in the starting lineup."

Elliot's mouth started to twitch.

"I'm happy to spend Sundays with your family—once a month. That's it. We need a little time to ourselves. I'm going to make a sign to hang on the front door. *Mr. and Mrs. Spencer are not receiving guests.*"

He leaned over and kissed her. "I've never seen my father wash a dish," he muttered. "Maybe he has, but I don't remember it. My mother will have a nervous breakdown if a husband—"

"Her precious Elliot."

"*Her precious Elliot* is in the kitchen doing dishes instead of mixing it up with the little kids." He sighed as though the whole situation were getting stickier by the minute. "I'm just telling you how it is, Nina. What you're proposing won't go down easily."

"And," she continued, "I'm through crying. I don't know what's hap-pened to me. I bawl at the drop of a hat. Completely out of character."

He shrugged. "You're pretty cute."

"Any chance you'll be home by ten?"

"I have that biochem test on Tuesday."

She knew what that meant. Elliot would ease in next to her around midnight, and the whole bed would shift like stressed tectonic plates. Asleep an hour later, they'd bump into each other, and Elliot's hands would wake up at least ten minutes before the rest of his body. He always apologized profusely the next morning when the purple circles under her eyes looked like they'd been painted with a brush.

Now as the weather grew colder, their sleeping arrangements became even more complicated. Elliot's feet weren't content to dangle over the edge of the mattress, and he thrashed around in his sleep until he was lying diagonally. That left her the upper right corner, which was about half the size of a crib. Neither one of them had noticed the bedroom was missing a heat vent—it hadn't seemed important in July—and now the bedroom felt like a cold storage unit. During the night, her breath rose in a frigid white mist. She woke in the mornings in a frozen fetal position. Elliot thought it was strange when he discovered her wearing ski socks in bed. "Is this some sort of Rushforth thing? Why do you wear socks?"

"Why do penguins have feathers? To keep from freezing."

Her response the next night was to leave the socks on the floor, and at 4:00 a.m. when her feet felt like a couple of snow cones, she put them on the small of his back. Shocked, he bolted upright in bed and then saw her shivering in her few square inches next to the headboard. He held her apologetically, tucked the covers around her, and rubbed her feet, but the next night her new husband was sleeping on the oblique again. All those years of mutual lessons and no one had ever addressed the real problems of sleeping with a man.

Nina was exhausted. She stumbled out of bed when the alarm rang. Bleary eyed, she groped through the two boxes of sweaters, the envy of her sorority the previous year, that had found permanent residence in the three-foot lane between the closet and the bed. She drove home from school with her windows down. She fell asleep at the movies during the opening credits with her mouth full of popcorn. Last Sunday, she snuggled against Elliot's shoulder at his home ward and fell asleep during the opening song. When his mother tried to prod her, Elliot shook his head.

Nina's persistent narcolepsy came to a dramatic finale during fourth hour on Thursday right before lunch. She'd been reading a story—a sad boy-and-his-dog story—that she had already read twice that morning to first and second hour. Even though her mouth was open and speaking, she realized she had no idea where she was on the page. It had happened before. Mitzi Olsen, an A student with immaculate braces, prompted her softly. "Second line, third paragraph." The room was silent. Every eye watched Nina's drooping head, and ten minutes later she was asleep. Rodney Hurt and Mickey Watson crept out of their desks at the top of the horseshoe and tiptoed to the back of the room. The air shaft. They shinnied up that shaft and crawled across the horizontal tunnel until their freckled faces were mashed against the grill. The last of Lyman Snarr, a black sneaker, was vanishing after the other two boys when Nina, struggling to open one eye, spotted his shoe.

"Okay," she said, jumping up. "Okay." These escapes up the air shaft were becoming a recurrent problem. Making it to the top had become a rite of passage or counting coup. A fuzzy memory pushed its way out of the deep recesses of her mind, something about extinguishing obnoxious behaviors she'd learned in Psychology 101. A woman, institutionalized but not dangerous, stole towels constantly. So the staff plied her with towels until her room was filled with them, until she was swimming in them, until she quit stealing them. Nina thought of her father and reminded herself not to react.

She just said as calmly as possible, "Is there anyone else who would like to go up the air shaft? I'm thinking twenty or thirty would be a good number." And trying to sound urbane, she said, "Fifty students in San Francisco stuffed themselves into a telephone booth." In a flash, every kid in the room was jammed in the shaft. Elbows and knees wedged against the dirty walls, they inched their way up until thirty-three bodies were crammed inside. Only Mitzi Olsen and Mary Margaret Stultz, sitting demurely at their desks, were left behind.

Nina wasn't sure how the telephone booth happening ended, and she was starting to be apprehensive about a surprise visit from "the boss" or a delegation from the district inspecting her leaks. A missing seventh-grade English section was sure to be noticed. And then, eight or ten feet up, Nina heard a boy gag and someone else groan, "Who farted?"

"Gross. Rotten eggs."

Legs, elbows, and bodies crashed down in a huge heap. Nina was sure a few heads were going to roll out the opening and across the floor. It was like Santa, all the reindeer, a handful of elves, and the sleigh had plunged down a dark chimney and shattered on the hearth. It took a few minutes for the participants to locate missing body parts and examine their wounds proudly and a few minutes longer for them to return to their desks. When they did, Nina was ready.

"We're going to write a couple of paragraphs. Here's your title: 'What I learned about my classmates while in the air shaft.' Perhaps some things you didn't want to know. Hmm?"

After the bell, Jerry stuck his head in the back door. "Did you lose anyone?"

"Nope. I did a nose count."

She sighed and sat down at her desk to eat the peanut butter sandwich Elliot had stowed in her purse. She'd gotten off lightly. If she'd fallen asleep during sixth or seventh hour, they would have tied her up like poor Gulliver in Lilliput. She grabbed a piece of scratch paper off the pile and made a list:

> *Sleep. Where to find it. How to get it.*
> *School Play. Find script. Yesterday.*

She rested her palm in her chin and closed her eyes.

* * *

During sixth hour while the rest of the class drafted intricate sentence diagrams with rulers and long glances toward their neighbors' papers, Robin Shelton tiptoed her way to Nina, and with her finger touching her lips and her back to the class, she whispered, "I need to talk to you." Robin was one of a handful of ninth-grade girls who belonged on the cover of the *Sports Illustrated* Swimsuit Edition. Maybe puberty had arrived too quickly for Robin's mother to start buying size nines, or maybe there was an argument every time Robin walked out the door. Nina had no way of knowing, but today, an upset young girl fluttered her eyelashes anxiously, and she glanced up furtively when Nina said, "What about?"

"Can you excuse me for the first ten minutes of seventh hour?"

Nina raised her shoulders.

"It's my birthday," Robin said, "and I have type seventh period." As though that should explain it all.

She was not looking for warm birthday wishes; she was pleading for help. The bell rang. Nina reached for the pad of tardy excuses. "Sorry, but I don't get it." And she didn't, but maybe she did.

Robin's face flushed a bright pink. "Mr. Fletcher spanks us on our birthdays."

But those meaty hands weren't going to touch this girl on her birthday. Nina could imagine Mr. Fletcher holding Robin over his knee at the front of the room while the boys salivated and the class counted out fourteen lingering strokes. Humiliation shouldn't be a requirement for a passing grade.

"Does everyone get the same treatment? Do the boys get spanked?"

"No. And not all the girls."

"You've said enough. I understand." Furious, Nina's heart hammered away. She was ready to march out to Beginning Type and tell Marlo exactly what he was, a lecherous bully and a poor excuse for a man. And then what? She took a deep breath and tried to envision what her father would do. "Have you talked to your parents?"

"No, Mrs. Spencer. My dad's the dean of education at Utah State. He'd have a fit, and that would make it worse."

It. Nina knew all about *it.*

"Well, Robin, you're going to be indisposed and need to spend seventh hour in the sickroom. Or in the library. Which?"

"Library."

Nina wrote a quick note to Mr. Bromley, the librarian, and another to Marlo Fletcher. She wanted to tell him that today's diversion had been canceled on account of bad taste, but she stopped herself. She kept it simple, but she'd drawn a line in the sand.

Sleep, she thought as she was driving home. She felt a bit frantic. She had to get more sleep. She had to keep her wits about her.

Dropping her things on the floor when she arrived home, she plopped down on the couch and stretched out her legs. She tucked a striped pillow behind her head and tried to think. She heard a small scratching noise. She wasn't alone.

She'd heard a soft noise, almost a twittering, two days ago. She'd called Elliot over to press his face against the couch and listen.

"Nothing," he said, but he'd brushed at something with the toe of his shoe. "You should vacuum in here. Right away." A rather cryptic response, but he was always encouraging her to be tidy, so she didn't pay much attention.

Sleep was the issue. The bathtub or the couch after Elliot fell asleep. That seemed to be the solution. Unfortunately, she'd received three silver pitchers and a dozen place settings of her Lennox, but no woolen blankets. She felt a moment's envy for friends whose mothers made elaborate quilts. Her mother made a perfect quiche lorraine. She thought of begging a little extra bedding from Rachel, but the explanation would be difficult to choke out. And the very thought that she didn't want to share a bed with her adorable new husband felt like two column inches in "Can This Marriage Be Saved?" in *Good Housekeeping*. She could diagram the Gettysburg Address and she'd graduated at the top of her class. Surely she could figure out sleep.

At 3:00 a.m., wearing her ski socks, her long blue coat, and wrapped in a couple of fluffy bath towels, she was blissfully asleep stretched out on the couch. A loud snap jolted her. She yelled, high pitched and terrified. Elliot raced in from the bedroom. She grabbed him around his neck and lifted her feet off the floor.

"Something's under the couch."

She cowered behind him, touching his back as he peeked under the slipcover.

He grabbed a piece of paper towel from the kitchen and reached under the couch and brought out a little mouse, still quivering, in a trap. "Got it." Barefoot, Elliot ran outside, and she heard the lid to the dumpster bang shut. Back in the living room, he stared at her.

He took in the coat and the ski socks and the towels. "Are you headed outside to take a shower?" He started to laugh. "You'd rather not sleep with me?"

She knew what he was thinking. "It's not about sleeping *with you*. It's about sleeping." He took her by the hand, and she followed him into their bedroom.

"Do you think he has friends?" she whispered, pulling the blanket over her shoulder.

"Who?"

"The mouse."

"Are you afraid they'll retaliate?"

"That's an awful thought," she said.

"Those socks are scratching the backs of my legs."

"Too bad."

◦ 19 ◦

Unscrupulous Characters

Mike's got to get some playing time." Elliot collected his notebooks off the kitchen table and shoved them in his backpack. "I should have helped him. Practiced free throws." Mike, the third Spencer son, hadn't exchanged three words with Nina in ten months. He just stared at her from a safe distance as though she were slightly terrifying.

Elliot had never seen her classroom, her labor intensive bulletin boards, or the infamous air shaft. He'd never met the cast of unscrupulous characters that starred in her monologues each evening at dinner. That would all change this afternoon. It was the season opener. The Clear Creek Horsemen versus the Logan Jr. High Mountain Men. Unfortunately, Mike, the skinniest Mountain Man, was clumsy to boot.

She kissed Elliot's cheek. "Remember I'm on the main floor. South side. East of the office. Condemned girl's gym." He nodded absently. She grabbed her books and raced for her car.

At noon she borrowed a cleaning cloth from Mr. Mumford. The moment the final bell rang, she was running the cloth over the top of her desk as students headed for the game. Wrinkling her nose at the thick accumulation of dust, she opened a window and waved the cloth, emitting a small gray cloud in the crisp November air.

Her head swaying back and forth and the cloth in her hand, she started to sing,

"I saw her today at a reception,
A glass of red wine in her hand.

159

I knew she would meet her connection
At her feet was her footloose man."

She danced over to the file cabinet and pulled out a half dozen manila folders and scribbled on the tabs. She loaded in leftover assignments. Alone on her side of the building, she belted out the rest of the chorus,

"No, you can't always get what you want."

She loved the Stones. She slammed the file drawer shut and dusted the top of the cabinet. Dancing around the room, she sprayed cleaner on the desktops and wiped off messages, doodles, and a couple of caricatures of her that were surprisingly good.

Her classroom door open, she heard the roar from the boy's gym. The game had started. She dropped the cloth and walked over to the window. Only a few activity buses remained, but the parking lot was jammed with cars. Four or five parents, late to the game, hurried across the gravel. She spotted the Spencers' yellow VW van. Her shoulders sank as she glanced around her vacant room.

Sitting down heavily at her desk, she drew loops and curlicues across the side of a lined sheet of paper for fifteen minutes before she picked up a stack of essays that needed correcting. Her chin in her palm, she glanced up at the clock. It must be the half because the roar in the gym had quieted. No echoes reached her. She'd dressed carefully that morning, a pink turtleneck under a multicolored, poor boy vest and long, corduroy bell-bottoms. Elliot hadn't noticed.

She jumped up. The second half was starting. She'd run over to the game for just a minute. Maybe he was waiting for her.

Concealed by the second tier of bleachers, she saw the line of folding chairs on the edge of the wooden floor for the visiting team and their parents. Sitting next to his mother, Elliot punched his fist into his palm, cheering against the skinny boys in maroon who comprised most of her seventh hour.

He was wearing his off-white Aryan knit and a light blue shirt. She'd ironed that shirt, at least the part that showed—the collar and the cuffs. She felt a jolt of attraction, a tug at her core, and thought for a minute of elbowing her way into the adjacent chair and taking her rightful place at Elliot's side, but he wasn't scanning the crowd for her. He was focused on the gym floor, because Mike had thrown the ball away, again. The Mountain Men's coach called a time-out, and Robin Shelton and the other cheerleaders bounced onto the floor to lead the students in the hand-me-down fight song, a relic from Clear Creek's high school days before it was condemned to be a junior high. Nina knew most of the words, and stepping out from behind the bleachers, feet firm on the concrete landing, she sang loudly,

"Clear Creek's Horsemen charging,
With our honor bright
Proudly wear our colors
Of Maroon and White
Fight, fight, fight!"

Walter Nibley, the youngest in a family of eight lackluster students, dribbled the ball down the court. The hair on the back of his neck was stringy with sweat as he launched the ball off the tips of his fingers and scored. Nina raised her hands over her head, clapping loudly and cheering, "Go, Walter!" Elliot's head swiveled around, but his mother grabbed his hand. Mike was back in the game.

Nina stayed long enough to watch Walter score eight more points and see Bevan Godfrey make an impossible three-point shot from mid-court. Robin caught her eye, and Nina gave her quick thumbs-up before she hurried back to her room. One minute was left in the game; she didn't want to miss Elliot in the crush of students racing for the last buses.

Whistling the fight song softly, she stood at the window leaning her elbows on the grimy ledge, her slim hips swaying back and forth. Through the glass, she waved happily at Walter and his parents. Walter waved back, a huge grin on his face. And then there was Elliot with his arm around a dejected Mike walking toward the van. Elliot was leaving? She pressed her fingertips against the cold window as the van pulled onto the road. Its taillights blinked at her from the only intersection in town with a semaphore.

Collapsing into the nearest desk, she hugged one knee. A few locker doors slammed. She heard buses pulling out. Jerry stuck his head in the door. "Great game. Have a good weekend." She managed a weak smile. Checking the back door to be sure it was locked, she turned off the lights. She knew she was being silly, but it seemed to her that given the choice between old family and new, she'd lost the jump ball. Jerking open her bottom desk drawer, she reached for her purse. Gone. She searched the back of the drawer with her fingers. No purse. No keys.

Sitting in the gloom, assailed by a deep sickening rage, she inhaled several times. A dirty trick. Marlo was retaliating. The only phone in the building was locked in the office. Ruth was gone. Nina bit off a piece of skin on the side of her thumbnail. She'd left her room unlocked when she'd hurried over to the game. How stupid was she? She couldn't call Elliot. He was driving in the van with his mother. She'd have to walk a half-mile to the gas station and sit in the grungy office by the cash register until she could locate Elliot with the extra set of keys.

She heard the rattle of empty bottles coming down the hall. The noise stopped abruptly outside her door, but she turned away. She had a pretty good idea of who had stolen her purse, but he'd deny it with a wicked grin on his face and relish her impotence. Maybe she'd head out to the portables and steal something from him, swipe a dozen of his typewriters. Escalating dirty tricks.

"Mumford, you still here?" Marlo called out. Then the rattle made its way down the hall.

Mr. Mumford pushed his cleaning cart into the room and flipped on the light. He stopped, barely moving his gray head, and nodded at Nina. Slowly, he pushed his broom across the wooden floor, making a tidy pile of dirt and candy wrappers. He swept the pile into a dustpan and poured it into the garbage, a small trickle of filth. Nina scurried over and touched the old man's faded work shirt.

"My purse isn't in my desk. Have you seen it? Navy with a strap? My car keys are in it. I need to go home."

The old man raised one grizzled eyebrow.

She clutched his spindly arm. "Maybe you could unlock the office so I can use the phone?" She'd call Mel. He was always at the store. He almost lived there. He'd bring the delivery truck. She knew he would. He liked her. But when she glanced at the clock, she remembered it was Friday, his day to deliver in Tremonton. She pressed her palm against her forehead. "Never mind, there's no one to call. No one's home."

Mumford lifted a spray bottle of cleaner from the middle shelf of his cart and wet a blue cloth from his back pocket. He wiped the surface of a desk she'd cleaned two hours earlier. It took him five minutes. Nina stared at the clock and wondered what to do. By the time the old man was starting the fifth desk, she heard the click of cowboy boots striding down the hall. Nathan stepped through the door. The fluorescent lights felt artificial, as though the classroom minus children were a set for an amateur theatrical. He didn't speak. A muscle jumping in his jaw, he gazed at her and then glanced over his shoulder.

Mr. Mumford stuffed his rag in his back pocket and rested a hand on Nathan's shoulder. "Her purse is gone. No keys." He pushed his cart into the hall. "I'll keep an eye out for that blue purse of yours," he muttered, his eyes on the floor.

Nina made herself breathe in and out slowly. *Don't react*, she thought. Treat Nathan like a friend. Pretend he's Lars stopping by for a chat.

Her heart was hammering away. "Hey, that was some game." She tried to smile. "Did you see Bevan's three-point shot?" She grabbed her jacket off the hook in the cupboard.

He took a quick look out the window at the parking lot before he turned toward her. "He didn't even know you were there."

She knew exactly who *he* was, and it wasn't Bevan. Nathan had been watching her, following her. She could pretend confusion, but he'd know and be irritated. "I'm disappointed," she said, "but basketball is big in Elliot's family. It's okay. Thanks for noticing."

"Everyone's noticed. You've lost your sparkle from the first of the year."

Sparkle? Her sparkle was being discussed in the faculty lounge? "Well," she huffed. "This is a tough job. Harder than I imagined."

He didn't answer. His eyes traveled over her—every inch from head to toe. Her skin crawled.

"My dad's an attorney, but I don't think he's ever worked as hard as we do." She'd horsed around with the guys on the tennis court; she knew the right tone, the casual male banter, but it wasn't working.

Her sweater rose with each ragged breath. He was strong. For weeks after her pathetic tripping episode, second-hour students regaled her with Nathan's superhuman feat of strength. He'd plucked her off the floor with one arm as though he'd hit the bell with the first swing of

163

the mallet at a carnival. His back, ramrod straight, looked like he had a Harrington rod shoved down his spine.

"I've misplaced my purse. Does your wife ever do that? Elliot's always on my case for losing things." She yanked open her drawer searching frantically with both hands. "You have kids, don't you?" She was almost pleading. "Is your wife from around here?"

"The first one was."

How many did he have? Was he some cowboy reincarnation of Blue Beard? Through the door she glimpsed Marlo striding down the hall, a scowl on his face. Nathan gave him a quick salute.

She glanced past Nathan toward the door. She'd never get around him. Two or three more steps and he'd have her boxed into the corner between her desk and the chalkboard and the filing cabinet. The back door lock was stiff and slow to open. But at the end of the room, thirty feet away, past the concentric rows of desks was the air shaft. She'd read the student essays. Three feet square. Using her hands and her knees, she could shimmy her way up until she hit that horizontal space. She slipped off her shoes.

She'd never seen him just walk. Nathan swaggered. He strutted. But could he sprint? He didn't have a bootjack. She'd be halfway up while he was sitting on the floor struggling to pull off those boots.

Trying to be inconspicuous, she slid the stapler across the desk and tucked it in her pocket. If she could just make that horizontal shelf, she'd have something to throw. She fingered the box of paper clips and wished she still had that apple from lunch. *Joke with him*, she told herself. Pretend this isn't a confrontation.

"You know, Nathan, there's something you should know about me." She brushed her blonde hair off her forehead as she forced a laugh. "I hate horses. I always have. My parents used to take us to the Days of '47 Parade every year, and those horses pooping their way down Main Street disgusted me." Her hands were trembling. "I mean they didn't even have the grace to wait for a field."

If she could just get up the air shaft, how long would she have to wait for someone to come, for Elliot to call the police, for the "where was she last seen" conversation to take place? Isn't this where they'd bring the dogs to pick up her scent? She'd yell down from the grill, "I'm up here!"

And Nathan, circling around the opening of the shaft, what would his explanation be? "Young gal shot right up that air shaft and won't come down. She's lost her mind. I've stayed right here. I was afraid she meant to harm herself."

With what? A stapler?

Ready to run, adrenaline racing in her veins, she pushed the sleeves of her turtleneck past her elbows.

Hands in front of him, palms up, Nathan stifled a smile. "You're as skittish as a two-year-old in the starting gate. I'm not going to harm you, Nina."

Her fingers fluttered against her throat. "Well, of course not. I didn't think you were."

"We'd both know I was lying if I said I didn't find you attractive, but I don't force myself on women. I've never needed to." All those teeth reflected the light, along with the pearl buttons on his shirt.

"Thanks. That's nice of you to say." She tried to sound casual as though he'd complimented her shoes.

"Honey, your husband's a fool."

"No. No, he's not." A line from a folk song flitted through her head and nearly fell out of her mouth, *He's a young thing and cannot leave his mother.* "You're friends with Mr. Mumford?" she asked.

"Not much about this old school Mumford doesn't know."

Moving slowly, she eased around her desk. "I think I'll just walk down to that Texaco station on the highway and call my husband to bring me the spare keys."

"Can't let you do that. What say I give you a ride home, and you can send your husband out in the morning."

"Thanks, but I don't want to put you out. I'm sure you have plans."

He shook his head deliberately. "None more important than seeing you safe."

The sharp rap of high heels echoed in the hall. Marsha, with two cheerleaders in tow, stopped at Nina's door. The young girls spit retorts at each other, but Nina didn't care. Her shoulders relaxed, and a smile stretched across her face. Marsha's sharp eyes surveyed the empty room, Nathan, and Nina standing in her stocking feet.

"Time to go home," Marsha announced in a voice that said the woman's patience was spent. She glared at Nathan, but he just shrugged.

"Her purse's been stolen. I offered her a ride."

"No." Marsha shook her head. "I'll take her. I've got to take these little twittle-butts home anyway. I can swing through town and drop off Nina."

Nina hated feeling helpless, or maybe it was hapless that she was feeling. Either way, she loathed being referred to in the third person as though she were a broom or a vacant chair or a woman in a vegetative state, but she kept her mouth shut and switched off the lights. Nathan held the heavy exterior door open with old-fashioned formality. Cold air chilled her skin. Someone was burning leaves down the road.

Following Marsha across the gravel parking lot, she listened to Nathan's rambling story. Jeff Wilkinson set a Bunsen burner under the gas tube and started the lab on fire. Well, maybe not the whole lab, but a couple of textbooks and four or five lab manuals, and he singed Marie Viebel's bangs and eyebrows. Nathan doused the table and kids with foam from a fire extinguisher he'd never used before. "Ninth-grade science," he said. "Every day's a rodeo. That Wilkinson kid? Trouble follows him around like he's got candy in his pockets." He held the door as Nina climbed in Marsha's car.

The sky was deep blue as they passed the brightly lit Texaco station, and distant lights across the valley twinkled on cue. After the Scotch blessing the cheerleaders received for mean girl antics—dropping chewed gum in a rival's hair—Marsha drove silently, frowning at her own thoughts. But when she stopped in front of Nina's apartment, she rolled down her window as Nina circled the front of the car. Marsha's voice, low and intense, cut through the darkness. "Anyone who can see the parking lot knows you're still in the school. Go in early if you have to, but don't stay late. Ever." And then she hit the accelerator and was gone.

* * *

The next day Nina hiked up College Hill, determined to laugh with Lars and Cindy. Elliot worked until four, and after last night's spat, she felt cast adrift and needed her friends. She slid into the booth and set down her lunch tray. Forty minutes later, a stricken-looking Lars said,

"If that Marsha person hadn't come by, that guy could have hauled you up one of those canyons, and no more doubles tennis. The stolen purse was a setup."

"I don't know." She examined a french fry before dunking it in ketchup. "Nathan's charming in a rough sort of way. Not a murderer. He'd be more inclined to toss a woman over the front of his saddle and ride off into the sunset. Very John Wayne."

"Enough with the junior high," Cindy said. "Quit. Monday morning, eight o'clock."

Nina struggled to keep the bitterness out of her voice. "We don't need any more complications—like unemployment. Being married is hard enough." She forced a laugh. "The guy does not know what to do with me."

Lars hooted. "That's a surprise."

Nina pulled her mouth to the side. "No, no, no. That's none of your business." She ran nervous fingers over the edge of the table as though she were playing a scale. "Have you ever had a dog chase your car?"

Cindy shook her head.

"Well, it happens a lot in the country. Dogs run loose and dogs chase cars. They bark and tear along next to the wheels, running for all they're worth. Whenever I get chased, I always wonder what would happen if I just stopped the car and said, 'Here, dog. It's all yours. Take the stupid car.' I mean, what would the dog do with it?"

Lars gave her a cross-eyed grin. "Where are you going with this?"

Nina shrugged. "Elliot's like that dog. He wanted me badly, but now that he's got me, he doesn't know what to do with me. I'm in the way. He wants to spend Sunday with his family. He doesn't want to quit being the alpha son. He wants to be free to study. He likes having someone else do the laundry and pay the bills, but spending time with me? Not a priority, unless it's three or four hours on Saturday night. A date once a week. He came all the way to Clear Creek and wasn't even curious about where I slave away every day."

"Those obsessive science guys are all like that," Cindy said. "If they're not studying every second, they think they're getting behind."

"Did he explain?" Lars asked.

"Oh sure." She rolled her eyes. "His little brother was devastated by how badly he played, so they took him out to get a milkshake, and then his mom was rushed for time." Nina raised her shoulders. "Dumb me. I thought being married would be like being engaged."

"Well, girls. The times they are a changin'." Lars sighed. "ERA's going to get ratified by the states, and then it's open season on all this gender stuff. You'll both get drafted."

"No more draft." Nina laughed. "I don't think the ERA's going to get ratified. Everything's going to get tossed to the courts."

"So," Cindy said, "what have you decided about law school? Are you going to take up the cross?"

"I don't know." Nina pursed her lips. "But interesting things are happening. Dad says exciting cases are in the pipeline headed for the Supreme Court."

Cindy pointed a finger at her. "He's tempting you."

Nina raised one eyebrow. Why hadn't that thought occurred to her? Because of course it was true.

"I talked to Nola Mortensen last weekend." Cindy shook her head. "She quit after her first year of law school."

"You're kidding," Nina said, her chin dropping.

"The males in her class were hounding her to death."

"Nola?" Nina said. "She's the smartest girl I've ever known."

"That was the problem. She didn't know her place."

Lars's eyes met hers. "I don't know, Nina. Who needs law school? It sounds like you could get in enough trouble right where you are."

"Nola quit." Nina exclaimed. "That is just so wrong." Someone had to step into the ring. Someone who wouldn't quit.

When she got home, she lay down on her stomach and reached under the bed. Wrinkling her nose at the dust, she pushed a boxed fondue pot to one side and found the long white dress box. Wednesday morning on her way to school, she shoved six large envelopes through the slot in the post office box. She made the first application deadline by three days.

❧ 20 ❧

Thanksgiving

Nina quit worrying about her missing purse, because the mouse onslaught commenced on Wednesday. Typically Nina avoided the faculty lounge, but she had to pick up her order from Scholastic Books. Ruth had nagged her about it twice. Fifty ancient wooden cubbyholes covered an entire wall, and as Nina reached around the package wedged in her box, a mousetrap sprung and broke her ring finger above the second joint. She yelped, but she didn't scream. Elliot iced her finger when she got home, and she groaned looking at a finger so swollen her ring wouldn't slide over her knuckle.

Two weeks later on a dreary November day during seventh period, she was writing on the chalkboard, *Let's eat Grandma.*

"Can a comma save this poor woman from being gobbled up by her grandchildren?" she asked, as a stealthy hand opened the back door. Four mice skittered across the floor. Girls screamed and jumped up on their desks. Boys swatted at the rodents with textbooks. It was a lopsided battle, but breathing slowly, Nina stood quietly, immune to the mayhem. She didn't have the energy left to hyperventilate. One energetic rodent raced to the front of the room. Nina lifted her foot, and with split-second timing, dropped it on the mouse's tail.

"Walter." She nodded at the boy as though she were asking him to sharpen a pencil. "Take it away." She wondered, as Walter cupped the mouse in his palms, if she should send it out to Beginning Type in the portable, but escalation was not in her best interest. "Put it in that large trash can by the office." Then she whispered, "If you could break its little neck, it won't have to starve to death."

Walter nodded seriously and started out the door.

"Wait, Walter," she said. "Take it outside and let it go. And wash your hands on the way back in."

Shell shocked was how Elliot described her face as he held her on the couch after dinner before he vanished into the labyrinth of the library. He stroked her shorn hair and told her mythical fairy tales about Christmas holidays she was sure would never come. How could she look forward to Christmas when that huge barrier blocked her view? THE SCHOOL PLAY. She hid her face in his soft wool sweater and listened to the rhythmic beating of his heart. The muffled sound had become something of a mantra, and when he left for the library, she was bereft.

A dubious Elliot had negotiated a Thanksgiving and Christmas Eve truce. "Masses of relatives," he'd tried to warn her, moving his hands in ever larger arcs as though each person represented a single spark in a tremendous fireworks display. It was hard to imagine someone setting off fireworks in Rachel's immaculate living room and kitchen, but Nina got the general idea. Christmas Eve, he'd indicated, was a much smaller affair, but she held firm. Thanksgiving with the Spencers and five pre-Christmas days in Park City with no one. She wasn't going to vacate that borrowed condo until the last possible second. Elliot's forehead developed a perpetual crease. If he knew about the Thanksgiving seating arrangements, he didn't tip his mother's hand.

The Tuesday before Thanksgiving Elliot tried to warn her again, but Nina looked at him blank faced, "Do I have to cook it? You know, the turkey?"

"No."

"Then nothing else matters. It's a day away from school." She gave him a wan smile. Her food assignment was a broccoli casserole. She was being set up—little kids hated broccoli. She glommed bacon, cheese, slivered almonds, and broccoli florets into a dish and glued the whole business together with cream of mushroom soup. Perfect.

Holding their sacrificial offering with floral oven mitts, Nina and Elliot arrived at noon on a cloudy Thanksgiving Day and were met by dozens of folding chairs stacked on the front porch, benign chatter, and the pleasant sounds of laughter. The smell of a turkey roasting wafted out the front door. Nina closed her eyes and inhaled. She didn't need to eat a thing; breathing the delicious smells would be enough.

Rachel had replaced the couch and chairs with seven long tables arranged throughout her house with an effect not unlike a crossword puzzle. Winifred and Sharlene had covered the tables with paper printed with small cartoons of pilgrims hunting, pilgrims eating, or pilgrims plucking wild turkeys. It was festive and fun, and Nina started to smile, encouraged, particularly by the place markers, small turkeys made from Oreo cookies, candy corn, and a red gumdrop wattle.

Getting around the tables was like wiggling past people's knees in a crowded movie theater. Extended family laughed good-naturedly and winked at Elliot, who kept a protective grasp of Nina's arm. When his grip suddenly tightened, she glanced at the man edging around the corner of table number three.

"Ralph." Elliot shuddered. "He's married to Aunt Vivian." The man's face was pockmarked, and a hard, wrinkled mouth made him look older than his fifty years. A shapeless polyester plaid jacket hung from his angular shoulders as he extended his hand.

"Hello, Uncle Ralph."

"Elliot. This must be the new bride everyone's talking about." His face loosened when he spoke. He leaned back as though he were gazing up at the Empire State Building; then he gave her a smile, but it wasn't friendly. She smiled back and then drifted away, down the edge of the table, looking for her name attached to a turkey. Ralph turned his shoulder away from her, but his hushed remarks to Elliot were loud enough to hear.

"Every time I see an eighteen-wheeler with that green Interstate Trucking logo, I think of you. What's she worth? Four or five million? And you're living in a shoebox, 'cause her old man's steamed." He threw his head back and laughed, as though Elliot had been outfoxed in the deal, a bargain betrayed. The room started to shrink. A hot flash worked its way up Nina's neck and circled her ears. Family members glanced at them as though a fight in a parking lot was about to erupt.

Elliot's face blanched. "I fell in love with Nina before I knew anything about her family."

"Right. When you were a missionary." Ralph feigned a chuckle. "How many American families can send daughters on a jaunt to Scotland? But you stick with your story. It's a good one." He cuffed Elliot's shoulder and tried to saunter away, except the maze of tables impeded his progress as he tried to meld into another clutch of men folk where he could repeat his clever remarks.

"Say something nice, Ralph," Elliot muttered. "Knock yourself out."

Fussing with their toddlers, two or three of Elliot's cousins averted their eyes, quit studying Nina's navy pantsuit and coral earrings, and edged toward the kitchen. A family narrative had grown up around her new marriage, bits and pieces of truth turned sideways and upside down to fashion an explanation, a plausible reason for Elliot's choice. She could almost hear the whispers: *He's always been ambitious. His mom says he'll be sorry. And Nina's so tall.*

Elliot pulled Nina into his sisters' bedroom, closed the door, and studied her face intently. "I'm sorry you heard that."

She'd slept in until ten, but now she felt exhausted, too tired to smile, so she kissed him on the cheek instead. "That's what everyone's saying, isn't it?" She could feel it. "Elliot, the family favorite, the returned missionary, All-State basketball player, and smart as a whip—that Elliot. And those snobbish Rushforths don't think he's good enough for their daughter? Who do those people think they are?"

He fingered the tied quilt on Diane's top bunk. His eyes flickered away.

She touched the sleeve of his sweater. "They all know, don't they? Dad was opposed."

"It's not like it was a secret. He tried to buy me off."

And of course, a humiliated Elliot had gone to his parents for consolation, and his mother had gone to her world.

"Ralph's always been a jerk," he muttered.

"Every family's got one." She felt like an invisible hand was pressing down on her head, trying to squash her. "Let's change the conversation. Let's stay in here for a half hour and then go back out totally rumpled. Scandalize everyone." She raised one eyebrow. "Or we could grab a pumpkin pie and make a run for it. Head for the hills."

His entire face drooped. "That would only make things worse."

"Then help me find my spot for dinner."

She discovered her name on a small turkey on a round table out on the back porch next to the washer and dryer and realized Elliot would be sitting in the living room. She squeezed his hand and kept a stoic grin on her face.

Rachel lifted the hand mixer out of a vat of mashed potatoes long enough to introduce Nina to her older sister, Vivian, the poor woman married to loutish Ralph. "This is our Nina. Elliot met her in Scotland." Rachel gave her sister a knowing look as though Nina kept a bagpipe hidden under her coat or was a wild-eyed Scottish Wiccan grafted onto the family tree when no one was paying attention.

Her cookie turkey was surrounded by other birds of a similar style, and as Nina read the names, she realized *all* the women had been relegated to the back porch, including a gaggle of teenage girls. Dinner was a gauntlet.

"We let the men sit in there so they can talk about world affairs." Rachel laughed, gesturing toward the living room.

"Scotland?" Vivian, a plump woman with an endearing smile, patted the back of Nina's hand. "I'm the family genealogist. We have several Scottish branches. And I think the Spencers do too." Her purple wool dress was old, and her frayed linen cuffs had been starched once too often, but kind eyes were taking Nina's measure.

Nina inched closer and whispered, "I'd love to see pedigree sheets on those Scottish lines some day when you have an extra minute. Maybe over Christmas break?" A pedigree chart, one that went back six or seven generations. She knew who she'd find: Robert Burns. Those genes had filtered down through the generations and found each other in Elliot's nearly perfect DNA. She smiled, she couldn't help herself, as she heard his clear voice in the living room sounding more like Walter Cronkite every day.

"Nina studied in Scotland for a semester," Rachel said.

"Studied Elliot," Diane whispered.

"I studied Robert Burns." Her mother always said when you're on stage and every eye is focused on you, it's too late to be inconspicuous, so Nina laughed and started to recite.

"O, my luve is like a red, red rose,
    That's newly sprung in June."

"Does Elliot read poetry to you?" Diane snickered.

Nina turned toward Diane until her face was only inches away. "You'd be surprised." She gave her an exaggerated wink.

Nancy, the only sister Nina had met at the wedding, laid down her fork. "I bet those little children love you." The two aunts smiled at her with wide-mouthed approval.

"Actually, they're not so little. I teach in a junior high."

"Teaching is a good thing to be doing until the babies start coming." Rachel nodded.

No storkish metaphors for Rachel. No adorable bundles dropped down a chimney or discovered under a cabbage leaf. The babies start coming. An invasion. Nina had visions of small troops of zombie-like toddlers moving across a windswept plain. Silent, eyes round, their small heads swaying from side to side as they trundled, stiff-legged, looking for a place to attach themselves and suck the blood out of their hosts. Nina shuddered. Rachel gave her a stern look out the corner of her eye.

"Babies." Nina nodded. "It might be good to start with a puppy and gradually get into the whole responsibility thing. We had a beagle when I was growing up. If I didn't remember to keep my bedroom door closed, it was mayhem in the closet."

Winifred sighed. "We've never had a pet. Except the rabbit that boy gave Diane."

"A dog ate it," Diane said. "A beagle cross."

Rachel got up to pass the platter of turkey one more time and lift a tray of rolls out of the oven, releasing a draft of hot air and wonderful smells. "I draw the line," she said, "at anything furry that urinates."

Nina heard men's laughter from the other room and wondered what was all that funny. This self-imposed segregation was like blacks opting for separate but equal because they liked crowded schools and antiquated bathrooms.

Winifred started to whine, a sound like fingernails scraping down a chalkboard. "Mom, if we got a puppy for Christmas, I'd take care of it."

"No. What we'd love is a baby," Rachel announced emphatically. Every eye bypassed the turkey and the dressing, the cranberry sauce, the green beans, yams, and the untouched broccoli casserole and zeroed in on Nina's abdomen as though three months were plenty of time to get down to the serious business of being married.

"Whoa." She held up a protective hand. "Don't look at me. I'm the breadwinner, remember? I go to work every day. I can't do that and take care of a baby too."

Nancy leaned forward. "Rachel would love to take care of your baby while you work."

These three women had planned more than the menu.

Vivian patted her hand twice to get warmed up and then kept up a steady rhythm, sort of like tapping out Morse code. "You'd love having a little baby." She nodded seriously. "And a baby would help you reconcile with your father."

Nina straightened her shoulders. "My dad and I are very close. We don't need to reconcile." Everyone quit talking for several long minutes. Rachel pinched bits of roll between her fingers.

Finally, Nancy spoke up. "You've got a lovely bosom, dear. You'll have plenty of milk."

Nina glanced up from the paper napkin she'd been shredding in her lap and suppressed a scream. Vivian and Nancy smiled, waiting for her response. "I'm sure I will, but I'm only twenty-one." She'd watched dark circles blossom on her sister-in-law's blouse when she heard her baby cry. It was like a pipe had broken in there somewhere. "There are a lot of years to start a family when Elliot's further along in school. And I'm planning on graduate school too."

The smile on Rachel's face thinned until it was little more than a line. Here it comes, Nina cringed, the slap down.

"If you're old enough to marry, you're old enough to start a family."

Vivian dismissed her sister with a wave. "I know exactly how you feel, Honey. I felt the same way until the nurse put little Davy in my arms."

Nancy laughed. "He's six four."

Vivian said, "And he's a CPA. The best in the business."

This felt like a full-court press, and Nina had just lost the ball. She put her head down. How long could this dinner go on? How long until the buzzer rang? And then the birthing stories began.

"I was only twelve or thirteen," Vivian said, switching the patting over to Sharlene's wrist, "not much older than you are now. I hid behind the couch eavesdropping on my mother and her sisters. My cousin Lucille was two weeks overdue." She stretched her arms out over an imaginary distended abdomen. "Aunt Mary told my mother that Lucille had her bags packed three times. I was horrified. I stood straight up and said, 'What do they do to you when they pack your bags?'" Vivian rocked back and forth. Her eyes twinkled, and her laugh was infectious.

"Lucille, poor thing—she'd given up waiting at home—was standing at the lunch counter at ZCMI when her water broke. She thought she'd lost control of her bladder!" They all howled again.

Nina's mother never discussed any of this maternity trivia. Her mother told funny stories about foppish waiters on cruises or cajoling police officers out of speeding tickets. Nina had never heard the grim details of the labor that produced her or any of her brothers. The specifics of her sisters-in-law's travails were reduced to "she had a difficult time, poor thing. Let's send more flowers." Nina didn't know that waters broke in a rush at the ZCMI lunch counter. It was a startling idea, an uncomfortable idea she didn't want to consider.

Nina glanced around the table. They were looking at her, waiting. If she wasn't reproductive, she was nothing. No story worth telling. She was just an empty womb sitting on a straight-backed kitchen chair.

Or was she the audience?

Perhaps it was the bits of gristle and the bony carcass on the cutting board, or perhaps Nancy had saved her gruesome tale to up the ante, but whatever the reason, she started talking about RaNae's tumor. "She thought she was pregnant. Hoped she was pregnant. But the doctor never did find a heartbeat. She was growing, no doubt about that. Finally, they operated and found a fifteen pound tumor, and right in the middle of the thing was a jawbone—with teeth!"

Horrified, everyone under thirty dropped her fork on a china plate in one collective squeamish response, which made Vivian giggle. These stories were so familiar that one sister would begin and another would deliver the punch line. Family myths punctuated with laughter that came right on cue as if a director were holding up cards. Vivian reached over and put her arm around Rachel's shoulder.

"Of course, there was poor Nancy with those twins." Rachel's laughter filled the back porch as she nodded at her sister. "The Sunday they blessed the babies, a young husband came up to her and said, 'I'm glad to see you had twins. The last time I saw you, I said to my wife, look dear, that girl's having a pony.'" Rachel wiped a tear or two off her cheek with her napkin. Nina glimpsed softness in Rachel's face, relaxed and happy, not making reproving pronouncements or marshaling the troops but with Elliot's brown eyes and his tender smile on her lips. Their stories, repeated over and over, bound the women together, connected the generations. Not interested in mingling a magna cum laude in her gene pool, Rachel just wanted a baby, Elliot's baby, not only to have a darling grandchild to love, but also to collect fresh material, a new story about blood and pushing and dramatic C-sections in the dark of night.

It was as though a curtain had been pushed back, if only for a second, and there was Rachel caught in a vice, knowing she should love a girl whose family she despised, a family who'd had the audacity to reject her wonderful oldest child. All during dinner, Vivian and Nancy, smiling and nodding at Nina while touching her hand, were passing on their family's memories, including Nina in their storytelling and signaling to Rachel, their youngest sister, that it was time to let go of her disappointment and induct Elliot's wife into this circle of women. Time to include her in the secrets of the most elemental experience that women share, the birthing of babies. Even if those deliveries happened now under fluorescent lights in a sterile environment, the wonder and drama of new life was still on their lips.

Elliot wandered in from the other room, rested his hands on Nina's shoulders, and kissed the nape of her neck. Vivian patted the back of Nancy's hand. Knowing smiles stretched across their faces, but Rachel stood silently, her back to the oven.

"Do you want to have pumpkin pie on the front porch?" he whispered.

Nina gave him a coy look. "I'd rather stay in here and hear about Rosemary's triplets. The second two were breech."

∽ 21 ∾

The Play's the Thing

The last mini course listing before the Christmas break included two new offerings: Play Production and Stage Crew. Students flocked to sign up. Nina wasn't sure why, but she had her suspicions. Tensions were escalating with the bad boys, Marlo and Zach. Kids wanted a front-row seat. Now days before the class was scheduled to begin, Nina still didn't have a script. She spent long hours searching the stacks in the university library. *King Lear for Children* was too long. *George and Mary Search for Santa* was too juvenile. A musical was out of the question without tryouts and a few solid voices. She was starting to panic. On a Wednesday evening when the first snowstorm of the season was howling outside, Elliot grabbed her hands across the kitchen table and looked her in the face. "This has got to stop. Go to the theater department. Talk to the dean. Talk to anyone. Someone sometime has produced a children's play."

"I need a junior high play."

"Okay. A junior high play."

The next afternoon, wearing her new boots, Nina wandered up on campus and nosed around the theater department, immediately intrigued with the smells of wig spray and the rolls of garish fabrics in a room full of sewing machines. Costumes swung on racks lining the hallway. Loudmouthed college students made flamboyant gestures in the lounge. A boy dressed in black sat in the corner and strummed a guitar with such a tragic air that he looked suicidal, which was, of course, what he'd rehearsed in front of a mirror. English majors were less self-involved, but she still had an overwhelming feeling of homesickness. These were her people, kids her own age.

She stood in the hallway and sighed. She could hide out here incognito, pretending to be a seamstress, and no one would find her until she leaped on stage to give a stunning performance in *Cat on a Hot Tin Roof* or *A Street Car Named Desire*. The university was doing Tennessee Williams in the spring. She could do crazy or lustful angst. All she needed was an open audition.

A woman with a loaded pincushion attached to her wrist turned away from her sewing machine and asked if she could be of help. When Nina explained her desperate predicament, the woman smiled. "LaRue Malstrom," she said. "She's in charge of the Children's Theater Workshop. Room five."

Mrs. Malstrom had a large, pear-shaped bottom and an exotic past. Mysterious photos of a younger, thinner version of herself adorned her walls, and stacks of scripts and small pamphlets with dog-eared covers filled shelves that covered an entire wall. Long salt-and-pepper hair swooped off her neck in a loose bun that threatened to cascade down her neck if anyone removed the jeweled sticks holding it in place.

In October, Nina had dragged Elliot to see *Macbeth*, and she was certain this woman had played the chief witch. Mrs. Malstrom poked around until she pulled a faded script from the bottom of a pile. "It's a television drama. General Electric Theatre. *The Other Wiseman*. It's short. Minus the commercials, only forty minutes." She tapped her bottom lip with her finger. "Although that could really be fun, if you had the kids come up with some commercials."

"Could you talk me through this?"

"You're a sweet little thing, aren't you?" She clucked at Nina. "I wish I had more time, but I have fourteen drama majors student-teaching this quarter. I've got my hands full. But don't be afraid to alter the script. Who will know?"

Nina tucked the script into her purse and backed out of the office. It was a treasure.

That night, her electric Smith Corona typewriter on the kitchen table, she went to work. She considered her class list. Thirty-three students were registered for the mini course, and there were only five parts in the script. She'd have to embellish. Before Artaban, the lost wise man, could find his way to the humble home of Ishmael and his mother, who was dying from leprosy, he needed several adventures that involved a lot of people. Nina wound paper and three carbons into her machine.

The first students on stage would be the three original wise men, glancing angrily at the stars and complaining that Artaban was always late. How long could they be expected to hang out at this oasis? Three lines each. That was probably enough. They'd take off without him, following the star. She typed several lines.

Enter Artaban. Disappointed in his friends, he wanders around the desert for a couple of lines, until he's beset by thieves. They beat him to a pulp, steal his camel, and leave him for dead. Three thieves, two kids to play the camel. But—frowning, she twisted a lock of hair around her finger—if Artaban is robbed, he won't have any money or jewels to give to the poor boy and his mother. Nina x-ed though the last line. The trusty camel, who loves his master, escapes from the robbers during a blinding dust storm while the robbers are hiding in their tent. The jewels are sewn into the leather of his bridle, because what robber in his right mind would look there?

Artaban, delirious in the desert, is found and taken to an inn by a good guy and his two buddies. She was working the Good Samaritan angle hard, but the kids would never notice, and who ever heard complaints about plagiarizing the Bible? After two thousand years, it had to be public domain.

She typed in more lines and some set directions.

After Artaban miraculously recovers, he and his camel set out to track down his fellow Magi. A lavish courtroom scene with Herod could save her. She could pack kids in and give Herod a cynical remark about babies with illusions of grandeur born in mangers. The kids would love it. Junior high kids loved heavy-handed irony. Nina clapped her hands together.

Finally, Artaban leaves the royal court and the dancing girls behind and sets out across the desert, but not alone. The Good Samaritan has become a loyal sidekick. Together they become lost. Near death, they come upon the home of a humble widow wrapped in rags to hide her disintegrating facial features and missing fingers. She lives with her small son and lots of relatives—it was the holidays, after all. The widow gives Artaban and Sam—Nina was tired of typing "the Good Samaritan"—her last crust of bread and cup of gruel. They revive and give the widow riches beyond her wildest imaginings. Everyone lives happily ever after, except the poor widow who is terminal. The true meaning of Christmas is dramatized, and the curtain comes down.

She was typing Artaban's soliloquy at 11:30 p.m., but she wasn't tired. She was on a roll. Standing alone in her postage-stamp kitchen, Nina cheered. *It will be fabulous,* she thought. I've got three acts. Act I. The Desert with the Other Magi and the Robbery. Act II. Herod's Evil Court. Act III. The Home of the Humble Widow. Every kid had at least one line except the camel, but the camel kids had a lot of time on stage. The costumes would be a cinch, bathrobes and head gear. Nina would ask the home economics teacher to make a papier-mâché camel's head and a cloth body for two.

Nina could do this. It would be okay. She would survive the school play. She rolled the carbon copies out of the typewriter, touched them lovingly with her fingertips, and danced into the bedroom when Elliot called her name.

* * *

Mr. Summerhays, a teacher she'd never seen, stopped by a week before the mini classes began. A reluctant smile on his face, he said, "I always did the sets for Janice. We collaborated."

Nina raised her eyebrows. "How?"

"I teach the stage crew mini course."

Pressing her hand against her chest, she sighed. "How wonderful. I happen to have a copy of the script. There are three acts."

They agreed a desert oasis could be suggested by tall, cardboard palm trees. Herod's palace would be a little more difficult, but a throne painted with gold spray paint and a few pillows would look nice against a three-sided structure that the crew could decorate with brightly colored lines and zigzags. A widow's hovel was easy. Mr. Summerhays had done something like that for Janice before. He suggested making a list of necessary props to send home with the cast. What they produced amazed Janice every year. He looked a little wistful.

"So, tell me," Nina said, "where is this Janice who never complained about leaks and blackboards and who produced amazing theatricals?"

A bitter smile on his face, he shook his head. "It's not my place to say."

Mr. Summerhays was right about the props. The back of Nina's classroom slowly filled with bathrobes, cardboard crowns, a few authentic headdresses from the Middle East, throw pillows to decorate Herod's court, and dozens of silk scarves. It looked as if Nina were operating a flea market on the sly.

Peeling an orange, she sat at her desk at lunch and grabbed a piece of scratch paper to write her "to do" list. It was a tardy note Karl Warner, ninth-grade algebra, had written the previous day excusing Walter. She flipped it over, saw what was written, and almost choked.

The time and date were noted in the upper right hand corner.

Karl,
> *Excuse Gary Wolford. He had to make up a test.*
> *Take a look at the dress Robin Shelton is wearing.*
> *Drop your pencil and ask her to pick it up.*

Marlo

She stared at the note. A smoking gun. Well, maybe not smoking, but enough of a gun to get Marlo in a truckload of trouble. What would Robin's father say? He was the dean of education at the university. She picked the note up by the corner as though she were being careful not to smudge fingerprints and filed it away between seventh-grade vocab and quizzes for *A Separate Peace*. Looking out the window at the black ribbon of Rural Road 84 cutting through the snowy fields, she wondered about Karl Warner. A nice guy, but if he were a part of this, the pernicious disease had invaded the entire school.

Fifth hour, she called Robin and Herod's other dancing girls over to her desk. "Tell me about your costumes."

"A gold drapery cord around our heads with scarves attached. Big chiffon squares that go from our shoulder straps down to our fingers," and Robin demonstrated by waving her arms from side to side.

"That's great, but no cleavage," Nina said. "Absolutely none." She sliced her hand across her throat. They all blushed. "I'm not being the mom here. I'm being a friend. I'm dead serious about this. No cleavage and nothing tight." She wanted those girls to look like bolts of cloth twirling across the stage.

Robin and Nina exchanged a glance. Robin nodded.

Nina rolled her eyes. If they only knew.

* * *

Assembly schedule B allowed the entire student body to see the play during the day, one performance in the morning and one after lunch. Sitting in the last rows of the auditorium, Nina's regular classes got to see the play twice. The dress rehearsal had gone without a hitch. No one fluffed a line, and there were plenty of lines. The actors were ready, chomping at the bit.

The students filed nosily into the auditorium. The curtain was raised, and the play began slowly but seemed to gain an energy of its own. Everyone came in on cue but at lightning speed. It was as though a record meant to be played at 33⅓ was suddenly spinning at 78 rpms. Nina waved her arms and hissed loudly, but this train was roaring down the track, and nothing she did slowed the momentum. Just forty-three minutes and the curtain came down with a thump. Her heart racing, Nina ran her fingers through her short hair until the blonde halo stood on end. She had three hundred and fifty adolescents packed in the auditorium for forty minutes with nothing to do. She peeked out the curtain. Already excited about the upcoming vacation in less than thirty-six hours, students would take this place apart before the bell rang. A row of eighth graders were already rocking in unison, loosening the bolts holding the seats to the floor. A dozen ninth-grade boys were heading for the exit. She couldn't just open the auditorium doors and flood half the student body into the halls. Mr. Killpack was going to kill her.

Mr. Martin, the chorus teacher, ran out with a book of Christmas music in his hand. "We have to get them singing. Can you play?"

"Throw me the book." Her fingers flew across the keys of a dusty upright, pounding out flourishes and trills. She sounded like she was playing a "Jingle Bells" duet. Then she transposed into a minor key and played it again, "Jingle Bells" in Transylvania. Quieted to a dull roar, the students were easily led by Mr. Martin as she played Jingle Bells for the third time. "Silver Bells" was next, then "Jolly Old St. Nicholas." So far so good, but could it last?

Mr. Martin called a few members of the ninth-grade show choir out of the audience. They stood around the piano and sang a few numbers, and then minutes before the bell rang, the entire crowd sang "We Three Kings" with gusto but not much else. Her heart was pounding and her recently damaged finger was throbbing, but she had been saved by Mr. Martin, twelve years of piano lessons, and a tyrannical mother. As the last students filed out the double doors and headed to the cafeteria for lunch, Nina rested her forehead on the keyboard and nearly wept with relief. Mr. Martin walked down from the stage.

She smiled up at him. "Thank you. You saved me."

"Well," he said, "we're not all like Marlo Fletcher."

* * *

Nina drove home after school slowly, reliving each second of the day. She wanted to take off her shoes, eat a banana, lie down, and maybe close her eyes for a minute before returning for the evening's final performance.

Walking in the apartment, the odor of Pine Sol assaulted her nose. All evidence suggested Elliot had been cleaning, a capitulation of major proportions. Her clothes were hung in the closet. He'd scrubbed the bathtub. He'd even washed the towels. What was up?

An hour later Elliot returned. When he came in with a smattering of snow melting in his hair, she was standing in the bedroom overdressed in an iridescent sheath with Juliet sleeves. It shimmered blue or pink as she moved, depending on the light. He carefully laid the sacks he'd been carrying onto the bed as though he were afraid something might shatter.

"The storm's getting worse," he said. "You should probably give yourself extra time."

Feeling his disquiet, she turned slowly on her heel. "You're not coming?"

"I have to work. I traded last week so I'd have an extra night to study for biochem."

Her back straightened. "But this is *The Play*." She held her hands out to her sides. "I've been talking about it for months."

He tried to zip up her dress.

"Leave me alone. I'll do it myself." She waved him off. "And since when do you zip things up. You're all about zipping things down." She sprayed perfume on her wrists. "I know the play's not like one of Gordy's basketball games"—which he never missed. Her breathing was shallow—"but it's important to me."

"It was the only day I could trade. We're leaving for Park City tomorrow." He put his hands in his pockets and leaned back on his heels.

"This goofball play is the only good thing that's happened to me at school this whole year, and you don't even care enough to come and see it?" She turned away from him. "I don't believe this."

"I needed that extra night to study."

"Everything's always about you, isn't it?" She hooked a pair of crystal drop earrings in her ears. "You have no idea what's going on with me. What I put up with. Do you know what happened to me yesterday? A kid crept into my room and set my mail on the desk, because I never venture into the faculty lounge." She paused to take a deep breath. "Of course, Marlo and Zach were too excited with their latest little trick to wait. They assumed I'd leaf through my mail in front of the class."

But she hadn't. She'd waited until the room was empty and took out her yellow rubber gloves, her tongs, and her can of bug spray. Worried about an explosive device, she'd checked under each piece and lowered the junk mail slowly into the garbage can.

"They put a pair of sleazy red silk panties—trimmed with black rabbit fur—in with my mail. If I'd found those panties standing in front of a room full of fourteen-year-old boys, those kids would never have gotten that picture of me out of their heads. It's something like that all the time. I can't even leave to go to the ladies room without hearing some jerk whistle at me." Her hands were trembling.

"Are you afraid Marlo will be there tonight?"

Elliot was irritating every nerve ending in her body. "No. Marlo would never come to something like this. You don't get it. I'm leaving."

He blocked the bedroom door. "I don't want you driving if you're upset. The roads are too slick."

Cheeks burning, she pushed past him, grabbed her coat, and hurried out into the storm.

185

* * *

Hidden by the heavy black curtains, Nina stood in the wings at the beginning of Act III and scooted students on and off the stage. She followed their lines on her copy of the script. Everyone enunciated their parts slowly and looked directly at the audience. Robin, covered from head to toe in a dozen chiffon scarves, gave Nina a kiss on the cheek as she fluttered past.

With Artaban holding his hand and his mother wrapped in tea-dyed rags limping along behind him, Ishmael—typically referred to as Billy Zlotnick—walked to center stage and spoke the final line, "God bless us, everyone." The curtain dropped with a whoosh. Walter Nibley mouthed at her, "It slipped out of my hands." He pulled it up again for the cast to take a bow.

A freezing hand touched her shoulder. His hair was damp. He'd borrowed a car and abandoned his post at the hospital. He didn't have a dozen red roses in his arms. He only had one, and he'd probably bought it at the hospital gift shop, but she didn't care.

"I got here for the last act. I've been standing in the back." Elliot wrapped her in his arms and whispered, "I'm so proud of you." He kissed her. Never one to let an opportunity pass him by, Walter pulled the rope for the side curtains and included Mr. and Mrs. Spencer in the final curtain call. The applause wasn't overwhelming. No one jumped to his feet and shouted bravo, but more than one eye was misty at the sight of the tall, young husband kissing Mrs. Spencer.

Nina wondered on the drive home if Elliot was marking his territory, demonstrating a husband's prerogative that he wasn't about to share, or perhaps he was swept away by the moment. She wasn't sure and didn't ask, but the next morning in the faculty lounge, the kiss was all anyone could talk about.

22

Park City or Bust

Nina relaxed against the red vinyl cushion in the booth in a secluded restaurant in Park City as she watched Elliot wind a thread of melted cheese from a bit of enchilada around the tines of his fork. She stabbed at an occasional black bean and smiled on cue, laughing in all the right places, but her eyes gave her away. Over the last six months, he'd learned to read those blue eyes. She was humoring him, pretending to be interested in his friendly chatter about winter in Dundee or his little brothers stacked on a sled or sliding off the road in a car with bald tires. But what was she really thinking? He reached across the table and snatched a cherry tomato off her plate. His finals were over. The next five unencumbered days were front and center in his head blocking out anything else. Work, school, and Christmas seemed light-years in the future.

"Let's go." He slipped a dollar tip under his plate. "Let's wander up Main Street and look at the lights."

The temperature had dropped, the air was crisp, and snowflakes, big and slow, settled on their shoulders and hair. Strings of multicolored lights crisscrossed the steep main street, and the shops' Christmas displays shone brightly against the deep quiet of the storm. Elliot put her arm through his as a rowdy crowd of happy skiers, coming out of a cowboy bar, jostled them.

"No one's going home," Elliot said, glancing ahead at throngs of people on the sidewalk.

"They're just getting started. Snow equals party." She laughed.

"You're sure you can find the condo?"

"I've been there before."

He brushed the snow out of her hair.

* * *

The front door opened to a room with a huge rock fireplace—it filled an entire wall—and picture glass windows framed a mountain. Brown leather couches, splashed with a half dozen ethnic-looking pillows, faced the hearth. A long, rough-hewn table separated the living room from the kitchen. Very Western.

Elliot dropped their suitcases inside a bedroom door and nodded his head at the interior. "The master suite is bigger than our entire apartment."

"The bathroom is bigger than our entire apartment," Nina said as she plugged in a Christmas tree that had to be twelve feet high.

Elliot stacked kindling in the grate. "Are they coming for the holidays?" The family that owned this spread.

"No. They're in Palm Desert. Maybe Hawaii."

So the tree and a stocked refrigerator were organized by Nina's mother or maybe the generous friend via a subordinate, a Mrs. Thatcher type or some overworked secretary, who made a few calls and transferred a list: Tree, decorated. Fridge, loaded. Sheets, fresh. Towels, clean. Who were these invisible people? His gratitude was undermined by queasy discomfort. He felt like he'd sneaked into a movie theater without a ticket, and any minute a teenage usher would shine a flashlight in his face and ask him to leave.

The match caught. A flame leaped under his hand. He turned and saw Nina's expectant smile. That damp blonde hair fanned around her face. She was so beautiful she took his breath away. He sighed. No alarm clock in the morning. No racing up College Hill late for class. No shifts at the hospital lab. Four and a half days. She lifted the edge of an afghan and patted the leather cushion. He slipped in beside her. Kicking off her wet shoes, she curled up next up to him.

"I have a surprise," he whispered into her ear. "I checked my grades. Before you got home." A deep satisfied breath escaped him as he stretched his long arms across the back of the couch. "A four point," he announced. She laughed and squeezed his leg. "Your brother was right. Getting married makes all the difference. I always blow at least one class. I don't know why. But not this quarter."

She stared into the flames.

He nudged her. "What are you thinking, Mrs. Spencer?"

"That you're wonderful." She flipped off the lamp. "You know, Elliot, I never got to see the play from the auditorium. I was always in the wings. I never got the total effect."

That's where she was, still rehearsing *The Other Wiseman*. "Those little kids had a great time," he said. He was glad her play was a hit, but his GPA was their ticket to the train labeled "future."

Every night for the past week, he'd sat at the kitchen table and worried about his answers to difficult test questions, covering the same turf again and again. He'd overlooked the meager offerings—referred to as dinner—because she was anxious and distracted about her play, her goofy bunch of kids in homemade costumes racing around the stage until they landed under mics hanging on wires to deliver their lines. Some skinny kid was the lead, but Nina was the star, tall and slender, standing in the wings with her fluff of hair looking like a crown.

Maybe a four point was a given in the Rushforth clan. Maybe she didn't worry about his grades because of the mysterious safety net strung below this high-wire act they'd been performing. He'd like to punch his creep of an uncle, because since Thanksgiving an imaginary trust fund pricked at the back of Elliot's mind, like a memory he couldn't shake, like the centerfold in a *Playboy* magazine passed around at scout camp when he was fourteen. Why didn't Nina talk to him about the family finances? Why? Was he still probationary? Not to be trusted?

Let it go, he told himself. Watching the fire, he leaned his head against the back cushion. "Do you know what today is?" he asked.

She shook her head.

"It's been a year. Since we were together in Scotland. A whole year."

"Oh." She didn't remember to smile until he arched his eyebrows. "I forgot the mistletoe."

He rustled around in the pockets of his jacket and pulled out the green sprig. "Here it is."

She held the mistletoe gently in her palm. "A talisman, a magical promise—or a bit of a weed." She laughed. "This year has jarred my whimsy loose."

He touched her cheek. "This little plant saved me from disaster. It was my last best hope. After the airport debacle, I thought we were done." He kissed her palm, waiting for her to explain that they were destined for one another or recite a few lines of poetry, but she gazed out the window at the storm.

"It's strange stuff," he said. "It doesn't root in the soil. It sends roots through the bark of a tree. It needs a host."

She climbed over and sat on his lap. "Just like love. Love needs a host."

"And," he said, holding it over her head, "it's an aphrodisiac."

"I thought it was poisonous."

"Only if you eat it. When a man holds this over a girl's head, his heart's on his sleeve." He tucked the sprig behind her ear and kissed her. "That last night in Scotland my heart was on my sleeve, in my throat, breaking in two. I thought you were some sort of Scottish apparition ready to vanish into the mist and I'd never see you again. I was holding on to this little bit of mistletoe—with all my heart."

"Too many heart metaphors." She tickled his ear.

"After you left, I kept thinking about Bothwell and the queen and how much he loved her. I hauled Twitchell up to the castle on P-day and tried to picture you with your long blonde hair hidden in a cloak, wandering through those rooms. It's a miracle you're here with me and not lost in a mist coming off the North Sea or sitting in a pub with Colum." He stroked her velvety skin under the edge of her sweater. The log popped and shot a spray of fiery sparks up the chimney.

"Do you realize tomorrow," he swallowed hard, "is the first day in four months that neither one of us has to get up to go to work or school or church?" Deep shadows settled around them. Snow pelted the windows, and the street lamp across the road was nothing more than a soft hazy glow in the storm. Hundreds of lights glittered in the Christmas tree. Sitting in the dark, he felt like a little kid on Christmas Eve.

She sighed. "What a year."

"You're here, and you're mine."

The fire didn't give off much heat, and she pulled an afghan over her shoulders.

"Four nights," he whispered. "Just us."

He could feel her heart pounding. He kissed the tip of her nose. "Next year will be even better. I'm going to get into dental school. I can just feel it." He ran his fingers through her short hair and traced the scar. "Your hair's almost grown back in." But the back of her head didn't hold his interest for long. He touched her hand and led her into the bedroom.

* * *

He left her sleeping, buried in a half dozen pillows. Glaring daylight filled every inch of the kitchen and reflected off the hanging copper saucepans. Sunshine sparkled off two feet of new snow outside the glass sliding door. Frost on the windows announced the bitter cold, but the sky was crystal blue. Starving, he opened the refrigerator and poured a glass of juice. The high-ceilinged room felt empty, drafty. Glass in hand, he wandered over to the Christmas tree, looked out the window, and then noticed an index card sitting on the coffee table. The Brigham Young quote, written in Nina's tight script, was hard to miss. Jaw clenched, he breathed in and out through his nose. He grabbed his coat off the back of the couch, borrowed some boots he found in the closet, and stepped out the front door into air so cold his lungs ached. Shoveling snow felt honest, worked his muscles, and cleared his mind.

* * *

Blinking several times, Nina clutched the doorjamb and squinted through her coke-bottle glasses at her reflection in a glass cupboard door. Showered and shaved, Elliot turned away from the newspaper on the kitchen table and grinned at her. Her hair was flattened against her head, and she tied her robe more securely. "I'm sure I'll find my pajamas again someday, maybe in April when the snow melts."

He laughed.

"Can't handle the glare coming off that white T-shirt." She held up her forearm to shield her eyes. "What time is it?"

"Twelve-thirty." He held in another laugh. She looked like a doll that had been left on the front lawn for a week or two.

"How long have you been up?"

"A couple of hours. I made a path down to the gas station to buy a paper. I wanted to see the game scores. There's no way we're getting your car out until the plows come through."

She eased herself slowly onto the padded kitchen chair and stole a sip of his juice.

"I've been waiting for you so we could make breakfast together."

She looked at him warily out of the corner of her eye. "Not a lot of together required for a bowl of Wheaties."

"I thought we could scramble some eggs," he said, determined to be cheerful. A positive attitude was half the battle in dealing with Nina.

She moved her jaw slowly from side to side. "My neck's stiff."

"I love that neck—stiff or not." He wanted to wrap her in a quilt and hold her on his lap, but his stomach growled, so he said, "Come stand by me. I can't believe anyone can live for twenty-one years and not know how to scramble an egg. It's so simple."

"I hate it when you show off in the kitchen," she grumbled, "like you're fluent in five languages or something." She put her arms around him and rubbed her nose against his shoulder. "Truth be known," she said, "I'm not overly fond of eggs. And I'm not really into breakfast."

Laughing, he bumped her with his hip and leaned over to kiss her.

"No kissing." She resisted with an upturned palm. "My lips are raw." She sniffed the square of butter sizzling. "What's all this stuff?" A pile of grated cheese and chopped green onions stood ready to leap into the pan. "You haven't been waiting for me to have breakfast; you're making a point, an omelet object lesson." She pinched some grated cheese between her fingers.

"Variation on a theme. Cooking is fun." He smiled at her. "But you have to plan ahead. If you're making meat loaf on Tuesday, you have to check Monday to see if you've got an onion and ketchup."

"And salt. Wasn't that the big problem with my meat loaf? I forgot the salt—once. Just a misdemeanor, not a felony." Bing Crosby was singing "White Christmas" on the radio. Elliot expertly cracked an egg on the edge of the pan.

"What is this?" she complained. "Now you've got the time, you're going to take me in hand, train me up? Is Rachel, the domestic consultant, hiding in the closet behind parkas and stretch pants, ready for the afternoon class on ironing and spray starch?" She nibbled his ear-lobe. "That graduate seminar in the bedroom last night left me a little fatigued. I was thinking we could just relax by the fire."

Pressed against him with her arms around his middle, she rested her chin on his shoulder. He was having a hard time concentrating on the eggs and eyed the jumble of blankets and pillows through the bedroom door.

"You know, I drive past all these cows every morning on the way to Clear Creek," she mumbled lazily. "They've never done anything to me—never committed an offense that would justify tossing them in the ovens. Some of those men I work with? We could grind them into sausage or stew them in a Crock-Pot, but cows are so peaceful."

"I'm not going to be a cannibal." Elliot moved the eggs expertly around the pan. "Plus, eating is social." He refilled his own glass of orange juice, poured one for her, and kissed her on the nose.

She held up a finger. "That's why delicatessens and takeout were invented."

He slid the eggs from the pan to plates he'd heated in the oven. "I'm not going to come home after working all day to a row of serve-yourself white cartons on the kitchen counter." With his arms crossed against his chest, Elliot leaned against the fridge. The spatula in his hand stuck out like a silver flag.

"Well, maybe I don't want to come home from work to a pound of ground round." She tossed her head from side to side. "That I'm sup-posed to magically transform into something that pleases you."

He shook the metal spatula in her face. The eggs, topped with fes-tive green onions, steamed unnoticed on the plates. "Your mom's a great cook. I don't understand why you won't even try."

"Hey, I do try, but everyone has different talents. My mom and me? Different people."

He'd handed her an opening, and she came in right on cue, as if she'd been rehearsing for days. "There's a great Brigham Young quote, 'Women are useful, not only to sweep houses, wash dishes, make beds and raise babies, but they should stand behind the counter, study law,'" she paused, "'or physics, or become good bookkeepers and be able to do the business in any counting house.'" She took a deep breath. "'In following these things, they but answer the design of their creation.'"

She said, "Ta-dah!", stretched out her arms, and did a small dance step.

"I like it better when you recite poetry. I read that quote on the coffee table—where you wanted me to find it. You should have stuck it on the bathroom mirror with a glob of toothpaste. That's what you do at home."

She recoiled as though she'd been slapped.

"I'm sensing an agenda here. Why the quote? Why now?" His eyes grazed hers, and she looked away. The anger he felt surprised him—and he was starving. Standing beside the table, he forked a bite of eggs into his mouth. "You're pulling that quote out of historical context," he said and swallowed hard.

Nina enunciated each word. "Even so, everyone's suited to different things."

"It was a rough time. Families had to eke out a living any way they could." His fork raised in one hand, he finished the speech he'd rehearsed while she slept. "You're not going to have to kill yourself working and trying to raise our family at the same time. I'll provide for you." *Maybe not condos in Park City and Hawaii, but a decent lifestyle— with or without a trust fund.*

Pushing her hands down on her thighs, she spoke slowly, as though she were explaining restrictive clauses to a slow ninth grader. "Working isn't just about money. It's about self-worth, about making a contribution, about being involved in positive forward motion." She wound her forearms in circles. "Brigham Young gave women the vote nineteen years before the rest of the nation. He would have loved Title IX. He could have written it."

Elliot rolled his eyes. "You've been talking to your dad."

"No," she insisted. "This is what I see every single day. Those darling little girls think they're second-class citizens; they think athletics are male terrain and the most they can do is decorate lockers and shake pom-poms." She lifted both palms. "Title IX is going to open all kinds of doors. No more discriminating against girls at school."

"That's the dumbest thing I've ever heard. You're going to have girls try out for the basketball team? What genius came up with that?" He tossed the spatula into the sink, narrowly missing her. "This is a silly conversation. That's not going to happen."

Breathing hard, she pushed her glasses up her nose, and her eyes looked huge, as though she'd suddenly become some lethal insect. "There's a math teacher at the high school who doesn't think girls should be allowed to take geometry because female brains can't understand Euclidean proofs. I'm not kidding. The man should be shot."

"Nina." Elliot's voice dropped a whole octave on the *na* as he reached for her. "There are reasons men and women can't play football on the same team."

She jumped to her feet, but suddenly she was splayed on the floor, clipped from behind—a five-yard penalty. Laughing, Elliot pinned her hands above her head. Untying her robe with his teeth, he got a mouthful of velour fuzz. "Some playing fields can't be leveled," he muttered.

She twisted away from him, grabbed a green pillow, and clobbered him.

He pushed his hair out of his eyes.

Clutching the front of her robe, she sidestepped until the couch buffered the space between them. "You always do that when you're losing an argument," she sputtered. "You grab my hands or step on my toe. You use brute force to try and intimidate me, but guess what? It doesn't work." She adjusted her glasses and blinked twice.

"Brute force?"

"That's what I said."

"I'm not sure how we got from scrambled eggs to brute force."

"It's the same thing. Domination. You want to shove me into some stereotypical pigeonhole and leave me there forever." She leaped onto an ottoman and brandished her pillow.

"That's ridiculous." He shoved his hands in his pockets. "I just want a wife who knows how to scramble eggs."

"*A wife*? Not *my* wife. Not my talented Nina, the tennis star. I love the way you're dismissing me with an unspecific, indefinite article. Is that all I am to you—*a wife*? Interchangeable with dozens of other faceless egg scramblers." She gasped. "All those things you said to me last night, you'd say to someone else? Another *a wife*?" He reached out to her, but she twisted away. "I can't believe you'd do that to me."

"I'm not doing it." His cheeks burned.

She glared at him, shifting her weight from one foot to the other.

"Why are we fighting about a nonexistent situation?" he said, his hands empty at his sides.

"Because it's a character issue, or a *lack* of character issue."

"Hey," he raised his voice. "If we're going to fight, let's fight about something real—like the disaster you are at taking care of the apartment. Three rooms and a closet, Nina, that's all we're talking about. And you don't even make an attempt at cooking. You hack off a frozen chunk of macaroni and cheese and drop it in that double boiler. If you're feeling particularly gourmet, we have a few raw carrot sticks. You know, when you're cooking vegetables, there's a lot of ground between raw and sludge." It wasn't hard to imagine three or four little kids—his children—sitting at a dinner table, gagging in unison.

"You are a horrible person." She grabbed a ceramic apple off the mantle and threw it at him. He plucked it out of the air without looking and juggled it back and forth in his hands.

"You come out of the bathroom," he said, "and it's like you've stepped out of the eye of a hurricane. You look gorgeous, but the bathroom's got wet towels and dirty clothes all over the floor, and every inch of the counter is covered with all your little jars and bottles and brushes." He wiggled his fingers contemptuously.

Her cheeks were crimson. She fanned her face with her hand.

He raised both dark eyebrows. "If anyone in my family had pulled a trick like that, Mom would have loaded our junk into her canvas bag, and we'd have to pay a fine to get it back."

"Now you're criticizing the way I was raised?" Her bottom lip quivered. "Who are you? I don't know you."

"And the laundry. I dumped the clean laundry out of the basket yesterday, and it had been sitting in there so long it kept its shape on the bed. A laundry loaf."

Her chest heaved. A cloud burst was imminent. He reached for her arm, but she ducked around the corner of the couch and escaped into the bedroom. He heard the lock click.

"Crying, Nina?" he shouted through the door. "That's the oldest trick in the book."

Something hit the door—a pillow, a paperback, he didn't know. Sitting down at the table, he shoved dry, tasteless eggs into his mouth. Breakfast with Nina. What a joke. He glanced at the bedroom door. She'd starve before she'd admit he had a point, that he was right. He'd never met a girl so stubborn. Well, she wasn't going to trash the only vacation he'd had in six months. It was a beautiful day. He'd go for a walk, that's what he'd do. He slammed the door on his way out.

Knee-deep in snow, he cut a path across the fairway. Sounds of ski lifts broke through the stillness. He slashed at the snow with a dead branch. He'd known what she wanted from the start. She hadn't been shy about telling him yes to law school, iffy on domesticity. Nothing needed to change, he'd promised, because six months ago he'd had no idea what that really meant. Now he tweaked their agreement in his head, because for the last few months, Nina was so consumed with her play and her correcting and her lesson plans and the bumpkins at work, that everything else went by the wayside. Fifty or sixty more years of that? Not okay.

Two different scripts were etched in their brains of what normal ought to be. Like it or not, they each brought those scripts—that they didn't know they had—to this drama called marriage. Standing next to each other on the stage, he was reading lines from *Barefoot in the Park* and Nina was performing *As You Like It*, so of course the dialogue made no sense. It was one long confusing mishmash. Nina thought he was one of a half dozen men trying to steal her autonomy. And he needed her to grow up and quit being a deluded princess. What next?

Thrashing through the snow, he tried telepathy and visualized her showered, repentant, and wearing something clingy with her arms out-stretched when he stomped in the condo knocking snow off his feet. Didn't happen. He turned on a basketball game and cranked up the volume. Three hours later, he stared at the five o'clock news. The after-noon sky turned a milky white before darkness covered the mountains like a peaceful blanket pricked with stars. Pressing his forehead against the freezing glass, he wondered if the torchlight skiers paraded tonight. They'd planned on watching from the base of the mountain before she decided he was a scheming chauvinist.

He didn't make any effort at being quiet. Around nine thirty he cooked a hamburger. He'd delayed that lesson as long as his hunger allowed, but he succumbed before *The Tonight Show* began. He watched that too—when he wasn't pacing. He looked down at the line of light under her door before he walked down the hall to a half dozen bed-rooms. He'd flip a coin to decide where to sleep.

* * *

The next morning, it was quiet when Nina opened the glass shower door. With eyes swollen from crying, she stared at her reflection in the mirror. She'd promised her dad she'd tell Elliot about the law school applications while they had plenty of time to talk, but why escalate this battle to an all-out civil war when there was only a slim chance she'd be accepted? Maybe she should just give it all up. Be a hausfrau. Tat doilies. Make brownies. Birth a dozen fat, adorable babies. Twisting her damp hair around her finger, she sat on the edge of the bed and frowned at the locked bedroom door. A sheet of lined paper edged its way beneath. She stepped back as though the paper had teeth and might bite her. An apology? He was always the first one to blink, but yesterday he'd gone too far. Anger that hot had been suppressed for days—maybe weeks. Holding her breath until the footsteps receded, she heard the hiss of cushions depressed on the couch.

She picked up the paper. *I love you. Don't stay mad and spoil the vacation.*

Ha, she thought. Fishing a pen out of her purse, she dashed off an answer.

> *You despise the undomesticated person that I am. It's horrible to think that when you look at me, you see a slob who can't scramble eggs. But I'm not a house with a basement that you can remodel to suit yourself. So much for romance. You're the one who spoiled the vacation.*

She shoved the note under the door and didn't answer his gentle knock or respond when he whispered through the keyhole, "Nina . . . Sweetheart. I'm so sorry. I know you've been trying."

She was so hungry she was ready to chew on a bar of soap, but instead, she sat stiffly on the edge of the bed staring at her hands.

An hour later she heard drawers being opened and shut, then the front door slammed. She raced into the kitchen and grabbed a banana. Was he stealing her car and abandoning her? Going home to his mother? And what would her mother say? With a mouth full of banana, she buried her face in a pillow. A half hour later, motion on the fairway caught her eye. Elliot was pushing a snowball—half his height—onto the patio. She hid behind the curtains and watched him lever it onto another snowball with a snow shovel. Elliot lifted the snowman's head up onto its shoulders; then he plucked globs of dirt out of a forgotten flowerpot and stuffed them into the holes he'd made for a frowning mouth. The snowman looked like he was drooling chocolate.

Bitter cold near the window stole her breath. He knew she was watching, and he bowed gallantly toward his creation. "Meet Elliot," he called out, "a flawed, coldhearted man. He'll live in this penitent state until he dies—or melts." His warm breath froze in the air. *I love you,* he mouthed. Frozen bits of snow clung to his gloves. His cheeks were red and a single syllable of laughter escaped from his mouth before he closed his lips tightly.

She'd thought for a year that they were getting away with something when fate wasn't looking, a romance so magical and tender that they'd become their own fairy tale, but looking at her transparent reflection in the glass, she realized every marriage is a compromise. And peace never lasts.

～ 23 ～

Christmas at the Rushforths'

A fifteen-foot flocked white Christmas tree covered with burgundy balls and shimmering silver streamers and at least a million twinkling lights stood in the corner of the Rushforth living room. Even the presents, wrapped in silver foil with matching ribbons, had been artistically arranged under the tree. Elliot wondered if he'd been beamed into the Hotel Utah lobby. A nineteen-inch black-and-white television with a burgundy bow on top had "Mr. and Mrs. Spencer" printed on the tag. Oliver's baby was having a difficult time crawling in her little red velveteen dress with a stiff white lace collar. Benjamin held his little boy on his lap while Nina demonstrated how to shoot ping-pong balls out of his Galaxy Solar Recon Launcher.

"We can't hit you if you keep moving," Nina said.

Elliot shielded himself with a needlepoint pillow. The drooling baby crawled over to where he was sitting on the floor and pulled herself up on his arm and tried to stand on his leg.

Oliver laughed. "She thinks you're the Wasatch Front."

"Nina," her mother called from the kitchen, "can you help me for a minute?"

Benjamin shoved his little boy off his lap. "Quick, Justin, block her path or dinner is doomed." The three-year-old ran at his auntie, and she swung him back and forth in her arms.

Oliver picked up the refrain. "Incoming Nina. We'll have to order pizza."

"Why me?" She folded her arms in front of her chest. "Why am I the only one who has to help?"

"That was our point. Please not you," Oliver said.

"Well then, hustle yourself into the kitchen."

Holding the baby in his arms, Elliot rose from the floor. "Come on. I'll help too."

"This is clearly a case of discrimination." She threw a pillow at Oliver.

"Hey, Nina, even Gloria Steinem has Christmas dinner."

"Excuse me. Steinem? Probably not."

Oliver tossed the pillow up into the air. "You could just stand up and say, 'I am not a cook.' I mean, it worked for Nixon; of course, it might not keep working."

Elliot smiled at the thought of a serious Nina, both hands on the lectern, at the National Press Club, announcing that she was not a cook. He glanced over his shoulder at the brothers. "She could use a little encouragement."

Benjamin winked at his brother before he spoke, "Didn't you sign the disclosure statement before the wedding?"

"Anyone can learn to cook," Elliot said.

Oliver kept tossing the pillow over his head. "That's like saying people can learn not to be color-blind. Nina can burn water." He looked at Benjamin. "And she has, right?"

Time out, Elliot thought as he followed Nina into a kitchen filled with every conceivable appliance that Nina's mother used with such perfection she could be an exhibitor at a trade show. "Does this ever stop? The banter?" How would he respond if they fired at him?

"What banter?" Nina stood on tiptoe and kissed him and then the baby.

"Why are they bugging you about cooking?"

"I told Mom about the scrambled eggs. She thought it was hilarious and passed it along. But, of course, this morning while you're all playing basketball at the church, I get to chop nuts and onions."

Christmas dinner was more of the same. The flickering candlelight and an elegant table set with sparkling crystal and china and starched linens didn't elevate the level of conversation, which, this evening, seemed to be Nina baiting. Benjamin had given her a year's subscription to *Ms. Magazine*.

"We don't want you to lose touch with reality up there in the frozen north," Benjamin explained.

"You have no idea," Nina said. "It's like the Dark Ages."

"So," Oliver said. "You're getting everyone up to speed on women's lib?"

"There are no women where I work."

"What are you? A stuffed mascot?"

"Okay, there are six of us. The secretary, two home economics teachers, and two PE teachers, who never venture out of their rooms or the gym. If there's a school nurse, I haven't laid eyes on her."

"How many men?

"Maybe ten men. Plus a couple of dozen thirty-five-year-old adolescents and another dozen cowboys."

"Well," Oliver said, "those sound like fair odds. Nina versus forty or fifty men. What do you say, Elliot?"

"As little as possible." He rolled his eyes. Everyone laughed.

"What did you guys do in Park City? Did you ski?" Benjamin asked.

"Elliot doesn't ski. Yet."

"Go to any movies?"

"We thought about it." She glanced away.

A smile on his face, Benjamin asked, "My gosh, Nina, what did you do for five days? You look a little draggy under the eyes." He started to laugh and turned to his brother. "She's blushing. This is a first. Congratulations, Elliot!"

Oliver stood and raised his water glass, "I'd like to propose a toast to everything that Nina and Elliot did and didn't do in Park City. Viva la différence."

Oliver's wife, Dorothy, was spooning mashed potatoes into the baby's mouth. "That's enough. Give the kids a break."

Oliver sat back against his chair, upholstered in cream and pale-green stripes, and grinned. "So much for the Equal Rights Amendment."

"Just you wait." Nina pointed a fork at him. "Lars says it's going to pass."

"Lars is wrong."

"Maybe not. He's in the thick of it. He's going back to be on Bennett's staff after graduation if he doesn't stay in Salt Lake to work on Garn's campaign."

He hadn't heard Lars's name in a month or two. Elliot whispered, "When did you talk to Lars?"

She shrugged. "I talk to him all the time." He caught her parents exchanging a quick look across the length of the table.

Nina's father spoke up, "The Civil Rights legislation guarantees most of what the women's movement wants without all the negative elements that absolute equality would impose."

"Maybe," Nina said, "but it's not being implemented. You guys have no idea what it's like to be a woman out there. No idea." Her lips pursed, she thumped a knuckle on the table.

"There's just no body of legal precedents," Bill said. "No one's defined what constitutes gender discrimination. Racial discrimination we have figured out."

"Have them give me a call," Nina said. "I'll fill them in."

"You just need to learn to play the game," Oliver said.

"Bat my eyes and act dumb? That's like asking blacks to shuffle their feet and say, 'Yes, sir' and 'No, ma'am' just to get along." She adopted a thick Southern drawl. "'Show me to the kitchen so I can eat some of your fine crow.' Nothing doing."

Bill rubbed his jaw thoughtfully. "You know they added gender to the language in the Civil Rights legislation because certain southern senators thought it would derail the whole thing. The assumption was the country wouldn't support equal rights for women. Maybe we're still not ready."

"Isn't it interesting that discrimination against women—half the population—is invisible because we're not a different color."

"But you're pink," Benjamin said.

"But you're not funny," Nina snapped.

"Well, on that note," Barbara said, "I'm going to let Bill serve the pumpkin pie, and Oliver and Benjamin can clear the dishes. Elliot, your job is to calm Nina down. Dorothy, let me hold that baby."

No one responded because Bill, folding his napkin carefully, said, "This will all end up in the courts. These arguments about gender and equality will be argued by a cadre of bright young attorneys who will probably change our perceptions of men and women forever. It's going to be fascinating to watch."

Nina shoved her chair back from the table. "I'll have pie later." She

strode into the living room and sat down at the piano. Elliot tapped his
clean fork against the tablecloth. The conversation stalled. Not the first
time. Twice when he'd walked into the family room, voices had dropped,
but the vestiges of conversations hung in the air like onions cooking or
worry brewing. Elliot glanced down at the new wristwatch, a gift from the
Rushforths, more expensive than all the presents his family exchanged—
combined. The gift was generous, no question, but he felt uncomfortable
and thick-witted. He listened to Nina pound out a half dozen Christmas
carols before he excused himself and walked in the living room with pie
on a china dessert plate. He stuck a forkful in her mouth.

"Don't be mad," he whispered.

"Are you kidding? If Oliver found a dead mouse in his desk drawer
or got wolf whistles from the secretaries, heads would roll. He'd be in
their faces so fast it would make your head spin. You know what? They
don't have a single female attorney in that whole firm. That's really
revolting."

"More pie. Open up."

She glanced over her shoulder. "They used to steamroll John." The
favorite brother whose funny stories she didn't mention. "They talked
right over the top of him. I can't imagine what they'd say to him now
if he showed up for dinner with shoulder length hair and a beard." She
sighed. "They probably wouldn't say anything, which would be worse."

"Did you defend him?"

"Are you kidding? I'm seven years younger than Oliver. I'd tug on
John's pant leg, and we'd duck under the table."

Elliot took a bite of her pie and then gave her one.

Nina started to laugh. "At least you're not shoveling in mashed
potatoes. I thought that poor baby was going to pop."

He scooted her over on the piano bench. "How about a duet?"

"That would be like playing tennis with someone who's never held
a racket."

"Then play 'I'll Be Home for Christmas.'"

"Is that your favorite?"

"No, but it will do." Because he missed garland chains made from
red and green construction paper and a tree decorated with an odd
collection of ornaments: cardboard stars covered with macaroni and
sprayed gold, mismatched glass balls, and hardened marshmallow

snowmen. He remembered sitting in the midst of his younger siblings, worn out with excitement, as he assembled a gun or a castle or a doll buggy with paper instructions strewn on the floor beside him. His mom and dad were probably sitting on the couch right now, quiet but happy. He hadn't been home for Christmas in three years.

That evening, the dishes done and the baby asleep, Nina fingered heather green skeins of wool, her mother's gift. "There's a message here." She stabbed the wooden needles into the yarn.

"My friends that knit say how relaxing it is." Barbara smiled. "Something tactile about wool running through your fingers."

No one had mentioned his family all afternoon, but Elliot swallowed his reluctance. "My mom would be happy to teach her."

"Yes," Nina said. "No question about that."

He clenched his jaw and didn't respond. Oliver was whispering to his wife and Benjamin was reading *Frosty the Snowman* to his little boys. Everyone was tired, a little sluggish after a long day and a heavy Christmas dinner.

Nina lifted the long Gerber knife out of the flat box and turned it back and forth to catch the light from the tree. "I sense a conspiracy. The domestication of Nina Rushforth. Knitting, chopping, and Elliot's started a campaign to get me to pick up my clothes."

"Once a month would be an improvement," Elliot muttered.

Laughing, Oliver tipped over on the floor.

Nina pinched the inside of Elliot's leg. "You need to remember which team you're playing for."

Propping himself up on his elbow, Oliver said, "Watch out, Elliot. When Nina pitches a full-blown fit, she's something splendid to behold." But the side of Nina he'd seen in Park City wasn't splendid. Would she have stayed locked in the bedroom for days just to win a fight?

She gave Elliot a suggestive wink. "I've outgrown tantrums. I'm into plotting and scheming." With Cindy and Lars, no doubt, and perhaps her father. Something was in the works; he could feel it.

"Then," Benjamin suggested, "let's start the Monopoly game."

Elliot watched Bill rise slowly off the couch. "I'm going to wish you all a merry Christmas. Your mother and I are going to bed."

Everyone watched them climb the stairs, but it was Oliver who said, "They're a class act. No doubt about it."

* * *

Bill shut the bedroom door and turned to his wife. "Well, Mrs. Rushforth, what do you think?"

"She's lost weight. She seems nervous, anxious, and wound too tight."

He nodded.

"There was more to the egg story than she's telling."

"They're very different. Which is something of a surprise. Both Mormon and raised in homes with similar values."

"Oh, I don't know. I'm sure the Spencers think of us as 'Mormon Lite.'" Barbara twisted the ring on her finger. "I should have kept her home and taught her to cook instead of sending her to court with you."

"She only went with me three times, and she was bored every minute."

"Maybe not."

He touched his wife's hand. "If he keeps snipping her here and tugging her there, he'll end up with a person we won't recognize. And she certainly won't be the girl he fell in love with."

"And he'll spend the rest of his life wondering where she's gone," she said wistfully.

"Maybe Lars the Lutheran wasn't such a bad choice. They had a lot more in common. Maybe I should have encouraged that and not sent her to Scotland."

"All those years that kid was so in love with her." Her reflection in the bureau mirror spoke to her husband as she removed her rings. "And she never saw it."

"She didn't want to see it. She wanted an ally."

Barbara sighed. "Never lovers, ever friends."

"Has she told Elliot about the applications?"

"What did she tell me? 'No, but I'm going to.'"

"Nina's good intentions." He laughed softly. "What's with the yarn?"

"She needs to make friends with Elliot's mother. The woman's a zealot, but still." She set her diamond earrings in a black velvet box. "If Nina could just unwind at night. Watch a little television, do a little occupational therapy. Every single day is a tennis match or a debate tournament. That job is a battleground, and you know how she gets."

He watched her fold her pink angora sweater over a hanger.

"I think I'll keep her here for a few days," she said. "We can make a few batches of soup she can freeze and take home."

"What do you think of him?"

"He's completely adorable. I understand why she's so in love with him. He makes me think of a very large golden retriever puppy, but he doesn't understand Nina—not at all. When the honeymoon's over, they might not make it over all these hurdles. And if they do, there will be scars."

"I don't want her to get hurt."

"You can't protect her, Bill. You can't protect any of them."

24

The Birthday Club

Nina glanced at the round-faced clock and then back at the indignant girls standing in front of her desk. Five minutes left in lunch. A pretty ninth grader with long auburn hair shuffled back and forth, wringing her hands, waiting for her friend to speak, but the girl wasn't just apprehensive, she was titillated, excited about being attractive enough to be tormented.

"It's Jessica's birthday." Robin nodding significantly at her friend. This was the third girl she'd dragged into Nina's room. Life was handing these girls so many mixed messages it was amazing they didn't spend their mornings conversing in French and their afternoons speaking pig latin. Nina felt like an accomplice, a consultant, but certainly not the instigator. Robin had already cast herself in that leading role, and no one can perform righteous indignation better than an adolescent girl.

Nina looked up at the ceiling and let all the air slip out of her lungs.

"Will you excuse her?" Robin asked.

Nina thought quickly as her eyes swept her classroom. "Are you girls watching the news at night? Women aren't tolerating this sort of baloney anymore." Her finger tapping her cheek, she gauged Robin's defiant expression. She'd love to suggest a boycott of Beginning Type, but that suggestion would be too overt.

"Have you ever seen *Spartacus*?" Nina asked. "It's a movie."

The girls shook their heads, side to side, in unison.

"Spartacus was a gladiator in the Roman Empire who instigated a slave revolt. After they were defeated by the Roman armies, maybe a hundred slaves survived. They were standing on the side of a hill, and the Roman general said they were all going to die. But," she held up one finger, "if they would surrender Spartacus, the reward would be a merciful death. If they didn't, they'd be crucified. Of course, everyone knew what he'd do to Spartacus." She nodded her head to include the girls in her thought. *And so do we.*

"It was pretty intense, and then one of Spartacus's friends stood up and shouted, 'I'm Spartacus.' And everyone stood up saying, 'I'm Spartacus.' They won a huge moral victory because they stuck together. Not a happy conclusion, but making history has a price." She drummed her fingernails on the side of her desk. "It's a great movie. If you ever get a chance, you should see it."

Jessica looked down at the toes of her scuffed shoes.

"I'll write Jessica an excuse if you want," Nina said. "But think about it during fifth hour. Maybe you'll come up with a better solution." She couldn't keep excusing girls from another teacher's class. When she'd intervened for two other girls before Christmas break, she expected a summons to the office, a pre-holiday session with "the boss"; plus, Marlo had to be seething.

As the door closed behind Robin and Jessica, Nina felt a small sense of reprieve but not much else. Two months ago she would have been thrilled that historical information spurred a student into action—the wheels were clearly turning in Robin's fertile brain—but not today. Not now. Nina pulled out her checkbook and counted out the days on the little calendar on the back of the register. She bit down on her top lip. The numbers hadn't magically changed in the half dozen times she'd counted in the last two days. She was late, almost three weeks.

Her palm pressed against her mouth, she was sitting at her desk when students wandered in for the short story mini course. Giving the students a stiff smile, she flipped open an ancient anthology to "The Pearl Necklace," but pushing against the back of her mind were the ticklish dates on the little calendar.

She drove home slowly that afternoon. The overcast sky matched her mood. She'd forgotten to take one of the soup bricks out of the freezer that morning, so she hurried when she got home and tossed it in the double boiler, her best kitchen friend, and lay down on the couch.

No question, her life as she knew it was over. Eyes closed, she collected her impressions and took her emotional temperature, as though she were observing someone else, another girl, someone she didn't know. She wandered into the bathroom and gazed in the mirror. She understood the mechanics of pregnancy, she'd watched maturity films in the seventh grade, but the reality was just sinking in. She touched her nose to the cold mirror.

Staring at her blurry reflection, she considered all the things she couldn't do. Forget law school. That wasn't going to happen. No tennis this summer. Her body was going to explode. Postpartum, the lovely physical relationship with Elliot would require an appointment. Her time, her sleep—gone. Mentally, she eliminated the pieces of her life, one by one . . . except the one piece that would stay firmly in place. Work. No choices there. Rachel would glom on to the baby, and Nina would go to Clear Creek Junior High—every morning. She'd care for an infant every spare second and then she'd bounce up at six thirty to go to school. How would she manage?

She'd always thought about having a family—out there in the future somewhere—not a platoon like Elliot's family, counting off at parade rest, or Team Rushforth like her family, but more of a string quartet or maybe a jazz ensemble with Nina at the keyboard. She imagined this baby grown, shaking a tambourine, long blonde hair cascading over her shoulders, a beautiful girl singing folk songs at a mic.

A funny hissing in the kitchen caught her attention. The water in the bottom of the double boiler had boiled dry, or perhaps she'd forgotten to put any water in. She didn't know. And what about Elliot? She wouldn't say anything yet. If he'd noticed, he would have said something. He'd be thrilled, so excited, this handsome boy who didn't want the mother of his children to work. She gave her reflection a grim smile. You had to love life's little ironies. She turned her back on the girl in the mirror. She'd wait. Maybe in a few days, there wouldn't be anything to tell.

* * *

Friday, Robin stopped in during lunch to deliver news Nina had already heard from a dozen other kids. "Mrs. Spencer, it was pitch perfect. After he took roll, Mr. Fletcher asked if it was anyone's birthday." She huffed. "As if he didn't know."

Nina could see him rubbing his meaty hands together with his drooling mouth hanging open, his beady eyes searching through the rows of tables and typewriters and landing on Jessica, his hapless victim with her hands clutching the sides of her chair. He'd drag her, protesting and clinging to her friends, to the front of the classroom.

Nina nodded for Robin to continue.

"Five of us planned it during fifth hour. We got more help in type before the bell rang. We all stood up and said, 'It's my birthday.' It was great. His face turned bright red. A bunch of the boys in the class stood up too. A revolution. What could he say? Totally outfoxed." Exulting in her newly discovered power as a student instigator, Robin waved over her shoulder as she pranced out the door.

Nina wondered if anyone would write her an excuse, because this would all land on her. She glanced up at the clock over the chalkboard. Faculty meeting, five minutes after the last bell. She squeezed her eyes shut.

At three forty, Marsha's classroom was packed with tired, impatient teachers. Some leaned against the north wall and a couple sat on the heater as Marlo and Zach swaggered into the room swigging bottles of pop. Someone, Nina wasn't sure who, said, "Hey, Marlo, it's not my birthday." Four men, surely by prearrangement, stood and took turns saying, "It's not my birthday." Marsha jumped up, waving her arms as though the battered wooden desk were a huge cake covered with candles and frosting. "It's my birthday, Marlo. What are you going to do about it?" Everyone laughed—too loudly.

Red from his neck to the roots of his black hair, Marlo tried to josh his way out of it, but humiliation hung on his body like a wet T-shirt, and those fat lips flapped open and shut just like a fish wiggling on a dusty riverbank.

The meeting was brief. The boss read the only copy of the agenda while Ruth interrupted with useful details. A half an hour after it began, the meeting adjourned to the faculty lounge, where several teachers jostled each other as they collected their mail, and others, not in a hurry to get home, dropped onto worn couches for a faculty meeting rehash and another bottle of pop.

Peering into her mailbox for her paycheck, Nina heard her name.

"Hey, Spencer." Marlo's voice was gruff. "I hear your old man's an ambulance chaser."

Shoulders back, she sighed, turned slowly on her heel to face him, and spoke in a resolute voice. "Actually, he does complex corporate litigation." She gave him a broad, lingering smile.

Marlo poked Zach in the ribs. "Say, Zach, how do you know when a lawyer's lying?" Marlo's dark eyes glowered at Nina before he barked out the punch line. "His lips are moving."

The room quieted.

When she didn't speak, he continued, "They're all scum suckers."

"Well." Her cheeks were burning, but her precise voice arched over the crowd. "My father does a lot of interesting things, but there's one thing he doesn't do. He doesn't manhandle little girls." Then in a voice that was almost a whisper, she said, "You should be arrested."

She strode out of the room and heard Marlo shouting, "What did she say?"

Someone, Nina thought it was probably Kent Warner, said, "Relax, Marlo. You don't want to know."

* * *

After such a long week, the apartment smelled like a hamster cage that hadn't been cleaned. *I'll attack it tomorrow*, she thought as she locked the front door behind her and climbed College Hill to sit on the frozen grass under barren trees and wait for Elliot to get out of his chem lab. She covered her ears with her mittened hands and entertained herself puffing small white clouds out of her mouth, when a friendly voice spoke her name.

"Hey, Nina."

She glanced up. It was Lars. The guy was always dressed so perfectly: jeans, a plaid Pendleton shirt, and a leather bomber jacket. "Hello, stranger," she said. "Sit a minute. I'm waiting for Elliot."

He eased down on the crunchy yellow grass beside her. "How's life in the Land of Mayhem? What's the fat type teacher up to these days?"

When she got to the last, "It's my birthday," Lars was lying in the dead leaves, roaring with laughter, which was really very pleasant, because until that moment, she'd failed to see the humor in anything that had happened that entire week. But when she mentioned her ugly punch line in the faculty lounge, Lars quit laughing.

"Whoa, that's intense. Are you okay?"

She shrugged. "So what are normal people doing?"

"I'm headed back to Washington after graduation. It's going to be crazy. Bennett's chief of staff thinks this Watergate stuff is going to blow sky high. You know how everyone always wants to be the fly on the wall? Well, that's going to be me. The fly." He sat up, and she brushed the leaves off his back and out of his hair. "And what about you? Have you heard from any schools?"

"Law school might not work for me." She glanced toward a couple of girls climbing the concrete stairs. "It might not be in the cards."

He put his palm over his chin thoughtfully. "Whose cards? Elliot's?"

"Oh no. It's my fat that's in the fire." She gave him a shy smile. "A baby."

He put his arm around her shoulders. "Nina, say it isn't so."

She sighed. "Don't say anything. Promise?" Another puff of white breath floated into the air. "Obviously an accident. I haven't told Elliot."

"Telling Elliot would be a good idea." He patted her gently on the back. "It seems kind of funny that you're having all these experiences that I'm not."

"No kidding."

"What's it like?"

"Inexpressibly strange. Surreal."

An odd expression on his face, he said, "You'll forgive me if I don't hang around to see you turn into a balloon. I want to keep you a nimble nineteen in my head. And don't worry. Your secrets have always been safe with me."

He jumped up when they saw Elliot coming down the steps, and Nina felt like a conspirator, guilty and cold from sitting on the hard ground.

* * *

Saturday afternoon a brisk wind was blowing the muck out of the sky. A snowstorm was coming in, and Nina crossed her fingers and hoped for a blizzard. The storm of the century. A snowfall so deep and heavy that roads would be impassable for days, and school would be canceled until April. The first flakes were starting to fall as she stood at the kitchen window watching for Elliot and washing a sink full of dirty dishes.

Walking into the wind with his jacket pressed against his chest, he saw her though the window and waved. He closed the door, leaving the chill afternoon outside, and she dashed across the room to hug him. He smelled like cold air and the slightest suggestion of hospital antiseptic that the wind couldn't clean away. He kissed the top of her head and held her at arm's length. "We need to talk," he said. He pushed the laundry basket aside and stacked a pile of student essays neatly on the floor before he pulled her down next to him on the lumpy couch.

She squeezed one eye shut and waited. Once the words came out of his mouth, this would all become real.

He cleared his throat. "Are we going to be parents? Park City?"

"One slip and you scored a home run."

He whispered into her hair, "You wacky blonde. I love you—more than ever." The room was still. She gazed at the blank television screen. Slowly, he undid the top button on her jeans and slid his warm hand in against her skin as though he needed a physical confirmation with the baby growing there. She felt oddly excluded.

"Do you think this little person is going to be a boy or a girl?" A winsome expression on his face, she realized he wanted her to be pleased and thrilled. She cloaked her anxiety with a smile.

"Shall we call our parents?" he asked.

"Oh, Elliot, please, no." She opened her eyes wide to keep the tears at bay. "I need some time for this to settle in. I'm just not ready." Her organized thoughts dribbled away. "I get one thing sorted out, and then I open a cupboard door and twenty things fall down on my head. My life is out of control."

"You're not in this alone."

"What does that mean exactly?" she murmured. "You're going to stay home every night instead of going to the library? You're going to get up at 2:00 a.m. to feed a baby? You're going to come home at noon and haul diapers to the Laundromat? Which dreams are you going to put on hold?"

He looked at her as though she were speaking Portuguese and

he couldn't understand her. "Nina, you're overreacting. Thousands of women do this every day. We're going to love having a baby. You're wonderful with kids. Your niece and nephews are crazy about you. And my mom will help. She's told me that a hundred times. She'll tend while you're at work."

And that was true. Rachel had been lobbying hard for a grandchild since Nina and Elliot had strolled out of the wedding holding hands. "Maybe she can keep the baby, and we'll just visit on weekends."

He started to laugh. "That's the answer. Joint custody."

"No kidding, Elliot. If I save all my sick leave and my two personal days, I can stay home for two and a half weeks. Then I'll have to go back." Her bottom lip trembled. "What a great twist of fate, after everything you've said about not wanting a wife who works."

"We can figure this out. Maybe you could work half a contract. I could take a lighter load, work more, and go to summer school." He lifted her chin to kiss her but stopped when he saw her face. "Oh, Sweetheart," he said. "This is a happy, wonderful day. Don't cry."

"Every couple I know," she said, "are madly in love until they have a baby, and then they start bickering about who's going to get up in the night, who's going to walk a screaming baby, and who's going to clean up the poop and the applesauce stuck on the walls and the bazillion toys."

"So, let's call a moratorium on the bickering." He ran his knuckle down the side of her cheek. "We should be ecstatic, and you're borrowing trouble from who knows where. We can't go back on this, Nina." He pressed his palms together. "Forward is the only way through."

She knew that. In a few days she'd swallow her regrets and gather her resources but not today. She couldn't imagine herself as the fresh-cheeked mother in the Gerber baby food ads spooning mashed peas into a little rosebud mouth.

"Where will we put a baby?" She glanced around the cluttered floor. "There's no room. We'll have to hang a crib from the ceiling."

"It will be tight, but desperate times call for desperate measures. Maybe we'll have to work at picking up the junk."

Of course, the royal *we* meant *her*. In spite of her best efforts, the dam broke. Tears washed down her pale cheeks and dribbled down her neck. "We've only been married six months. This is too soon. I don't want to quit the crazy-in-love stuff."

He pulled her against his chest and stroked her hair. "That could never happen to us. I'll tell you what. We won't argue about who's going to get up with the baby at night. We'll get up together. We'll sit right here on the couch, the three of us, and I'll tell him about a beautiful girl I saw on a street in Scotland." Three on a couch in the dead of the night, an improbable configuration, and they both knew it.

* * *

Monday after school, Nina was daubing correction fluid on a mimeograph when Marsha knocked on her door. "Ruth put the W-2's in our boxes. Just thought you'd want to know."

"Yes," she whispered to herself. Last night, sitting at the bright red kitchen table, she and Elliot figured out an elaborate savings program, a budget in a lined ledger. A nice tax refund should get things started. She hurried in to pick up her form. Her mailbox was empty. She faced the couple of smirks sitting on the couch. "I'd like my W-2 back, if you don't mind."

Marlo put the tip of his tongue through his lips and shrugged. Zach turned his face to the side and giggled. Her fingers itched to grab Marlo and shake his sorry hide until his teeth rattled as loudly as his empty bottles.

She pinched the mimeograph to keep her hands steady. "I'll be back in ten minutes, and I better find my W-2 in my box, or I'll call the financial guy at the district and name names."

She didn't stomp, she didn't strut, but she did move quickly, her heart racing. Furious, she rounded the corner into the workroom, but not before she heard Jerry say, "Why don't you morons leave her alone? She's only a kid."

She stood still, the mimeograph fluttering in her fingers. The door to the office was open.

Marlo snickered. "There's a line, and you're not in it. Nathan's at the front." He guffawed loudly. "Unless you *butted* in." More loud laughter from three or four men.

Jerry raised his voice, "How would you like it if someone treated your wife like this? Or your daughter?" It was quiet for a few seconds before he spoke again, "You need to grow up, Fletcher. You can't hide in your dad's shadow forever."

Nina pressed her damp palms against the wall behind the mimeograph machine and didn't move. Mr. Killpack rustled around at his desk and then walked into the outer office and spoke quietly to Ruth, "The minute I laid eyes on her, I knew she'd be trouble. Those guys are like randy stallions fighting over a mare."

But she wasn't a filly; she was a mouse caught by the tail being poked and prodded by a long line of cats. They should just break her neck mercifully and toss her in the trash, or take her outside and let her run free.

~ 25 ~

A Miscarriage of Justice

S teer clear," Barbara Rushforth interrupted Nina mid-rant. "Send a
student to collect your mail. Nothing short of jail time is going to
change that type teacher, so don't engage."

"But he called Dad a scum sucker."

"Who cares?" She could almost see her mother's smile through the
phone. "Focus on something positive. Invest in your darling students.
Invest in that handsome husband of yours. And for heaven's sake, learn
to cook something edible."

And, like it or not, because her mother's advice was usually
sound, Nina tackled cooking as though it were honors chemistry
and a grade were involved. Each afternoon when she arrived home
from school, Nina felt like she was climbing a stepladder to dive
into the pots on the stove. She pretended competency as if it were
a costume she could wear, like a cheerful floral apron tied with a
bow. She'd conquered a tolerable hamburger stroganoff and a fair
shrimp creole. When Elliot walked in one evening to find her sauté-
ing onions with her nose buried in a novel, she scoffed, "My mother
says you can't read and cook at the same time. Ridiculous." Noodles
al dente were more of a challenge, and she preferred the rice she
could cook in her faithful friend, the double boiler, which seemed
to produce consistent results with little regard for the split-second
timing chops and steaks required.

She was making a valiant effort, but the first week in February, her dive into culinary creations became more of a leap into the deep end while she held her nose. The smells of garlic or onion, even tuna, made her nauseated. The second week in February, she couldn't force herself into the cramped kitchen. Watching her first sprints into the bathroom, Elliot murmured comforting words as she clutched the cold porcelain bowl, but after a few weeks of Nina racing to the bathroom like rush-hour traffic, he became more resigned. "Aim," he'd shout as she lurched by. He bought a few old blankets from the Deseret Industries and resigned his position in the double bed for reduced status as the sleeper on the couch. Each morning he folded his blankets and sighed heavily. That audible sigh became her signal that it was time to drag her body out of the warm covers and throw up while he shaved.

Elliot was studying her behavior, and she wasn't surprised when he started waking her at midnight, when he put his books aside, to hand her a glass of milk. He woke her at five-thirty every morning with a piece of dry toast and a small glass of orange juice, then he'd pat her on the head and tell her to go back to sleep. He tucked a lunch inside her purse and handed her a thermos of chamomile tea each morning as she raced for her car. Two boxes of saltine crackers were hidden in her drawer at work. "A small constant infusion of calories," he insisted. It helped, but she still teetered precariously in that miserable no-man's-land between perpetual nausea and violent spewing. Days blurred in a never-ending bout of flu-like symptoms until she forgot what it felt like to be well.

"This can't go on much longer," Elliot said as he watched her, a clothespin on her nose, gag down a miniscule mound of cottage cheese and a few apple slices. "This can't be good for the baby. What if this is the day you're making ears?"

"You better get used to the idea that I'm probably going to die." She stuck her tongue out of the side of her mouth making an odd looking Q.

"The funny thing is you don't look green. You're absolutely bloom-ing." He reached over and traced his finger along her clavicle and then played with the buttons on her shirt.

She held up her palms and closed her eyes. "Oh, Elliot. I just can't." The thought of all that jostling made the cottage cheese revolt.

"I understand." But he looked desperately sad, and she was pleased not to be suffering alone.

Arriving at school every morning, she remembered Marsha's admonition, "Don't ever let them see you cry." She wondered how much worse it would be to let them—whoever *them* happened to be—see her throw up, and she kept the wastebasket close by. Hiding her mouth with the flat of her hand, she stuffed in a saltine between each class, crumbs scattering onto her skirt, and she counted the hours until she could go home and climb back into bed. She was four hundred and thirty-two essays behind. Stacks of lined loose-leaf paper surrounded her desk, and she felt like a compulsive hoarder when she bothered to feel anything at all.

On a cold but bright blue Friday afternoon, she smiled at Walter, who was asking, maybe for the third time, if she was coming to the game after school.

"I'll try. I really will."

"It's the Swan Valley Lancers. They're our biggest rivals."

She opened her eyes wide and nodded. "A big game?"

"The last of the season."

"You'll be great, Walter."

He smiled sheepishly.

Walter's performance on the basketball court—he was the star—had miraculously translated into major academic improvements. Pleased, she gave him a large smile and said, "I loved your essay." She'd read it three weeks after he'd written it. "It made me want to visit Newton and listen to the birds." The point of his delightful piece was the wonder of a small town and a quaint belief that the birds chirped. "Newton is a very nice place to live." She could almost hear the lyric in the cheerful trill she heard outside her bedroom window.

As Walter's backside vanished through the door, she turned back the ruffled cuff on her favorite pink blouse and wondered how much longer it would fit. Other than her stomach's terrible aversion to food, her chest was the only part of her anatomy that had gotten the pregnancy message. Her pants still buttoned nicely, but when she studied her silhouette in the bathroom mirror, she couldn't help thinking of that Rogers and Hammerstein's song, "June is Bustin' Out All Over," because Nina surely was. In a couple more weeks, she'd need to invest in comfortable smocks and maybe a jumper or two. She'd confide in her mother; maybe she'd call her tonight. A secret announcement would certainly merit a shopping trip, maybe even crack open a stock portfolio an inch or two. She sighed, thinking what a serious infusion of cash would solve.

Five minutes after the final bell rang, she heard the last echoes of locker doors slamming as students raced to the game. She picked up another assignment packet and stapled the corner. The stack was shrinking but not quickly enough. Yawning, she stretched her arms over her head before she shook her thermos. Empty. Time to go home. Her head felt light, and her stomach grumbled a warning. No basketball game today. She squeezed the stapler. Two little indentations, but no silver staple. She pulled open her drawer to discover an empty box of refills. Picking up her keys, she strolled down to the storage room surprisingly cramped for a school this size. Her mother's walk-in closet was larger.

She pushed aside reams of colored paper and dozens of cellophane-wrapped workbooks piled on top of cardboard boxes. In the corner, two retired typewriters sat patiently on chipped metal tables with casters. She stepped over stacks of *The Utah Story* so old and dog-eared that the picture of Bryce Canyon on the cover looked like it had been left on the line too long and had faded from bright orange to an anemic pink. Standing on her toes, her arms reaching over her head, she felt along the edge of the shelf for the rectangular boxes she knew were there.

A silent hand flipped off the light as the paneled door clicked shut. The darkness was so dense she felt as if she'd been dropped into a roiling lake of blackness. Thick, musty air filled her nose. She couldn't breathe, couldn't move. Something rustled against a cardboard box. The faint rasp of heavy breathing filled the cluttered space. She turned slowly. Whoever this heavy breather was, he'd chosen his moment carefully. Her body trembled. A new smell—her own sweat—rose from under her arms. Her right hand dropped protectively over her abdomen. Her left hand groped along the shelf for something she could throw. Her toe did recon searching for a path until it collided with a stack of books. A floorboard creaked.

She spoke into the darkness, "I don't know who you are. I don't want to know. I'm going to walk out of this room and never look back. No harm, no foul." The door was on her left. A thin edge of light showed her the way out, a finish line. Her heart hammered. She sensed him, felt his close physical presence, before strong fingers bit into her upper arms and gripped her tightly. Lunch rose up in the back of her throat.

"Four women told my wife what you said about me," he whispered. "My dad told me to quit acting like a fool." Then he shook her, her head flopping back and forth like a cloth doll. Her back slammed against the shelf. He paused to catch his breath. Her scream shattered the quiet.

His fleshy hand over her mouth, he pushed his face next to hers. "Everyone's at the game." Flecks of spittle hit her cheeks. Shoving her back into the corner where the wooden shelves joined, he jammed his left forearm against her windpipe. Pain and fear ripped through her. She twisted, but his thick arm against her throat pressed her against the shelves. He pawed at her roughly with his free hand. The ping of a button hit a metal table. Pinpricks of light circled her vision, and her knees started to give way.

She made a tight fist around the keys in her pocket. She cocked her right arm and connected her fist with his jaw. He stumbled backwards. She grabbed a textbook and backhanded him, slamming the side of his dark hair and shoulder. Arms flailing, he clutched at her but lost his footing, tripped on a cardboard box, and went down, hard. A typewriter crashed onto the floor. She could hear the casters spin. More boxes tumbled. Someone pounded against the door.

"Marlo, unlock this door, or I'll break it down!" Nathan shouted.

She opened her mouth to yell, but her stomach lurched. The tangerine, a half thermos of chamomile tea, and a dozen saltines heaved out of her stomach. She spewed lunch down the front of herself and all over the floor and probably all over Marlo. Nathan pounded again with his fist. She spit out a stray bit of saltine and groped her way around a box.

"Help," she called weakly and waited for the sound of splintering wood, but instead she heard the jangle of keys in the lock.

The door swung wide, and Mr. Mumford stood in light framed by the opening. He wielded a long-handled broom as if it were a lance. Nathan stood on his toes behind the old man, staring over his shoulder at the body prone on the floor. A pool of bright blood growing under his head, Marlo's left foot was twitching.

"Nina," Nathan said. "I think you've killed him." He glanced at her. "And maybe killing is what he deserves."

Coughing and wiping her mouth with the back of her hand, she mumbled, "I'm having a baby," and threw up again.

Nathan flipped on the light. Veins stood out on his forehead and a sheen of sweat covered his face. He poked Marlo with the toe of his boot. Marlo groaned. "Not dead after all, but you've made a believer of him. No doubt about that."

She stepped over Marlo and stumbled across the hall. The pungent stink of her own bile overwhelmed the underlying odor of chalk, sweat, kids, and the lunchroom smells of canned peas and yeast. Her blouse soaked and sticking to her skin, she dry heaved again—and again. Her teeth wouldn't stop chattering. Her body shivered.

Her keys still clutched in her fist, she burst through the exterior doors into the cold March air and started to run. The parking lot gravel crunched beneath her feet.

"Nina!" Nathan sprinted across the road. His eyes passed over her quickly. The icy wind flattened the damp fabric against her skin. She couldn't speak. He reached out to touch her shoulder, but she jerked away. "Honey," he said, "you're more frightened than hurt." He dropped his hand to his side, but the compassion on his face bordered on tenderness. "He won't bother you anymore, and we won't speak of this again." Half of his mouth curled up in a sad smile. "And you're having a baby. You keep your mind on that." He was looking for some assurance from her, some signal she understood the pact they were making, as she fumbled putting the key in the car door.

"He's got kids, Nina. Two boys and a little girl—three years old."

* * *

Standing in her bathroom, she dropped her clothes in a pile and stepped into water so hot after five minutes her skin looked parboiled. The soap kept slipping out of her trembling fingers. An hour later when the drizzle coming out of the tap was finally lukewarm, she slipped under the water and felt her hair float around her face. *I should have called the police*, she thought for the tenth time. But justice in Bridger Falls was a deputy sheriff named Greg Maples, an old friend of Marlo.

She could imagine what he'd say. She'd seen him before—a tall, skinny guy with beige pants tucked into high leather boots. He'd have run his thumb and finger along the edge of his hat brim before he spoke in a halting voice.

"Mrs. Spencer, I'm sorry there's been unpleasantness this afternoon." And then as though rowdy hormones could explain it all, he'd mumble, "You're pregnant."

"I was attacked," she'd declare with a raised fist. "Marlo Fletcher attacked me. I want him arrested. Now."

In her mind's eye, she could see the deputy shift his weight uneasily from one foot to another. "That's not the story he's telling. He says he didn't know you were in the storage room. The two of you argued. You shoved him, he shoved you back, and you decked him."

The angry red bruises on her throat would have testified on her behalf, but Greg would have looked away, embarrassed, as though her behavior were unseemly. "A few days ago, you accused Mr. Fletcher of being a child molester." He'd clear his throat. "In our part of the country, those are fighting words, Mrs. Spencer. That's an ugly thing to say—to anyone."

"It's an ugly way to behave."

Deputy Maples would have just talked right past her as though he hadn't heard a word. "I can't blame Marlo—Mr. Fletcher," he'd have to correct himself, "for taking offense. And clearly, he got the worst of the set-to. You have a fierce right hook. He'll be drinking through a straw for days."

"I want him arrested. He turned the lights out. There were witnesses. Mr. Mumford. Nathan."

"They found Marlo out cold on the floor. If I arrest Mr. Fletcher, I'll have to arrest you too."

No one would believe her.

But in Marlo's farming village, whispers and raised eyebrows followed him, because she'd slapped a label on him, attached a handle to his behavior that allowed it to be passed up and down the rows at church. She'd robbed him of his good name and shone a flashlight on the sordid, dark corners in his portable classroom. She remembered her father's warning: Marlo can't endure the view of himself through her eyes. She put each hand on the side of the tub and pushed herself up, but she didn't feel clean. She stared in the mirror at the bruises on her throat.

Toweling her hair and searching for her jeans in the heap on her bedroom floor, she glanced toward the clock. Elliot would be home soon. She stretched a turtleneck over her head. Shuddering, she collapsed onto the couch, a disjointed pile of a girl, sick and miserable and somehow filthy as though she'd been trampled in farmyard muck.

Sitting on the couch, she clutched the stripped pillow to keep her hands from shaking. *I'm living in the Twilight Zone,* she thought, *but Monday morning by eight o'clock, every man on the faculty will know I'm having a baby, so I'll quit being Marilyn Monroe and become the young mother.* Hands off. Status change overnight.

Her life had been crazy since she came home from Scotland. An uncomfortable truth. How many other lives had been knocked off-kilter? Pam's, certainly. Rachel's. Her dad's. The cowboys at work. Occasionally, second thoughts stood out on Elliot's face in bas-relief. And her own life? She felt like someone was yelling, *Go Long, Nina* and then hurled a baby, wrapped tightly in a receiving blanket, fifty yards for Nina to pluck out of the air and hug tightly against her chest as she sprinted down the field past mothers in law and fat-lipped linebackers. Lars would block for her, but Elliot? He always had a test on Tuesday.

* * *

Monday morning, every cell in her body was on red alert. Nina hid in her room with her doors locked until forty-five seconds before the tardy bell rang. Tuesday was uneventful. No racks of pop rattling down the halls. They must be hauling them into the faculty lounge with a rope through the window. Wednesday was eighth-grade testing, but there was no extra action in the halls. Marlo was lying low. Listening at her door on Thursday morning, she waited for Marsha to arrive. She desperately needed a mentor, a guide through a minefield this slippery.

"Do you have a minute?"

Marsha nodded.

Irritated with herself for the shame she felt, Nina studied her hands as she described the previous Friday afternoon. Her stomach in a knot, she stared out the window, focusing on the clouds amassing across the valley. Thin-lipped, Marsha listened without asking questions, her eyes darting furtively around the room as though she were anxious about being overheard.

"I've been wrong about Nathan," Nina said. "He's been hanging around to watch out for me."

"He's had a crush from day one. We all knew it. He's been protecting you." As a handful of laughing boys crashed through the door, she put her arm around Nina's shoulder and whispered, "Because you're not the first."

26

Charades

Something had happened last Friday. Elliot was sure of it. Wearing a turtleneck pulled up to her chin and wrapped in a worn quilt, Nina sat shivering on the couch hugging a striped pillow when he'd arrived home. Her hair was damp and straggly, and she'd flinched when he kissed her. Wrapping his arms around her, he'd noticed her knuckles, swollen and bruises blooming. "What happened?" She'd snatched her hand back under the blanket. "I'm must be catching a cold" was all she would say.

"You hurt your hand."

She'd shrugged.

For the last couple of months, Elder Twitchell's voice in the back of Elliot's head kept repeating a phrase like a record with a scratch. *You don't know anything about her. You don't know anything about her.* But that wasn't true. He'd discovered a lot about Nina. She slept with one slender foot dangling out of the covers. She sprayed perfume in her hair instead of daubing it behind her ears. A shabby pink bear shared their bedroom. She loved the Stones and Elton John, corn dogs and raspberry shakes, and he was pretty sure she loved him. But he didn't understand her. Not for a minute. He loved her—with every breath he took. Every other thought in his head was about her, but he didn't know how to make her happy—and that worried him, all the time. In an apartment smaller than a single-car garage, he was terrified of misplacing her.

That Friday afternoon he'd smiled. "How was your day?" and she'd stared through him as though his innocent inquiry were an accusation, a request for a household accounting, in hours and minutes. She'd stood and walked to the precarious stack of dishes in the sink covered with dried cottage cheese or spaghetti sauce or Cheerios glued to bowls. Still wearing his jacket, he stood next to her not speaking, a dingy dish towel in his hand. He blamed her parents. How could you send a kid into the world not knowing how to scrub a tub, or sweep a floor, hang up clothes, or make a decent tuna casserole? It was like handing a child who didn't know how to drive a set of keys to the family station wagon. The kid would climb into the driver's seat and wait expectantly for spontaneous transportation.

"How did you hurt your hand?" he asked again.

"Bashed it moving a box of books." But she was trembling. This was more than the hormonal train ride through a winding canyon. She was miserable, probably homesick for crisp salads, a grand piano, and clean sheets that appeared magically on beds.

Tuesday daisies appeared on the kitchen table. "Lars brought them," she'd said, giving Elliot a quick glance over her shoulder. "He stopped to say good-bye. He's leaving at the end of the quarter." Good riddance, but Elliot wished he'd been the one to think of flowers.

That night after class, the winter wind slapping his face, he sprinted down College Hill, his chest bursting, punishing himself with the truth he could only face in the dark: he'd tricked her into marrying him, cajoled her, seduced her into giving up her posh life. He'd kidnapped a princess and carried her off to live in a hovel, and then sent her off each morning to earn his keep.

When he unlocked the door, she was awake, eyes wide. She stretched out her arms, but her face was pasty. Frightened and pale, a spasm crossed her face and she grasped the edge of the old quilt.

"What's wrong?"

"I'm having a miscarriage." Tears smeared her cheeks.

"Oh, Nina." He sat down on the couch and lifted her head onto his lap. "I've left you alone too much." He brushed her hair away from her forehead. "Did you call the doctor?"

"He was very nice. Not to worry. Nature's way of dealing with a problem. No aspirin. See him Monday morning at ten forty. He was just so ho-hum, but it doesn't feel that way to me."

"How does it feel to you?" He held his breath waiting for her answer.

"Like a theft."

* * *

Sunday evening, Nina's head resting on Elliot's lap, they watched Masterpiece Theatre with the volume turned low. Nina had been feverish all day, and she fidgeted against his leg, her face flushed and her eyes red-rimmed and shiny.

He touched her cheek. "You're burning up." He rested his palm on her forehead. "That's not normal."

She opened her mouth to speak but closed her eyes instead.

"We're going to the hospital," he said. "Now."

Nodding, she sat up and tried to put her feet on the floor, but she held out her arms instead. Elliot grabbed her, wrapped her in a blanket, and carried her to the car, but she was sweating and flailed her arms when he tried to talk to her.

Neon lights over the emergency bay glared in the darkness. Attendants wheeled her through the automatic double doors. Noises were too loud, colors too vivid. These were the halls where Elliot worked, where he walked with his tray of needles and plastic tubes, harvesting blood. But following Nina on a gurney, nothing felt familiar. The night was a blur of antiseptic smells and needles invading her skin, and snatches of conversations as he watched her fall in and out of consciousness. Dr. Markham examined her, speaking softly, his strong hand on her abdomen. Pushing the curtain aside, he spoke to Elliot in a quiet whisper. "Residual placenta," he murmured. "Infection." He shook his head. "Sepsis. Her parents should come quickly." Putting his stethoscope in his pocket, he gave Elliot a frank stare. "How did she get the bruises around her throat?"

An invisible hand squeezed his heart so tightly, Elliot could hardly breathe. Bruises? He shook his head. He didn't know. Minutes later, he felt his mother's arm around him, a Kleenex mopping tears on her anxious face. Who called her? Two o'clock, but the fluorescent lights chased shadows away. Then Bill and Barbara arrived frightened, but trying not to look frightened. Her dad moved in close and gathered Nina to him before the nurse gestured toward the door.

"I love you, Kitten," he whispered, tears in his gruff voice.

Elliot wandered in and out, touching her hand, touching her leg, glancing around the room, unsure of his surroundings.

A nurse adjusting tubing to the IV tree studied him. "You're the boy who works in the lab. I've seen you on the floor drawing blood."

He nodded.

"This your wife?"

He nodded again.

"She's one sick little girl."

Nurses strode past while Elliot stared at the white-faced clock on the wall; three thirty, four, four twenty. He sent his parents home. Lights above patient beds were dim, and the quiet whirs and whooshes of the monitors and machines were the only sounds. An older woman sat in the nurses' station making notes in a chart. Sitting on a metal chair outside Nina's cubicle, his elbows on his knees, Elliot grasped his head through his thick hair. Bill sat down beside him and offered him a Coke.

Elliot wiped his face on the sleeve of his sweatshirt. What if she doesn't make it? What if she never smiled at him again? Or kissed him. Or walked home with him through the park, swinging her arms, making jokes. "I should have been more careful," he mumbled. "I don't know what I was thinking."

"This is more than you bargained for." Bill inhaled slowly. "You'll have other children. She doesn't know it yet, but Nina will be a wonderful mother. Give her some time. She'll let you know when she's ready."

Elliot gripped his hands together tightly as he looked at the floor. Nina's dad didn't get it, didn't know how sick she was. He'd worked here long enough to know what sepsis meant. It was an ugly struggle, bacteria in her bloodstream. Vital organs shutting down. Curtains drawn. Sheets pulled over pale faces.

"She'll never be one of those moms who bakes chocolate chip cookies or sews Halloween costumes," Bill said, "but she'll be interesting and fun. She'll do things her own way. She always has. Your home will be full of music."

"But she's so sick." Elliot stared at the seams in the linoleum.

"She's young and healthy." Bill couldn't speak for a moment. "We can only hope in a couple of days this will feel like a bad dream." Bill's face was gray and dark pouches hung beneath watery blue eyes, but he stirred himself and patted Elliot on the back. "You know, I owe you an apology. I don't misjudge people often, but I misjudged you. You're something of a surprise to me. I didn't think you were right for Nina, but I was wrong."

Elliot glanced away and brushed tears off his cheek with the back of his hand. "You don't understand. This is my fault."

Bill shook his head. "Don't tell me things I shouldn't know." A redheaded man with pocked cheeks mopped the corridor with slow motions, back and forth. His name tag swung on a lanyard around his neck. The chemical tang irritated Elliot's nose. Bill sighed. "Did Nina ever tell you how I named the boys?"

Elliot shook his head.

"Well, they're all named for Supreme Court justices. Oliver Wendell Holmes, Benjamin Cardozo, and, of course, John Marshall."

"Marbury versus Madison?"

"That's the one." Bill stretched out his legs. "I was sure the boys would all be brilliant. I married the brightest girl on campus, and I'm no slouch, so I was feeling pretty confident. Expectations in our home were almost palpable. But it was all too much for John." He smiled sadly. "He was such a sturdy little soul. He'd trundle along and try to keep up. I kept thinking that if he'd just do what I asked, stretch himself, he'd be like the rest of us, but all I succeeded in teaching him was that he was inadequate. I needed to let him be who he was, love him for who he was, because you can't change people." He nodded toward Nina's room. "Plus, the poor kid was just a couple of years older than that blonde sprite who was speaking in very funny complete sentences when she was two." He cleared his throat. "I have to wonder if he'll ever forgive me." He paused, his hand on Elliot's shoulder. "We all make mistakes. The important thing is not to keep making the same mistakes over and over again."

Elliot studied his palms and prayed silently for a second chance. The two men sat not speaking for another hour as the soft pearl gray of dawn filled the corridor. Whispers from the nurse's station signaled the morning shift change.

His green scrubs wrinkled and his face a study in exhaustion, Dr. Markham stepped out of Nina's room. "Her temp's coming down. Although she's given us all a scare, she'll be okay."

27

The Return

Her sick leave spent, Nina returned to school. Her desktop was chaotic. Too tired to move, she sat staring at notes from three different subs.

Marsha rapped on the door. She took one look at Nina's face and said, "Oh my goodness, you've had a rough go."

Nina gestured at her desk.

"Don't worry about any of it," Marsha said, dismissing the paper clutter with a wave of her hand. "Start fresh. Toss it in the trash." She rested a hand on her hip. "Jerry and I tried to get a handle on it, but you can see it got away from us."

"What's the word on the street?"

"Elliot called and scared Ruth to death. She called the hospital and they said you were critical. She was about to drape the office in black crepe until Mr. Killpack told her to keep it quiet." She touched Nina's arm. "But the story's in your face. You look like death warmed over."

"I'll be better soon."

"Of course you will. I'll check on you later before I head down to the gym."

Nina allowed the momentary stillness to envelope her. She glanced at her colorful bulletin boards. She'd been so naïve, so ridiculously naïve to think she knew anything about being a teacher or a wife. She thought she could learn everything at once, grappling with the intricacies of

creating a handout, inventing three lesson plans every single day, stirring up sloppy joes that didn't taste like the old man in question, and
sleeping with Elliot and all that came with it. She shook her head and
started to hum, and then, almost silently, the lyrics tripped off the end
of her tongue.

Well, I'm on my way
I don't know where I'm going
I'm on my way, I'm taking my time
But I don't know where

She hummed the rest, drumming with two fingers on the top of
her desk. Pale morning sunlight filtered through the windows. The
bell rang. Children spilled into the room but the ruckus quieted
when they saw her. Her green jumper hung on her gaunt frame. She
should have brushed more color on her cheeks, tied a vibrant scarf
in her hair, or worn dangling earrings. Tomorrow. She'd do better
tomorrow.

Two days later, during seventh hour, she sat in the middle of the
horseshoe arrangement—Mr. Mumford had quit rearranging her
desks—and as she was turning to page fifteen, she heard the familiar
rattle of pop bottles. A subdued Marlo lumbered down the hall holding
the rack in front of him like a chunky kid selling hotdogs at a baseball
game. Walter sprinted to close the door, but he wasn't quick enough.
Marlo flashed a vile look her direction, but Zach, his sidekick from the
portables, jumped into the front of her room. Short, with glasses hanging onto a nose too small for his face, he grinned. "Where you been?
On a Caribbean cruise?" A handful of students giggled. She bit her
bottom lip. If Zach wasn't a clown, he was a nothing, a cipher with no
role to play. He sauntered out the door, but turned in the threshold, and
whistled, that long low sound that had plagued her all year.

The last straw. Enough was enough. The expression on her face
squelched the handful of twitters in the back of the room. A pop of
adrenaline propelled her out of her chair into the hall, where Zach was
leaning against a bank of green lockers, a sappy smile on his face as
though the Smothers Brothers were a trio and he was the clever brother
with all the best lines. Well over six feet tall in her high-heeled shoes

and splashy floral dress, she placed four fingertips on his chest and shoved him.

"Don't set foot in my room again—ever." The glass transom rattled as she slammed the classroom door and turned to face thirty-six startled fourteen-year-olds.

Walter tapped his watch. "Countdown to Armageddon."

* * *

Waiting until her seventh hour departed, she retrieved a manila folder secreted in the back of her filing cabinet. By four o'clock she was standing in front of the secretary's desk in the education building on the university campus.

Breathing hard, she said, "My name's Nina Spencer. Would it be possible for Dean Shelton to see me? I'm his daughter's teacher."

The secretary ushered her into an office with lackluster furniture, beige industrial-grade carpeting, and shelves crowded with books. A man this ruggedly handsome seemed oddly out of place as he stood up from his desk, extended his hand, and studied her face. "Mrs. Spencer. Robin said you've been absent. I'm sorry you've been ill, but I have to assume this visit is about my daughter. What's she up to now?"

Nina cleared her throat and recited the speech she'd rehearsed in her car. "I'm putting myself in a precarious position by being here. I need to remain anonymous. My husband's a student and I can't afford to lose my job, but the situation at Clear Creek is out of control, and I'm hoping that as a parent and a leader in the educational community, you might be able to intervene." She pushed the scrap of paper across his desk and started to explain.

Nothing on the dean's face betrayed what he was thinking as he fingered the tardy excuse inviting the recipient to drop a pencil for his daughter to bend over and retrieve.

"Someone sent this paper to you? Excusing another student?"

"I'm sure he didn't realize what was on the other side."

"There's a fair amount of discussion in our home about Robin's choices in clothing."

Nina raised her chin. "Robin could come to school painted green with feathers in her hair, and it wouldn't justify an adult male touching her. This isn't about Robin. And she certainly hasn't been singled out."

"Well," he sighed, "that's comforting. She's a bright girl, but she's grown up too quickly."

"Some do." Then she explained Robin's effort to defend herself and other girls plagued by humiliating attention on their birthdays. The dean took a few notes, asked a pointed question or two, and a half hour later stood, signaling the end of the meeting. "I appreciate you coming to see me. This is disturbing for multiple reasons. I'll give serious consideration to placing any more student teachers in that district. I'm not sure how to intervene as a father. This will require more thought." His tone was brusque.

Nina thought she might feel relieved. She didn't. She picked up her purse and walked into the outer office. The secretary told her to have a pleasant evening.

Exhausted, she walked into the apartment a few moments later and found Elliot washing a head of lettuce. When he saw her face, he placed the lettuce on a dish towel and wrapped her in his arms. She buried her head against his shoulder. Funny boy. He needed to touch her—all the time. It was like he couldn't help himself. Eating lunch or dinner, his fingers grazed her knee under the table. In the evening, his textbooks spread on the floor in front of the couch, he rested his hand on her foot. At night he held her against his chest until she fell asleep. When she mentioned his nonstop attention, he just smiled or reached over and tousled her pale hair.

Lettuce forgotten, he held her on his lap. "What's wrong?"

"I went to see Dean Shelton. I gave him that tardy excuse about his daughter. You know, the one I intercepted last fall." Her heart was racing.

"Why now? I don't understand. I thought we were going to coast to the end of the year."

She felt the muscles in his arms tighten. "Someone has to say *enough*. Someone has to say no."

A half smile curved on his face. "And that someone has to be you."

❧ 28 ❧

Consequences

No rumblings in the past month about her meeting with Dean Shelton, and diverted by happy thoughts of summer vacation, Nina wasn't anticipating trouble because the day was so perfect and the weather so delightful that the warm breeze coming in her car window felt like a kiss against her cheek. Nina loved April almost as much as she loved May. Thirty school days left in the year—that was it. The light at the end of the tunnel was almost flashing. She parked against the curb.

The foyer smelled of fresh paint and the patterned green carpet was relatively new, but the drinking fountains were only a couple of feet off the floor. Thirsty secretaries would have to get down on their knees like religious supplicants, because the building was a very old elementary school that had been converted into the district offices.

Her purse in her lap and her foot tapping in time to the music in her head, Nina waited for the assistant superintendent in charge of fiscal affairs. She inhaled. Nothing about this old building smelled like a school. No lingering miasma of chalk dust, no sour odors from the lunch room, no sweaty children bringing the smells of cut grass and spring into the halls, just the illusion of clarity and purpose. Clothes pressed and their hair sprayed firmly in place, secretaries typed, in triplicate, on large Selectric machines.

The conference room door opened and five or six men, smiling, chatting, clean-shaven, hair slicked back from a side part, and wearing dark suits and narrow ties, marched through the room in lockstep.

Nina would have been hard-pressed to single one out in a lineup. No one burped or gave anyone a high-five. No one jumped up on the desks or tripped the man walking in front of him. No one shouted a crude remark at any of the secretaries. How could they possibly make any sort of relevant decisions about education in such a pristine environment? They needed to hang with the cops on the beat.

Mr. Patterson, differentiated only by the impressive length of his nose, was almost to his office when he recognized the girl sitting patiently. He rubbed his palms together. "Nina, just the person I need to see. I was going to call you tomorrow for an appointment. Do you have a minute?"

"Of course." *What kind of a minute?* she wondered. Had he talked to Marsha? Mr. Patterson was so unfailingly pleasant whenever he saw her. He'd tiptoed out onto a limb when he hired her, something she remembered gratefully every time she saw him, but she didn't need any more complications. "I came for a duplicate of my W-2."

"Let me take care of that for you." His voice was too cheerful, his smile too broad. He stepped into the adjacent room and she heard him say, "Just bring it into me," before he gestured openhanded toward his office. Following her, he closed the door with a firm click.

He pulled her employment file toward him from its ominous position on top of a pile. Nina's palms started to sweat.

"Thank you for the flowers," she said.

"Don't mention it. You were in the hospital for a week?"

"It felt like a month." At least a month.

He opened her folder and flipped through several pages. "There aren't any evaluations from Mr. Killpack."

"He's never observed any of my classes."

"Not once?"

"No."

A kindly man, his lips made a firm line as he studied her. "There was a meeting here last night. A group of parents met with the superintendent to express concerns about your school." He paused, giving her an opening, but instead of speaking, Nina ran a small silver heart back and forth on the delicate chain around her neck.

He continued, "I knew what they were going to say, but it was something of a surprise to Superintendent Pratt."

Nina looked at him curiously. He knew everything. Marsha kept him informed, but he wasn't going to mention what Marlo had done. Why not? She bit her lip, unsure of this rocky terrain.

"One of the parents is an attorney," Patterson said. "He led the charge. I thought we could smooth things over until Dean Shelton, I believe you know him, spoke about his daughter. He was quite emphatic. There will be no student teachers from the university if we tolerate what's been going on at Clear Creek. He didn't frame it as an ultimatum, but everyone understood. If Marlo Fletcher stays, no student teachers. It's a terrible black eye for the district, and of course there are complications; Marlo's father sits on the school board."

"I know," she said. It had been obvious all year. Marlo was at the front of the line when free passes were passed out.

"Superintendent Pratt is in a difficult position, a school board member's son creating turmoil. Typically, Mr. Killpack's solution to problems between men and women has been to have all male teachers."

"Which ignores the half of the student body in skirts."

"That's true. Half that faculty should be women." He exhaled audibly. "Mr. Killpack caught the brunt of it last night, but Dr. Pratt and Mr. Killpack have gone duck hunting together for years, and he'll bank on that relationship. But Fletcher will go. There's no other choice."

She remembered chatting with Marsha between classes about animosity—prehistoric—between two old warhorses, Mr. Killpack and Mr. Patterson. The longer Patterson spoke, the more obvious it became that Marlo was a pawn. Nina grasped her hands together. Why was he telling her all this? Was he apologizing or did someone need to know how deftly he'd positioned his pieces? Had he known when he hired her, when he placed his queen on the board, what he was setting in motion?

"Mr. Killpack will receive a promotion and come to the district to manage student transportation. That will give me an opening to correct the problems at Clear Creek." Mr. Patterson sighed heavily. "It was apparent last night that someone has been speaking to Dean Shelton. Killpack's sure it's you. I wish you'd come to me first, Nina. I could have protected you. Killpack insists you've been divisive and a troublemaker. He thinks you instigated the female rebellion in Beginning Type." A grin stretched across his face. "Spartacus?"

Nina tried to smile, but the best she could do was pinch her bottom lip. This man had searched through dozens of applications looking for a pretty face, a high GPA, and a streak of independence. He'd known exactly what had gone on this year, and he'd let it play out, strung out enough rope until Killpack hung himself. She was trapped in a power struggle that had nothing to do with her.

Mr. Patterson leaned forward over the desk and patted her hand. "Principals determine which new teachers receive letters of intent, and you won't be receiving one. I'm so sorry. I wish there was something I could do."

Dumfounded, she stared at him. Fired? She wavered between wanting to scream and fainting. "A first-year teacher without a letter of recommendation from her principal is dead in the water."

"I'll be happy to write you a glowing letter."

"But if you had an applicant without a principal's recommendation, you wouldn't consider him, would you?" Her heart thumped wildly in her chest.

"There are just so many excellent applicants right now."

Did he enjoy this? Clobbering victims with a bat? "I haven't done anything wrong, and I'm the one being punished. This is classic murder-the-messenger retaliation."

"I'm sure it seems that way to you," he said. His smooth countenance didn't betray a thing, but she suddenly realized who she was in his eyes, a girl who would probably get pregnant again and leave midyear, an expensive week-long hospital stay costing more than her first year's salary, and a bone the superintendent could throw to placate Mr. Killpack. She'd played her role to perfection and was no longer useful. That was it. Done.

"Do you have any idea what my life's been like this year?" She ticked off the slimy pranks on her fingers. "It's all happened on your watch. On Mr. Killpack's watch. No one intervened. No one said stop." Red faced and ranting, she was making a spectacle of herself to this audience of one. "I've been a good teacher, but none of that matters. This is so completely wrong, so completely unjust."

He rose and shook his head sadly, a thin sheen of moisture on his nose and forehead.

"Would it be possible to get a duplicate of my W-2?"

"I'll have it sent to you in the morning."

"For heaven's sake, don't do that. I'll never get it. That's Marlo's first stop. 'Let's plow through Nina's mail and see what we can steal.' I've never reciprocated. I've never stolen his mail or his wallet, or sabotaged his room, or stood in the back of his class and made obscene remarks to undermine him in front of his students." She stopped. Or attacked him in the supply room.

She scribbled her home address on a scrap of paper and pushed it toward his hand. "If you could send the W-2 here, I'd appreciate it. It looks like we're going to need the refund." Her parting shot might sting for a second or two but no longer.

She collapsed on the curb next to her car and looked over her shoulder at the ugly yellow-brick building with "Oakwood Elementary" in carved concrete letters over the main entrance. She replayed the last half hour over and over in her head. Then she squeezed her eyes shut and tried to think of something she could tell Elliot. Telling Lars would be easy. He'd cheer. He wasn't dependent on her for food. Telling Elliot, however, was another matter.

* * *

Pounding the steering wheel and shouting at the dashboard, Nina circled the block twice before she slammed on the brakes in front of their apartment. Entering the front door felt like sticking her head in one more noose. Elliot was standing in the kitchen deboning a chicken, but when he glanced at her, his smile faded.

"Put down the knife," she said. "We need to talk."

He wiped his hands on a towel. "No W-2?" His dark eyebrows met in the center of his forehead.

"They're sending it," she hissed.

"What's wrong?" He turned off the burner and gave her a gentle shove. "Come sit by me on the couch."

"I'm not going back next year." There, she said it. The grim truth hovered in the air.

He chose each word carefully. "If you quit, that Fletcher guy wins. Killpack wins."

"No. I'm leaving them there to lose all by themselves. Marlo, Mr. Killpack, Mr. Patterson, the whole crew."

"What aren't you telling me?"

"I'm not being rehired. No letter of intent. No contract to sign a contract." She inched away from him to the end of the couch. "Mr. Killpack's retaliating against me because I talked to the dean about Marlo, but other things have been at play. I just ʌigured it out. They used me. Mr. Patterson. Mr. Killpack. In their petty little battle."

A raw quiet filled the room. His jaw was so rigid it looked like stone. Nothing moved except a twitching muscle in the side of his face, but his cheeks flushed an ugly red. His voice was so low she strained to listen. "The minute you walked into the dean's office, you knew this would happen. You sabotaged your own job and gave yourself a way out cloaked in some half-baked rationalization."

"Is that what you think of me?" She flexed her fingers and swallowed hard.

"You're friends with those two teachers," he said. "Marsha and Jerry. They've bent over backwards for you. Why? Because they're well read or have better taste? No, Nina, it's because you like them. They got to bask in the 100-watt Rushforth smile, and that's a great place to be. I ought to know."

Breathing hard, her chest rose and fell. "You don't understand."

"Sure I do." He shook his head. "You despised that Fletcher guy the first day you saw him, because he's a hick cut and teaches type."

Elliot siding with Marlo? Every time she stepped into the supply room, she felt that man's rough hands, smelled his stench, and felt his hot breath in her face. For the first time in her life, darkness was the enemy, and she slept with the lights on until Elliot came home. She pushed her palm against her forehead. *Tell him,* she thought. But she couldn't choke the words out of her mouth.

"So, what's the plan? You've always got one." His dark eyes glittered. "Does it include me?"

What did he mean by that? She clutched a striped pillow in front of her chest like a shield. "This just happened."

"So, the first of September we have no income and no insurance," he said. "Great. Thanks." He stood twisting the dishcloth in his hands like he wanted to stuff it down her throat.

"Did anyone ask why you waited three months to hand Shelton the smoking gun? Which is an excellent question. Why now? Right before letters of intent come out?" His eyes fixed on her for an explanation.

He didn't believe her. Suddenly she felt stranded by the side of her own life, trying to thumb a ride, but no one would pick her up.

"I feel terrible about losing my job." It was the only responsible thing to say.

"I don't believe that for a minute." He strode into the kitchen. If she were that angry, she'd grab that chicken and wrench the thing in two, spraying the kitchen with bits of gristle and fat, but Elliot wrapped it in aluminum foil, tucking in the corners as though he were wrapping a birthday present, and set it on a plate in the refrigerator. Then he collected his books, stacked each one neatly, largest volumes on the bottom, and slid them into his backpack. He was furious, white-hot.

She trailed him into the kitchen. "Sit down for a minute and let me explain."

"Would it have been so tough to keep your head down"—he bit off each word—"and hold on to this job for one more year?"

"I've tried, Elliot." She fought back hot tears. "For an entire year." Waving her arms, she paced between the kitchen linoleum and the worn carpet on the living room floor. "I tried to learn to cook, and I failed. I've tried to be a schoolteacher, and I failed. I sit here night after night—all alone trying to be a wife. None of this is a good fit for me, but I've tried."

He glanced past her shoulder toward the bedroom, the happy reprieve neither of them was willing to mention in the heat of battle. His hand twisted the doorknob.

She sputtered, "I hate going to work every single morning. I admit it. I fantasize about getting in a wreck and breaking my leg, so I'll have an excuse not to go. You haven't wanted to know, because that might get in the way of what you want, someone to pay the bills, cook and clean, and ignore. I'm not a person to you. You don't know me at all." She poked him hard in the chest with her fingernail.

Breathing hard, he frowned. "I know you better than you know yourself."

She leaned forward until she was an inch away from his face. "I can't believe I let you talk me into any of this. I'm on a trip to nowhere without a return ticket."

"Don't say that, Nina."

"I am saying it. This marriage is so one-sided. Have you given up anything?"

His eyes narrowed. "Are you kidding? Do you think you're easy?"

A sucker punch to the gut. She bounced off the ropes, and he hit her again.

"You're pampered and self-absorbed."

"I'm self-absorbed?" She flattened her palm against her chest. "I'm sick of you trying to stuff me into this little black box you call 'wife.' What about the promises you made? We'd be best friends. Roommates? Equals? I want all the same things you want. But everything is always about you." She took two steps back. "Maybe this has all been a terrible mistake."

He stared at her, the color leeching out of his face. "You don't mean that." He grabbed his backpack off the floor and lurched out the door as though he'd been shot. She stomped her foot on the floor and pummeled the pillows on the couch. Picking up a stack of ninth-grade essays and a green pen, she tried to concentrate, but she couldn't.

He was wrong, but he was always so sure he was right. An invisible contract in his mind had her signature on the bottom. A year ago, she'd handed him her heart and her head on a valentine-shaped platter. She'd determined to play the role of a dutiful wife, like thousands of other girls, putting husbands through school, but she was unhappy, so unhappy.

Hours later, she sat curled on the couch, a spoonful of peanut butter melting on her tongue and her heart aching. The telephone rang. Maybe it was Elliot leaning against a pay phone at the library, ready to beg her forgiveness. She raced into the kitchen and grabbed the receiver.

"Nina?"

"Yes."

"You don't know me, but my name is Janice Walker. I used to teach in your room. We need to talk."

29

Daddy's Darling

Bill stared at the receiver.

Barbara sighed and laid her book down on the bedspread. "Nina?"

"I can't believe what she just told me." Bill shook his head.

"What?"

"She's been fired."

She gasped. "You're kidding. "

"I wish I were."

She sat up a little straighter. "And you're angry."

"Very angry. She's been used and tossed aside. The assistant superintendent knew what's been going on all year. He didn't intervene. He wanted the mess to implode and destroy the principal. Our Nina was the fuse."

She patted his thigh. "Calm down. Nina will find another job."

"She was assaulted. Some creep cornered her in a storage room. A week before the miscarriage." He rubbed the stubble on his jaw. "Nina grew up in our home with an attorney for a father, but she didn't report it." He winced. "I understand that women don't, and I don't blame them—the whole he-said-she-said problem—but still."

"Oh, Bill."

"She didn't tell Elliot either." He raised both eyebrows. "He doesn't know."

"Oh no."

"That's the worst piece, isn't it?" He slapped his palm with a rolled magazine. "She didn't think the police would act, at least that's what she said, but I think she's humiliated and somehow feels tainted."

"And the miscarriage?"

"In her head the two are connected. Maybe that's why she's not telling Elliot. I don't know. None of this is rational."

"And she's just telling us now? My little girl's been holding all this inside?" She pushed her palm against her mouth.

"She's finally come up for air, starting to get mad. Another woman contacted her who had a nasty encounter with the same guy."

"This is ugly."

"It's more than ugly. It's illegal."

"What are you going to do?"

"I'll drive up on Saturday. I might have Rick Hamilton work on this. He's that junior associate from Yale. He loves a good fight, and that's what those men are going to get."

* * *

The large circular brushes on a street cleaner were sweeping up the winter's accumulation of leaves and litter as Nina hurried past. She was a few minutes late, something her father didn't tolerate well. She glanced up at the sign, *The Bluebird*, before she pushed open the heavy oak and glass door.

A pretty woman, dark haired and glancing anxiously around the restaurant, stood waiting near the cashier's desk. Her purse was tucked tightly under her arm and her worn navy shoes were polished to a dull shine. She clutched a small blue sack of jelly beans in her fist. Feeling the rush of chill air, she turned quickly.

Nina smiled. "Janice?"

The woman nodded.

"Marsha says hello." She addressed the hostess. "We're supposed to meet Mr. Rushforth."

"He's in the Pioneer Room." The hostess didn't say "sequestered in the Pioneer Room," but that's what her look indicated because the room was only used for homecoming, Mother's Day, and the Rotary Club breakfast on the Fourth of July.

246

Nina touched the back of Janice's arm as they walked down the aisle past the antique pink marble soda fountain and display cases full of assorted chocolates. They made a quick right turn between double doors.

Introductions were made, lunch was ordered and served, and Nina tried to ignore the frank appraisal a blue-eyed young man was making of her face. She'd spoken to Rick on the phone for over an hour, and now she had the unpleasant feeling he was gauging her appeal for a jury, and her height might be a distinct disadvantage. Forced chitchat about chocolates and jelly beans faded as Nina's father leaned toward Janice. She'd just stabbed a bite of chicken salad with her fork, but before it reached her mouth, he spoke, "Nina's told us about your situation, but we'd like to hear the story from you."

"I'm divorced." She set her fork on the edge of her plate and smoothed the cloth napkin in her lap. "That's why all this happened. People make assumptions about divorced women that aren't particularly kind."

Bill Rushforth smiled gently. "We don't. None of this is your fault." A master at orchestrating small details, her father was dressed in campus casual perfectly pressed by Mrs. Thatcher's practiced hand. Doors to the private room eliminated the possibility of gossip escaping into the high-ceilinged restaurant. He'd brought an attractive young man with longish sandy hair curling over his collar and an eager expression on his face. No wedding ring shone on his finger.

"Are you your boys' sole support?" Bill asked.

"Their dad lives in Montana. He's supposed to help, but he doesn't. What he really wants is custody."

"What can you tell us about Mr. Fletcher?" Buttering a roll, Bill spoke as though he'd asked her opinion about an impudent student or a questionable best seller.

"We grew up in the same small town. He was a big deal. One of those amazing kid athletes who can do anything with a ball. His parents thought he was the sun and the moon and the stars. I don't think 'no' ever came out of their mouths. They were always covering for him, making excuses for him, bailing him out." Janice sipped her water. "Because Marlo was mean. A real bully."

Nina caught the flicker in her dad's eyes, but his calm expression remained constant.

"I hadn't seen him for years when I started at Clear Creek," Janice said. "At first he was just obnoxious, but there was always an unpleasant undercurrent like I must be frustrated—not having a man in my life. Her hands twisted the napkin in her lap. "There are no boundaries with that guy. I didn't encourage him, but some men think I'm available until I make it clear that I'm not." Tears welled in Janice's eyes and Nina glanced away.

"He was livid when I didn't reciprocate," Janice said, "like I didn't think he was as cool as he'd been in high school. I do a lot of my prep at home after the boys go to bed, so I was usually the first one to pull out of the parking lot, but a couple of times when I had to stay late, Marlo cornered me in my room."

"What happened?" Rick asked.

"Oh, you know." She cleared her throat. "He'd try to get romantic. When I refused his advances, it wounded his pride."

"How did you respond?" The young man nervously tapped his pencil on the table.

"I'd tell him to leave me alone. Remind him he was married to a wonderful girl. Things like that."

"That didn't have the desired effect?"

"He didn't hear a single word."

"So what finally happened?"

"The play was in full swing, after-school rehearsals. It was December. The days were short. One night when I finally got out to the parking lot, my car had two flats. There was nothing wrong with those tires. I assumed kids were pulling a prank."

"Was anyone else around?" Rick looked up from the notes he was taking.

"No, it was after five. I was in a rush to pick up the boys at the babysitter's before her husband got home."

"And Mr. Fletcher happened by."

"In that monster truck of his. He offered to take me to the gas station to borrow their air tank. He was so nice, so completely sympathetic, that I got into his truck. Big mistake."

"What happened?"

"He was driving so fast I couldn't jump out. He was bumping all over the road. He didn't stop until he was in the middle of a field somewhere, then he was all over me. I finally got out of the truck, and by some freak chance, his fingers were in the door when I slammed it. I'm sure people in town heard him yell. I took off running."

"To the gas station?"

She nodded. "I stayed off the main road. It was at least three miles."

"You didn't call the police?"

"In that small town? No way."

"Nina says you told the principal," Bill said.

"The next morning. I told him everything."

Bill leaned back in his chair and set his napkin next to the lunch he'd barely touched. "How did the principal respond?"

"He told me I should quit wearing makeup. Cut my hair." She waited a minute to let that sink in. "But later that afternoon Marsha was in Ruth's office, and they heard Mr. Killpack reading Marlo the riot act. He left me alone after that. In March, Mr. Killpack brought me in to tell me I was going to be teaching in the young mothers' program at the district. I didn't want to go, but he told me that was the job. Take it or leave it."

"You've been unhappy there?"

"It's chaotic. The girls bring their babies. The funding is soft. If they lose it, I'll be out. I've sent applications to other districts, but the market's flooded with all these college kids who think they're going to change the world."

Bill tapped his finger on the table. "Let's order dessert. I understand the pies here are wonderful. Rick, would you grab the waitress?"

Poor choice of words, Nina thought, *considering the conversation*, plus she'd never liked pie. She opened her mouth to decline, but when she caught her father's eye over the top of his reading glasses, she said, "I'll have a piece of your strawberry chiffon, small." She held up her finger and thumb an inch apart.

Her father didn't start speaking until everyone else was eating. "Rick and I have discussed this situation with a couple of partners, and our firm would like to take this on. We all agree Clear Creek is a hostile environment for women—and girls. Janice reported it to the principal. Nina, you think Mr. Patterson was aware of your situation?"

She nodded, her mouth full.

"Janice, you've been damaged professionally for reporting an assault.

Nina reported illegal behavior to a parent. A case could be made that her dismissal was retaliatory." He pursed his lips together. "Our inclination is not to bring suit against individuals. There's not much to gain by going after Fletcher or Mr. Killpack. I'm suggesting we bring suit against the district for knowingly allowing the situation to persist and then damaging you instead of acting appropriately to solve the problem.

"We need to set the stage carefully. Rick's identified a reporter who might be an interested collaborator. He's going to call him Monday and mention the meeting at the district with the parents. We need the name of the girl's father who's an attorney. Do we have his name?" He looked at Nina.

She glanced at Janice. "Jessica. Redheaded ninth grader."

"Jessica Renlund. Her father's name is Carl."

Bill raised his eyebrows. "We hope he'll want to talk. Rick's coming back up on Wednesday to meet with the reporter and let him know a school board member's son has been fired—regardless of what they call it—and that an unnamed teacher has been let go without cause. Rick will intimate that if the injured parties file suit, it could have huge implications. There are a couple of similar cases wending their way through the legal system that could end up at the Supreme Court. That should get his attention."

Rick glanced at Bill as he took another bit of pie.

Bill wiped his mouth with his napkin. "We'll keep feeding the reporter information, incremental bites. Keep up the pressure on the school district, so they'll be motivated to settle out of court if that's the direction we want to take."

"Nina," He looked at her seriously. "I need to control the story we give the public. Do not answer your phone. Are we clear on that?"

"Okay."

"Hopefully, no one at school knows you didn't receive a letter of intent. Before that becomes common knowledge, you need to talk to Marsha and discover Mr. Patterson's other confederates. That's key. We need to establish what Patterson knew about you and Janice, and when he knew it." He leaned back in his chair. "The last week in May we'll file. We'll be deposing these jokers in June. If they have any sense, they should be very uncomfortable."

A strawberry dissolving on the back of her tongue, Nina sat

comfortably in her father's shadow, relaxing for the first time in days, until she remembered work on Monday morning. This could get ugly, quickly, and she'd be at Clear Creek alone, stranded in the middle of wheat fields covered with just an inch or two of green.

"Nina, Rick could use your input formulating questions for the depositions. You know the people. You know the situation." Bill tipped his head toward Rick.

A grin spreading across his face, Rick said, "Great." When Bill turned toward the waitress coming in with the check, Rick signaled Nina a quick thumbs-up.

Bill turned toward Janice. "There's one thing you both need to understand before we begin." His voice was quiet and low. "If we go to court, we'll lose."

Nina reached for her purse, an excuse to turn away. Of course they were going to lose. No one had poked out her eye. She had full use of her faculties. Sooner or later, someone would make the connection between Nina and Interstate Trucking. Millionaire would reverberate through the halls at district office. And Janice? What was her complaint? She had a job—for the moment. No visible harm; therefore, no foul.

Bill kept talking. "There's no body of law to support this litigation. We're relying on our own interpretation of the '64 Civil Rights Act." He shrugged. "But several things could happen. They might offer to reinstate both of you if we drop the suit. They might want to settle out of court. It's hard to say. This is new territory." He rubbed his jaw thoughtfully. "And it's an election year. After all the shenanigans, Fletcher's father's going to have a rough time getting reelected. I wonder if that was part of Patterson's plan."

"We'll appeal if we lose?" Nina asked.

"Of course." Bill smiled. A victory on a major social issue would be the capstone to a brilliant career.

Janice pushed her chair back from the table. "This is all exciting, and I'd love to be a part of it, but I can't afford to be a sacrificial lamb. Those guys will go after me, and if I lose my job, I could lose my boys. I wish you all the luck in the world, but I was never here, and I don't know anything about any of this."

She stood, and Nina's father did too. He took both of her hands in his. "I appreciate you coming. I know this is risky, but if anything should occur to you, or if you hear anything I should know, please call me." He pulled a business card out of his wallet, jotted down his home phone, and tucked it in her palm. "Believe it or not, this first shot over the bow is going to make your life easier."

He gave Nina a long hug. "You've had a rough year, but we're going to make these guys squirm, and maybe do a little good along the way. We'll see. Rick and I are going to head back, but the next time I come up, I'll bring your mom, and we'll all go out to dinner."

"Thanks, Dad."

Rick grinned at her. "I'll be in touch. I'll let it ring once, and then I'll call again."

She raised one eyebrow and forced a smile. "I'm home from school at four."

* * *

She dropped her straw purse by the front door and kicked off her shoes before she headed into the bedroom to slide out of her dress. Sitting on the perfectly made bed between two plumped pillows sat her shabby little bear. Nina's bottle-bottom glasses were perched on his nose and a *Ms. Magazine* was propped between his legs as though he were engrossed in a scintillating article. Someone, obviously the bear, had written in the margin, "Your husband is a jerk. I say we stuff him." Nina snatched the bear to her chest, the tension draining out of her shoulders and neck. She and Elliot hadn't spoken, not since their latest fight. She hadn't asked him where he'd gone that night, or where he'd slept, because he hadn't come home, which is a nasty way to run an argument. Nope, he'd left her alone, wide-eyed, listening in the darkness and remembering the desperation on his face as he fell out the door. He'd arrived home late the day after—she heard him settling on the couch—but not much in the way of words had passed between them since. She sighed. "Bear, what am I going to do? I love him."

Hours later, the windows open and curtains fluttering, the sound of the landlord mowing the lawn and the scent of cut grass filled the apartment. A big yellow sponge in her hand, the girl in 2-C was soaping her car, covering the asphalt with puddles of suds. A wary-looking Elliot opened the front door and found Nina sitting on the floor with sheets of paper, covered in her tight handwriting, spread in front of her. Killpack, Patterson, and Fletcher were written boldly on index cards.

Smiling at Elliot, Nina leaned back, resting her weight on her elbows. "Don't step on anything. It's all organized."

He moved cautiously as though he were tiptoeing through a minefield. "Don't tell me. You're writing a novel, and I'm the antagonist."

Nodding, she raised her voice over the sound of the lawn mower. "A murder mystery. A young bride stuffs her husband with sawdust, shoves big brown marbles in his eye sockets, and props him against the front window—so she knows where he is at all times. No one discovers the dirty deed until the Laundromat owner notices a significant reduction in his weekly receipts." She jumped up and put her arms around his neck. "I love you." It seemed like enough when she said it. "I had lunch with Dad today."

Elliot glanced around the room. "Is he still here?"

"No. He was with a junior associate, and they had to go back, but I'll tell you what we figured out."

After he kissed her behind her ear, he shoved dishes aside to make a space for his elbow on the kitchen table. He listened patiently for ten minutes, until Nina, smiling expectantly, stopped to catch her breath.

He held out his arms and invited her to sit on his lap. "I love you. Losing your job has been awful, but I need you to look at the bigger picture." She loved the feel of his arms around her, and when he spoke next to her ear, it tickled, but something in the tone of his voice sounded a warning.

She pulled back and looked at him evenly.

"There are a couple of things you haven't considered," he said. Those soft brown eyes were so serious. "The smaller the town, the longer the memory. Next to the university, that school district is the largest employer in the valley. Each employee has a family; aunts and uncles, cousins, friends, ward members. You get my drift. It's going to be difficult to set up shop if we've offended a third of the population."

She gripped the side of the table so she didn't fall on the floor. "You want to live here? Like, forever?" A shocking photo of her future flashed through her mind. She and Elliot and half dozen blond kids with straight white teeth standing in front of a comfortable ranch-style home with a two-car garage. They'd look like an advertisement for *Dental Hygiene Week*. Elliot would be the handsome orthodontist everyone loved, a Little League coach, president of the school board, and a pillar of the community. But what would she be? An appendage? A pleasant accessory standing on his left, doing his books and keeping stats at the games.

"Sure. Why live anywhere else? A small town is a great place to raise a family."

"You never mentioned this before." She jumped up, her arms tucked tightly around her body.

"I just assumed you understood."

"There's nothing here for me," she choked.

"I'm here. Our kids will be here. My family's here."

Sunday dinners at Rachel's, flaky piecrusts and censure stretched out on the horizon as far as her eye could see. Trust obstinate Rachel to live into her nineties, the equivalent of two thousand dinners, give or take a few lemon Jell-O salads. Nina's throat constricted, but this was not the time to gag.

"There's nothing here for me *to do*." Her pulse was racing.

"People in New York think that about Salt Lake. It's all relative."

"Actually, I get a little claustrophobic in Salt Lake," she said. "There's a big world out there, Elliot."

"People live in their neighborhoods. You think you're going to be involved in a million different things, but most people aren't. You'll be busy with the kids' schools and—don't look at me like that, Nina."

"An orthodontist's wife in a small town. You've got to be kidding." She tapped a staccato rhythm against the edge of the table. "I guess I could be the president of the dental auxiliary. Spearhead a drive to collect used toothbrushes to send to the peasants in Outer Slobovia. Host teas and luncheons with toothpaste themes." She gave him a toothy grin.

He rolled his head back and stared at the ceiling, that Elliot-under-siege look on his face. He didn't speak for several minutes, then he clapped his hands twice as though he were silencing the crowd for an announcement. "Kids here have incredible personal freedom. They ride bikes to the park or to get an ice cream cone. They float the canal. Everyone will know our kids, know us. My children are not going to grow up bawling behind some chain-link fence at a day-care center in

Milwaukee. I want them to grow up in a small town with grandparents and cousins. That's it. Bottom line. So nix on the lawsuit."

"Why do you always get the bottom line?"

He just shook his head.

"For the last two hours, I've been organizing arguments and documenting what's gone on this year. I'm fighting back, and it feels great."

Elliot mouthed, "No," at her as though silence wouldn't provoke a rebuttal.

"We should have pounded this out before we got married," Nina said, sighing. "What were we thinking? No way am I going to live here." Elliot needed to take a few new locales for a test drive, kick the tires, slam a few doors, and leave Rachel pacing in the parking lot. "People who live in Milwaukee love it. Big Ten Football down the road. Mosquitoes large enough to be house pets." She grabbed his hands and pulled him to his feet. Maybe she could win this argument in the bedroom.

He rested heavy palms on her shoulders and studied her face. "Nina, I'm sick of fighting with you." They teetered on the tightrope stretched beneath them.

"Then let's not fight. Let's do something else. Let's throw together a picnic and head up the canyon or adopt a puppy with sad eyes or plan a trip to China. Anything."

"I'm not going to change my mind about something this important. You need to call your dad and tell him 'thanks, but no thanks' on the lawsuit."

She ran her finger around the edge of his ear. "Can we negotiate a cease-fire?" she murmured.

"Maybe." He raised one eyebrow. "Every other Tuesday. Holidays and Christmas."

She glanced over her shoulder at the papers arranged on the living room floor. "You know, Elliot, you have a low tolerance for making history."

30

A Letter of Acceptance

Grabbing her sweater, Nina caught her reflection in the mirror on the inside of the cupboard door and laughed as though she were sharing an inside joke with herself. She felt deliciously alive. She strode into the faculty lounge as if she owned it—not a trace of chagrin on her face. If those men thought she was cowed, they were mistaken.

Marlo's bluster about supervising the building of his father's new truck stop fizzled on Monday as the first article appeared in the local paper, the first installment of the gathering storm.

> *At a private meeting at the school district, local attorney Carl Renlund demands the Beginning Type teacher go or face criminal charges.*

Personally, Nina thought it was a bit much. Marlo wasn't going to be prosecuted—everyone knew that—and she would have settled for having him tarred and feathered and run out of town on a rail, but that wasn't going to happen either. At least he had a job. Maybe he'd turn into an entrepreneurial whiz and make loads of money selling pop and junk food to long-haul truckers.

Driving home, Nina laughed again. She'd take College Hill steps two at a time and wait for Elliot to finish his chem lab. Maybe they'd spread a blanket on the slope under the trees and have a picnic, deviled eggs and strawberries. The possibilities seemed endless.

She had a list in her purse of Patterson's informants that Marsha had whispered to her between classes. Some she could have guessed (the choir teacher for sure), but others were a surprise. Kent Werner was playing both sides of the fence. The bounder. She'd give Rick a quick call before she changed into jeans and a T-shirt.

The lilac tree by their window was in full, fragrant bloom, but the front door wasn't locked. She took a step back, her lips pursed. Flipping the corner of the mat, she saw the spare key. Elliot never forgot to lock the door. Holding her breath, she nudged the door open with her toe. He was sitting on the couch, not moving, staring at an envelope he held between his fingers as though it were combustible material and might burst into flames. The University of Virginia Law School logo was the return address. Rejections were a single sheet, so they both knew what that fat envelope contained. The rest of the mail littered the threadbare carpet.

She dropped her purse and slowly, untied the white lace choker around her neck, and let it dangle from her fingers.

"Open it," he said.

Without speaking, she slid a thumbnail under the flap and removed several pages. A colorful pamphlet fluttered to the floor. Staring at the insert covered with photos of students with grins on their faces, Elliot spoke slowly, reluctantly, as though the words left an acrid taste on his tongue. "Some guy told me two unnamed women teachers were assaulted at your school. It was in the paper today." He stared at her. "You were one, weren't you?"

"Last winter." She pressed her fingertips against her temples. *How did the paper get that?* "I meant to tell you, but then I just wanted to push the ugliness away. Pretend it never happened."

"He choked you." He spoke quietly, but his face was rigid with the effort. "What else did he do?"

"He roughed me up a little." She whispered, "I wanted to tell you, I really did, but I didn't want that creep to be part of our story. I didn't want him between us every time you reached for me."

He was so worked up listening to the fight in his head that he didn't hear a word she said. "So I hear this from a kid in chemistry. I panic. I cut class and run down the hill, so I'd be here when you got home, and I find *that* waiting in the mail." His empty palms fell against the slipcover.

"Elliot, let me explain." She hadn't felt this panicked since she was a little kid standing on a high dive.

He stared through her. His face was cold and still as though it were a shell, as though he'd been hollowed out and what was left was just a brittle exterior, an empty mask.

"That first night when you were so sick, I was sure you were going to die. I wanted to die too. I didn't know how I could keep breathing or go to school or eat. Living without you seemed impossible. And now this?" He looked at the envelope crumpled in her hand. "You're leaving me." He leaned against the cushion, his eyes round and dark. "Without a backward glance, you're going a couple of thousand miles away to Virginia," his voice rose, "to law school?"

"Elliot, you've got to listen to me. This is not what you think." She glanced at her watch. He'd been sitting here for an hour judging her with only this flimsy bit of evidence, and he'd passed sentence before the defense opened her mouth.

"Give me a break," he muttered. "I'm not dumb. You've been lying to me, deceiving me." He pointed at the letter in her hands. "That says it all, 'Congratulations, you've been accepted.' I live here. You live there. That's not a marriage."

"No." She shook her head. "You're overreacting."

"You didn't even tell me you'd applied."

"I didn't tell you because getting in was a long shot. Why have a big fight over something that might not happen?"

"I bet Lars knows everything. And your parents? And your brothers? Everyone knows—except me. They must think I'm a fool."

She clutched her throat with her open hand. "I needed to see, to know if I was good enough, if I could get in. I didn't think much beyond applying. I tried to tell you at Christmas, but you didn't want to listen. You've put up a wall about all this. And when we were going to have a baby, there didn't seem any point in telling you, because there was no way I could go. I put it out of my mind." She didn't mention the rejections in the box under her bed. She didn't tell him she raced home every afternoon to intercept the mailman.

"You're lying. You've been lying all year. This whole year has been a lie."

"Don't say that. It's not a lie." She tried to smile. "I love you."

"Does Lars know that pig went after you at school?"

Nodding slowly, she winced.

"Lars is the one you trusted. Not me." His shoulders collapsed.

"Lars always makes time for me."

"And he's in Virginia."

"Northern Virginia. Not Charlottesville." *Stupid thing to say.* She edged toward the couch. "I'm not in love with Lars. I'm in love with you."

"Stay where you are." The light drained out of the room that suddenly seemed so shabby and small. "I loved you so much."

The past tense slapped her face. "Elliot. Sit down. Let's talk through this. We can."

"I'll never trust you again. I can't stay here." He grabbed his backpack. The echo of the door slamming filled her head.

The telephone rang once. In a few seconds, it rang again. She didn't answer.

* * *

Hours stretched into long days. She washed the dishes and went to the grocery store. She picked up all her clothes and pushed the vacuum until she had a blister on her palm. She organized her sock drawer until it was almost as neat as Elliot's. Screaming, she grabbed handfuls of socks and tossed them in the air. She felt better—but only for a minute—then she collected the socks off the floor and arranged them in plastic baskets. Capitulation to socks, she'd achieved a new low.

Loading the laundry hamper into her car, she drove to the Laundromat, and as she watched the suds and the clothes go round and round in the front loader, she tried to think. Maybe if she could impress Elliot with her amazing ability to juggle all things at once, school and domesticity, she could drag him into the seventies. When she got home, she folded everything and ironed Elliot's shirts—with spray starch. What further proof could he want? But he wasn't there to see it.

Sunday afternoon, she covered the table with a pale pink cloth and stole a tulip from the neighbor's flower bed and arranged it in a budvase with a lilac sprig. She set the table with her wedding china and silver and cooked up a storm, but he didn't come. Around seven, Rachel called to say they were making homemade ice cream. "Don't stay home," she said, her voice was warm. "The kids would love to see you." *So*, Nina thought, *Elliot isn't hiding out at his mother's house*. Where was he?

A three-by-five card stuck in the edge of her mirror read, "Fortune sides with she who dares." She ripped it into a hundred tiny pieces and flushed them down an immaculate toilet bowl. She fell asleep that night and woke alone. She dreamed she heard Elliot's key in the lock. Stumbling to the door, she held it open, but only the spring breeze coming down from the canyon touched her as she stared into the darkness. "Where are you?" she whispered. Night after night, she woke repeating the 3:00 a.m. vigil with the wind ruffling her hair.

Assuming he'd come home during the day to eat and change clothes, she left a sandwich and a note inside the refrigerator. *Elliot, I love you*. She taped a piece of red thread on top of the front door so she could tell if it had been opened. When she got home on Tuesday night, the thread was loose, but the note was sealed.

Thursday afternoon, she knew he'd be working. She painted her toenails pale pink and fluffed out her hair. She stopped at the bakery and bought a small offering, two brownies with a half-inch of fudge frosting. Who could resist chocolate in a crisis?

Feeding specimens into the auto analyzer, Elliot didn't look up when she walked into the lab. "Elliot . . ." She smiled. "I brought you a treat." With a fair amount of trepidation, she held out the white sack. He glared at her for a couple of seconds before he strode into another room. There was a silence, past awkward, as the two other techs exchanged glances but couldn't meet her eyes.

"He's angry," Nina said stupidly.

"He mentioned that," the girl responded, sticking her pen in the bun on top of her head. "He's sleeping in the call room. There's a shower in there."

Nina dropped the sack on the desk and backed through the door. Hurrying down the hall, she touched icy fingers to cheeks that were burning. *Humiliation*, she thought, *isn't all that fun, even if you are a liar and a sneak*.

Every afternoon the telephone rang once, and then again. It was Rick. The firm had cut him two or three hours each day to work on the filing and the depositions. He'd started calling her "girl genius," and she didn't know if he liked her or if he was buttering up the boss's daughter. Either way, when she talked to him, her laughter surprised her. But after their superficial banter, he pressed her hard, made her question her own assertions, and defend the logic of her assumptions. Gradually, they refined their list of questions, and Friday afternoon, he announced the suit had been filed.

"Did the tape recorder come?" he asked.

"I've got it in my hand."

"I'll be amazed if *the boss* doesn't call you in. Probably Monday or Tuesday. He's going to be a caged beast, so you've got to be ready."

"I understand."

"These tape recorders are sensitive. If you're wearing jeans, it won't pick up. You need to keep it in the pocket of something loose, a light cotton skirt. Can you manage that?"

"Sure. But I thought you couldn't use tape recordings if the person didn't know they were being recorded."

"We'll use it in the depositions to keep the guy honest. It's a surprise, sort of like a left hook coming out of thin air."

She took a deep breath.

"Nina, are you okay? You don't sound good. I know this is scary, but honestly, what can the guy do that he hasn't already done? He can't fire you twice. Socking you in the face would be handing us a gift wrapped with a bow. All he can do is bluster, and that's what we want."

Glancing at the buttons on the tape recorder, she said, "I'll be okay."

"Everything steady on the home front? I need you focused next week."

Was her voice so easy to read? "I'll be ready."

"I'll call you on Monday. Keep your chin up."

She fingered the daisies she'd arranged in a mason jar. Elliot had been here today. What did he think when he walked into such an immaculate apartment? She made the bed every morning. And fluffed the pillows. Her clutter in the bathroom had vanished. No panty hose hung on the towel rack. What else could she do? Feeling desperate, she sank onto the couch and played with the tape recorder. She turned it on and off inside her skirt pocket and recorded her voice telling Elliot how much she loved him.

* * *

She didn't expect to see him at church on Sunday, and Rachel didn't extend an invitation for Sunday dinner. That was a dead give-away. He was boycotting her but not his family. She could imagine *that* conversation around the dinner table. They'd close ranks. Maybe she should have gone home this weekend, but she couldn't give up. Not yet, not while there was a chance.

She ducked down the hallway after Sunday School. Dodging several men in dark suits standing around the clerk's office, she knocked lightly on the bishop's door. The leader of their congregation, a kind man with a lined face and silver hair, was her last best hope.

"Could I speak to you for a minute?" she said.

* * *

She hadn't seen Elliot in two weeks. She perched on the sofa in the church foyer waiting for him to come through the glass doors and ignore her. It was one of those soft evenings in May everyone loved, but she felt like she was tiptoeing across a trapeze wire so high that the earth below had vanished. She'd arrived five minutes early, but now it was ten after seven and still no Elliot. He wasn't coming. Eyes closed, she played a Chopin prelude on the end table and wondered how it would feel to be unmarried.

The door to the bishop's office opened. She blinked. The bishop walked out and grasped her hand. "Come in, Nina."

Elliot was sitting in a chair opposite the large standard-issue desk. The wall behind him was pebbled cinder block painted off-white. How long had he been here? The other folding chair was so close she inadvertently brushed against his knee. He flinched, but when she muttered, "Sorry," he glanced at her with those soft brown eyes that looked like a couple of milk chocolates. Her heart leaped into her throat and her knees felt like mush.

The bishop sat across from them. Before their lengthy conversation Sunday afternoon, she'd only met him a time or two. Last fall he'd stopped by their apartment to meet the young couple, and he'd visited her in the hospital twice. He'd been great last Sunday, mopping her face with Kleenex and sharing half of a Three Musketeers candy bar. What had Elliot told him tonight?

Fingering a pen, the bishop paused a few minutes until the silence weighed heavily, then he spoke, "You'd be surprised to know how many marriages fail in the first year. You kids are teetering on the brink."

He paused again, but neither of them spoke or glanced at each other. "Okay." He took a deep breath. "Elliot, there are hundreds, thousands of girls on campus—a stone's throw away—who would love to stay at home and raise children. Why on earth did you choose Nina?"

Elliot looked up, flustered and surprised.

The bishop continued, "Obviously she's a pretty girl, but there are hundreds of pretty girls."

"I don't know. I fell in love with her the first time I saw her."

"Love at first sight? I don't buy that. Give me the particulars."

"She was sprinting down the street in Scotland to save me from some toughs." He fidgeted in his chair. "I've wondered this last year if we've had all this trouble because I was breaking mission rules, not literally, but certainly in spirit."

"You think you built your house upon the sand?"

"Yes, I do."

"Were you ever alone with Nina?"

"Just once, for about five minutes."

"Did you kiss her?"

"No, but I wanted to."

The bishop laughed, a deep full-throated laugh that made Nina smile.

"She wouldn't let me," Elliot added.

Still grinning, the bishop nodded at Nina. "Good for you." Then he looked back at Elliot. "So you choose a smart girl who's gone to Scotland—all by herself—to study poetry at a foreign university. Come on, Elliot. Why did you fall in love with Nina?"

Elliot flushed. "I know where you're going with this. I fell in love with Nina because she's bright and inquisitive. And amazingly independent. We were standing on top of Rule's Tower looking out at the North Sea, and that was just it. I was in love."

The bishop looked at Nina. "And what about you? When did you know you loved Elliot?"

"That same moment." She glanced at Elliot, but he was staring at their translucent reflection in the window. "Getting married was the last thing on my mind. And suddenly there he was, like it was meant to be, climbing the tower steps. I was supposed to meet a friend, an Irish guy I was dating, but he was late. And Elliot and I stood there together and . . . what can I say? It was magic."

The bishop gave Elliot a serious look. "But now, because Nina's bright and inquisitive and independent, you're through. Toss in the towel and move home?"

"It's more than that." For the last two weeks, he'd been building a case, layering each incriminating brick side-by-side, walling her out. Now, sitting here speaking to the bishop, Elliot didn't sound angry. He sounded stone cold, analytical, and Nina felt like her skin was being sliced off one square inch at a time. He spoke as though she'd been raised in Windsor Castle with an army of servants to do her bidding; and consequently, she'd been delivered unprepared, and worse, spoiled, like something disgusting from the back of the fridge. Nothing in the opening salvo was a surprise; she'd heard bits and pieces of this litany before, but what came next astonished her.

"And I'm sick of the whole Interstate Trucking thing, sick of the insinuations. I would have done anything, said anything to get Nina to marry me. I was that kind of infatuated. Head over heels. Money had nothing to do with it. Her dad and brothers think I'm a fortune hunter, and to tell the truth, members of my family think that too, but it's a lie. I wish she didn't have a dime."

"I don't. I won't till I'm thirty-five."

"So why didn't you tell me that? Why didn't you tell me about that pig attacking you? And law school? Doesn't moving to Virginia involve us both?" He was breathing hard and grasping the edge of the desk as though he needed support. "I guessed she was pregnant *two weeks* before she admitted it."

She winced. Her hands felt like dead weights banging against the chair. She stared at the pictures of past bishops on the wall, trying to focus on the bad haircuts and thick-framed glasses.

The bishop smiled sadly, his brow furrowed. "How do you feel right now, Nina?"

"Worthless." But what she really felt was sideswiped by this accident Elliot called a marriage.

"How do you feel, Elliot?" he asked.

"Like this is a waste of time. If Nina's moving to Virginia, we're done."

A moan escaped her before she could stifle it. *This is over,* she thought. *Let him have what he needs. Someone to blame.*

The bishop laced his fingers together on top of his desk. His knuckles were white. "Physical intimacy is an adventure; learning to please each other is very pleasant. Emotional intimacy, which is just as important, is more difficult. It takes time and effort to put each other first, to create trust and understanding."

Nina held up one hand, her fingers extended. "I'm number five. On Elliot's list." She started with her thumb. "School. Work. His family. Church. Finally, Nina, tied for a distant fifth with Sunday dinner."

The bishop's mouth curved up. "Urgent things get done, but important things rarely do. Why Virginia? Seems far away."

"I was rejected at the other places I applied. Wait-listed at the U. I probably fill some administrator's idea of an affirmative-action three-in-one. A token woman, Westerner, and Mormon. A walking case for broad-mindedness." She held her breath and touched Elliot's hand. "Come with me."

Elliot rolled his eyes.

"This is why I couldn't talk to you. I knew it would be a nonstop fight all year over something that might not even happen. What's the point?"

"Integrity."

"Oh, please."

The bishop sighed and looked over their heads at the chalkboard hanging on the wall. "Let's change direction here. Imagine a canyon," he said. "A young couple is down in the valley making their way through the rocks and the brush. The families of origin are on the hillside. They're either applauding or they're throwing rocks. Elliot, how has your family treated Nina?"

"Mostly rocks. But her family was firing arrows."

"His mother disliked me from the first minute." Nina spoke so quietly she almost didn't hear herself. "She wanted you to marry Pam."

"Pam?" There was softness in his mouth when Elliot formed the word. "You're never going to forgive Mom for that, are you?"

"It's not just Pam. Your world, Rachel's world, is so black and white. You assign a moral value to things that are inherently amoral."

"Wrong," Elliot said. "Some things are clear cut. Moms need to be at home. That's it. If a husband falls off a cliff or gets desperately ill, that's another thing, but raising children is a full-time job."

"But not for you," she said.

"I'm not a woman."

"That offends me."

"You've made that clear."

The bishop signaled a time-out. "Nina, describe your father's role in your family."

"Sometimes it felt like he didn't know what was going on, and then he'd show up at a critical tennis match or pick me up at school and take me to lunch. My mother was his eyes and ears, but he was behind the scenes moving the props around. He wasn't above incentivizing us to get us to do what he wanted."

"Bribes," Elliot said.

"Bribes," she agreed. "But he was always in our corner."

"How would you describe Elliot's father?" The bishop leaned back in his chair and laced his fingers together."

"He's a sweetheart, but he functions in a parallel universe. Rachel's the only power player."

"Nina, do you want to have children? A family?" The bishop leaned forward.

"Of course I do. But I don't want to do it the way Elliot's mother did. She raised a big family in a small house on a shoestring, and it's worked because Rachel's right there with her hand on the rudder, and everyone is sure if she lets go, for even a minute, the whole ship will sink beneath the waves."

Elliot ran his fingers through his hair until it stood on end, but he didn't speak. This wasn't the end of the world, but there was a bombed-out crater where her heart used to be, and a single word ricocheted inside her head. *Infatuated.* He'd dismissed his feelings as though an infatuation were a virus, curable with sleep, a variety of fruits and vegetables, and a crew of old friends.

The bishop sat up straight in his chair. "Okay. I'm going to make some assumptions and give you some assignments. The first assumption is that we all want this marriage to work. The second assumption is that it's going to take some compromise and adjusting. Elliot, no drawing lines in the sand.

"The first assignment is that you are not to talk about *anything* you've discussed with me—*not with each other or anyone else.*" He raised one finger. "And that will be tough. No arguing. Bite your tongues if you need to. No third-party stuff. Do not involve your parents. The second assignment is I want you to sleep together, or whatever kids call it now days. Nobody's on the couch. Is that clear?"

Nina squeezed her eyes shut.

"Are you praying together?"

Elliot shook his head. "Not lately."

Nina said, "And when we do, they're not prayers. They're small horizontal lectures. 'Please bless Nina that she'll see the light and do what I want.'"

"Okay." The bishop held up a finger. "For the next week, you're going to express gratitude for at least five things you appreciate in the other person. And they have to be a different five each night. And the only blessing you're going to ask for is to feel love for each other.

"One more thing. Who's in charge of Nina?" They both raised their hands. "Brother Spencer, we're going to release you from this calling with a vote of thanks. The only person's behavior you can really change is your own." He handed his scriptures over the desk to Elliot. "Read Moses 3:24."

Elliot cleared his throat. "'Therefore shall a man leave his father and his mother, and shall cleave unto his wife; and they shall be one flesh.'"

Raising one eyebrow, the bishop gave Elliot a stern look. "I'm your bishop. You've got to trust me on this. Will you do what I ask? For a week?"

Elliot sat not moving for too long, studying his palms, before he chanced a look in her direction. "Okay. For a week."

Nina was surprised when the bishop stood and placed a hand on both their shoulders and offered a simple prayer. His touch felt more like a blessing. Then he shook Elliot's hand. "Go home with your wife. No detours."

~ 31 ~

Tape Recordings

Sitting at the kitchen table across from his parents, Elliot looked at the BLT next to carrot sticks and a pile of potato chips. He was starving, but the price of lunch had yet to be paid.

"What did the bishop say, Son?" Rachel asked.

"Well, he made an interesting request. He asked us not to discuss anything we'd talked about with anyone or each other." He placed his hands around half the sandwich and carried it carefully to his mouth. He sighed and closed his eyes. *How does Mom do it? How can she consistently make such a great sandwich?*

"It's times like these that parents can really help. Talk through things," his mother said. "Set a better course."

"I gave him my word."

"So you went home last night?" his dad asked.

"I did."

"And how was that?" his mother nudged a carrot stick toward him with her fingertip.

"Awkward."

He was suddenly grateful for the bishop's assignment. He could hide behind it. The tense moments in the living room as he and Nina stood looking at one another, unsure of themselves, not knowing what to say or who should be the first to say it, were not his mother's business. He wasn't proud of the way he treated Nina, rolling away from her in bed and listening to see if she'd cry.

His mother leaned forward as though she were going to pry his mouth open, just like she did when Gordy swallowed a goldfish on a dare and started to choke. Calmly, as though she retrieved fish every day, she reached her long fingers down Gordy's throat and grabbed the tail of that fish and saved Gordy's young life. She was ready to do the same with him—reach down his throat and pull the story out, word by word, examine it on the kitchen table, poke it with a fork, and see if she could make it wiggle. No thanks.

Her strong fingers touched his arm. "Do what you need to do, Son, to live without regrets."

Which regrets?

She sensed his confusion. That maternal intuition could focus in like a laser given any opening—a twitch in his left eye, a dropped syllable, or a few hairs pulled askew.

"I understand why you fell in love with her." Rachel sat back and brushed a few crumbs off the kitchen table. "She's beautiful and warm and interesting, but you didn't know her. Going to law school might be a better fit for her. There are some women—perfectly good people—who aren't cut out for marriage and family. A temple marriage is a sacred commitment, but it shouldn't be a life sentence."

He bristled at the disdain in her voice.

She retrieved a milk bottle from the fridge and refilled his glass. "I can't see you living in a city, picking up a couple of tired, cranky children at day care or a babysitter's, coming home to a dirty, cluttered house, and tossing a couple of TV dinners in the oven. That lifestyle would make you miserable."

He picked up the second half of his sandwich. "I promised I wouldn't talk about this."

"Well, we don't need to say anything else, but remember one thing, lots of marriages flounder in the first year or two. I can think of six or seven. They were accidents—no one's fault. Accidental marriages." She patted his shoulder awkwardly.

The one unfailing constant in his life was how much his mother loved him. She'd cut off her arm if he needed a spare. If push had come to shove and his mother had needed to work, she would have been a great heavy-equipment operator. A hard hat on her head and wearing a pair of striped overalls, she could have driven a steamroller and made highways through granite mountains. She was a strong woman.

"Well, I've got to be getting back to work," his father said. "Can I give you a ride up the hill?"

Elliot glanced at his watch. "Sure. I've got a one-thirty class."

He sat in the grimy cab of his dad's truck with the faded Spencer's Feed and Seed logo on the door. Neither of them spoke until his dad stopped in front of the physiology building and Elliot swung open the door.

"Losing Nina would be a mistake, Elliot."

"It doesn't seem like it should be this hard—not all the time."

His father just smiled.

* * *

Later that afternoon as he was running down the stairs on College Hill, Elliot thought about what his dad had said. Did he want to lose Nina—or punish her? It was a beautiful May afternoon. Pink blossoms from crab apple trees covered the sidewalk, and tulips were in full bloom. Maybe he'd grab Nina by the hand and they'd go for a walk. He'd apologize for last night. They could stroll down to Baskin Robbins for an ice cream cone. He examined the jumble of change he pulled out of his pocket. Maybe they could stop at the elementary school playground and he'd push her on the merry-go-round. He pictured her laughing and all that blonde hair blowing around her face. They'd stopped there last fall. She sat on his lap on the swings, and they buried their bare feet in the warm sand. She'd recited bits of a poem, Robert Frost talking about swinging on the branches of a birch tree. The motion reminded her, and she'd repeated it twice.

One could do worse than be a swinger of birches.

Maybe that's what they'd do, swing higher and higher. Maybe they'd laugh and play in the soft spring evening and clear the cobwebs out of their heads. Remember how it felt to be carefree and in love.

* * *

He called out her name as he strode through the door. But the apartment was still. He glanced around the immaculate interior; only a neatly piled stack of her schoolwork was out of place and a funny-looking cylinder not much larger than a cigarette lighter sitting on the kitchen table next to a mason jar full of daisies. She'd taped a note on the fridge.

At a job interview. Catch you later.

Sitting down on a chair, he fiddled with the small machine. It was a recording device. He flipped it on. "*Pushed around by a little girl like you.*" The tinny voice dripped venom. What was Nina up to now? He pushed rewind with his thumbnail. The whirring noise stopped, and he pushed play.

> *Elliot, Elliot, Elliot. Where are you, Elliot? I love you, you big lug. I miss you.*

There was a singsong quality to her voice, and he couldn't imagine why she was leaving him such a strange message on this little machine.

> *I want you to come home. I want to throw you on the couch and pounce on you. I am so sick of all the fights. You need to buck up and join the rest of the human race. It's the seventies, for crying out loud. I'm not your servant. I'm a person too, but I love you. I miss you. I want you to come home. I want to kiss your goofy face. Right now. Come home right now.*

Happier than he'd felt in days, he rewound the tape and listened again. He listened to *right now*, then there was a shuffling noise and a couple of clicks and he heard Nina speak.

> "*You wanted to see me?*"
>
> "*The superintendent sent this over this morning. He's plenty mad, and he asked me if this was going to go anywhere, and I told him no. Do you know why I could tell him that?*"
>
> "*No. I don't.*"
>
> "*Loyalty. There's not a person on this faculty who will back you up. In fact, they'll line up to say you've been nothing but trouble this entire year. This mess started at my school, and it ends right here—today.*"

Elliot heard the sound of paper ripping.

"That's not the only copy."

"It is as far as you're concerned."

"Wrong. You dismissed me without cause."

"Oh no. I had plenty of cause because you don't understand loyalty. Walking into that dean's office showed a clear lack of understanding."

"You never observed any of my classes."

"I know what's going on in my school."

"Marlo assaulted me."

"What did you expect? Calling him what you did."

"And Janice Walker? Was that her fault?"

"Janice will keep her mouth shut or she'll be out of a job."

"This place is a zoo. You knew what was going on in Marlo's classes and you didn't do anything."

"You got those little girls riled up over nothing."

"That's not true. Those girls came to me for help. They were being manhandled and humiliated. You've made no effort to control Marlo, and I've been victimized by continuous dirty tricks this entire year."

"And every man on this faculty will swear that you haven't. Call your dad and tell him to call off his dogs. This is going nowhere. No one's going to risk losing his job for you. In two weeks, you're just a bump in the road."

"You wouldn't pressure people to lie if you hadn't done anything wrong."

"I'm not going to be pushed around by a little girl like you."

There was a pause on the tape. Elliot leaned forward and stared at the device in his hand.

"The thirty-first of May, five minutes after the bell rings I want you out of this building. Now get out of my office."

So much anger. He envisioned Nina in that old office, circling around the desk with a knife in her hand, getting ready to grapple with a grizzly bear. But that wasn't what she called him. She said he was a shark, all cartilage and no bone. Nina was in way over her head. How was she going to finish the year? Two more weeks?

The telephone rang once, but when he picked up the receiver, no one was there. It rang again.

"Hello."

"Is Nina available?"

"Who's calling?"

"Rick Hamilton. Hey, if this is a bad time, I'll give her a call tomorrow."

"She's not here."

"Well, just tell her I called."

Rick, the junior associate in her father's office. The muscles in Elliot's neck tensed. What had gone on the past two weeks while his back was turned? What he'd said about the lawsuit had fallen on deaf ears.

He heard Nina's footsteps on the concrete stoop. She hurried in the door. Dark circles under her eyes looked chalky. She seemed skittish, wary.

"Rick called." He didn't like the guy and he'd never even met him. "I guess your lawsuit's underway."

"Dad thinks it might pressure the district into reinstating my contract next year." She gave him a tentative smile.

"And how's that going? Everyone behaving nicely?" He placed the tape recorder on the table.

She ignored the gesture and glanced at the fridge. "Did you see my note? Congratulate me. I have a job. Two, actually."

She wasn't going to tell him the truth, and she wasn't going to talk to the chummy guy on the phone. Not until tomorrow when she had the kitchen to herself.

"Aren't you interested?" She pushed herself up onto the kitchen counter and sat there swinging her legs.

He nodded his head but his mouth twisted. *No arguing and no sleeping on the couch.* "How can you be mad already?" she murmured. "I haven't even said anything."

"I'm not mad." He gripped the back of a chair. "Tell me about your job."

She grabbed a banana and gave it a forehand swing. "I'm going to teach group tennis lessons for City Parks and Recreation. Three one-hour sessions each morning, five days a week. If I get enough repeats, maybe they'll add more sessions. They called me last week. So that's good news."

"Where did you go this afternoon?"

"I got a job at the Peppercorn Grill. They have a liquor license, so evidently the tips are great. At least that's what one of the other girls told me. And here's the kicker, I get to choose one entrée from the menu each night. Think of what we'll save on groceries."

"When do you work?"

"I'll start Memorial Day Weekend. I'll work Friday, Saturday, Sunday, Tuesday, and Wednesday. Four o'clock to midnight." She set the banana on the Formica and lowered herself off the counter. Turning away from him, she grasped the edge of the sink. Students, strolling down the street, laughed and called out to each other. "I thought you'd be pleased," she said. "Clearly, you're not."

"I thought we'd have evenings together." It wasn't a thought he'd entertained until the prospect was removed, until he'd heard the familiarity in Rick's voice. Now all he could think about were long summer evenings walking on campus, sitting on the side of the hill and watching the sunset, listening to Nina, holding her hand and kissing her to interrupt the flow of her talk.

She didn't turn back toward him. "You're always gone at night. I thought you were going to summer school."

"Just one class. And I'm always home on Friday night. I have been all year."

"I know that, but I thought you'd be pleased."

"Why would I be pleased not to have you here?"

She walked away from him down the tiny hallway. "I've got a miserable headache. I think I'll lie down for a little while."

He followed her down the hall and grasped the doorjamb. "I thought we could go for a walk. Maybe get an ice cream cone."

Her head on the pillow, she turned away. "I had a really ugly session with the principal this afternoon." He heard tears in her voice. "I just can't do any more."

Any more? Was that what he'd become? He picked up his backpack and thought about going to the library. Finals started next week. He stared through the window screen. School was almost out. Evening air, soft and warm, reminded him of last spring and slipping that little diamond onto her finger.

He walked into the bedroom quietly. He stood over the bed until she felt his presence and turned toward him, mascara smudged under her eyes. Sitting beside her, he didn't speak; he just tapped the side of his face until she finally laughed. "What are you doing?"

"This is the goofy face. You know, the one you wanted to kiss."

She gave him a blank look.

"I listened to your tape. The whole thing. I'm sorry about the principal. He's horrible."

"You weren't supposed to hear that. I meant to erase it."

He touched her cheek. "Don't be embarrassed. I did hear it. I played it three times." He lifted her up against his chest and smelled her hair. "Come on, Nina. Let's leave trouble behind for a little while and see if we can find a circus that needs a couple of lion tamers."

Part Three

The End
of the Beginning

~ 32 ~

Magic Isn't Magic

Dry, record-breaking temperatures didn't make the summer any easier or tempers less volatile. The newlyweds were primed, ready to argue, all the time. Their pain and disappointment hovered near the surface as though each had been cheated by the other. He'd been certain she'd capitulate, repent after the boldness of her deception, but she didn't. She nursed her anger, and so did he.

Elliot sat on the bed on a hot Sunday afternoon and watched her hang her dress on a padded hanger and run the zipper up the back.

"I'm sorry about dinner," she said over her shoulder, trying to look nonchalant. She knew he was watching her.

"It was fine."

"Your salad was delicious, but the pot roast was a mess. I don't know what went wrong. I followed the directions exactly."

"Following a recipe isn't like building a model airplane. You have to taste as you go."

And suddenly she was furious. Zero to sixty in five seconds. He couldn't believe it.

Sitting beside him on the bed, she yanked on her panty hose and wiggled into her uniform. He tossed the passbook next to her on the bedspread. She gave it a cursory glance.

"Amazing. I made more in tips over the Fourth of July weekend than I earned in a whole month teaching."

"How do you do it?" He leaned over to tie his shoes.

Frowning, she settled the elastic waistband over her hips. "I never write anything down. It makes people nuts and becomes something of a game. They're sure they can trip me up, and when they can't, they leave a bigger tip." She tied on the frilly white apron.

"So how do you do that?"

"It's a piece of cake," she huffed. "Excuse the food metaphor. People look like what they order. Skinny women order Shrimp Louis with dressing on the side. Red-faced, imminent heart attacks always have the prime rib. University types have pasta. Fat blondes over fifty order the pork roast and mashed potatoes. It's not rocket science."

"That's it? The ten-dollar tip?"

"Oh no."

She brushed more color on her cheek bones. "That's just the beginning. With university types, I sound like a Rhodes Scholar, who happens to be a spunky student-wife slaving away putting her husband through school. 'Yes, ma'am' and 'No, sir' come out of my very demure mouth every third sentence. When I serve rednecks, I drop all my *g's*. You know, *goin', sayin' pleasin'*. When men say something crude or pinch me when their wives aren't *lookin'*, I just giggle and wink."

The bitterness in her voice knocked the wind out of his chest, a body blow to the solar plexus. "Quit the job," he said.

"I just flutter my eyelashes, and say 'Whatever you want, darlin'.'" She painted her lips red. "Isn't that what pretty girls do to get what they want? To earn big tips. If I'd learned all this ten months ago, I'd still have the pleasure of teaching at Clear Creek come fall." She grabbed a couple of cheap, jangly bracelets out of her drawer. "And maybe you'd still be in love with me." She glanced at him, waiting, but his jaw clenched, and he turned toward the harsh western sun streaming through the window.

She raised her voice. "But this clinches a good tip." She undid the two top buttons on her uniform. "I lean way over when I put their food on the table. 'Careful, honey, these plates are hot.'"

He grabbed her wrist. "Stop it. You're punishing me, and worse, you're punishing yourself. This isn't some game you're playing."

She pushed his hand away. "Sure, it is. I just never knew the rules." She ran a brush through her soft flyaway hair and sprayed perfume on her wrists. She checked the bedside clock. "I've got to go, but I'll tell you what, Elliot, we're both home tomorrow night. Why don't you plan *somethin'* fun? Maybe a lesson on cooking the perfect pot roast or scrambling eggs."

The slamming door shook the walls. She adamantly refused invitations to his mother's Sunday dinners, so he stayed home with her, and this was his thanks? He waited a few minutes to walk down the hill to the hospital to his quiet job in the lab, drawing blood and feeding specimens into the auto analyzer, something he could understand.

She got home late the nights she worked, past midnight. She peeled off her aqua uniform and dropped it on the living room floor before she curled up on the couch. If he was awake, waiting for her to come home, she sensed it and stayed away. If she heard the regular sounds of his breathing and knew he was asleep, then she came to him in the darkness, the smell of a deep fat fryer in her hair. Lifting the sheet, she slipped inside his dreams. Bleary eyed, he woke to her light touch tracing his arm and the gentle pressure of her lips on his face.

Later, drowsy and spent, he'd hold her tightly and whisper how much he loved her until they both drifted away. Waking in the morning to sunlight filling the room, he'd reach for her, expecting a smile, some knowing wink, or raised eyebrow—suggesting a change in the marital climate—but nothing in her face betrayed her. Except for the occasional erratic outburst, she was unfailingly polite, but the eyes above that sunburned nose evaded him. If he smiled suggestively, or made some casual reference, joking or appreciative, to her nocturnal visits, she turned away as though it were a secret to protect, a shadow that couldn't bear the brunt of day. And then she was gone, in the shower and out the door on her way to the courts at 7:45.

Stretching and yawning, he'd wander into the kitchen, but her food-stained uniforms were never left on the floor. Her towel was always hung, folded neatly in thirds, from the rack. The bathroom counter was wiped clean, and her bottles and potions were nowhere in sight. She left her tips in an envelope in his drawer, bills, nickels, and dimes, like an admission or an apology—or penance. Her cereal bowl was washed and put back in the cupboard. It was as though he lived in the apartment alone. No trace of Nina, but she was everywhere.

He met her at the bishop's office, their weekly session, late in July. She nodded at him as he walked through the door. The bishop stood to shake his hand. Taking off his glasses, the man made the ear pieces into a triangle that changed shape nervously. "I've been thinking hard about you two. A couple of things occurred to me." He set his glasses on the desk, cupped his chin in his palm, and studied them both. "You come from such different family configurations, and like it or not, those patterns, those scripts, create your expectations."

Nina laughed sadly. "And Elliot says he doesn't need me to be like his mother."

"I'd take it a step further. After listening to you both for a couple of months, I'd be willing to bet you and Elliot's mother are very similar. A couple of generations apart, but both strong, independent women. I think that's what attracted Elliot to you. You're a person who can run the domestic side of his life so he's free to pursue his goals." Nina stared balefully at the off-white walls.

Uncomfortable, Elliot cleared his throat. "And how do I fit into Nina's script? Her father's incredibly busy. He's got about a million irons in the fire."

"I'm not sure, but I bet Nina's father gave her permission to follow her aspirations. He opened doors, gave advice, paved the way, and then stood back ready to pick her up if she fell or applaud if she succeeded. I don't see you stepping into that role. But like I say, I'm not sure, but I'm worried about Nina." He gazed at her gently. "It's my sense you're struggling."

Elliot answered, "She's vanishing." Every time they argued, each time she erupted, and every time he didn't bite his tongue, she got a little smaller and seemed a little further away.

"Vanishing or retreating?" the bishop asked.

"You both make me sound like a cloaked woman waiting on the strand for the ocean to wash me out to sea." She glanced over the bishop's shoulder to the open window. "It's just so sad when the magic isn't magic anymore. When I was a little girl, a magician did an assembly at my school and showed us his tricks. His bouquet of roses came out of a tube in his sleeve. The rabbit's mashed in a compartment in a hat. The dove doesn't work alone." She shrugged. "I loved the illusion, but now it's gone." Her hands folded in her lap, she sat in the chair not moving. "Whimsy's gone. So sad."

Elliot glanced at her. "I'm not a reincarnation of Robert Burns?"

"Nope. You're Rachel's firstborn son and you grew up on Maple Avenue. And I'm not Mary, Queen of Scots. I'm just a girl who spoils everything I touch. You should have married Pam."

"Pam." The bishop nodded, remembering the name.

"The girl who waited, and then I stole Elliot and ruined his life."

Elliot touched her fingertips. "Pam would never have made me happy."

She gave him a half smile. "No law school for perfect Pam."

"You can still change your mind."

Frustrated, the bishop pressed his palms down on the top of his desk. "You two want the same thing, a happy marriage and a family, but you've let one problem escalate until you've built a wall between you that feels insurmountable." He bumped his chair back and dropped his hands in his lap. "I can't help you until you're committed to being married to each other." He frowned, and deep creases crossed his brow. "My flawed wife and her flawed husband are going to take our crew of demanding, spoiled children to the beach. We'll have a wonderful time, and then we'll come back in ten days sunburned and grumpy. I'll be waiting to hear what you decide you want to do. I'd like you two to go to the temple a couple of times while I'm gone."

Elliot closed his eyes, knowing what Nina would say, *No more promises that I can't keep*, but instead she shook her head silently. The bishop sighed.

* * *

Two days later, sitting at the kitchen table staring at the same equation he'd been trying to memorize for an hour and a half, Elliot snapped his pencil in two. The kitchen was hot, and a fly was buzzing against the window screen. He'd flipped it twice with a dish towel, but it evaded him and made a frantic dash around the room every five minutes. He glanced at the clock. Nina was just starting her third lesson. He could watch the end of her class and maybe take her to lunch, but he'd have to hurry.

He ran down the stairs behind the high school to the canal bank and stood under the trees catching his breath. Slender and tanned with a yellow visor pushing back her hair, Nina was on the courts, patiently hitting the ball across the net to ten little eight-year-olds who took turns stepping forward to swing at the ball. There were loose balls, at least two or three dozen, all over the painted green surface. Elliot didn't know how the kids kept from tripping. They must have radar in their toes. He heard Nina laugh and watched her tousle their hair, correct their grips on the rackets, and hit more balls over the net.

In a few minutes station wagons started to arrive. As the kids collected their bags, Nina called out to the mothers—more tomorrow, same time, real progress. She stood waving as they drove away. Then she walked onto the court. She bounced a ball with the flat of her racket until it rose waist high, then she smashed it into the other court. She dropped the other balls in her basket. Standing alone, she tossed ball after ball into the air, and in one graceful, fluid motion, brought her racket down with a fury that drove the serve into the opposite court. She was laid bare in the glare of the sunlight. Elliot had no idea her arm was so strong. If he got in the way of one of those balls, it would kill him. She collected the balls, changed sides, and pounded dozens of serves into the opposite court. Finally, she tore the visor off her head and threw it on the grass. She dried the sweat on her face and the back of her neck with a towel she'd flung over the net. Finding shade under a tree, and with her knees pulled up to her chest, she looked past the court into the trees bordering the canal.

Surprised when he sat down on the grass next to her, she flashed him a quick smile.

"I'm taking you to lunch," he said, "and to see where you go during the day when you're avoiding me."

"I'm not avoiding you. It's just that apartment's too empty." She lay back in the grass and looked up through the branches of the willow tree. "Sometimes I go to the city library. It's air conditioned and quiet. I read the *Washington Post*. See what's happening. It's hard to get my head around Nixon resigning. And no blood. No guns." She glanced at her wristwatch as though his presence were tedious, interrupting her routine. "Sometimes I fall asleep in those big leather chairs behind the stacks."

He plucked at blades of grass. "What else do you read?"

"Lots of things. Everything's changing. What does it mean to be a woman? No one knows." She tapped his knee with her tennis racket.

"You and I are caught in the crosscurrents. People like your mom hold onto the way things were done in the past, but you can't rein people in with nostalgia. There's nothing intrinsically valuable about baking your own bread or making jam. You want to live your life as though we still lived in the fifties. Good luck."

"I don't know, Nina. There are some constraints. Men and women are so different."

"That's a myth."

"No, it's not."

"So," she said. "You're going to tell your daughters they have to be nurses, but your sons can be doctors? How are you going to explain that? What if your daughters are more capable or smarter than your sons?"

Your instead of *our* knotted his stomach. "I'll tell my daughters that if they want to be doctors, someone else will raise their children." He couldn't seem to help himself and kept poking that sore place between them. He lay down next to her and propped himself up on his forearm. He felt the muscle in her bicep with his free hand. "You're amazingly strong. What do you do after the library?"

"I go home and get ready for work. Pretty boring."

They both sat on the grass without speaking for several minutes, marshaling their thoughts for another round.

"Did you do the bishop's assignment?" He'd asked her to question a young mother juggling a professional career and small children.

"I talk to Betty at the restaurant every night," she said. He'd heard about Betty before, met the heavyset bleached blonde once. She shared Nina's shift at the restaurant. "She rails at her ex-husband on the phone, but he just hangs up on her. It's a mess. He quit sending child support even though the judge told him he has to come through."

"Why doesn't she haul him back into court?"

"She'd have to hire an attorney, and she doesn't have five extra cents. So she's stuck. She and the kids are sinking below the poverty line, and that jerk just bought a new car. She leaves her four-year-old with her eight-year-old when she comes to work. How's that for scary?"

He traced her profile with a blade of grass.

"That tickles." She knocked his forearm from under his head and he hit the ground.

He rolled over and stared up into the leaves. "My last test is Friday. The bishop will be back next week." And he'd want a commitment.

She shook the grass off her white skirt. "Where are you taking me for lunch? I'd love a raspberry milkshake. And french fries." She took the hand he offered to pull herself off the grassy slope. "You know, there's no one to help someone like Betty access the legal system."

"Why don't you call Rick? He's doing your suit pro bono."

"Dad's firm doesn't do family law." She tapped the button in the middle of his shirt. "There needs to be legislation to stop those men from ducking their child support by hiding in another state."

He lifted her chin so she had to look him directly in the eyes. "Now you want to run for the legislature?"

She jerked her head away. "No, but I could craft legislation."

He wasn't sure how to respond. He wanted to reel her back in, but she was like a kite played out to the end of his string. One strong breeze and the string would snap, even if he managed to hold on. He knew she was leaving, long before she did; he'd known it all summer.

* * *

The day before she left, he knew, sitting on her right in sacrament meeting. Only the noise of an errant bee broke the dense quiet. A pen in her hand, she drew lines and squiggles or random words in the margin of the program. She let the sacrament tray pass by her. He took the pen from her fingers and wrote, *Why?* Then he handed the pen back to her.

I'm not a good person, she wrote.

He rested the paper against his knee. *What have you done?*

Nothing bad, but we both know what I am.

I love you, he wrote and underlined it twice.

No. You love a girl you invented who happens to have my face. We both know what I am. I'm a girl who misplaces babies. I'm not to be trusted.

He grabbed her hand and tucked it under his arm next to his chest.

Elliot knew that night when he held Nina in the double bed with his feet hanging over the edge of the mattress. He held her until he felt her quiet, rhythmic breathing, but his chest was damp. Tears he couldn't hear, he felt.

She left all her things and took only her purse as though she were running an errand, making a quick stop at the grocery store, or dashing into Parks and Recreation to grab her last check, and she'd be right back. It was as though she hadn't known she was leaving, been surprised to find herself headed south on the highway, but once she found herself going that direction, the momentum carried her away.

The next morning the restaurant called. "Nina didn't come to work last night. Is she coming today? We're shorthanded."

He would have been frightened, called the police, alerted the highway patrol, or searched for Marlo's truck—if he hadn't found her note on his pillow.

33

A Chick Named Joan

Barbara set iced lemonade on the glass tabletop next to Bill, who was sitting in a chair next to the pool.

"Is Nina in her room?"

She nodded.

"How is she?"

"Her hair's gone. She went to that five dollar barber on Fourth South. It's short. Maybe an inch on top. She's quit wearing her contacts and no makeup."

"Coke bottles in a gold frame?"

"She looks like a cross between Joan of Arc and a baby chick." Barbara sighed. "Not a radical feminist."

He watched a beach ball floating in the pool near the drain.

She ran her finger down the condensed moisture on the side of his glass. "He left her last May—for two weeks. She's convinced he wouldn't have come back if their bishop hadn't intervened."

"How did I miss that? I was up there in June a couple of times."

"She's playing this close to her chest," she said.

"Or else she doesn't know what she wants. That's probably closer to the truth."

Barbara walked over and grabbed a beach ball and tossed it onto the grass. She stood staring down at the water. "She didn't bring anything with her. There's nothing in her car. She just picked up her purse and stepped out of her life."

"Leaving poor Elliot in the mausoleum."

She nodded and sat down on a wrought iron chair.

"What's she been doing all day, besides the haircut?"

"Playing the piano." She drummed both sets of fingers on the table. "I can handle the classical stuff, but when she played Gershwin, I closed the door to our bedroom and just bawled." She murmured the lyric, " 'Someday he'll come along, the man I love. And he'll be big and strong, the man I love.' "

"More drama at the Rushforths'."

"She'll go back in a minute if he calls," Barbara said.

"I'm not so sure." He traced his finger around the rim of the glass. "She's finally encountered someone more stubborn than she is." He looked up at her. "If we'd pushed the marriage, she'd still be single. I'm surprised Elliot hasn't figured that out, the way she digs in her heels."

"Be fair." She raised her eyebrows. "New marriage. New in-laws. New job. New town. A miscarriage. It was too much—for anyone."

"I reviewed Rick's depositions," Bill said. "That school was a snake pit. How much of this trouble with Elliot is fallout?" He sipped his lemonade. "I sat in on the deposition with Marlo Fletcher and with the principal. It made them very uncomfortable."

"A furious father glaring at them."

"I didn't glare. I just passed Rick a few terse questions."

"Sorry. I know you."

He stood up slowly and ambled out onto the lawn. She followed him and put her hand on his shoulder. He covered her hand with his own.

"The poor kid's a lump of modeling clay. Everyone's tried to shape her into something she's not." She gave a genteel snort. "Those male teachers wanted an in-house fantasy in room seven."

"Well, it's payback time," he said.

"And Elliot—and that mother of his—wants Nina to be a cross between me and some perfect sitcom mother, June Cleaver or Harriet Nelson."

He gave her a sharp look.

"And you." She poked him with her finger. "You've pushed a legal career since Oliver taught Nina to lisp the Pledge of Allegiance when she was three."

"Are you angry with me?"

"She can't spend her life pleasing you. Let go."

"It's just that she's so bright."

"Oh, she can take an idea and run with it, but she doesn't have much in the way of common sense, and we both know it."

"Don't be too hard on her," he said. "She's only twenty-two. Just a girl."

"Your little girl." She smiled sadly. "It's so hard to listen to her cry, Bill."

"I know, Sweetheart, I know."

* * *

Sweaty and tangled in the sheets the next morning, it took Nina few seconds to realize she was in her mother's redecorated guest suite. She flopped on her stomach and glanced at the clock. Elliot would be in the shower getting ready for church. What would he say if she called? What was he thinking? If she got in her car, she could be there before noon, but she wouldn't call today, and that would make it easier not to call tomorrow. One day at a time. That's all that she could do.

She wandered into the kitchen and leaned against the counter. Her mother handed her a glass of orange juice. "Your dad wants to talk to you."

"No surprise there." Pushing up the sleeves of her pajamas, she strode into the study. The musty smell of books and furniture polish enveloped her. The furniture hadn't been rearranged since she and John fit in the knee hole under the desk. His tortoiseshell reading glasses balanced on his nose, her dad was sitting behind his desk studying the outline for his Sunday School lesson. Documents with the firm's letterhead were stacked next to the blotter. He was shaved and impeccably dressed, a white shirt and yellow tie, and his suit coat was tossed over the green leather chair.

He doesn't know how long this interview will last, she thought. Racing around at the last minute to get ready for church was not his style. She plopped down on the ottoman and waited.

He gave her an appraising smile. "The depositions went well. The attorney for the school district was better than we expected. They denied the assault." Reading the expression on her face, he leaned back in his chair before he spoke. "Rick wonders if you can come down to the office tomorrow and go over a few things with him."

"That's easy."

"Yes, compared to the other things going on in your life. What are you thinking?"

"I'm mostly just reeling." Her head throbbed, and she was pretty sure last night at 3:00 a.m., her heart had broken in two.

He nodded slowly. "Not making a decision is actually a decision." He tapped his pen lightly on the moss-green blotter.

"What makes you think I haven't made a decision? It's over." He didn't believe her, making her more miserable if that were possible. "All summer we've both been waiting for the other guy to blink. Elliot's not going to back down. I'm supposed to drop the lawsuit, but no one should ever be treated the way I was treated at Clear Creek. It's just wrong. There's a fight coming over these travesties in the workplace, and I'm going to be in it."

He sighed long and slow.

She stood. "Listen, Dad, none of this is your fault—not the lawsuit, not anything. If God wanted women to be an inferior subspecies, he would have created a mumbling bunch of grovelers. And we're not. The proof's in the pudding."

"Nina—" he started to say, but a cork had popped out of her mouth and words tumbled off the end of her tongue.

"I'm sick of being treated like a not-too-clever little girl who needs remedial lessons in scrambling eggs or putting salt in the meat loaf, who comes from a morally challenged family."

She paced across the floor, gesturing with her hands. "But it's not just about me. The crown bypassed Elliot's dad and landed firmly on Elliot's head. He's more than just his mother's pride and joy; he's the family alpha male, and the sibs defer to him. He's not even aware of it, but he expects the same from me. He announced where we're going to live. He announced he's applying at Oregon like it's a done deal. No discussion about all that rain, just pronouncements—like it doesn't involve me. I'm not on the team. I'm not even a cheerleader. I just play the tuba in the pep band."

He smiled. "A tuba?"

She collapsed on the ottoman and wrapped her arms around one knee. "There's only room in our marriage for one person to have dreams."

"I'm so sorry."

"You can't steal another person's dreams. Not if you really love that person."

He came around his desk and hugged her. She crumpled in his arms.

"But I love him, Dad. I love him so much."

"I know you do. And he loves you too. I'm sure of it. He's sitting in that little apartment, hurting as much as you are."

Her voice caught and trembled. "Trust me, he's not."

He patted her on the back. "Where did my little girl go? I used to fix your hurts so easily." He handed her one of the peppermints he kept in the front of his desk drawer. "You have several options," he said. "You talked once about getting a graduate degree in English lit. That might be more palatable to Elliot. Or you could put graduate school on hold and focus on your marriage."

She glanced up quickly, warily. "Capitulate?"

"No. Compromise."

Her mother stepped into the room and closed the door behind her, shutting out the music from the Tabernacle Choir's Sunday morning broadcast that she'd been listening to in the kitchen. "Don't mind me," she said.

Bill gave his wife a quick look over the top of his glasses before he continued. "You'd be an excellent attorney, but the price might be too high. A lit degree might be safest, but I can't make these choices for you, Kitten."

"I'm going to law school." She imagined herself in front of a crowded courtroom with a judge peering down from the bench as she pounded a wooden stake in the chest of a male chauvinist pig with thick lips and a curly black hair. She'd wipe the blood off her face and wave her mallet at the cheering crowd. "And I'm not staying here," she announced. "I'm going to Virginia."

"I can call in a few favors and bump you to the top of the waiting list at the U."

Nina and her father were both startled by her mother's crisp voice. "There are valuable lessons to be learned in Virginia."

The last two people in the world she really trusted were on opposite sides of the room glaring at each other. What kind of a cruel joke was this?

"I don't want to be who I've been," Nina spoke quietly in a measured tones. "I need a fresh start." Someplace where she wouldn't have to explain the white line on a suntanned finger. And those phones all over her parent's house—she needed to be someplace where those phones wouldn't stare at her, humiliate her with their silence, Elliot's silence.

"You're too vulnerable right now, Nina. Stay here for a while, where you have a support system. People who love you."

Nina shook her head. Not a chance.

"Leaving now would be a mistake. I can't finance a mistake." He rested his palms on the top of his desk. Case closed.

Her mother sighed audibly and crossed her arms over her chest. "I can speak for the Franklin England Foundation, and we'd be happy to finance the education of a young legal scholar." She smiled at them both. "We need to leave for church in a half hour."

* * *

Rick had laid out the depositions on the conference table before Nina arrived at Rushforth, Rushforth, Brewster, and McGregor.

"Whoa, I wouldn't have recognized you on the street," he exclaimed, his crisp blue shirt rolled up to his elbows. It was funny how he'd adopted all the little catchphrases he thought would tag him as Western. He hadn't said "howdy" yet, but she expected to hear it soon.

"We brought in a half dozen teachers, plus the principal and the students you suggested." Rick upended his pencil over and over. "The men were surprised they were being deposed, that their behavior was even in question. They didn't think they were doing anything wrong.

"Start with the best," he said. handing her an official-looking document. "The Deposition of Marlo Fletcher." He'd underlined a few sections with a yellow marker.

"You recognized student birthdays in your classes?"
"A spank for each year, and one to grow on. Who doesn't like a little attention on their birthdays? It's important to have some fun. I try to avoid drill and kill. I don't want the kids to hate type."

"Did you spank all of the students in your classes on their birthdays?"

"Not all."

"Did you ever spank a boy?"

"Never did."

"Did you spank all the girls in your classes?"

"No."

Rick tapped his pencil next to another question. "This was great. This Fletcher guy looks around the room like, 'Hey, we're all men here. We know which girls get paddled.'"

"And how did you choose which girls would get spanked?"

"Well, it would depend on the kid. I didn't want to embarrass anyone that was shy or didn't want the attention. It's pretty easy to tell."

"Did you choose the most physically developed girls?"

"No."

"How often did you discuss this birthday spanking in front of the principal?"

"Maybe once or twice."

"Your friend Jerry and Kent Warner put it at more like five or six. The principal knew what was going on." Rick gestured toward the silky red underwear in a plastic bag sitting on the table. "I thought the rabbit fur was a nice touch."

Nina groaned. "Can you imagine going into a store and actually buying the things?"

"You've never been in Fredrick's of Hollywood?"

"No, and I'm not going."

Rick laughed. "This next part is great. He just wanted to be your friend."

"Who purchased the red panties?"

"Zach."

"Did you place them in Nina Spencer's mailbox?"

"Yes."

"And when she didn't retrieve them, did you have a student

take her mail to her room while she was teaching a ninth-grade English class of fourteen-year-olds, mostly boys?"

"Yes."

"Did you do that to humiliate Ms. Spencer? To disrupt her class?"

"We were just trying to joke with her a little. Get her to feel more comfortable and maybe get her to smile every now and again. She was one unhappy girl. We all liked Nina, but she's not a good teacher. She can't control her classes."

"Was the principal aware of your jokes?"

"He might have been."

"Was he aware that you were out of your class in pursuit of these jokes?"

"I'd give the kids their assignment. I didn't need to be there every minute to watch them type."

"Skip over this next part. That's just foundation." His hand on the back of her chair, Rick leaned past her to point at the sheet. She could smell the starch in his shirt. "Start right here."

"Did you release four live mice in the back of Ms. Spencer's classroom on December 4?"

"Yes."

"What effect did you think that would have?"

"It was a joke."

"A joke that involved girls screaming and boys chasing the mice, turning the classroom into essentially chaos. Was that your objective?"

"We were just having a little fun."

"Did you ever release mice in any other teacher's classroom?"

"No."

"Has anyone ever caused similar disruptions in your classroom?"

"No."

"Ms. Spencer was the only recipient for your jokes last year, correct?"

"Yes."

"Describe her for us."

"Young. Pretty. She loved the attention. If she'd complained, we would've left her alone."

Rick tried to look nonchalant. "Fletcher denied the assault, said it was just a frank conversation that turned unpleasant, and then you decked him."

She shoved her hands under her thighs to stop the trembling. "What did Nathan say?" Her protector. She tried to picture him flanked by attorneys in dark suits. With his brow furrowed under that two-tone tan, he'd smile and tell the truth, the whole nasty truth, and nothing but.

"He heard you scream, and when he and the janitor got the door open, Marlo was out cold on the floor." She realized she'd been holding her breath.

Rick pushed another deposition toward her. "Marsha Lundgren was nervous, but she nails the assistant superintendent. Patterson knew about everything." He gave her a tentative smile. "I don't know how you stood it. I would have gone to work with a baseball bat."

She laughed nervously. "Ignoring it just goaded them on."

"Of course. Snotty Nina won't play." He winked at her and ran his fingers through his hair. "Hey, would you like to head down and grab some lunch? Look at a few more of these?"

"Sure." She nodded and smiled.

Following her out to the elevator, he pushed the button. "There's a little sandwich place on Third South. If we're lucky, maybe we can finagle a table on their patio. I want to hold on to these summer days."

"I leave next week."

"Right, that's what your dad said. Law school."

The sun was warm on her shoulders as she stepped in and out of the light under the red bud trees planted along Main Street. She glanced up through the plate-sized leaves at the flickering sunshine. A year ago she'd been meeting Killpack for the first time. What new teacher was staring out her grimy windows at those ancient maples and wondering about surviving the ninety-degree temperatures? And the bulletin boards, how did they look? Marlo was long gone. No more bottles rattling in the hall. Mr. Killpack was transferred to the district, but wonderful Ruth would still be in the outer office. Who would they corral to direct the school play? The faculty lounge would be buzzing about the lawsuit, but would anyone miss her?

Rick held the door open and tried to hide handing the hostess a five dollar bill. "Do you have a table outside?"

"I'm sure we do. I'll be right back."

He tapped the manila folder on the counter next to the cash register. "That school was out of control. You've got to wonder just how common this type of harassment really is." They followed the hostess wearing sandals and a loose skirt down the aisle. He kept his hand on the back of Nina's chair after he sat down next to the trellis covered in blooming wisteria. Frowning, she traced her finger down the edge of the menu.

"The other side," he said, "is going to ask why you didn't report the assault."

"I know."

"How are you going to handle that?"

She set her glasses down on the table and looked at the blur his face had become. "I never took a backseat to my brothers. We skied the same runs, took the same classes, shared the same kitchen duty. Being younger and a girl just meant I tried harder—it was never an excuse." She was silent for a moment, wrestling with her own thoughts and choosing her words carefully. "I was too proud to admit that I was losing every battle, that I couldn't defend myself." She glanced at the waitress serving the adjacent table. "But mostly, I didn't want Marlo's ugliness to be in Elliot's head when he touched me."

He looked at her but he didn't smile. "This whole case hinges on your testimony, and you'll be great. There's not a juror in the world who could listen to you and look at that Fletcher guy and not understand what was going on. I don't know what's up with your new look, but glasses or not, you turned every head when you walked into this restaurant." The corners of his mouth curved up slightly.

She gave him a wry smile. "I'm through being a pretty face." She tapped the menu with her fingertip. "I'll have the Waldorf salad."

34

Letters and Cards

On a Friday afternoon, the second week in September, Elliot pressed three stamps on the corner of the thick manila envelope—Admissions, University of Oregon—and leaned against the mailbox. Was there something more he could do? Attach some charm to the envelope, send a recommendation from the governor, or secret a million-dollar bribe into a willing palm. Something. But he didn't have any money, didn't know the governor, and the magic had vanished out of his life. He grasped his application firmly for several long moments, then he closed his eyes, held his breath, and shoved the envelope through the slot. He ambled out of the student union and headed down the hill to have a late lunch with his parents before he went to work.

His mother waved a striped dish towel in the air when she saw him. "So, it's in the mail? This is so exciting." Beyond solicitous, she fluttered around him, trying with obvious compliments and odd clucking noises to coax a smile onto his face.

He nodded as he sat down at the kitchen table and bit into tuna on rye.

"When do you hear back?"

"A couple of weeks before the first deadline for the regular applications." She'd asked him these same questions probably nine or ten times in the past two weeks. It was starting to wear thin.

"How many boys will they take early decision?"

"Not more than ten, but they don't have a set number. They take the applicants they're sure they want. Usually a couple from Utah."

"After an interview?"

"Yes."

"In Salt Lake?" she asked.

Elliot bit down on a sweet pickle.

His father shook his head at her. "Leave it be."

"You're not going to see Nina, are you?" She stepped beside him, refilling his glass of milk.

"Mom, I don't even know if I'll get an interview."

"Have you heard from her?"

"Nina's in Virginia." He swallowed hard.

She blinked in surprise and eased into a kitchen chair. "How do you know?"

"Her brother called me."

Sighing heavily, she propped one elbow on the table. "You need to end this. You need to move on."

"Nina's dad will handle this. I'll sign somewhere and that will be it. It's not like we have any assets." Dreading the white envelope with the firm's logo, he grimaced as he checked the mail each afternoon.

"I'm glad she's in Virginia," Rachel said. The weight of her anger settled on his shoulders and made him feel tired. Anger was easy, but it's not what he felt.

"Don't start in on her," Mel said.

Elliot didn't want to hear it again. How the last year had been one big mistake. How no one would blame him. How people in the ward would understand. He was still chewing when he hoisted his backpack over one shoulder and turned toward the door before she could begin on her other obsession—moving back home. She wanted him here under their roof, up there on the top bunk listening to Gordy breathe through his mouth.

"Sister Brubaker thinks an annulment might be simplest," she said, speaking to his back.

He settled his backpack on his shoulders and turned around. "I'm not going to pretend the marriage never happened."

* * *

Elliot avoided old friends. He didn't want the slap on the back and empty assurances. He didn't want to hear the latest on who was getting married, the massive march toward matrimony that started on the east end of campus and ended on Temple Hill. His very presence made the newly engaged squirm; and frankly, friends avoided him. No one wanted to entertain the possibility that they might pull a "Nina and Elliot," the synonym for newlywed disaster.

How did other couples skate through the first months of marriage? Things had always come so easily to him; why not this? He'd been a prize, a friend worth having, a member of that caʹre of straight-A student athletes. Now everything he thought he knew about himself was wrong. He was a failure at marriage, banging his head against Nina's stubbornness. And so, as the leaves started to change color, and the morning walk up the hill grew chill, he spent more and more time alone, studying at the red kitchen table.

* * *

One hazy October afternoon, kicking through the leaves as he cut across the quad, he heard a voice he recognized.

"Elliot?" Pam ran to catch up with him. Her long brown hair was tied back with a green ribbon and her cheeks flushed a pretty pink.

"Are you headed down the hill?" She hurried along beside him, chatting about a paper she didn't want to write for children's lit. He didn't pay much attention to the particulars of what she had to say, but the sound of her familiar voice eased the weight in his chest and made him feel a little less lonely.

"I don't think Laura Ingalls Wilder was really into political commentary. When you read about her married life, it was grim. Terrible poverty. She picked up a pen to pay the bills, not out of some romantic notion about settling the American West." Pam took two steps for each of his long strides.

He needed to say something, respond politely, but he was so used to being alone that his tongue felt stiff, unused, like a rusty tool on a shelf in the garage.

"They moved a lot." He remembered that. When he was little, his mother gathered her children before bed and plowed through the Little

House books—the whole series. He was relieved when the little girl grew up and got married and they could read something he liked, *Treasure Island*.

"That was the story of her life, one continuous move. No roots." She looked up at him and smiled. "But my favorite class is the child development lab. Those little kids are a scream. It's all about potty training and learning to share."

As they walked along, she gossiped about people in the ward, and his monosyllabic replies didn't seem to bother her. They were down the hill and standing in front of his apartment when he realized for the last ten minutes he hadn't thought about Nina. Pam waved and strolled on down the street.

Two days later she caught up with him again. And then it became something of a routine. Monday, Wednesday, and Friday, she seemed to arrive just as he was leaving his physiology class. If she suggested stopping at the dairy to get an ice cream cone, he managed to have the correct change. She didn't question him about his plans, didn't interrogate him about his applications, and didn't reproach him about the afternoons he wasn't there. He found himself looking forward to seeing her, noticing what she wore, or the way she combed her hair. Occasionally, she held his hand for a minute or two, and her palm was always soft and warm. Quick memories of her in his car or sitting on the grass at the park came unbidden into his head, and he pushed them aside, until he didn't.

He stood outside the library, waiting for her on a Friday afternoon. The maple trees were a dusty red, but the quaking aspens had already dropped their yellow leaves that he kicked through on the sidewalk. Leaves might signal the coming of cold weather to someone else, but for him it meant any day he'd be getting a letter in the mail, a rejection or an acceptance. His stomach clenched.

Pam hurried across the lawn, a giant flip board in her arms. *Cat, Mat, Bat, Sat,* and *Pat* were written in bright colors on the top sheet.

"I've been packing this around all day. I've got sore muscles I didn't know existed."

She looked so funny, so cute, trying to manage the huge board that he laughed. He took the flip board from her and stuck it under his arm.

"Thanks," she said. "I nearly killed myself on the stairs in the education building."

He reached down to grab his backpack with his free hand. When he stood, he was face to face with nasty Marjorie, Cindy's old roommate.

"Elliot." She sang each syllable. "Good to see you." But it wasn't good to see her. She looked at him as though he were a worm on the sidewalk, a filthy bit of trash, a faithless husband all of twenty-three years old. Whispering behind her hand to her companion, Marjorie stomped on by.

"Whoa. Who was that?" Pam asked.

"A friend of a friend of Nina's. I tripped over her one night, and she's never forgiven me." How long would it take for the long-distance calls between Logan, Utah, and Charlotteville, Virginia, to connect? What would Nina think? Would she care? Probably not.

They crossed the quad and strolled around Old Main without speaking. Pam sat down on a concrete retaining wall in front of a bed of pansies planted for early spring blooming. Elliot stood, the flip board resting against his thigh.

Pam spoke softly, "That's the first time you've mentioned her name."

"I figured you've gotten the blow-by-blow from Diane."

"But you haven't told me how *you* feel." Her brown eyes gazed up at him without blinking.

"I don't want to talk about Nina." He nodded toward the steps and started to walk. She followed him, quiet and pensive, until they stopped in front of his apartment.

"Can I leave the flip chart here? I'll run back up with Mom's car to get it."

"Sure. No problem."

"We could make a pizza."

"I'm still married."

"I'm an old friend, and it's just a pizza. I'll come around six." She walked away swinging her free arm. He stood on the sidewalk watching her, and halfway down the block, she turned and waved.

She arrived prepared. The dough was rising in a bowl covered with a red-checked cloth. She had candles in brass holders and ran back to the car to retrieve a chocolate layer cake. She was all brisk efficiency as she opened drawers to find Nina's knife and opened cupboard doors and touched Nina's dishes. She ran a fingertip around the double row of tiny raised tulips on the edge of the dinner plate before she set it on the table. Nothing in that small gesture should have made him angry, but it did. Another girl touching Nina's dish towels, or Nina's spoons, or Nina's bottle of olive oil, or her crushed basil, or her garlic salt, felt like an assault, a hostile intrusion of enemy forces determined to widen the gap. And what if Marjorie, her interest piqued by the afternoon's encounter, decided to spy and report what she'd glimpse through the kitchen window? Or worse, what if, by some miracle, Nina's heart softened, and she'd chosen today to fly home? What if she opened the door and found him with Pam, a competent cook, fixing a dinner that smelled so delicious he was already salivating? Nina would be devastated—and furious. He'd eat in a hurry and use studying as an excuse to send Pam on her way. But the candles? How could he eat the pizza and refuse the candles?

Every bit of lettuce in the salad stood fresh and ready to be eaten as though some inside deal had been made with a garden. Pam whisked the dressing together with a few no-nonsense strokes, and then, *she tasted it*. So simple, yet so critical, but he'd never been able to convince Nina to take that final step, tasting and then correcting the seasoning. He'd never understood her reluctance, and here was Pam tasting as though it were the most natural thing in the world. Tasting to a good cook, it was like breathing to a lung. He shook his head.

The pizza was perfect. The crust was crisp. The cheese refused the temptation to be greasy. He was reaching for his fourth slice when Pam touched the back of his hand and said, "Leave room for chocolate cake." He gulped and watched her reach for the knife, but she could have cut through that fudge frosting with a feather. She set two large pieces on clean plates, and his head followed her as she moved into the living room and sat on the couch. "Let's have dessert in here," she suggested as though the eating of cake required a different locale, a more relaxed environment away from the kitchen, or softer lighting. He didn't know which.

She started in the middle of the couch, but by the time he was pressing the last crumb on the edge of his fork, she was significantly closer. She lifted his empty plate out of his hands and leaned across him to set it on the floor.

She straightened up and kissed him. She tasted like chocolate. He probably did too, and that in itself was not wrong. Her mouth was so soft, and Pam had always been willing. But gone or not, Nina was his wife, and the weight of the ring on his finger kept his hands at his sides as she pressed against him.

"Pam, I can't do this," he mumbled. One hand on her shoulder, he gently pushed her away.

"I've never quit loving you," she whispered. "Nina was a terrible mistake, but that's all she is—a mistake."

But Nina wasn't a mistake. She was a presence. She was standing in the kitchen not tasting the dressing. She was right here on the couch, flat on her back with a book in her hand. She was standing in front of him straightening the prints on the wall; he could almost reach out and touch her. And that disastrous macramé plant holder hanging from a hook in the ceiling, he laughed every time he saw it. She'd made it at a Relief Society meeting, but it looked like a neophyte spider's failed attempt at web construction. Nina had stuffed a sweet potato in a mason jar filled with water, stood back, and said, "Grow, you obstinate thing." But the potato just looked like a fly caught in yards and yards of white string. Her attitude toward all things domestic was adversarial. But sitting on the couch with this girl who would happily spend the rest of her life making his life comfortable, his food delicious, and teaching his children how to read and go potty, all he could think about was Nina.

"I love her," Elliot mumbled. "You don't want me." And he waited to hear all the clichés he knew were available for such moments. *What does she have that I don't? She could never make you happy. I can give you children. All the children you want. Sons, half a dozen.* But Pam stood up and walked into the kitchen. She covered the cake with aluminum foil and set it on the counter. In one smooth motion, she collected her bowls, her candles, and her checked cloth. She stood with her back to him, waiting for several seconds with one hand on the doorknob, before she said, "You're crazy."

And maybe he was, completely out of his mind. Nina had pushed him over some indefinable ledge and he was falling, his arms and legs thrashing as he dropped through empty space. He didn't know when he'd hit bottom. Maybe never. Maybe that's what it meant to love Nina. No top, no bottom, no sides, and no landing. Just the journey.

* * *

Monday afternoon he was sitting on the curb watching for the mail truck. He felt more than a little foolish because he hadn't waited for the mailman like this since he was seven and had ordered a Roy Rogers fan club kit with an autographed photo. He paced back and forth, glanced at his watch, and sat down again. He should hear from Oregon today or tomorrow at the latest. Finally, the white truck rounded the corner. It spent a half hour at each stop. The regular guy must be on vacation, and they called in a ninety-year-old man to cover the route. Or maybe the mailman was with the FBI checking the campus for student radicals getting mail from the SDS or the Black Panthers. Who knew? But this guy was the slowest mail carrier in the history of the world.

Elliot couldn't wait another minute. He strode to the neighbor's mailbox, and smiling as pleasantly as he could, he said, "Have you got anything with my name on it?" He wanted to snatch the stack of letters out of the guy's hand, but he stood patiently until he saw The University of Oregon in the corner as the letter slipped past.

"Stop. That's it." He grabbed it, took two deep breaths, and ripped the end of the envelope.

> *Dear Mr. Spencer,*
> *We are happy to inform you. . .*

He laughed. He read the letter again. Then he read it out loud to be sure he wasn't delusional. Grinning, he rushed into the apartment and flopped down on the couch with the letter in his hand and stared at it. His heart was racing. He was in. He was in early. He couldn't believe it. He picked up the phone and stared at the receiver. The person he wanted most to call was Nina. He rotated the dial four times to call her mother and get Nina's number, and then he stopped. He dropped the receiver back on the hook. He leaned his head back, closed his eyes, and bellowed, "Nina!" He wanted her to hear him. He wanted her.

He strode into the bedroom and yanked open her drawers. Grabbing a silky blue nightgown, he pressed his face against the soft folds and breathed deeply, then he flung it into the air. He opened her sweater drawer and tossed the pretty knits all over the floor. He threw T-shirts and slips and scarves onto the bed. Then he went into the bathroom and dumped the contents of her makeup drawer next to the sink. All the little pots and tubes and brushes scattered over the counter. He sat down on the edge of the tub and flipped open her shampoo and inhaled deeply the way kids did when they were sniffing glue, because he was addicted. Addicted to her.

He calmed down and looked around. For the first time since she'd left, this apartment felt like home. Gazing at the mess, he pretended Nina was in the next room. He shouted, "Hey, Nina, I got into school." He imagined her walking through the door unzipping her jacket to add to the pile of clutter. She'd slip past him to run a comb through her frizzy hair or tuck a tube of lip gloss in her pocket, and because he'd rehearsed her every motion in his head when he couldn't sleep, he knew she'd sit on his lap, laugh, and give him a kiss so tantalizing he had to remind himself to breathe. He set the shampoo on the floor and rested his head in his hands. "Nina," he whispered. "Come back to me."

And then it hit him, sitting on the edge of the tub, that Nina's letter of acceptance had been received with less celebration. He remembered the panic on her face. He'd stolen her moment. No congratulations; instead he'd berated her and left, and then she left, leaving only her shadow behind.

The next week, on a day surprisingly sunny for the first part of November, he collected the mail and gingerly flipped through the letters, always dreading a return address from Rushforth, Rushforth, Brewster and McGregor, but surprise—the third envelope was a hot pink card. Her name written in her funny script and a Charlottesville address were in the upper left hand corner. He fumbled for his house keys in his pocket before he dropped onto the concrete step and tore it open.

Elliot,

I'm so pleased for you. All your hard work has paid off. A friend of mine in the sophomore class has been checking, and when he told me you'd been accepted, I smiled all over. Good for you. You deserve the best.

Nina

No *dear* in the salutation. No *love* and row of *xoxo*'s before her name. There was more of a message in what she didn't write than in what she did. She'd chosen her words so carefully. It looked like she'd just dashed off a note, but she hadn't.

He studied the envelope and smelled the card. No perfume. When he'd opened her letters before they were married, a cloud of her scent filled his head. Now she was being cautious. Maybe this was just a kind note from a friend, but she wasn't just a casual acquaintance. She was his wife. For the past two weeks the words of a scripture had been bouncing around inside his head like the words of a song, or a verse from one of Nina's favorite poems—or the answer to a prayer. *Influence ought to be maintained by persuasion, long suffering, gentleness, meekness, and love unfeigned.*

Two days later, when he should have been studying developmental physiology, he was making two lists, side by side. Nina's pros and cons. He crossed things out and he underlined other things twice. But how could he equate her smile with scrubbing the tub? Or the smell of her hair on a summer afternoon with scorched peas? He scrunched the paper into a ball and started another list. His own list of pros and cons. Why would she want to come back to him? He wasn't patient. He wasn't a brooding Irish author. He did look like Robert Burns. Scribble a star there. He was smart. He nagged her something terrible, but he scratched that out. In fairness to himself, he decided all the things he'd never do again weren't going on the list. That created a considerable improvement. He stuck the list to the bathroom mirror with a glob of toothpaste.

Standing at the refrigerator, he poured himself a glass of milk. He reached up and touched the ceiling with his fingertips. He could do this, but convincing her would take some planning.

35

The Last December

No wreath on the door, but the key fit the lock easily and why that should feel like a surprise, she didn't know. Shivering, Nina knocked, then opened the door slowly as she stepped out of the wind. Elliot had the thermostat set at 60. The apartment was silent and felt shabby and a bit forlorn, impressions she didn't remember. Worn through at the doorways, the carpet, nevertheless, had been vacuumed, probably recently, and Elliot had plumped the striped pillows on the couch, a thought that brought a lump to her throat. No sign of Christmas. No tree. No twinkling lights draped around the window with duct tape. Only the bright-red table and chairs stood out in the pale afternoon light.

She'd forgotten how wind rattled the kitchen window. A storm was forecast; she could have picked a better day. Her heart pounding, she glanced at her watch. If Elliot was at work, and he probably was, she had three hours. If he walked through that door with Pam, what would she do? Edge past them? Run out into the snow? Scream?

Her knit hat on her head, she ran back to her car and, fighting the wind, brought in an armful of flattened boxes and the roll of strapping tape. She felt like she was sneaking around in another person's house, as though the girl who had lived here were an old friend, but they'd lost touch. Why had she come? To give herself a hard pinch to wake up and realize Elliot was gone? To poke through the rubble of her marriage— for what? What did she want? Not much. She stood in the middle of the kitchen. Her mother had insisted on the wedding china and sterling silver as she pushed Nina out the door. She said Nina would want it again someday. Not likely.

She shrugged off her coat and tossed her hat on the floor before she ran her hand along the titles on the bookshelf. She set several in the box. An album she'd bought last January, in a short-lived stab at organization, fell open, and pictures of Scotland scattered across the carpet. Scooping them into a pile, she tried to avert her head, not look, but she was caught by the cathedral ruins and the North Sea, pulled back by funny Elder Twitchell mugging for the camera, as he stood by a pile of chiseled red stones. And there was Elliot, tall and handsome, with an expanse of dark blue sea behind him and a mischievous grin on his face. Her bruised heart ached at the sight of him, and she touched the picture gingerly with her fingertip. There was another snapshot of him outside a tea shop, and another, waving over his shoulder. Two years ago. A hundred years ago. She shoved the pictures inside the cover and set the album in the box.

Her Charlottesville apartment, on the third floor of a house built in the twenties, had new carpet and fresh paint. Her most recent acquisition, an overstuffed easy chair, sat in the corner and a half empty closet extended along the length of one wall. The kitchen was too small to count for much, but overlooking the yard was a big old window with paned glass. She'd shoved her bed under it so she could look out at an oak tree taller than the house. She'd been sitting on her bed when Cindy called to repeat what Marjorie had reported: multiple sightings of Elliot holding hands with an old girlfriend. She lay there for hours that October afternoon, counting each leaf as it drifted past the window, until she hauled her body across campus to attend a late afternoon seminar on contracts.

A lined piece of loose-leaf paper was folded over twice and stuck in the edge of their silver-framed wedding picture. She unfolded it cautiously and adjusted the glasses on her nose.

Nina,

If you're reading this, you've come and I'm not home. Please take whatever you want. The lease is up in January, and I'll be moving into my parents' attic over the break.

I need to see you. We need to talk. I'm so sorry about everything.
Please wait for me to come home. Or call me at the lab or at
my mom's.
I'll come.
Elliot

She hesitated, pressed the page against her knee, and read it again. *I need to see you.* Why? To discuss the logistics of the divorce? To tell her the distressing bit of news face-to-face: "I'm getting married when the divorce is final." She didn't need to count on her fingers; it had been almost four months. Why speak to her now?

Wrapping dish towels around the frame, she placed it carefully next to the album. She didn't blame Elliot; she blamed herself. She could have swallowed her pride and made this little apartment a home. How tough would it have been to hang up her clothes and make the bed? And her secrets? She should have trusted him. She wound strapping tape around the first box and, with her back to the wind, carried it out to the trunk of her car. An old flatbed delivery truck, Spencer's Feed and Seed, pulled into the driveway. The truck door slammed, and there he was, standing in the snowstorm. Elliot.

Her glasses fogged. She pushed them up on her forehead and squinted in his direction. She felt faint, thought she might collapse in a heap on the snowy driveway. His hood and shoulders were covered with white and his cheeks shone red with the cold. His mouth opened. "Nina." But the wind carried his voice away. Shaking his hood off his head, he noticed the box. Hands on the trunk lid, he slammed it shut. "I was coming to see you tomorrow."

Her heart flipped over in her chest. He was thin. Deep hollows under his eyes said he'd not been sleeping or he'd been sick. The storm whipped the snow and stung her eyes. Elliot followed her into the apartment and pushed the door shut with his shoulder.

"I thought you might come." He nodded at the note. "Hoped you might come." He couldn't look away, and she squirmed inside her bulky red sweater.

"Your hair." He touched the crown of her head softly. "You look like a cancer survivor."

She blinked away tears filling her eyes.

He tugged off his mittens and dropped the heavy parka, protection from frigid Scottish winters, over the back of a kitchen chair to dry. The pungent smell of wet wool filled the kitchen.

"Can you stay a little while?" he said. "I could fix lunch. Nothing exciting." With eyes soft and expectant, he gazed at her but didn't smile. They were both ill at ease. Had they ever been married?

"I was just going to grab a few things." She glanced around the room and then down at her hands. "I should have called before I barged in, but I thought you'd be at work." She couldn't meet his frank stare. "I'm not hungry."

She gestured toward his creased note on the floor between them. "I'm not sure what's left to say," she muttered. "I didn't think being here would be this hard. I need to go." But legs made of rubber wouldn't move, and she sniffed loudly.

He reached out and touched her hand. "Please stay."

"I just can't." She felt like such a dope, standing here with tears in her eyes, waiting for the crushing finale. "I can't be your friend. I can't keep in touch."

Tears unbidden dribbled down the side of her nose as she grabbed her coat off the floor and felt the sharp outline of keys in the pocket. "Can I leave the boxes? I'll come back after Christmas while you're at work." She tugged on her hat and turned toward the door. "I understand you're back with Pam. I guess that has a kind of symmetry."

"No," he said. "Not a chance."

Her hand faltered on the doorknob. "That's not what I heard." She steadied herself against the door and closed her eyes.

"What you heard was wrong." He ran his hand though his wet hair and it settled in damp curls. "I understand you being uncomfortable." He stared at her as though trying to read a message hidden on her face. "This is hard for me too, but we need to talk, and I need to see your face when we do." His eyes pleaded with her. "Give me five minutes."

Shoving her hands in the pockets of her peacoat, she leaned against the door with her jaw clenched. "Okay, shoot."

But apprehensive or unsure of himself, he paused before he spoke and took a deep breath or two. "We're a complicated mess, Nina." His voice was gruff. "We made every mistake in the book. We were too young. Too much family interference. We tried to do too many things at once, a setup for catastrophe." He waited for her to respond, and when she didn't, he plowed ahead. "But I'll never think of Scotland without thinking of you." He cleared his throat. "Mistletoe and our wedding and everything in between and everything after. I know last summer was awful, but I'm not ready to give up."

She made herself close her mouth. When he left her in May, she knew the marriage was over. When a hesitant Cindy called in October, she knew he'd slipped back into the comfortable, predictable life he wanted. When he didn't answer her note, it confirmed what she already knew.

"What's changed?" she asked.

He glanced past her out the window at snow blowing in horizontal waves. "Everything's changed. Nothing's changed." He sighed. "I was boxing some things and found my old missionary journal. Our wedding was the last entry. That day. It was just so right. You felt it too. I know you did." He waited, but she didn't know what to say. "I've checked the mail every day waiting for the envelope from your dad's firm, but when it didn't come, I started to hope that maybe you were having second thoughts too."

Second thoughts? She turned that particular idea over in her mind. Standing here next to him, she ached to feel his arms around her, but she knew she'd never survive another descent into the war zone.

"So how was it?" he said. "Law school?" There was a ragged edge to his voice.

"Three women in a class of a hundred. The homegrown chauvinists around here have nothing on those good ol' Southern boys." She drawled, "Sweetheart, do you realize you're taking a job away from a *man* who needs to support a family?" Elliot's eyes tightened at her bitterness. "After about twenty guys sidled up to whisper the same thing, I finally told one I gave up a marriage to be there. After that I was a pariah." She spoke, almost under her breath, "But I'm going to make law review and bury those guys." He reach d for her mittened hand, but she pulled away. "I've gotten cynical and laconic. Not the girl you knew. I've chewed through two mouth guards. I don't sleep. I snap at my friends and I'm nasty to my family. No one likes me. And I miss Walter."

"Walter?"

"And Robin, and Jerry, and Marsha, and I really miss Ruth, and that dump of a room." Angry words careened out of her mouth. "And that cold air return, and Mr. Mumford and Nathan, and Amanda Church." She stretched her hat between her hands. "I miss diagramming complex-compound sentences on the chalkboard. How ridiculously stupid is that?" She held up one finger. "But we have a potential marital asset, something to divide. The district's willing to give us a fair chunk of change if we drop the suit and agree never to disclose."

Elliot's eyes traveled over her face. "Are you happier now? Was it worth it?"

"Not yet." Maybe not ever. But one thing was sure, she'd never settle that suit. There wasn't enough money in Fort Knox.

He turned away. Rustling in the kitchen, he dumped milk in a saucepan and clunked it down on a burner, a wooden spoon in his hand. Milk sloshed over the rim as he stirred in spoonfuls of cocoa. His clear, emphatic voice carried over the din. She watched his lips forming words as he waved the spoon in his hand like wizard sending flecks of chocolate onto the floor, but she couldn't make sense of all he was saying. Only the abstract nouns: fights, too many, commitment, compromise, common goals, respect. A recipe for happiness she didn't believe.

Elliot wrapped her fingers around a steaming mug. "I have a proposition for you." He took a deep breath and let it out slowly. "What about spending next summer together? One more try on neutral turf. No friends or family, just us. We'll have to depend on each other. We could learn to listen. No hit-and-run conversations. If we end up fighting again, we'll call it quits in September."

"Are you kidding? You must be straight-up nuts." The steaming mug burning her palms, Nina collapsed slowly on her end of the couch and stared at him. She could start her second year like she'd started her first, a blithering emotional head-on collision. "If it's great, at the end of summer, I head to Virginia brokenhearted and you go to Oregon alone, and if it's horrible, I pack my guts in a suitcase and step in front of a train. No thanks."

"No." He shook his head. "If it works, I go to Virginia with you. I'd defer school a year and work. We'd be together."

"You'd do that for me?" She tipped her head toward him suspiciously.

313

"Where is the real Elliot, and what have you done with him?"

"I promise. I've thought about this a lot."

"And the year after that?"

"It won't be perfect, but we'll figure it out as we go along."

"Maybe I'm not cut out to be a wife." She sighed, set the mug on the carpet, and stuffed her hands in her pockets. "Last year was different for you than it was for me," she said. "I was dishonest from the beginning with you and with myself. I was a disaster—at everything."

"Not everything." His mouth curled up on one side. "Too much was thrown at you. I know that now. I should have seen it then."

"Slow down." She rolled her eyes. "You've blindsided me. For the last three months, I thought you were back with Pam. You didn't answer my card. I don't know what to think."

"Listen. I'll admit it. The week after you left was like R and R from Vietnam." He shook his head. "After that I was miserable. I tried to reconnect with Pam. She was handing me everything I thought I wanted you to be, but being with Pam was like putting a key in the ignition and nothing happens. The engine won't turn over."

He'd traveled around this corner a month ago, but it was all a surprise to her. She sat hunched with her knees bent and her hands in her pockets. "I was expecting a wedding announcement." She couldn't look at him, so she covered her face with her palms and tried to think. She could hear the soft clicking of the second hand on the kitchen clock. She sat not moving for five minutes, and then fifteen. His breathing next to her ear turned her thoughts into a jumble. "I've barely started spitting the water out of my lungs and you want me to jump in the deep end—again. I can't believe I'm sitting here."

But she was sitting on the couch and not moving toward the door. He tried to smile at her, but there was fear in his eyes. "We can make this work." He rested a tentative hand on her shoulder.

The snow blanketed the tiny apartment in soft quiet. She finally spoke. "There's a blizzard out there, and I need to get on the road before it gets worse." She didn't trust herself. He believed what he was saying, but did she believe him?

What did her mother always say? *People change, but not much.* This roller coaster ride wasn't going to slow down for the curves. On the other hand, it would never be boring—no chance of that. Elliot wasn't going to quit being stubborn, but he also wasn't going to quit being adorable. She touched the side of his cheek. Surprised, his eyes widened and his lips parted.

She could live without him, stumble along on her own, but he'd carved out a place in her heart that only he could fill. She loved him. Convenient or not, she loved him, enough to do battle in the kitchen with lobster bisque, or chocolate mousse, or New England pot roast. Enough to compromise.

Elliot glanced out the window. "It's not letting up."

"I'm at a loss," Nina offered. "Where do we go from here?"

He stood up. "Wait just a minute."

He bumped around in the bedroom closet and she heard drawers open and close. He returned with her boots in one hand and a scarf tossed over his shoulder. "Let's go for a walk. Neutral ground."

She glanced at the snow pelting the window and then over at the macramé hanging from a hook in the ceiling, the potato long since shriveled.

He grabbed her hands. "A walk in the snow. For a half hour. Give the plows a chance to clear the snow in the canyon."

"It's a blizzard out there."

"Put on more layers."

She edged past him into their bedroom, and standing there stole her breath away. Nothing had changed from her necklace on the dresser to her shoes piled in the closet. The pillow shams were perfectly aligned, and her little stuffed bear, so faded the pink was only a suggestion, sat expectantly between them. Smiling to herself, she stripped off her sweater and rifled through her top drawer looking for a navy turtleneck she was sure was there. She felt Elliot watching her from the doorway.

"I've missed you," he said in a gruff voice. He closed his eyes and turned away.

"Someone dropped a grenade in this drawer," she whispered.

"I used to bury my face in your things." His back to her, he pressed both strong hands against the doorjamb.

* * *

It wasn't a light fluffy snow, no Bing Crosby singing "White Christmas" in the background. A fierce wind drove the storm, and she wrapped the scarf over her mouth and chin, but snow crystals grazed her cheeks. Christmas lights swung dangerously against houses.

A half a block away, they could hear children, out of school for Christmas break, shrieking on College Hill, racing their sleds down steep slopes in the midst of the storm. Tall trees, their trunks and branches a wet black, looked skeletal against the white of the blizzard.

"I've climbed this hill a million times," he said. "I'll close my eyes in twenty years and feel concrete steps under my feet."

"Almost done."

"Two more quarters." Laughing, he squeezed her hand. He brushed the snow off a bench and they sat, without talking, watching little daredevils speed down the hill. He fished two quarters out of his pocket before going over to a boy holding a red plastic sled. "Three trips for fifty cents?" Grinning, the boy nodded.

"Come on." Elliot tugged her off the bench. "This will be great."

Feeling his arms tight around her middle, she leaned against him. His warm breath tickled the side of her cheek. Flying down the hill, going at least forty, he stuck his heels off the edge of the sled, and stinging snow sprayed her face. They tipped over at the bottom, and she rolled away, laughing, a half inch of wet snow sticking to her cheeks. It had been so long since she'd laughed out loud she didn't recognize her own voice. The weight pressing against her chest started to ease.

"You did that on purpose." She shook her fist at him.

"Never. Let's go again."

On their third trip, they hit a bump and spilled into a drift under a tree. She lost her hat and one mitten. Elliot picked up her glasses and tried to straighten the bent earpiece. He looked through the lens. "If we were playing hide-and-seek, you couldn't find me if I were sitting on the couch." He perched the lopsided glasses on her nose as she lay sprawled in the snow. He dropped down next to her and laughed. "You look very funny. 'Men don't make passes—'"

She finished the line, ". . . 'at girls who wear glasses.' That's the point."

"Glasses have become a feminist statement? Not in my book." He wiped the snow off her face and kissed her gently. "You don't have to pretend to be someone you're not. I'll love who you are." He pulled her against his chest. "What about it? Should we give it another try?"

She took his snowy cheeks in both of her mittened hands and kissed him until the snow down her neck started to dribble. "I'm going to be a summer intern at the Department of Justice in DC."

He swallowed hard. "Great. I was thinking Yellowstone, but Washington, DC, works just fine. We can sublet an apartment and set up shop." He jumped up and reached for her. Then, not moving, he held her tightly until a skiff of snow covered them both. "Let's go home," he whispered. "I'll lead you unless you have a white cane hidden in your pant leg."

She brushed the snow off his shoulders. "What was all the hand-holding with Pam?"

"She was holding my hand."

"I've heard that before." Nina watched a little boy hit a bump and go sailing into the air. "How far did it go, Elliot?"

"Nowhere, because I'm married to a blind girl with a shaved head. I must be crazy."

Giving him a shove, she strode down the hill. A snowball splatted behind her left ear.

Arms waving above his head, he shouted into the storm, "I love you." Several boys pointed at him and jeered. He sprinted up the hill to return the sled, and she was halfway down the block before he caught up with her.

"Two inches in the valley means a foot of snow in the canyon," she said. "I should go."

Snowflakes on his eyelashes, he grinned at her. "You don't honestly think I'm going to let you leave."

The comfortable weight of both his hands rested on her shoulders. She looked into his dark eyes. "I'm sorry, Elliot. About everything."

"We both made mistakes."

"How is this going to work?"

Shivering, he dropped his hands to his sides. "One day at a time."

He kicked his boots on the side of the step and brushed the snow off her hat before he followed her through their front door. "You're smart and independent, but it's clear, you need me."

She punched his shoulder. "That's fairly egotistical."

Standing together in their living room, he looked her straight in the face. "You drove up here today because you love me. The stuff, the possessions, just an excuse."

He lifted a small sprig of mistletoe out of his inside coat pocket. "I was headed to Salt Lake in the morning. I was going to plant myself in front of your house until you honored your obligations."

"This will never hold up in court."

"Nevertheless, you know what this is," he said, the mistletoe resting on his palm. "It's an IOU. A promise made in Scotland. No statute of limitations, and I'm going to hold you to it."

She dropped her coat on the floor and tossed her hat on the couch. "Well then, Elliot, convince me."

Acknowledgments

*W*riting a book is not a solitary endeavor; it is a collaboration of friends, and so, many people deserve my gratitude. First the writing goddesses, Terrell Dougan, Kate Lahey, and Sally Robinson for years of laughter, valuable insights, and incremental deadlines. I am grateful to willing readers and dear friends, Cindy Badger, Kim Bouck, Kathy Merkley, and Shawna Wilde, who read early drafts, spoke honestly, and changed the shape of the novel. Angela Eschler at Eschler Editing provided content guidance and professional advice that was very helpful. Jan Smith, Sue Kaelin, Steve Dunn, Kathy Peterson, Lana Jeremy, Kris Goll, and Janet Jensen offered unwavering encouragement and support. Vida Gines was a wonderful mentor during my early years in the classroom and is certainly the most "put together" redhead I've ever known—an affectionate thanks to Vi. Leah Miller has been my patient tech wizard and has endured many blank stares with good humor. Always willing to share his talent, Randy Haws grasped the book's concept quickly and sketched ideas for the cover art. The main character's mother is a wise woman, and much of her wisdom is borrowed from Leslie White. The world's greatest cousins, Julie Markham, Georgia Miller, Laurie Priano, Karen Therios, Rosanne Nieto, Mary Elizabeth Cannon, Susan Forsberg, and Sid Kimball, have cheered me on from the sidelines. Angie Workman is the person responsible for seeing the possibilities in the manuscript and guiding it to publication.

I'm grateful to her and the wonderful staff at Cedar Fort Publishing & Media for their professionalism, patience, and kindness.

And where would authors be without the ladies who read, think, and discuss? Sincere thanks go to friends in my book clubs: Martha Blonquist, Sally Larkin, Phyllis Griffiths, Clytee Gold, Liz Gloeckner, Becky Harding, Kathy Newton, JoAnn Miner, Kaylynn Nielson, Jenny West, Liz Goodell, Karla Wilson, Tracy Bigelow, Deanne Curtis, Penelope Harris, Nancy McDonald, and Carol Haymond.

A big thanks to my wonderful kids, Pete, Andy, Betsy, and Charlotte, who are always so pleased (and a little surprised) when their mother does something out of the ordinary. I have to mention Ben Haws, because he's my favorite fan. My first reader and best friend is my husband, Charlie, who willingly tosses aside his golf magazines in favor of a red pen. And to the two people who believed all things are possible—thanks, Mom and Dad.

Discussion Questions

1. Three days post nuptials, Nina and Elliot experience a time crunch. Work, school, family obligations, and the intricacies of making a new home demand more time than the day allows. How much time does a healthy marriage require?

2. The wise bishop compares a new marriage to a couple wending their way through a mountain valley. The families of origin are gathered on the cliffs above, and they're either applauding or they're throwing rocks. How much damage did those rocks inflict on Nina and Elliot's relationship? Or did those rocks make them more determined to build a life together?

3. Purchasing food, chopping food, cooking food, and eating food consumes a fair amount of time in the life of a family. Is the significance Elliot places on food ridiculous or reasonable and important?

4. The emphasis in Nina's family was on accomplishment and education. Did that emphasis handicap Nina and her ability to function in a rural school environment or did it help her?

5. Every family has secrets. What are the undercurrents in Elliot's family? Are the secrets in Nina's family more compelling or more easily understood?

6. The numbers may vary slightly, but it's safe to assume that between 30 to 35 percent of all women will be the victims of a sexual assault. Two-thirds of those women will know

their attackers. Eighty percent of those women won't report the attacks to the police; and surprisingly, 30 percent won't tell their friends or family. Nina is an educated woman who grew up in the home of an attorney. Why didn't she report the assault? More important, why didn't she tell Elliot?

7. What consequences would Nina have faced if she had been more truthful with Elliot?

8. Influential senators added gender to the 1964 Civil Rights Legislation because they believed that inclusion would derail the legislation. They supposed the country wasn't ready for equal rights for women. In view of Nina's experiences, was that supposition correct?

9. What could Nina have done to be more successful as a schoolteacher? Was she doomed from the beginning?

10. How influential are families of origin on new marriages or on second marriages? Should young couples move away from family and friends for the first two or three years? How important is mutual dependence?

About the Author

After fourteen years teaching in the public school system, Annette Haws set aside her denim jumpers and sturdy shoes to pursue her interest in writing fiction. A native of a small college town on the northern edge of Utah and a people watcher from an early age, Ms. Haws examines the tribulations and the foibles of characters playing their parts on a small stage. Her first novel, *Waiting for the Light to Change*, won Best of State, a Whitney Award for Best Fiction, and the League of Utah Writers award for best published fiction. She's been published in *Sunstone* and *Dialogue*. She is the mother of four above-average children and is the spouse of a patient husband. She would enjoy hearing from you at annette_haws@yahoo.com. She blogs at annettehaws.com.